Further Praise for *Saltblood*

'Masterful . . . The characters, both colourful and sordid, who passed through Mary's life were superbly drawn, the historical setting deftly painted' James Oswald, author of the Inspector McLean series

'Like some great, lost eighteenth-century adventure novel, *Saltblood* is a thrilling, gender-shaking roar of a tale every reader will enjoy. Moll Flanders answers back' Neil Blackmore, author of *Radical Love*

'An absolute treasure trove of a book . . . Deserves to be huge' Anna Mazzola, author of *The Clockwork Girl*

'*Saltblood* is a complete triumph. A glittering jewel of a novel; a treasure chest of delight. I cannot bring myself to put it down – it's so utterly absorbing. Told with a spareness that captures the time and place perfectly, it is also rich and gorgeous with imagery, dripping with love of the sea and the tides, and told in a unique voice – at once modern and yet also deeply evocative of Mary Read's own time. The infamous but scantily documented Mary is rendered so human I am with her on every step of her piratical journey. I adore this book' E.S. Thomson, author of *Beloved Poison*

SALTBLOOD

FRANCESCA DE TORES

SALTBLOOD

BLOOMSBURY PUBLISHING
LONDON · OXFORD · NEW YORK · NEW DELHI · SYDNEY

BLOOMSBURY PUBLISHING
Bloomsbury Publishing Plc
50 Bedford Square, London, WC1B 3DP, UK
29 Earlsfort Terrace, Dublin 2, Ireland

BLOOMSBURY, BLOOMSBURY PUBLISHING and the Diana logo
are trademarks of Bloomsbury Publishing Plc

First published in Great Britain 2024

A catalogue record for this book is available from the British Library

ISBN: HB: 978-1-5266-6133-3; TPB: 978-1-5266-6132-6; EBOOK: 978-1-5266-6136-4;
E-PDF: 978-1-5266-6137-1

2 4 6 8 10 9 7 5 3

Typeset by Integra Software Services Pvt. Ltd.
Printed and bound in Great Britain by CPI Group (UK) Ltd, Croydon CR0 4YY

To find out more about our authors and books visit www.bloomsbury.com
and sign up for our newsletters

For APN, who knows when to be an anchor
and when to be a sail.

Author's note

Mary Read and Anne Bonny are real historical figures –
but I am not a historian.

'Now we are to begin a History full of surprizing Turns and Adventures; I mean, that of *Mary Read* and *Anne Bonny*, alias *Bonn*, which were the true Names of these two Pyrates; the odd Incidents of their rambling Lives are such, that some may be tempted to think the whole Story no better than a Novel or Romance [...]'

A General History of the Pyrates, Volume I, Captain Charles Johnson

'It's better to swim in the sea below
Than to swing in the air and feed the crow [...]'

'A Sailor Song on the Taking of Teach or Blackbeard the Pirate', attrib. Benjamin Franklin

Prologue

March 1721

Tell me your crow name. Tell me the name you will wear to the bottom of the sea. The name shaped to fit every part of you, instep and underarm and the exact curve of your ear. Tell me the name you hear someone calling in a dream, and wake with your mouth already open to reply. Tell me the name that the crows would say, black-voiced, because everybody knows a crow cannot lie.

I've had many names – some were given to me, and some I took. Each of them was a lie, big or small. The wrong name, or the wrong form, or the wrong time. Sometimes all three.

In the main, they call me Mary Read. If I am to be remembered at all, it will likely be by that name.

As for my true name? Go ask the sea.

A reverend comes to the gaol to see me. He wishes me to make my final testament – says he's concerned with my soul's salvation. Perhaps that's the truth, although he has a greasy way about him, so I suspect he is more concerned with selling an account of my life. Many a condemned pirate has had their last words published after their death, but few would recognise themselves in the accounts published. Some such testaments are full of contrition and godliness. Other accounts are imagined entirely, pamphlets crammed with details chosen to scandalise.

Even if I were to give this man my story, how can I put into words this life of mine – its unruly sorrows and its pleasures, more unruly still? Words cannot capture Anne Bonny nor Jack Rackham, nor the way we set out to make a republic of pirates and ended up making something altogether different.

How can I make in words the sea, or the singing of the ships? Such things I learned not through language but through my hands on the lines and my bare feet braced against the deck, my eyes squinting against the salt spray. I have swum deep, the sky a distant thing beyond the veil of sea. What words could tell the truth of this?

'Go,' I say to the reverend. 'I've nothing to give you.' He looks over his shoulder as he walks away.

A word is the wrong tool for knowing, but it is all that I have. If this story is to be told in words, they shall be my own.

1

I am born Mary, but not allowed to be her. I must be Mark, because Mark is dead, and I must take his place.

As I grow, Ma says I must hide my womanliness, my womanly softness, and I don't know what she means, for she is the only woman I know well in all this world and I have never seen any softness in her. Not when she drowned the mice that we trapped in the pail; not when a cat crept in and whelped three kittens under our bed, for she drowned them too, before their eyes were opened. Such softness as Ma ever had, the world has seen fit to rid her of – or perhaps there never was any, for she is hard from her raw knuckles to her cracked heels that scrape my shins at night when we nest together for warmth. So when Ma says I must hide my softness, I don't know where such softness is to be found – not in her, and not in me neither.

Here is how I became a girl who became a boy:

Ma's husband skipped out on them, and on the navy too, when my brother Mark was still a suckling. The man died soon after, and his family felt badly about Ma – bad enough to send her money every month to help her raise baby Mark, their grandson. Then Ma got with child again, by somebody else, unseemly fast with her husband barely gone, and she had to leave Plymouth and have the baby in the countryside, so her husband's family wouldn't find out and stop the money.

That is me: born in 1685 in a rented room in some stranger's cottage. I picture Ma biting down on a twisted rag so as not to make too much noise. A pail of boiled water, a bloodied towel. Maybe some local woman roped in to help her. Maybe she did it alone. But as I was being born, my half-brother Mark was dying. Ma's sister sent a letter from Plymouth: Mark died from the flux, having lived only a little over a year. Ma always says that I came quick and hard, so when I picture my birth it gets muddled in my head – the blood and sweat and screaming of my coming, and of Mark's going.

A dead child is no rare or special thing – but Mark having lived past a year, which many children do not, I think Ma had dared to count him safe, and love him, as well as she could love. It was not a mistake she was to repeat with me.

To keep the money coming, I had to become Mark. He hadn't much of a head start on me: as long as Ma kept me from her husband's family for the first couple of years, it was an easy enough trick to pull. Mark was dead, but I was the one who had to disappear. Mary had to become Mark.

'You understand?' Ma said, dressing me in boy's clothes and teaching me, over and over, that my body was a secret. 'We need this. You're doing this to help us get by. My good little helper.' The panic sitting just under her breath, along with the sour whiff of gin.

I understood very well. I understood that I hadn't stepped into somebody else's life; I'd stepped into somebody else's death.

For the first year or two, Ma was able to plead illness and to keep me from my grandmother. When I am no longer a baby, and she calculates I'm old enough to pass for him, the visits begin. Once a year, sometimes twice, I am taken to be presented to my grandmother, who is not my grandmother at all, but my dead brother's grandmother – and I go as him. Ma's stories about my

4

sickly infancy go some way to explaining my size, a year and a half younger than the boy I am supposed to be.

My brother's grandmother takes my face between her hands and stares at me, and declares herself well pleased. 'I thought him sickly last time – simple, even. But he's bright enough now, and I can see my Robert in the shape of his nose. The hairline too.' She traces my brow with one finger. 'Yes. He's the dead spit of Robert.' And my mother murmurs agreement, and says indeed, and what a mighty comfort it is to her to have the memory of her dear husband each time she looks upon his son, and the old woman rolls her eyes a little.

'There's no need to colour it too rich, Agnes – we both know you were neither of you paragons during his life.'

Nonetheless she cuts me a narrow slice of sugar from the loaf, lets me eat it straight from the knife, and presses money into Ma's hand when we leave.

And if she does not care for Ma, she never holds that against me – or perhaps it makes her more inclined to like me. Once, I reach out to touch the unlikely white of Grandmother's table-cloth, and when Ma slaps my hand away Grandmother smiles at me like the two of us are a small conspiracy against Ma. But I pity Grandmother, for I know it to be the other way about.

I call her Grandmother, and she calls me Mark, neither name our own. I am old enough to know that the affection she shows me is not for me at all, but for Mark, who is dead, and for her own son, who is dead too. Mark was named after his father's father, Grandmother's late husband – thus Mark's name is doubly dear to her, and doubly removed from me.

So I wear her love like borrowed clothes and know they do not fit me. But what does?

At the corner, near the alehouse, two sailors are singing: 'And the seabelow is waiting, waiting.'

For days I hum the tune to myself, trying to picture this mysterious beast: a *seabelow*.

I ask Ma what a *seabelow* is, and she teaches me, very fast and not scrupling to use the poker, not to be a damned fool. And while I see now that it was only the *sea below*, I like my version too: that great heavy thing, the *seabelow*, awaiting me somewhere.

———————————

Ma is pitted in a constant battle against colour. Despite the money from Grandmother, we have to take in washing. Most everything we take in is supposed to be white, but the world conspires to dirty it, and our grubby rooms conspire even more. The linens come in with marks and stains, and Ma boils and beats and scrubs, but even when the sheets are out on the line, smuts drift across from Mrs Fegan's kitchen fire next door, and if the pigeons have a shit on the sheets, Ma takes it very personal. Once a dog gets into the yard and runs about with its tail like a muddy plume, leaving mud streaks all over the bottom of the sheets. We are up most of the night trying to get them clean again by the stink of tallow candlelight. Ma stretches a sheet close to the candle, examining its stubborn stains. 'It shouldn't be like this,' she says, and I don't know if she means the sheet, badly soiled, or all of it: the rooms; the damp; her hands, cracked and ruined, an old woman's hands that she cannot recognise.

There are women beaten down by their lives – as if life is a husband too ready with his fists, and they've learned not to argue back. Mrs Fegan next door is that way, and Ma's friend Elsie too: quiet women, their gaze kept always low. Ma is never like that. She shouts back at the bailiffs that come to the door; she mixes the lye with a mighty clattering of the paddle against the tub. 'I wasn't raised to this,' she tells me, letting the pails drop to the floor with outraged thuds. She will not forgive her life for what it has dared to become.

———————————

Ma teaches me my letters and numbers, for it is what Grandmother would expect of Mark. I learn my own names first, both of them: Mary and Mark, though the truth is that Ma mainly calls me Mark. The public pretence fast enough becomes a private habit, for what is private anyway, with the walls of our lodgings so thin we can hear Mr Fegan's snoring, and the smell of his wife's cooking is a fuggy reminder that even our air is not our own. With a stick I write in the dirt of the yard: *Mark, Mary, Mark.* How close the words are – the same at a glance, barely two strokes of the final letter between them. And *Ma* is there at the root of both of them – whichever name I go by, there is no escaping her.

We have one book in the house – not even a book, in truth, but a mere gazette: *An Almanac of the coasts of the British Isles, including Observations, Draughts, and Anchoring places, Invaluable to Merchant Adventurers and all Gentlemen belonging to the sea.* This is what Ma uses to teach me to read. Over and over, I sound out those words: 'Gentlemen belonging to the sea.'

'Was it my father's, this book?' I ask Ma. She spits on the iron to test its heat, and its hissing answers me where she does not. I dare not ask her again, for she never speaks of my father. But I hold close to me the thought that it was he who left the book. If the almanac is my father's, it explains why Ma has never sold it. And I cling to the notion that he is a seafaring man, same as Ma's husband, because it explains why he is no longer here. It gives my father all kinds of alibis: storms or pirates or war or marooning. A thousand reasons to be anywhere but here with us.

We can afford no other books, but from time to time Grandmother will lend us one, to help with my lessons. She lets us borrow an old reader, whose author swears in the preface that all the tales within are true, and taken 'from my own knowledge, or from reverend godly ministers, and from persons that are of unspotted reputation, for holiness, integrity and wisdom.' I trace my finger over 'unspotted,' and in my mind the salvation of my soul is all bound up in Ma's war with smuts, and with the starched whiteness of the linen at Grandmother's table.

More than any other of its litany of sins, the book abjures lying: 'O that is a grievous fault indeed! And whither do such children go when they die, do you think?' But the very same book also

7

enjoins me to 'Do what your father and mother bid you cheer-fully; and take heed of doing anything that they forbid you.'

Thus I know that in keeping or breaking the secret of my own body, I am bound to disobey either God or Ma. But Ma's punishments are much closer to hand than those of God, since Ma is very ready with the laundry paddle or anything within arm's reach.

Once, when she has been at the brandy, she puts both hands to my cheeks, and I don't know if she is about to kiss me or spit at me, nor which would be worse. Then she gives a great weepy smile and says, 'Look at that face. You could've made a lovely girl.' She says it as though the girl part of me is put away for good and there can be no summoning it back.

For myself, I do not find it strange to be raised a boy. I know nothing different, and for many years I think the world is made thus. Grandmother lends us a book of ancient myths, and so I believe all bodies are as loose as the bodies in those stories. Zeus changes into a swan to have his way with Leda; Daphne changes to a tree to escape some other cockish god. I figure there is a truth running through these tales like a thread of gristle through meat: that you can be one thing, and then another. Sometimes it's a threat; sometimes it's a promise.

My brother was a boy without a life; I am a girl without a name. I live inside his name and inside the life that was meant to be his. We are two people trying to cram into one person-shaped space. I miss the brother I've never met, for I am lonely – our secret means that Ma keeps me close, and I quickly learned that playing with other children in the street will bring her out in a righteous fury, to drag me back into our rooms. I understand, too, that my mother has barely enough love for one. If I am to get any of it, I had better be Mark, for he was there first and such warmth as she has was shaped to fit him.

When I am six or seven a fever takes hold of me. For days and nights I sweat and shudder, my bones trying to shake themselves loose of skin. When Ma spoons water into my mouth, my teeth clatter against the spoon. I vomit until there is nothing left inside me but bile, and I keep vomiting nonetheless, black-green pooling in the bottom of the bowl.

'Mark,' my mother cries. 'Mark.' I have not seen her cry before and I wonder if I am dreaming, or perhaps already dead. And I do not know if she is crying for me, or for my brother who is already gone, or for both of us, since I am more him than I am myself.

And when I cry, who am I crying for? And who is crying?

The dysentery wrings me out, but I am stubborn. I have been granted little and have learned how to cling to what I have. I cling all the harder because I know this life was never really meant for me. I am the accident, the troublemaker, the proof of Ma's sluttish ways. Maybe it was me that caused my brother to fall sick in the first place, because he was still small – too small to be left behind by Ma, and me taking her milk all for myself.

So I do not die. I come back into my body, which for weeks is reluctant to do as I ask.

'You're weak.' Ma says it like an accusation, but she buys meat to add to our pottage. It's the leavings from the butcher – the cheapest she can get, more gristle than flesh. If Ma's love comes as gobbets of bone then I take it nonetheless, and gladly. The walls by the fire drip with steam and when she looks away I lick the side of my bowl.

I am eleven and my breasts have barely started to come in, but we can afford no risks, so Ma buys some reed stays, not too soiled. She stands behind me, yanking the corset strings tighter – *yank* – tighter – *yank*. We do this daily for a year, and at the end of it she casts the corset aside for my breasts give no sign of growing at all. I think she will surely be happy, for it means the end of the daily ritual of lacing my stays. 'And you can sell the corset,' I say, for nothing gladdens Ma like coin. But when she takes the stays to sell, she slams the door so hard I think the latch will come right off, and I see that in some way I have failed her – that in not growing breasts I have got womanhood wrong. She has often railed at me for not being boy enough; today I discover that nor am I girl enough.

———————————

Grandmother falls ill. We visit her but she cannot speak. Ma's lips are pressed so tight they disappear in a single, set line, for it is clear the old woman is dying, and our allowance with her. I am sorry to see the old woman thus, with a tremor that will not let her hands rest, and each breath the sound of a stick dragged through gravel.

'Recite your lessons, Mark,' Ma says. 'Show your grandmother how well you've attended to your studies.' She leans closer to Grandmother, and speaks loud. 'For he is bright as his father was. Willing, and quick to learn.'

I do not want to join in the usual performance, and instead I stay silent, and let the old woman stare at my face, which she does very intently. She is no fool, my brother's grandmother. She keeps her eyes on my face, and her mouth opens and I fancy she is about to speak. But her voice will not answer her summons, and Ma is talking over her now.

'Recite your catechism, love,' Ma says to me. 'It's not like you to be shy – not with your own grandmother, whom you hold so dear.' Her voice has crept to a higher pitch. This is her final show, she knows – the last chance to squeeze some kind of bequest out of Grandmother.

I manage to stumble through a catechism, from the book that Grandmother lent us:

The books of every man's doings shall be laid open, men's consciences shall be made either to accuse them or excuse them, and every man

*shall be tryed by the works which he did in his life time, because they
are open and manifest signs of faith or unbelief.*

It makes no difference: Grandmother is dead in a month, and
leaves us nothing. I wonder whether, in that final visit, I let her
stare too close and too long.

———————————————

It is the end of the money that used to come each quarter, and
Ma says it will for sure be the end of us too. 'We'll starve,' she
says, over and over. She is always one for dramatics, as long as the
news is bad. 'We'll starve. We'll be on the streets. We'll starve for
sure.' And it is true that since the war ended, the docks are full of
sailors in need of work, and I can no longer distinguish between
the beggars who gather by the market, for hunger makes all their
faces look the same.

Ma fights very vicious against change, for change has never
been good news for her. Change was her husband leaving, and
my father too; a daughter she wasn't supposed to have; her son
dying. Change for Ma is a series of damp greasy steps that she's
stumbled down, angry all the way, from the clean house of her
parents to this damp room.

So she curses prodigiously, abusing Grandmother's name until
both the Fegans pound on the wall. Myself, I cannot summon
any anger for the old woman, though in truth I cannot summon
much sadness either.

'Aren't you angry at that sour old bitch?' Ma demands. But
Ma's anger doesn't belong to me – it is all hers. I have tried
hating Ma – sometimes it comes easy, but most of the time I
don't know how to hate her, because she is my Ma and her
anger is the nest I grew in, and is my home as much as those
two rented ground-floor rooms with their stubborn stink of lye
and tallow.

It isn't only Grandmother she is raging against. It's the mound
of laundry in the corner; her husband; my father; the life she
used to have and has lost. I can understand that anger. I know

why she spits on the ground after she speaks of men, and of how they passed through her like a harbour but never thought to stay.

She has raised me to be a boy, and she says it is for the money, but sometimes I wonder if it isn't also so the world will treat me kinder than it has treated her. But that means she hates me too, now that I am a boy and on my way to becoming a man. The older I get the angrier at me she becomes, and I never know if it is because I am not good enough at playing a man, or because I am too good at it.

2

I keep waiting for Ma to say it is the end of me being a boy. My grandmother was the reason, and now she is dead, so it must be time now for Mark to be put away like an outgrown coat. But I have been Mark for every one of my twelve years. Do I even know how to be Mary? I don't ask myself about whether being Mary is what I want – with Ma, wanting doesn't come into it.

'I've been up to the big house,' Ma says, when Grandmother has been dead for two weeks. 'You're to go into service.'

'As Mary?' I do not say, *As myself*, for what would that be?

'As Mark.' She doesn't meet my eyes. 'You'll bring in more as a boy.'

'Unless I get caught.'

'So don't get caught.' Her voice softens a little. 'You'll be safer as Mark. It'll keep you out of trouble.'

'What trouble?'

'You won't get boys sniffing around you like dogs.'

She takes me to the back door of the big house to present me to the butler. Mr Twiner stands over me, as grand and square as the grey house itself. He has a narrow mouth and a prodigious sense of his own importance. He looks me over from his great height, and says I shall earn five pounds a year, working as an underfootman, and it will be more if I prove myself a keen lad, and more still if I grow tall, because Madame fancies the look of tall footmen with her coach.

Before I am to return the next day, Ma gives me one final gift. 'Put this in your drawers,' she says. It's a rag sewn around a bundle of dried beans, the whole of it the size of a small fist, and she has stitched three neat buttonholes, with matching buttons inside the men's drawers that I wear.

'Nobody's going to be looking that close,' I say.

'You'd be surprised.'

I believe her, for I know Ma to be an expert in scrutiny.

So I tuck the bag of beans into my drawers, and fiddle ungainly with the buttons until the parcel is fastened into place. It feels strange – a weight where no weight had been. I stand differently too: my legs apart, and when I walk it is with more of a swagger.

Ma says nothing, but nods. Before bed, when she changes her shift, she holds it in front of her breasts with one hand until she has the fresh one ready, and turns away from me as she drops it over her head. She does it quickly – maybe she doesn't even know she's done it. But I know.

I am due back at the big house at dawn. At the pair of yews standing sentry on the back lawn, Ma pulls me close and I think she might embrace me but she just whispers, 'Don't mess this up,' and pushes me on my way. Halfway to the door I turn – she is still there. She watches me right up the back steps, as though she thinks I might run away.

They give me some livery – a jacket and stockings, very fine. 'If you don't last six months, you'll have to give them back,' says Kitty, the maid. Having never worn clothes so extravagant, the stockings alone feel almost reason enough to stay, if Ma and the laundry paddle weren't sufficient already.

At first I feel that I am there on sufferance, and may at any moment be discovered and expelled, stripped from my boyness as well as my fine new stockings. But I have lived so many years in fear of Ma that fear is not strange to me, and soon enough I learn the shape of days in the big house.

I am lucky, the others say, to have mainly indoor work. But I prefer the mornings, when I do the dirty work outdoors – cleaning the shoes, and chopping the wood to set the fires. Later, when Madame is up, I am to come indoors and wear my white neck-cloth that must be kept clean and stiffened or Mr Twiner gives my ear a yank.

'He jerks my ear fit to take it right off,' I confide to young Kitty.

'He's a proper tartar,' she whispers back, all sympathy, which is a new thing for me after Ma's company.

There is a lot of standing about. The trays are my particular terror, for each one is loaded with glasses or chinaware worth more than my year's wages, and when I think about dropping them, my hands start to shake and the glasses set to jangling and Mr Twiner gives me a look sharp enough to pin me to the wall behind.

I have much to learn. The first week, Madame drops a knife and I scurry to fetch another and make to pass it to her. I have never seen Mr Twiner move above a stately pace, but now he swoops across the room and grabs that knife from me like a gull snatching food. Then he puts it on a tray and passes it to Madame thus. I don't know if she even notices this tiny drama, for she has an abstracted air and views the world with a look of mild surprise. We are all to call her Madame, but her right name is Mrs Norton. Her husband was English and died in the late war so she is tolerated here despite being so very French – and she has her late husband's name, and his money too, which counts for more. But she lives extremely quiet and very retired, or perhaps no company is offered to her. At any rate I have seen her sit at a window with needlework untouched on her lap, and stare outside for an hour at a time.

There must always be something coming between me and Madame, I learn. If I pass her a letter, or a glass, it must be on a salver. Makes no difference that I clean her boots and help Kitty turn the handle on the mangle for Madame's sheets. I must pretend that I don't begin each day with my hand inside her shoe as I polish it, which is a surprisingly intimate thing, the curve of her instep and the small dents in the leather from her toes. Once, when she is caught in the rain between the church door and her carriage, her pale blue boots are brought down for cleaning straight away, and when I slip my hand inside them they are still warm.

———————————

For the first time in my life I have a room to myself, though it is way up in the eaves, and so small that to look out of the little window I must kneel on the narrow bed. In spring, swallows make a nest under the eaves and from my window I watch the clutch of five tiny chicks growing and I don't tell a soul. I never knew that birds hatch bald, looking nothing like birds at all. I watch them gradually take on their bird-shapes, and then their proper feathers, and I tell nobody – not even Kitty. It is a novel feeling, to have a secret that isn't a sin.

———————————

Ma never took me to church, but here we all accompany Madame every Sunday, when we sit at the back and she settles alone in her pew at the front. There's a great deal of talk about lying and truth, which seem to much preoccupy the vicar, or God, or perhaps both. 'Speak every man truth with his neighbour: for we are members one of another.' Each week I walk through the double doors carrying with me that big lie, which is the whole shape of my body.

One Sunday the vicar reads from Luke and says, 'For nothing is secret, that shall not be made manifest; neither any thing hid, that shall not be known and come abroad.'

Each Sunday I sit there, feeling the cold from the flagstones even through my shoes, and kneeling when the others kneel, and standing when the others stand. I wait for God to strike me down, for I am a lie and therefore an abomination to the Lord. But no striking comes – and after enough months have passed I start to enjoy the singing, and when the psalm climbs higher and higher I even allow my voice to go along with it, trusting it will be lost in all the other voices singing alongside me, and with the flute and hautboy and bassoon all clamouring along.

And so it happens that I don't believe in God anymore, and I believe in the lie instead. I am Mark – I believe it because I live it each day. We believe what we see and touch, and so my boy-self is as solid to me as the beams of the church itself.

On the first wage day, at the end of the quarter, Ma comes and takes my money.

'That's it?' she asks, when I give her the coins. A guinea and a crown, the guinea new-minted, fresh as a warm egg.

'That's all of it.' More money than I've ever held at once; less than she was expecting.

'What about vails? You should be doubling your wages, if you're attentive to visitors.'

'Madame doesn't have any visitors.'

I try to explain what it's like: the quiet of the big house, when the greatest excitement is the weekly outing to church. Ma simply clamps her hand tight around the coins and leaves.

After six months at the big house, the little beanbag that I wear fastened tight in my drawers grows grimy, and has taken on the rich salty tang of cunny. I sniff it and catch myself smiling – it feels like a joke, or a trick, that this parcel, of all things, should smell most of woman. I wash it by hand with the pitcher and basin in my room. Then I fear that I've made a mistake, and that the washing may cause the beans inside to sprout. For days I wait for those green tendrils to creep through the cloth, curly and springy as new hair down there. But nothing grows, and I am relieved and disappointed.

You may imagine that I am at all times preoccupied by my secret, but the truth is that if you live long enough inside a secret, it concerns you little at all. I am busy with my work, and I do it well. 'Unobtrusive,' Mr Twiner tells me again and again. 'A good servant is attentive, but unobtrusive.' I don't know at first what *unobtrusive* means, but I know I don't want to be looked at. My livery is a disguise – not because it makes me look like a boy, but because it makes me into a servant, which means I am part of the household and nobody in particular, no more than a broom or a tray or a poker for the fire. That suits me well enough.

Kitty sidles up to me on the servant's stairs. 'Can you keep a secret?' she asks, holding out her hand. Three preserved cherries, staining her palm red. She's stolen them from the jar in the cool-room.

'Of course I can,' I say. Kitty little knows how much I deal in secrets.

She gives me one of the cherries, still warm from her hand. I eat it right away so my palms or pockets won't be stained telltale red. I suck every bit of the flesh off the stone, and then I don't dare to spit it out in the courtyard in case the cook or Mr Twiner catches me. For an hour, as I clean the drawing room fireplace, I keep the stone in my mouth like a dislodged tooth. In the end I swallow it. For days I dream a cherry tree will grow in me. I think of Grandmother's book of myths, and the picture of Daphne, half woman and half tree, taking refuge in her own branches. I think of the hardness of women and the softness of wood. I remember the sour-sweetness of the cherry and how it split under my tongue. At night, in my narrow bed, I clench my hand then unfurl it like a leaf, and imagine how boughs might grow from me.

When Ma next comes to the back door for my wages, she looks all around to be sure we are alone, before darting a hand into her pocket and pressing onto me a new parcel of beans. 'You may burn the other,' she says, low-voiced, 'for I hate to think of the state of it.'

I mutter my thanks, and I mean it, for these furtive bundles are the closest I have had to a gift from Ma. I have barely turned from her, the beanbag in my hand, when Kitty pounces at me in the kitchen corridor.

'From your ma?' she says, reaching out. 'Oh share, won't you?' She is whispering, as though this is a secret between just the two of us.

I yank my hand away from her. 'It's nothing,' I say. 'Nothing worth the sharing.'

'What is it?' she says, laughing, and snatches again at my hand. I'm clutching the cloth bundle tight but my hand is too small to hide the whole of it, and her fingers are strong and the thing drops to the floor with a thud. I don't know if she has a chance to see it before I dart to grab it, and even if she did I warrant she could never know its purpose — but she is furious nonetheless.

'Fine,' she shouts. 'Keep your secrets. But don't expect me to share my treats with you again.'

'It's not a treat,' I say, hasty. 'Nothing like that. Only a compress of dried lavender, to help me sleep.' I look down at the floor.

She crosses her arms. 'Then why hide it so?'

I don't have to make a show of my embarrassment — my blushing is real. 'It seemed unmanly,' I say, avoiding her gaze, 'to have my ma bring me such a thing.'

'Well I think it's touching,' she says, once again in the intimate whisper of earlier. 'And kind in your mother too.' She touches my arm. 'Why, if you'd asked, I could've made you one myself.'

'Please don't tell the others.'

She presses my arm again. 'Of course not. Not a word.' And all day she is smug and sends me meaningful glances and fancies herself my particular confidante.

After that I stop wearing the parcel of beans altogether. It's not just the fear of discovery — it's that I have learned to stand as men stand, and to walk as men walk. I have learned that this is nothing whatsoever to do with anything hidden in my drawers — rather, it's a way of being in the world. I have seen how a woman moving through a crowded street will shrink from the bodies of those she must squeeze past. A man, crossing the same place, will shoulder them aside, or if he's more gently inclined, put his hands on the small of a woman's back to ease her out of his way. I see it in the kitchen: how Mr Twiner and Mr Lincoln move through space without thinking, and how Kitty and even Cecile, Madame's Abigail, make way for them. This is the way of it: women making space, and men taking it. So I hold my shoulders back and my knees apart, and if I meet Kitty in the corridor I do not move aside.

In summer I find sprigs of lavender slipped under my door, and on those days Kitty looks at me very knowing and shy. And though she is young and foolish and I would not dare touch her, still I tuck the sprigs of lavender beneath my pillow. If this is the womanly softness Ma warned me against, it smells sweet nonetheless.

In the kitchen, Cecile is fiddling to fix some pins that have come loose from her bodice. She always fancies herself grander than the rest of us, on account of getting Madame's cast-off clothes to wear, and of being above the lowly work of cleaning.

She is from London but her ma was French so she moves between the two tongues. When she speaks to Madame in French, Cecile's voice is uncommon genteel, and she is very pretty-behaved. Below stairs, with the rest of us, she is cockney, and speaks nothing like as dainty as she looks. She contains two different people, and I watch her closely, to see how she manages the jostling of those two within her.

When I see her fumbling her pins, I take them from her without thinking. 'Let me,' I say, and set to pinning them, just as I've done a thousand times for Ma, though the fabric of Cecile's bodice is thicker, brocade stiff under my fingers. She smells of newly pressed cloth, and I can see a dusting of Madame's face powder, or maybe hair powder, on her skirt.

I've barely got the first pin lined up when she grabs it from me, stepping back towards the hearth.

'What're you at? Keep your grubby hands off me.' I must look as ashamed as I feel, because Cecile softens her sneer to a giggle, and says, 'Leastways until your voice breaks, lad.' She goes back to fixing the pins herself.

After that I speak little, and when I do I make an effort to speak low.

———————————

My greatest secret isn't that I am not a boy. My greatest secret is that I like it. I have learned to relish this in-betweenness. I am fourteen now, and then fifteen, and my monthly courses have begun and in my room I must wash privately the rags Ma has given me. My breasts have still not grown – I do not know if it is Ma's savage corsetwork that kept them from taking root, or if I was always to have no breasts to speak of. Yet I find I like my body: the places where it is soft and the places where it is hard. It does not disgust me, not even when it bleeds.

3

1701, and there is a new war. When the Spanish king died, he left his throne to Philip of Anjou. 'He will bring France and Spain together for sure, and overrun all of Europe,' says Mr Twiner, 'and I for one will not be ruled by a Frenchman.' He seems mightily troubled by the notion, for a man who serves a French mistress, and spends so long each day checking her table setting, straightening and straightening again so that all the silverware is lined up just so.

For kings and emperors, it is a war. For me it is a chance to get away from my stiff neck-cloth and the tyranny of trays, and Ma coming to take my money and stare at my face as though it is not what she expected. I am newly sixteen, and I know I am becoming part of this huge, hushed house, as Mr Twiner has. I have worked so hard and for so long at being unobtrusive that I have become unobtrusive even to myself. One day, standing with my back to the wall, hands clasped behind me to keep them still, I shall melt into the wallpaper altogether.

Kitty has become what I think may be called my friend – the first I have ever had. Sometimes she still gazes at me in her moony way, but she has long gathered that nothing shall come of it, and thus over these four years we have become allies against the whims of Mr Twiner, and the airs of Cecile.

For all her staring, Kitty has never seen the truth of me. Yet do I know myself any better than she? Am I Mary, or Mark, or *Read*, as Mr Twiner calls me? And are these my only choices?

If I wish to find my real name, it is not to be found here, in the scullery, or in the corners of the drawing room where I stand watching Madame eat. I will have to seek beyond the familiar walls of this house to find the name that fits my skin.

A war is a strange place to go to find a name – but it seems no more odd than going to war over a Spanish prince, and anyway I have nowhere else to go. So it is to be war, and I am to be in it.

When I give Mr Twiner my notice, I ask him to see that my wages are given to Ma when she comes for them. He gives me a guinea for myself, for good service, and I buy broadcloth to make trousers in the sailor style, and a short jacket too. In my final weeks I sew them in the kitchen every evening, and Kitty insists on helping me, though I am forever having to stitch over her careless seams while she prattles on, oblivious.

I am to enlist at Deptford, for I long to see London before joining the navy. Mr Twiner has offered to pay for the stage-coach from Exeter to London, a luxury I had not thought to have. He pats me heartily on the back and tells me he is proud of me; he seems to see his generosity as a patriotic gesture, though I do not know that the navy will see me as any great prize. When the household finally gathers to see me off, Kitty pretends to cry, and enjoins me through her bunched handkerchief to return safely. I've no intention of returning, but am glad to give her the chance at some theatrics, which she heartily enjoys.

If the news that I am to leave has reached Madame, she has made no sign of it. The French are once again our enemy, as well as the Spaniards. When I walk away from the big house for the final time I think of Madame and her quiet life there, and I wonder if she too is accounted an enemy now.

The roads are so bad and the journey so toilsome that I begin to believe that whatever hardships are to found in the navy, they cannot match the long trudging days to reach Exeter by foot, nor the violent jolting of the stagecoach on rutted roads. By the time I reach London, eleven aching and wretched days since

I set out, the bag of food pressed upon me by Mr Lincoln is exhausted, and what little money I had is all spent on the coaching inns, where I slept amongst strangers and the industrious fleas. I do not stay to marvel at the city's loud and crammed streets, but waste no time in pressing onward to Deptford.

At Deptford Docks, half the boys enlisting are lying about being old enough to get a seaman's wage, instead of a boy's. My lie goes the other way, because I am small and my voice not deep. I take two years off my age and say I am fourteen. When they ask for my Christian name, I say *Mark*, for it is what I am used to – though I could have told them any boy's name of my choosing.

They send me to the *Resolve* as a powder monkey.

'Don't be getting any notions of boarding parties and heroism,' the officer warns me. 'You'll be swabbing decks and running powder from the magazine.'

I, who had no such grand notions, am glad just to be admitted into the war, for a war is such a big thing that a person and their secrets may easily go unnoticed. The *Resolve*, too, is vast: a third-rate ship of the line, one of the navy's mighty battle-ships, with eighty guns and more than 450 men aboard. From the dock it strains my neck to stare at the whole of her, for the masts reach up fit to puncture the sky.

The carpenter's mate catches me ogling the awful height of the rigging. 'She's but a third-rater. A first-rater carries a hundred guns, and near four acres of sail.' He nods sagely, enjoying showing off to a new lad like myself. 'Six thousand trees, a first-rater takes. Oak, mainly – all to be chosen and cut and laid down for seasoning years before the ship can ever be built.' It has never occurred to me that a man might plant a tree and never know that in truth he is planting a ship.

The *Resolve*, with a mere eighty guns, is smaller than those mighty first-rate ships, but to me she is nonetheless so huge that the fact of her floating seems a daily miracle. She is a world entire, with a language all its own. I learn quick, for I have no choice – a ship has no patience and a bosun even less. Under his shouts, I learn of clewlines, buntlines, and reeflines, and 'hitching the lizard.'

On the second day we are all mustered on deck, and the captain reads us the Articles of War. Bored, he wades through the regulations like chest-high water:

No Person in or belonging to the Fleet shall utter any words of Sedition or Mutiny nor make or endeavour to make any mutinous Assemblies upon any pretence whatsoever upon pain of death . . .

It is treason even to mutter against the captain. Likewise we are enjoined, on pain of death, to shun cowardice. But there is a general snickering and rolling of eyes when the captain reads the part about food:

If any of the Fleet find cause of Complaint of the unwholesomeness of his Victuals or upon other just ground he shall quietly make the same known to his Superior or Captain or Commander in Chief as the occasion may deserve . . .

After just two days of navy food, I am already thinking fondly of the food in the big house: Mr Lincoln's suet pastry, eaten fresh with the marks of his fingers baked into it. Here on the *Resolve* a carpenter named Abernathy, who fancies himself a great wag, wears a ship's biscuit rigged on a bit of string like a medallion beneath his shirt – swears blind that he's worn it since the last war and would not be without it, for he claims it saved him from a shard of exploded cannon in the battle of Lagos. He proudly shows me the damage.

'It looks like nothing so much as the gnawings of a rat,' I say, for Ma and I lived in enough cheap lodgings that I know the sight. But Abernathy remains cheerful and swears to his story.

A lad named Marston is quartered close by me, and shares the same shift and the same mess at meal times. He is fresh to the navy as I am, but he is a sailor's son from a family of fishermen, and thus bred to the sea. On the third day we are scrubbing the decks as we must each morning, with a flat soft sandstone that the bosun calls the *holystone.*

'Don't see what's so holy about these things,' I say to Marston, when the bosun has passed us.

'It's because we serve on our knees, as though at prayer.' He glances across at me. 'Though I never met a sailor spends as much time praying as he does scrubbing.' His loud laugh sets gulls squawking from the mast to join in.

We fall to talking, and Marston tells me his father was drowned in the last war, at the battle of Camaret.

'And you still wanted to enlist?'

He shrugs. 'I might as well be drowned by the navy, and see a little of the world, as stay a fisherman in Whitstable and be drowned there.' Then he lets out another of his mighty laughs and the bosun comes stamping up the deck, roaring.

Marston is patient with my many questions and shows me knots without ever grudging it. He seems to step light-footed through days, and all his noise and bluster carves a space where my own quietness can pass unnoticed, like a small boat being towed by its ship. He has a winning way about him, so that before a week is out even the cook knows him by name and after a wet shift will let us dry our coats and gloves by the galley stove, a boon not granted even to the officers.

'Where do you think we'll be headed?' I ask Marston. The ship is full of rumours, but Marston has a knack for confidences.

'Farleigh, one of the bosun's mates, said we're to rendezvous with a convoy. But he won't say where.'

Some of the men are chafing at the uncertainty of not know-ing where we are headed, nor for how long this commission will last. For me, after all those years in the big house, each day neatly obeying its rituals, this not-knowing is a gift.

'Wherever we're headed,' I say, 'it won't be home. And that's something.'

Marston meets my grin with his own. 'That's something indeed.'

The river takes us eastward, past Tilbury, towards the sea.

'See that?' says Lewes, a thin lad with a mouth puckered tight like an arsehole. He points further downriver; on the northern bank, something hangs up high, so heavy it does not even shift in the wind. 'That's Kidd.'

William Kidd the pirate, whose capture a few years back was such monumental news that it even penetrated the thick walls of the big house.

'Rope snapped clear in half, first time they tried to hang him,' Marston says.

A ship's corporal comes near on his way to the forecastle; we fall silent.

'That's just a story,' says Lewes in a low voice, when the corporal has passed.

'It's the sworn truth.' Marston nods very earnest. 'Took two goes to kill him right.'

'Were you there?' I ask.

'Heard about it. Then, before they strung his body up there, they tarred him, and hanged the gibbet low, so the tide would cover it. Three tides' worth. In. Out. In. Out. In—'

'We get it,' I say.

'Hanging him twice wasn't enough?' asked Lewes.

A shrug. 'S'pose not. Anyway, I'm just telling you what happened.'

'You weren't there,' Lewes says, making fast his end of the line. 'You talk nothing but trumpery.'

The *Resolve* has passed the gibbet now, but Marston keeps his eyes on the caged figure. 'He'd have some stories to tell.'

'Whatever stories Kidd has,' I say, 'he ain't telling them to us.'

I used to think Mr Twiner a hard master, but I knew nothing then of officers and captains, and most particularly of our bosun. The captain is the ship's God, but for lowly powder monkeys such as us, he is a remote figure. In our daily business it is the bosun, and the bosun's mates, who keep us at our work. The bosun, Mr Flyte, is always at pains to call us 'Mister,' but there's nothing genteel in his way of speaking.

'The water butts, if you please, Mister Read,' Flyte yells.

'That man has a gift for making a name sound like an oath,' Marston whispers to me.

For the first few days I believed all our scurrying was to get the ship sea-ready. I awaited the time when it would all be done: the swabbing of the deck, the checking and rechecking the lines and yards, and fixing chafing gear where the lines are rubbing. I figured that when all was done well enough, the *Resolve* would be sea-trim and all set. It is not until we've rounded Broadstairs and are at sea that I realise shipboard work is never done. Even on the rare, snatched moments when we might dare to stand, or lean against the rail and talk awhile, down sweeps the bosun to make us polish brass or pick oakum. Oakum is the worst of it: the endless job of unpicking tangled and spliced cordage to use afresh, or sometimes merely because the navy hates nothing so much as idleness. We pick oakum until even Marston, who has worked his uncle's fishing boat for years, has fresh blisters to compare with mine.

'I could scour the deck without the holystone, my hands are that rough.' I hold up my palm to show him.

He claps me on the back and grins. 'Then we'll make a sailor of you yet.'

We pass two nights off Portsmouth, awaiting the wind. When at last we weigh anchor, the whole shift is set to hauling, and it seems an age before the anchor breaches the surface, dripping and reluctant as some outraged beast of the deep. My hands on the messenger rope are growing stronger. I think of Ma, and her tough hands yanking my corset strings. She would've made a good sailor.

Marston was right: we're heading south to rendezvous with a Dutch convoy on the way back from Cape Town, and are to escort them back to the Low Countries.

'Didn't join up just to play nursemaid to Dutch cargo ships,' mutters Lewes.

'I'd like to meet the nursemaid who could take on a Spanish man-of-war,' I say.

'And we need the Dutch,' says Beadle, an able seaman nearing fifty. 'If the enemy strangles the Dutch trade, we'll all be speaking Spanish before too long.'

'That may be so,' says Lewes, 'but this isn't what I enlisted for.'

'You near pissed yourself when the mail packet fired the signal shot,' says Marston, with his hand on Lewes' shoulder. 'Don't be in such a hurry for action.'

Lewes shrugs off Marston's hand, and continues his muttering. For myself, I am glad to be on a ship of the line, which sees less action than the frigates and other smaller ships. The sea is enough for me.

Marston is with me when, for the first time, the bosun sends us up with the topmen, to learn the knack of balance. Up here the very air feels different. The men call to each other, mast to mast, and I stare down upon our wake, spreading behind us like the train of a lady's skirt.

'Are you not afraid?' asks Marston, who has no love of heights, for all his experience of sailing.

'No,' I say. Then I say it again, louder, for I am as surprised as he to find that it is true. 'No,' I shout into the wind.

When the bosun orders me to the tops, I like nothing better than to swing myself up to the crosstrees where the air is a draught fit to make me forget that I ever lived in those damp rooms with Ma. You could almost be drunk on the freshness of it. I, who have never been greedy, take great gulps, denying myself nothing.

The bosun sees how quick I have become at gaining the tops, and how nimble I come down again. 'Mister Read,' he says, pleased for once, 'you're more ape than boy.'

I think: *You do not know the half of it.*

There's no privacy on a ship – leastways, not for a powder monkey like me, nor for any but the captain or most senior officers. But keeping my secret is not as hard as I'd feared. The great pace and bustle of naval life is a boon to me. There is rarely a moment of rest or pause, and all is done in such a hurry. Each change of shift is heralded by impatient shouts, 'Out or down! Out or down!' so dressing and stowing our hammocks is done in a flurry and a rush, each of us concerned only with getting out to the muster and avoiding the bosun's fury. The navy is full of boys pretending to be men. Is it such a big difference, one girl pretending to be a boy?

As for doing my business at the heads, I make sure to let my shirt hang long, and from years of practice I've trained myself to piss man-wise, standing, my hands cupped around nothing but a stream of my own piss. And while I cannot aim as neat as a man, I warrant I am still neater than Lewes, who thinks it rare sport to spray all about like a dog. For shitting I foster the habit of hanging my arse low enough that none can see what goes on below the wooden seat, though Marston jokes that the sharks will have my balls if I hang my arse any lower, and I laugh along with him.

I am handy now at washing by passing the wet cloth quick beneath my shirt. Twice, when we are becalmed, the captain has a sail lowered into the water to form a kind of great bath where the men may bathe – but I am far from the only one who does not join that naked crowd, and those that do are enjoying their larks and splashing too much to trouble themselves over those of us who wait adeck.

We are changing for Sunday muster and Lewes is strutting about naked and I am doing my usual busy work of changing beneath my long shirt and Lewes says, loud for all to hear, 'What are you hiding that's so rare and precious, Read? Are your balls made of gold?'

Marston jumps in at once. 'Jesus, Lewes, it's a mercy to be spared the sight of Read's balls, for God knows we see enough of yours. If you had your way you'd hang yours under the mantel like my ma's Christmas puddings.'

And now all the men are making sport of Lewes, for it's true he parades about as though his tackle were a prize to be admired, and Marston shoots a smile at me across the hammocks and I smile back, and though he does not know my secret we are conspirators nonetheless.

My man's stance, practised over years in the big house, comes ever more natural as I take on the shipboard sway, the sea forcing us to brace our legs wide as we walk. I talk little, and make my voice as gruff and low as I dare. Given the many young servant boys on the *Resolve*, some barely twelve, mine is far from the highest voice aboard.

I have slim hips, and all the shipboard work keeps my middle stout with muscles, instead of a nipped-in lady's waist. And after years of waiting for my breasts to come in, half dreading and half curious, I've accepted that they're never coming. There are many men on ship with bigger breasts than my own, though even those men shrink after a few weeks of shipboard victuals. After the first month I don't even need to smuggle the bloodied rags of my courses, for my body is too thin and worn to have any blood to spare.

There's a midshipman called Havers who boasts of his prodigious sense of smell. He says it makes life below deck a sore trial for him, with the bilge stink and the sweated stench of many men and little air. But some days Havers makes a spectacle of his talent, and has Marston bring him a pile of shirts so he can sort each one to its owner, from a sniff alone. It's a good trick but I get the notion that he might sniff me out, my cunny and its smell distinct from the fug of men that thickens the air below deck. So though Havers seems a decent man, I make sure to avoid him, even leaving the mess table early if he sits too close. I fear the betrayals of my own body, or of his.

Yet if you think it's all watchfulness or fear, this queer business of being in my body, then you're missing all the joy: joy so big I might split my lungs with it. When I am clambering up the shrouds, or hauling with the others to raise the sheets, my body is as much a marvel to me as the mighty machine of the *Resolve* itself.

4

1702

Beadle, the able seaman, shows me how to use a backstaff to measure the sun's midday angle to figure our latitude. I pick it up quick, and with a clear sky, I can soon take my reading and calculate where we lie, north to south, more or less.

'But north to south's the easy bit,' says Beadle. 'Doesn't take a ship's master to figure latitude. Now, east to west? That's where the real skill lies.' He explains the almighty looseness when it comes to east and west, which don't submit to any sailor's measurings. 'And if you're but a few degrees off, you can find yourself hundreds of miles from where you reckoned.'

I pester Beadle to teach me more of navigation; I pester Marston to teach me more knots. When Flyte, the bosun, sets us to wetting down the sails when the wind is weak, I ask Marston: 'Why, though? Doesn't it make them heavier, and more sluggish?'

'I've never concerned myself with *why*,' he says, hauling the full pail. 'It just works, is all I know. Now mind those shrouds.'

'And another thing,' I say, ducking under the shroud lines. 'Why do so many shipboard words sound like death? *Shrouds, hanging blocks, throat seizings.*'

'Don't you be taking a word for a prophecy,' says Marston. 'They're just words, is all.' He lets the empty pail fall. 'You know, I thought you a quiet one, when first we came aboard. But, indeed, you're a barrel of *why*.'

He is grinning, but I counsel myself to stay quieter, for few men are like Marston, who will share his knowledge as readily as he'll share his tot of grog. I daren't risk drawing attention to myself, or drawing the ire of the bosun, who swoops down quick on chatter. And I should know my place, for I'm no midshipman – not even an able seaman. But I take it all in, nonetheless. I take it as greedily as I gulp down the sharp clean air of the tops.

———————

Our convoy safely delivered, we are sent south, to patrol against the Spaniards. But in the Bay of Biscay, the sea unleashes a storm. I have forgotten what it is to be dry, and I am soaked through, anchor-boned. The *Resolve*'s tremendous height is as nothing now to the height of the waves. Between each crest we pitch into a black trough so deep you cannot see the grey sky anywhere but straight up. At the base of each trough I hold my breath, and it seems impossible that the *Resolve* can ever rise again, and not founder. Each time she climbs from the darkness, the breath shudders from me; then it begins again, over and over through the limitless night. The captain and the officers keep us scrambling, for they must find a precise balance: too little sail, and we shall be overset in the chasm between waves; too much, and wind will crack a mast like a spine, and we'll be done for.

'You ever seen a blow like it?' I ask Marston.

'In my uncle's ketch?' He snorts. 'I'd be a dead man.'

'And us? Are we dead men?'

'Not yet.' He spits saltwater. 'Not if you quit your questions a moment and help me with this mainstay.' Then he grins, and I feel an answering grin rising on my own face, as unlikely as a ship rising up the face of these great waves.

Near dawn the wind eases a little, but a sudden gust wrenches the crosstrees clear off our mizzenmast. A lieutenant is struck and is carried below with his head smashed out of shape, and not like to live. A trail of broken cordage hangs limp above us. Aloft, men scuttle to repair the mast, but the ship is still pitching something fierce, and a young midshipman slips from the tops.

I am close enough to hear him land, a hard and soft sound at once. The surgeon is called but there is no physicking that body, broken as it is, and so we swab the blood from the deck instead, and it takes four pails to clear.

When the waves have settled, the dead lad is sewn into his hammock, weighed down with shot, to be sent overboard before he takes to smelling. The chaplain reads a prayer, solemn but hasty, before the assembled company.

'This bible talk never seems to have much to do with us, somehow,' Marston whispers.

I keep my eyes forward as I reply. 'Nor with what happened today to that wretched fellow.'

They hoist the body over the rail. I watch the sea close over the shroud, the water all about and never-ending.

'Excepting Noah,' I say, keeping my voice low. 'That's a bible story I could come to believe in.' That tale at least has the salt tang of truth in it. Anyone who's sailed beyond sight of land must know that feeling, when all the world is water. From the *Resolve*'s decks, it's no stretch at all to believe that the sea has risen up and claimed the world for its own.

'Aye.' Marston dares a small sideways smile. 'Only part of the Noah story that's hard to credit is the bit where they find land again.'

The storm has rinsed the sky clean — a vast blank sky, above a sluggish sea. By dawn word comes that the injured lieutenant has died. He too is sent overboard, and this time I fancy the chaplain rushes the prayer even more than yesterday, and he is finished by the time the water has taken the shroud.

The sea ignores the sailor. You must get used to that fast. Crabshell or stone or bone: it's all the same to the sea. If you can learn that, you might learn to survive.

When I left the big house, Mr Lincoln, the cook, told me the navy would be the making of me. If he'd ever been to sea himself, he'd know it isn't like that — not even one bit. 'Going to sea has been the unmaking of me,' I would tell Mr Lincoln. And whether you take to a sailor's life or not depends on whether you can handle being unmade.

'Make you regret signing up?' Marston asks, once the last bubble has risen from the lieutenant's shroud.

'No,' I say, for the only way to love the sea is recklessly.

I think of Ma less often now, and of the big house little at all – the sea has a great knack for forgetting. On a clear day the *Resolve* casts its reflection on the water but the sea holds on to nothing.

Nine weeks have passed and still we have seen no action. We are escorting another Dutch convoy, this one to the south.

'I enlisted to fight Spaniards and Frenchies,' Lewes says, 'not to polish decks and wait.'

Marston rolls his eyes. 'You enlisted for the same reason as the rest of us – for a wage.'

On the dawn watch, we are employed filling the water butts on deck. Young Flett is telling a story of a woman whose lover discovers that she slips into the sea at night, and takes on the body of a seal. A *selkie*, Flett calls her. He is from Orkney where such things are spoken of very serious, so when Lewes and the others make sport of his tales, Flett takes it ill, and will not tell us the ending.

'Don't pay any mind to Lewes,' I say. 'Tell us what became of the selkie.'

But there is a cry from above, for the lookout has espied a sail to the south. Soon enough it is confirmed: a French ship of the line.

I had thought battle was a thing that happened quickly. Now I learn that a battle at sea can be a drawn-out thing. For a day and a half the enemy ship haunts our horizon. The captain's orders are passed down the ship and we obey, and sometimes we draw clear and the French ship recedes; sometimes we slow and she comes on fast. When dark settles our whole convoy labours upwind, all lights extinguished, and Lewes crows that we have lost the French ship for sure, but come the dawn there she is, closer than ever. There is a grim patience to her pursuit, and after our night's ruse failed there is no doubt she will catch us, for she is free to set as much sail as she likes, while we can go no faster than the slowest of the Dutch merchant ships, which is slow indeed.

'No battle could be worse than this waiting,' I whisper to Marston.

'Let's hope you prove right.'

By noon she has gained on us so that even without a glass I can see the individual lines of her rigging. Now of a sudden all is action: the decks must be cleared of anything loose and wooden – for everything can become deadly when shattered by shot. We shunt benches and mess tables below, and lower the boats aft, to be towed. We fetch the cross-bar and langrel, bundles of old nails and bolts to be used as shot, for tearing to pieces the enemy's rigging.

The French fire when we are well out of range and Lewes scoffs that they are wasting shot and time. These are two things always in short supply in a ship – but I don't mistake the French for fools for I think they merely wish to show us they are ready for a warm action, and indeed they are, for they come about swift, so that they will cut between us and the convoy, and the bosun shouts, 'Mister Read, be ready with the sand,' and gestures at the pails laid ready.

I shout 'Aye aye, sir,' for this response comes quicker than breath to a sailor – but I don't know what use sand will be in a battle, and the bosun must see my blank face.

'To stop men slipping,' he says.

I take up a pail, hefting its weight, but I still don't understand.

'In the blood,' he says impatiently, and is gone, harrying Marston and Lewes.

The French get off another broadside but they time it poorly on the pitching sea, which rolls their gunports too high and they largely shoot at the sky, though the screeching of shot overhead is a noise I will not soon forget for a battle at sea is a very clamorous thing, a great catastrophe of sound.

In our hammocks, Lewes and the other lads have yarned about the heroics of battle, but now I see that for powder monkeys such as us, most of our task in battle is staying out of the way. On deck I must needs run hunched to keep my head below the gunwale if I don't want it blown off. Carrying powder up from the magazine to the guns, we must dart clear of the gunners who dash about with linstocks, priming-irons and rammers, and we're as like to be crushed by the crew running out the gun as we are by enemy fire.

I'm halfway up the ladder from the magazine with a load of powder and there is a mighty lurch, a blow as sharp as Ma used to smack me on the back of the head.

'Are we hit?' I yell to Marston, as I try to regain my footing.

'It's only our own broadside going off,' he calls from just behind me, and he is right for when we get back up to the gundeck there is the reek of powder and all the guns on the larboard side already being reloaded.

Back on deck I can see our broadside clipped their mizzen-mast, its top spar hanging by the sheet. They have done us but little damage, yet someone is yelling, for abaft our mainmast young Flett has taken a blast of grapeshot from a swivel gun, and has gone down in a wet mess of blood and saltwater and is dead.

'Jesus,' says Marston, when the bosun yells for us to scatter the sand. 'You would not believe so small a lad had so much blood in him.'

All the blood is gone out of Flett, and his stories too. I toss the sand where his blood has leeched and think how we shall never hear the end of his tale: the woman remains a seal always, and cannot return to her lover, nor even to her own body. The story ends with the teller.

The French ship crippled now, we have no difficulty in running her down, and she is boarded neat and the French make no great heroics of resisting, and the captain sets a prize crew aboard her and she is a fine prize indeed.

We have nine dead to be sunk before sundown. It falls to me and Marston to shroud young Flett.

'It was a quick death, at least,' Marston says. 'That's a mercy.'

'Aye,' I say. Such small mercies as we are granted, the sea has taught us to take.

Marston winces as we hoist Flett's body onto the canvas, then says, 'We've no need to weigh the shroud down with shot, for there's so much in him still.'

I find that I laugh too, for laughter is the only way to navigate days like these. Nevertheless, we do load the hammock with heavy shot before we sew it about Flett, for the sea must take down our dead or how will we be forgiven?

The secret of ships is that they sing.

Marston confides this to me the day after Flett's death, when we are together in the tops, put to work on setting the topgallants. All around us the high keening of lines vibrating against the wind.

'They sing, you know,' Marston says. 'Each ship different.'

'They do,' I say quickly, for he is looking abashed, not being one to talk poetic. I pat the mast. 'Though sometimes her singing is none too tuneful.' The *Resolve* is older than most ships her size – and though a fine old lady, she creaks something grievous under topsails. But I know exactly what Marston means when he speaks of the singing of the ships, for I have grown accustomed to the *Resolve*'s particular song. The slap of a slack sail against itself. Wood against water, water against wood, the deep-down groans of the hull yearning for the forest of its bones. The wind in the sails is a roar barely to be imagined. A hundred lines, a thousand, each straining, stretching, and the great heavy rush of the mainsail being let out, the mighty drop of canvas from the yard.

'Tell me about your uncle's boat,' I say to Marston. 'Tell me how she sang.'

Reassured that I will not mock him, Marston recounts for me the song of his uncle's fishing ketch: the hiss of her narrow hull splitting the water; the neat crack of her staysail catching the wind.

'I can get used to the sounds of a ship,' I tell him, 'but I can't find it in myself to care for her smells.' And Marston grins, for it's true that smells make a tremendous din on any ship. No smell in the world like ship-smell. The fry of burnt rope ends, and the lingering tang of powder from the last exercising of the guns. Then, below deck, the man-stink of sweat and breath on greasy air. The nasty farts of Lewes, who farts mighty big for a small fellow. Worst of all is the bilgewater, but when Beadle, the kindly able seaman, hears me groan at the stink, he says, 'You get sweet bilgewater, that's a sure token she has a leaky hull. You'll learn to be grateful for the stink, lad.' And over and under everything, the sea's own smell: salt to cut through the air and make my chapped lips sting.

The ship has reshaped my body, these months aboard. What fat I used to carry has dropped away. On navy victuals I am stripped down to what the navy needs: muscle and bone. I learn how to tap my biscuit against the bulkheads to knock the weevils loose, and to scatter sand evenly before we holystone the deck. Though I am not, like Marston, bred to the sea, I am quick to learn. I copy Marston's hands until I, too, can close my eyes and read a knot with my fingers.

You might think it a poor friendship, and me a poor friend, for not confiding my secret to Marston. Indeed if I were to tell him, I would swear he would not betray me. But his friendship does not need to be bought with secrets, and he demands no price of me. And I will not allow that I keep anything from him – for he knows me as no other has. He knows of Ma, her sudden anger and her appraising stare. He knows of the hushed world of the big house, and of how when I climb to the tops I feel that the world is opening out before me. I know that he wears his dead father's jacket and will not change it though the elbows are worn clean through; I know of the song of his uncle's ketch. Our friendship is such that he knows the whole of me, and I him – and what has that to do with the business between my legs?

If you were to ask me the greatest change I ever made, it would not be going about as a boy, for I was raised thus and it has never felt a big matter. No. The greatest change in me was going to sea. I could pass again as a woman, and may yet in years to come. But I will never not be a sailor.

5

Our captain is Turnbull. He is accounted a good sailor but if ever he was a keen one that was many years ago, and now he fancies himself a man of science, and is more concerned with sea creatures than with the French or the Spaniards. He sets boys to trawling with nets and hooked lines, to pull from the water all manner of creatures better left to the dark. His great prize is a polypus. I am on deck when he hauls it from the net, a weighty, slack beast with flesh spongy as a ball of risen dough. Its many legs are lined with round suckers, a row of blind eyes. The captain is jubilant: 'I will author a paper for the Royal Society,' he says. 'A new lineage altogether.' He calls for one of the topmen, an able seaman named Ellis, who has a talent for drawing, and sets him to sketching the creature, which is laid on the deck, pulsing. The captain has made of Ellis a kind of factotum, bidden to follow the captain about with parchment and inks to draw the speci-mens. I have heard Flyte, the bosun, mutter that a topman like Ellis is wasted trotting after the captain all day, when he is needed aloft. For myself I am glad of it, for more and more the bosun sends me aloft in Ellis' stead, and though Flyte is not one for praise, when he calls 'Mister Read,' his voice has less venom in it.

The captain calls often upon the surgeon, too, even when the sick bay is loud with men ill or wounded. The captain will summon the surgeon to his quarters, or to the deck where some new creature lies flapping and slapping wetly on the boards. The surgeon, Carson, gives him no encouragement but Captain Turnbull says loudly, 'Come, we men of science understand that there are graver concerns than the Spaniards,' which is a fine thing to say on a clear day with no Spanish sails about, but less persuasive when we are harried by the Spanish privateers, or when we've weathered a foul storm overnight and are left limping with a damaged foremast.

Daily, Captain Turnbull has men carry his specimens from his great cabin to the deck, in barrels and in earthenware jars, and the polypus in a huge glass bowl of the captain's own design. 'She's an extraordinary creature,' he announces to Ellis. 'You would not credit it, but if a limb were severed, she could grow a new one entirely.' He leans closer to the glass. 'I am thinking of attempting an experiment.' He oversees the men carefully as they haul up fresh water and top up the containers, upbraiding them if they jostle his specimens.

Does he know that the polypus is watching too? I see it when I pass: its massive eyes, and its tender flesh pulsing, pulsing – the sea's vigilant heart.

Thick winter. Below deck our breath steams and our wet clothes never dry; above deck we wrap mufflers about our faces, and hunch with our hands in our armpits for warmth.

We meet a navy frigate bound for Southampton and the officers come aboard to dine with the captain, and will take our letters for home. I write to Ma:

I am in good health, and find this navy life suits me well. You needn't worry on my account . . .

Which would be a fine thing, I think, but I must fill the page for it will cost the same if it were empty and God knows Ma decries a waste.

I hope you are well and they say this war shall be ended before the year is out and that at sea we have the better of them. If you could see the Resolve *in full sail you would agree – and we are but a*

third-rater and some are newer and larger but few so fine I believe,
and her men of stout heart and willing, and we do not fear the enemy.

I fear the enemy no more than I used to fear Ma. Indeed I fear them less, for I could never conceive of fighting back against Ma, whereas a man may at least take arms against the Spaniards or the French.

I did not mean to grieve you by going so sudden to the navy but was very eager to be gone and you will grant I hope, Ma, that neither of us is a great one for leave-taking – but I wish you heartily well and Mr Twiner vouchsafed to give you the last of my wages which I trust he has done.

I go to sign myself Mark, for Ma's sake as well as mine, should anyone else see the letter. But in the end I sign it *M*, which serves very well, for it stands in place of both Mary and Mark, neither and both. The way I have scrawled it, the *M* might be a bird in flight.

I am not the only woman aboard. The captain's wife has stayed ashore, but some of the warrant officers' wives sail with us. We see little of them, for they're quartered in the lower deck with their husbands. By day they stay out of the way, often down on the orlop deck, where although it's dank they have peace. Some men pay them a few shillings to do their washing, but I steer well clear of the wives, for fear their women's eyes will espy me for what I am. I mend my own clothes too, and my knack with a needle does not betray me, for I discover that every sailor knows his way around a needle, from mending sails to making their clothes.

There are servants to attend the officers' wives – just two lads, Belling and Lorimer, perhaps twelve or thirteen years old. The purser's wife, Mrs Tandy, has made of Belling a kind of pet and favourite. She takes turns about deck with him, arm in arm and ruffling his hair, which sees him roundly teased whenever he ventures into the seamen's quarters.

'They say her own children both died,' says Marston, as Mrs Tandy passes, little tallow-faced Belling arm in arm with her.

'If it's true, I think Belling a poor substitute,' I say. He is known to steal, and once he takes one of Mrs Tandy's dirty skirts and charges the men to sniff it. Then he wears the skirt himself, mincing between the hammocks and playing at being Mrs Tandy, some rope balled down his shirt for her dugs, 'though I'd need more, and to have it hanging about my knees, for she's a slack old baggage.'

Even as he parades in the skirt, Belling looks about him with an alertness that I recognise well enough. He has been raised poor – poorer than me. His sharpened face and stunted body tell the story of mean rooms and unwholesome food, and not enough of it. So while I mistrust young Belling and his designing ways, I know why he scans each face, each cabin, for his chance. Perhaps he is no more dishonest than I, for I keep my own secrets.

———————————

Five months out, the scurvy begins to stalk us. They say it is a lazy man's disease, but I watch it take Hanson, a young seaman so full of vigour that many times we have had to pelt him with whatever we can reach from our hammocks, to shut him from yammering when we're trying to snatch the four hours of sleep that we're allotted between shifts. He sickens fast, and one morning he doesn't even get up and Lewes is sent to rouse him and unhooks Hanson's hammock for a jest, but Hanson falls to the deck without even bracing himself or uttering a noise.

The bosun grudgingly grants me leave to visit Hanson in the sick bay. The lad's gums have swollen and turned black, and his breath is enough to make you gag though we sailors are no strangers to stench.

'Look,' he says, and ushers me close, and draws a tooth from his own mouth like a wooden peg from its slot.

'Don't,' I say, and I close my hand over his. 'Rest easy. The surgeon will soon set you right.' But Hanson is impatient to show me what is happening to him – he is ardent for witness. He wheezes as he casts aside the blanket and shows me his leg.

'That's where it was broken, eight years back,' he says, his voice clattering loose in his swollen mouth. On his leg, the old scar has opened as if freshly made, and he can no longer walk, for the snapped bone that had knitted strong is come undone. Dark patches bloom on his skin.

He holds out his tooth on his palm like he is offering me a coin. He can barely speak. Scarcely a month ago he won our whole shift's ale ration on a dare and drank too much and spoke very free about a girl he saw only once, as she hawked her wares at market. 'It's the oddest thing,' he told me then, 'for ever since, whenever I wake with my cock straining at my smalls, it's her face I'm thinking of, and I hear her yelling, *Cabbages cabbages get your fine fresh cabbages.*' And Hanson was no great storyteller but I understood how, for all his short days, that girl's hoarse voice had been the sound of desire.

The next day he is dead and the sea takes him. I watch his shroud slip unresisting down down down, and I wonder will his loose teeth make their way out of the shroud, and what do we grow when we scatter teeth on the sea floor like seeds?

———————————

I am approaching seventeen, and find I am coming into the season of my yearnings.

Aboard ship we have a surfeit of touch: we are forever jostled together, bodies pressed tight as we haul together to wind the messenger cable around the capstan, or rush up the ladders under the bosun's yell. Yet of tenderness we have none, and while I have no particular fondness for Mrs Tandy, I am so starved of softness that when she takes a turn about the deck with young Belling scuttling beside her, I cannot even see the brush of her skirt against the boards without envying that gentle touch.

It is a cruel thing that this age, when I am suddenly so sorely aware of my body, should also be the age when all of us lads are barnacled with pimples. Marston's forehead is thick with them, and he picks them cheerfully using the polished brass of a lantern as a looking glass. I think we are an ill-favoured, ugly lot, crowded together below deck with our loneliness and our pimples and our lusts. The loneliness none will admit to, but both the pimples and the lusts are made sport of, and when Lewes wakes with a stand hoisting his trews to the wind, Marston says, 'Lord man, you'll have someone's eye out.'

'The girls at home didn't complain, I'll tell you that much,' says Lewes.

'Lewes would have us believe he spent his youth servicing every lass in Brighton,' I whisper to Marston as we stow our hammocks.

'Their mothers too,' Marston replies, and Lewes pauses his bragging to demand why we are laughing.

There are noises at night sometimes – a creaking in the dark just a bit too rhythmic, and rumours of gropings and suckings. A man would swing for such a thing – thus even Lewes does not joke of it. Sometimes I catch myself staring at Havers, the midshipman with his sharp sense of smell. He has a scar through his plump top lip and when I look at it, I find myself tracing the same place on my own lip with my tongue. So I redouble my efforts to avoid him, for I have better reason than most to avoid the whip.

Turnbull is not known for a flogging captain, being more concerned with his specimens than with ship's discipline – but discipline a ship must have, and Flyte, the bosun, is not a forgiving man. Last week Lewes missed a morning muster and Flyte took his name, and today the ship's company is gathered to witness his punishment, along with six others – guilty in the main of drunkenness, or sloth. Lewes is first, and being not yet eighteen he is spared a proper flogging and instead the bosun uses a cane on Lewes' bare arse. For all Lewes' brashness, I will allow that he takes his ten strokes well enough, and does not cry out. Next, though, a midshipman takes twenty lashes on the back from the cat-o'-nine-tails, for gross drunkenness and insubordination, and shrieks with pain. By the ninth stroke, each time Flyte draws back the whip, droplets of blood spray those of us in the front row. We dare not flinch, but when we are dismissed and Marston is helping Lewes down the ladder, I carefully wipe the spatter from my face.

Of course I fear the pain – I am a creature of flesh like any other. But it's the exposure that I fear more. To have my trews wrenched down before the assembled company, and to face my own shame and their fury.

Belling, the servant boy, is trying to fence some things he stole from Tandy's wife. They are only trinkets: a riband; a kerchief; and a pamphlet, entitled *The Blessedness of the Poor in Spirit: A Sermon, Preached Before the King*. Lewes, who cannot read, has said he will pay Belling a shilling for the pamphlet to wipe his arse on.

I feel no sisterhood with Mrs Tandy – I've never spoken to her, and what I've seen of her makes me think her a sour and timid thing. But I dislike the needless cruelty of Belling, who has not the resolve to cheek Mrs Tandy to her face, yet mocks her amongst the hammocks to amuse the men.

When Marston cautions Belling that he could hang for thieving, Belling only scoffs and says, 'The old shrew's too stupid to know anything.'

'Yet I notice you don't talk so free around her, do you, Belling?' I say. 'You're happy enough to play at being her pet. If you were a year older I'd tell the bosun about your thieving, and we'd see you hang.'

He wheels around. 'You're a snitch, then?'

This is not a matter for jesting: we've seen men whipped for mere drunkenness, and thievery is reckoned worse.

Belling presses his face close to mine. 'Or is it that you fancy the old dame yourself? Is that why you've taken against me?'

'I've seen you simpering to her every day. Playing at being her sweet little lad. You're nothing but a lickspittle.'

Is it fair of me to scold the boy for dishonesty, when I'm lying to all of the ship?

'You fancy yourself quite the gentleman, don't you, Read?' His bared teeth are small and sharp, surprisingly white. 'You won't cry rope on me. And I'm warning you: don't make an enemy of me.'

'What has Mrs Tandy ever done to you, other than show you kindness?'

'What business is it of yours? And if you snitch, you'll have no friends below deck, and the morning shift will find you hanging one morning, afore I ever swing.'

He snatches up his stolen trinkets and leaves. His threats are only bluster, I tell myself – he is little liked amongst the men, and I could best him in a fight, for he is the merest scrap of a boy, and his work as a servant has not given him a sailor's muscles. But I distrust the curved blade of his smile. An enemy aboard is worse than an enemy on land, for there can be no escape. So I keep a watch for Belling and his small white teeth.

6

For the second time this year we dock at Portsmouth, which is crowded with seamen's wives, waiting there in hope of word from their husbands. In the harbour the whores and the wives await the ships with the same desperation. Sometimes the whores and the wives are one and the same, for how else are poor wives to feed themselves or their children, when the navy pays us only at the end of each commission, if at all?

The women are allowed aboard while we are in Portsmouth, for if the navy allowed shore leave, the pressed men would surely desert, and so would half those who enlisted, now they know the truth of a sailor's lot. Lewes swears that the real reason women are allowed aboard is because the officers fear the men will otherwise turn to buggery, after so many months at sea.

It is not just the women who rush aboard, for others come too: moneylenders and merchants, a great tide of bumboats loaded with all who think to wring some profit from our time in Portsmouth.

In the pictures on ballad sheets and pamphlets, the whores are bonny, stout women with big breasts and strong arms. In truth, they are mainly girls, and often sickly. By law they should be no younger than twelve, though some are so thin that it's hard to tell. Instead of the leering grins of the women in the pictures, these girls have pale faces, half afraid and half bored.

'You needn't be shy,' Lewes says, when he sees how I avoid them. 'You might be a scrawny bastard, but these bitches can't afford to be fussy.'

He cannot know why I shrink from these girls and their knowing eyes.

'We don't all need to pay for it,' says Marston to Lewes.

Wives and children come aboard too, so one sailor may be talking with his wife and son, while the next hammock along is creaking with another sailor and his whore hard at it. We're allotted sixteen inches for each hammock, but in truth at sea we have double that, for one shift is always above. In dock we're all here, the hammocks pressed tight, and men sleeping on their trunks and the floor too. The space is filled with grunts and chatter and the crying of children who barely recognise their fathers.

Lewes takes a girl to his hammock. For months he's been talking about nothing else – all that big talk about what he'll do when he gets to have a woman again (though Marston rolls his eyes whenever Lewes says 'again.') Now it's happening but Lewes is all aflush with panic and excitement, and he works away at her very industrious, as if he's manning the pumps. She is staring blank-eyed over his shoulder, towards me. I risk a small smile.

She smiles back. She has a black gap in her mouth where her front teeth should be. 'You want to watch, it'll cost you.' I turn away quick.

Two days later the ship is readying to leave when the captain's wife is brought aboard, along with a great quantity of trunks and other dunnage. I catch only a glimpse of her as she is helped aboard: a curl of pale hair beneath the ruffles of her cap; a down-turned cast of the head; a pale cheek. She looks young – barely more than twenty, though the captain is forty if a day.

'What must a gentlewoman make of all this?' says Marston, gesturing at the bumboats still being loaded with whores, harried from the ship by officers, amidst all the clamour of the ship's final loading.

But what she makes of it we have no chance to see, for Mrs Turnbull is hustled at once to the captain's cabin, young Belling rushing to help with her trunks, while Captain Turnbull, by way of greeting, is loudly complaining that she has too much in the way of baggage, for 'the specimens in my cabin are arranged by my particular design.'

As we weigh anchor to leave Portsmouth, I find myself thinking of the captain's wife, and her cheek set with a dimple, neat as the slit in the top of a piecrust.

———————

We are to rendezvous with another Dutch convoy, headed south to catch the trade winds that shall bear them to Suriname. For these weeks we see nothing more of Mrs Turnbull. She does not stir from her cabin, and Belling says that she is so seasick that the surgeon has had to attend her. Belling seems to take it as a personal affront that he himself has not been called upon to serve her, for I don't doubt that he wishes to curry favour with the captain's wife.

Our surgeon, Carson, is a steady-handed man. We ought to be grateful, for he is a proper surgeon and not a carpenter nor a barber, such as serve on many navy ships. Nevertheless I fear that being a surgeon, fluent in bodies, he must surely spot my secret, so I shrink from him when he passes. But he spares me no glances, for he has his work to do, and plenty of it, and the captain's whims and sea creatures too.

'The captain called the surgeon to look at his polypus,' Marston whispers to me. 'He's convinced it's ailing.' He grimaces. 'How would you tell, with such a creature?'

'From what I've seen of the surgeon, I can't imagine him humouring the captain in this.'

'He's the captain,' shrugs Marston. 'What choice do any of us have?'

———————

'You were lately in service, Mister Read?' The bosun has a way of coming up behind very quiet, then speaking loud and sudden.

'Aye, sir.' I keep at my work as I answer, double-lashing the boats on deck, for Mr Flyte will not abide idling.

'Look at me when I address you,' he barks, and I straighten up sharpish and say again, 'Aye, sir.'

The bosun has been watching me. I had thought him pleased with me of late, because I've taken so quick to the work in the tops. Yet in these weeks since we left Portsmouth, his gaze follows me about the ship, and his mood is foul, and aimed most particularly at me.

'In service to a woman, I gather?'

'Aye, sir. A footman, for a widowed lady – Mrs Norton, outside of Plymouth.' I'm careful to call her 'Mrs,' though in the house itself she was always 'Madame.' Could Flyte have heard, somehow, that Madame is French, despite her husband's name? Does this cast suspicion on me, now that the French are the enemy?

'And were you much in her company?'

I swallow. Has he seen something of the woman about me? In which way has my body betrayed me?

'Little, sir. At least, I was often near her, but it was not my place to speak.'

He talks over me. 'But you served her, yes?'

'There were many others in the household, sir, more directly—'

'Jesus, Read – did I ask about the goddamned household? Just answer the question. You served this woman?'

'Yes, sir.'

'For some years?'

'Yes, sir.'

'Now get on with your work.' He strides away.

Marston passes me his end of the rope. 'What've you done to get him so vexed?'

'Christ knows.'

'Watch yourself,' says Marston quietly.

But he has no need to warn me of the bosun's wrath – I fear it already. Have my years of service to a French woman cast me in a treasonous light? Or does Flyte suspect my private treason, the lie that I have smuggled onboard like contraband? What punishment would be deemed fit for such an audacious trick? Whipping, or hanging? All through the forenoon watch, each time I handle a line I imagine its rough caress on my own neck.

The bosun marches up to me at the dawn shift, and while he's never been a man inclined to sunniness, today his scowl is a fearsome thing.

'Mister Read. Captain's cabin – now.'

Marston raises his eyebrows at me, but I have no answer to offer him, and when I hesitate, the bosun's voice is dangerously polite: 'Do you think it wise to keep the captain waiting, Mister Read?'

The great cabin, where the captain has his rooms, is astern, below the poop deck. I walk there like a man walking to the gallows. I knock, and the captain's steward ushers me in, but absents himself quick. The captain himself is at his table, and does not look up from his papers, nor speak. Nothing disturbs the silence but the scratching of Turnbull's quill, and the wet sounds of the endless specimen barrels, arranged all about the bulkheads. On the table before the captain is a huge glass bowl. Something within it moves. My eyes adjust to the light, and I see that it is the polypus. In the dank bowl the creature has turned grey-black, the colour of the mould that grows atop the water barrels.

I wait, and the polypus waits too, heavy with its own awful patience. Still the captain does not look up from his writing. With the bright light of the enormous windows behind him, I cannot make out what he is working at. Is it a letter to the Admiralty, denouncing me as a French spy, or as a woman? Can a few words on a page do so much? Can they snatch the sea from me?

He places his quill down, very precise, and looks up.

'Read.' He looks me over, taking his time. 'The bosun says you're prettily spoken, and not rough as so many of the boys are.'

I do not know how to respond. From the polypus' bowl comes a squelching sound.

'You were in service before enlisting, I gather?'

I swallow. 'Yes, sir.'

'In a woman's household, I am given to understand?'

'A widow, sir.' Fixed to the bulkhead behind Turnbull is a glass-fronted case, with eight butterflies pinned to a felt backing. I focus on that, and try to keep my breathing steady.

'And you know the ways of women, then?'

Despite his words, he does not look angry. He looks rather bored than otherwise.

'I was raised by my ma, sir. And in service, I hope I gave my mistress no cause for complaint.'

He takes up his quill again, his eyes once more on the pages before him. 'My wife has been stricken with seasickness, and still refuses to leave her cabin, though both the surgeon and I have told her she would do better by taking some air. I'm persuaded that the unwholesome air below is as much the cause of her illness as the ship's motion.'

I don't know why he has changed the subject – nonetheless the relief hits me like a new wind in the crosstrees.

'The other wives insist on staying in their own quarters,' Turnbull continues. 'They barely come on deck. They lack the scientific mind, you see, to heed my advice.' He gestures towards the closed door on his right. Is his wife in there now? Can she hear him discussing her like this, with a stranger?

'I worry for her,' he says, though he does not look worried, and nor has he ceased his writing. 'It does her no good, to be cooped up thus.'

What this has to do with me, I cannot fathom, and so remain silent.

'You will accompany Mrs Turnbull for a few hours a day, on the deck. The task falls outside your normal duties, I know. But I've spoken with Mister Flyte.' He smiles blandly as he glances up at me. 'He was none too pleased when I told him. He begrudges me your time, for he says you're useful in the tops.'

'I don't know that I'm fit company for a gentlewoman, sir.'

He gives an airy wave of his hand. 'You shall do very well. The deck of a ship of the line is an intimidating place for a lady, and I have not the time to spend with her that I might wish. I cannot spare any of the young midshipmen – and the servant boys are overburdened, especially now Lorimer has the scurvy.

'You'll be sent for each day. Accompany her to take a turn about the deck. Read to her, perhaps. Flyte tells me you can read well enough?'

'Yes, sir.'

'Then it is settled.' His eyes follow the scratch of his quill on his papers. 'And give Mister Flyte my compliments and tell him I should be obliged to see him.'

Of course I am relieved not to be exposed, for I have seen what the whip does to flesh. But escorting Mrs Turnbull about the deck holds its own terrors for me. She is a woman, after all – will she notice things that the men who surround me do not?

I am summoned that very afternoon.

The captain's steward opens the door to the great cabin, where Mrs Turnbull awaits me. She is indeed pale – her face is pinched, and the dimple that looked bonny when she came aboard just a few weeks ago now looks like a stitch pulled too tight in her skin.

'Mister Read,' she says. 'I gather you have been kind enough to agree to accompany me on deck.'

Kindness has little to do with it, for a captain's orders are law. Nonetheless I nod, and say, 'Yes, ma'am.'

I wait as she puts her shawl about her shoulders. The polypus' glass bowl has been placed amongst the other specimen barrels, carefully fastened in a wooden case that keeps it affixed to the wall. The creature's suckers press against the glass, like a child playing at kissing a window. I used to envy the captain his grand cabin, but despite the splendid array of windows, there is a smell in here of damp and must, and slurping sounds from within the casks and barrels, so that the crowded gundeck where I sleep seems fine indeed, no matter that Lewes is still farting fit to kill us all.

Mrs Turnbull sees me staring at the polypus.

'Do you share my husband's fascination with these creatures, Mister Read?'

I am not sure how best to answer this – not in front of her, nor in front of her husband's steward, busy with papers at the table. 'I'm sure they are fascinating, ma'am. Though I think I prefer them in the sea, and not in a cabin.'

She leans close to the glass, her nose wrinkling as she peers within. 'Then we shall get along splendidly, for we have that in common.'

I open the door for her and we make our way up. When she is through the hatch and on deck, she hesitates, turning to face me.

'I thought myself a hardy creature, but I find I have taken ill to shipboard life,' she says, with a small, forced laugh. 'Indeed, I confess the staring men rushing about the deck frighten me as much as the rolling of the ship itself.'

'We are not rolling, ma'am,' I say. 'This is pitching, for we rock stern to bow. Rolling would be starboard to larboard.' Her face is blank, so I demonstrate with my forearm. 'Side to side, ma'am.'

She raises one eyebrow. 'I see that I have much to learn.'

'Forgive me, ma'am. I am new myself to a sailor's life, and overfull, perhaps, of all that I've learned.'

'Then you must teach me in turn,' she says. When I offer her my arm to steady her, she takes it.

The poop deck is usually the domain of the captain and officers, but orders have been given that I may accompany Mrs Turnbull there. A chair has even been set out for her use, yet having been in her cabin so long, it seems she is keen to walk – we march back and forth, at a pace that barely allows for conversation.

'Do you care to sit awhile, ma'am?'

She shakes her head. 'Thank you, but I have been idle too long. My husband was right, perhaps – I ought to have been more on deck.'

'You have more colour in you already, ma'am.'

'Indeed?' She presses her palms to her cheeks. 'And you, Read? Were you poorly when first you came aboard?'

'I had not the time to be ill, ma'am. The bosun would not countenance it.'

She laughs, a sudden clear sound. 'Perhaps I should have been under the bosun's orders all along.'

'I fancy you would not enjoy it, ma'am.'

We walk side by side in silence – as much silence as the deck of a ship of the line allows. The men gape at Mrs Turnbull, for on any ship a pretty young woman is a tremendous novelty. They stare so nakedly that I understand why she has stayed below – and I cannot but feel a gratitude for my disguise, and the freedoms it has won me.

When she has walked enough, I escort her back to the great cabin.

She thanks me solemnly. 'The same time tomorrow?'

'Yes, ma'am.'

From within the cabin I can hear the voices of the captain and his steward. Mrs Turnbull steps inside and I close the door behind her, glad that I do not have to enter, nor be subject to the scrutiny of either the polypus or her husband.

———————————

You may conjecture how my fellow sailors react to the news of my new duties.

'All your fine airs are paying off now,' Belling sneers, when I come below after the third day of accompanying Mrs Turnbull. 'How do you like the view from the poop deck, amongst the officers?'

'I would rather be working the pumps,' I say. 'Unlike you, I'm interested in honest labour, and not in currying favour.'

'You say that,' he says. 'But we all see you taking her arm and talking sweet to her.'

'Would you have me refuse the captain's orders?' I ask.

Yet even to Belling I cannot deny that I enjoy those strange hours with Mrs Turnbull. Amongst my shipmates I feel foolish and full of questions, but to her I am a veritable expert in all matters of the sea, and she listens very attentive, her bottom lip tucked beneath her front teeth, as I share with her what I know of the ship and its workings.

The bosun does not forgive me for what he sees as a defection on my part, and during my other shifts is at pains to set me the worst tasks. Lewes and the other lads make sport of me for promenading with the captain's wife. Even Marston is curious.

'What do you speak of?' he asks.

'Little enough.' I shrug. 'She takes an interest in the ship, and how she sails.'

Marston scoffs. 'Then that's more than her husband does, I warrant, for he bothers only with his creatures.'

And I hush him quick, for such talk could see us whipped.

The next day, I see that Belling has found an excuse to come on deck whilst I walk with Mrs Turnbull on the poop deck. I see him abaft the mainmast, watching us. He lingers there a long while, watching us as we take the air and talk. As usual, the other men watch Mrs Turnbull, and make an indifferent job of hiding their stares. Yet Belling watches only me.

These are oddly peaceful weeks, the Dutch convoy following the *Resolve* like so many ducklings. I walk with Mrs Turnbull daily, except when the roughest weather keeps her below. Late spring is giving way to summer and the weather uncommon hot, so that the air below deck is stifling, and on deck Mrs Turnbull carries a parasol, which catches the wind like one more sail.

Once I ask if she would care for me to read to her, as her husband suggested, but she waves an impatient hand. 'Reading, reading, reading – it's all I do in my cabin. My husband has provided me with a tower of books.'

'That must provide some diversion.'

'If I were a naturalist, with a great interest in scientific literature, and in fishes most particularly, I'm sure that it would.'

I permit myself a smile, but make no reply. To criticise my captain could be accounted treason – though such rules do not seem to apply to wives.

'For the love of God, do not threaten to read to me,' she continues. 'I am done with fishes.' She turns her suddenly bright face to me. 'Tell me instead of something new. Tell me of yourself.'

And so I do. I tell her of the big house, and of the swallows that nested near my bedroom window, and Madame's silent days in the drawing room.

'She was lonely, you think?' Mrs Turnbull asks.

'She was alone. I think it doesn't follow that she was lonely.'

I tell her of Ma, though I say nothing of Ma's moods, nor of our great secret. Thus what I give Mrs Turnbull is only a sketch of my life, not coloured by the messiness of truth.

'And you are happy now, as a sailor? In all of this?' She waves about us, to the deck below where the men scurry – and beyond it, to the green and churning sea.

'Yes, ma'am. It suits me very well.'

She stares across the waves. 'You are lucky, then.'

'Indeed,' I say, though I think: *such luck as I have had, I have made.*

'And you, ma'am? What of your life, before you came aboard?'

'My life?' She has been tugging at the fringe of her parasol, and now she tosses a loosened thread into the wind. 'I am sick to death of my life.' Again that brittle laugh, and the words a little too fast. 'Tell me more of your time in service. How many horses did Madame keep, and what sort of carriage?'

And so we fill the hours with talk. I tell her how Kitty used to be afraid of horses, and how the big grey gelding used to reach over the stable door and take a quarter of apple from my palm, so gentle you would fancy he didn't have teeth at all. I reach my hand out flat before me to show her, and she reaches hers out just the same, each of us offering a palmful of air.

'There's talk,' Marston whispers from his hammock to mine.

'There's always talk.' We're four hundred and fifty men trapped in a small space. What currency have we but talk?

'You know what I mean. Talk about you and the captain's wife.'

I shrug. 'What are we supposed to have done? We're never even alone.'

'If you ask Belling? All but the deed itself.'

I laugh. 'And what would Belling know of that?'

Despite my laughter, I fear that Belling's sharp eyes may have discovered what I myself have learned: that when Mrs Turnbull turns to me with her head cocked to one side, and her dimple deepening into a smile, intimacy may be found even on a crowded deck.

'Just be careful,' Marston says. 'Belling likes nothing more than to stir up trouble.'

'There's no trouble to be had,' I say. 'Mrs Turnbull is bored, that's all.'

'That's what I feared.' Marston is rarely serious, but now his face is grave. 'A bored woman is a dangerous thing – and a bored woman on a ship full of men, even more so.'

I say nothing, so he continues. 'Look. You're nothing like her. She's a gentlewoman. For all your pretty way with words, you're just a ship's boy. Don't let her make of you a plaything, for it'll be you that pays the price.'

Marston turns back to his work. Another man might have demanded something in return for such a warning; might ask, even if only for his own curiosity, what it is that passes between me and Mrs Turnbull each day. Marston is not such a man – his friendship keeps no accounts.

You're nothing like her, he said. He is right of course – and wrong, in ways he cannot know. Does Mrs Turnbull recognise something of the woman in me? I do not know. I know only that the next morning when a brisk westerly spurs the waves, I find myself glad, for Mrs Turnbull will take my arm to steady herself as we walk about the deck. That I am careful to touch her gloved hand as I pass her the shawl that the wind has snatched from her shoulders.

I think, at times, of Kitty, and how she found ways to brush against me in the corridors of the big house. I could have been kinder to her – for I understand better, now, how skin calls to skin.

7

The Dutch convoy safely dispatched west, we are set to patrolling the Bay of Biscay again, to intercept the Spanish trade ships, loaded with the riches from the New World that are funding their war.

'I had not thought so much of war would come down to trade, and money,' Marston says.

'What else should it come down to?' I say. The notion of sovereignty is a very loose thing, it seems to me, compared to coin, or cargo.

Yet we've met with no enemy ships since last leaving Portsmouth.

'If the captain bestirred himself to seek the enemy like he seeks his bloody fish, we'd be rich by now on prizes,' says Lewes.

'Or sunk by a Spanish gunship,' Marston says, and then nods towards the bosun, who is looking our way. 'Anyway, keep your voice down.'

Oftentimes Mrs Turnbull and I pass her husband on deck. Sometimes he gives her a very proper bow; if he is busy with his specimens, he does not seem to see us. Today he is instructing Ellis, the topman with a skill at drawing. Turnbull is bent over a fresh-caught fish, laid out dead on the deck. 'Be sure to capture the bifurcation of the fin,' he is saying. He does not look up as we walk by. 'And the gradation of colour on the underside.'

'I am a miracle of science,' Mrs Turnbull says to me in a low voice, when we have passed them. 'Did you not know? The first woman to become entirely invisible.'

She wheels about, and we pass the captain once again. Still he does not look up.

'See?' she says.

I do not dare respond. In the Articles of War which the captain himself reads to us most Sundays, it warns: *No Person in or belonging to the Fleet shall utter any words of Sedition or Mutiny upon pain of death.* The more Mrs Turnbull confides, the closer she steers me towards the reef. The lads may tease me for my new, soft duties – but balancing on the crosstrees, bare feet on a rope slick with grease, is less treacherous by far than this conversation, which could lead me to the gallows.

'The captain is much occupied with his duties, I'm sure,' I say.

She cocks her head to one side as she watches him leave the deck. 'If I could contrive to grow some tentacles, he might find me fascinating.'

'In fairness, ma'am, I think every soul aboard would be fascinated were you to do so.'

She laughs – that high, clear laugh, so that the men by the mizzenmast turn to stare. I change direction, guiding her so that our backs are to the men.

'May I ask, ma'am, why you chose now to come to sea? Many officers' wives do not. Weren't you afraid?'

'I didn't intend to come. We knew when we were wed last year that my husband must needs be at sea. And he seemed to find that no hardship at all.' A silence. 'But I found it intolerable to be at home.'

'You were alone?'

'My sister came to live with me, for a companion.'

'That must have been a comfort.'

'You would not say so, had you met her.' Her dimple deepens when she smiles. 'My sister was always reckoned the pretty one, and has not forgiven me for marrying first, when she has not.'

Her looks are much improved these last weeks, since she emerged from her cabin – but still she is pale and thin. When I take her small hand to help her up or down the ladder, her knucklebones are sharp beneath her gloves.

'Can you not pass time with the other women aboard?' I ask. 'Mrs Tandy and the others?'

'They are good women, I'm sure. But they're all at least ten years older than me. And they are always deferential – always aware of my husband's office. It's quite impossible for me to speak unguardedly with them.'

Yet she does not hesitate to speak thus to me. She is careless of my opinion – I am a mere ship's boy, after all, and of no account.

I escort her down the ladder. She slows as we approach the great cabin. I fancy I can already smell its close air, despite the windows, and hear the stifled sounds of the specimens banked against the bulkheads. She stands before the door and says nothing.

'Ma'am,' I say quietly. 'The bosun will see me caned if I am late.'

'Of course,' she says. 'Forgive me, Mister Read. Of course.'

I open the door for her and step back. The captain is within, and looks up briefly. 'Back so soon?'

One of the tarred barrels is open before him. His sleeves are rolled to the elbow, and he lifts from the water a creature not unlike the polypus.

He sees me staring.

'A cuttle-fish, Mister Read. She is a marvel.'

'Indeed, sir.' I wonder how he can tell that the creature is female.

Mrs Turnbull passes behind him. When she reaches the door of her own cabin, she begins to remove her gloves. She takes each finger with the tip of her other hand and eases it loose, and then draws the whole glove. Her pale hand is startling in its nakedness. I cannot stop watching her. As for her, she is watching her husband.

Tenderly, he lowers the creature back into the barrel. 'To escape predators, she can pour forth a black ink,' he says. 'Truly remarkable.'

Mrs Turnbull closes the door of her own cabin behind her.

At mess that night, Lewes asks: 'What do you find to speak of, you and Mrs Turnbull, for so many hours together?'

'Nothing that signifies,' I say. I am no Belling, to be sniffing skirts and selling secrets.

'I'll warrant she's lonely,' Beadle says, crumbling biscuit between his fingers.

'She must be,' snorts Lewes, 'to find Read's company so diverting.'

———————

I report to the great cabin the next afternoon and find the captain hunched over his table, and Mrs Turnbull not yet emerged from her cabin.

The captain does not greet me.

'Can she possibly thrive, thus?' he says suddenly. 'Can she be happy?'

I swallow – I do not know how to answer such a question, least of all to my captain. But he goes on, without waiting for an answer. 'You can observe the persistent greying of her colour? The slackness of her limbs?' And I see that he is standing over the glass bowl of the polypus, placed before him on the table.

'I'm afraid I have no knowledge of such beasts, sir.'

'My wife accounts you a clever lad,' he says. 'Bright and well-spoken.'

'I'm grateful for her notice, sir.'

'Well then,' he says, impatient. 'What say you? Does she look ailing to you?'

I step closer. The polypus lies at the bottom of the bowl in a pool of its own flesh, like so much offal tossed by a butcher.

'Yes, sir. I fancy she looks sickly indeed.'

'Yet she has the finest care. I have her water changed daily, and she's fed on the freshest fish.'

I think of the dry rations of my own mess: biscuit, dried peas, salt beef.

'Perhaps she is pining, sir?'

He snorts. 'It does not pay to be fanciful about creatures,' he says. 'The rational mind admits no such temptations.'

'Yes, sir.'

He fastens the wooden lid atop the glass bowl, and carefully secures the whole of it in its casing against the bulkhead. He takes his time, screwing fast the contraption.

The door opens and Mrs Turnbull emerges. Does he ever go there, to her bed? Or does he stay always thus, with his specimens?

'Read is here for you,' says Turnbull.

'So I see,' she says. 'And you? Do you care to join me for a turn about the deck? I am sure Mister Read should be glad to be excused, if you were to take his place.'

'I regret that my duties don't permit it,' he says. From another casing he has unscrewed a smaller glass bowl, which he carries to the table. Something moves in the water within.

She draws her shawl more tightly about her shoulders. 'The Admiralty is fortunate indeed, to have so devoted a captain.'

If he hears the sting in her words, he does not show it – only leans forward to peer more closely into the glass bowl, so that from where we stand his eye is a great distorted thing.

On deck she turns her face full into the wind.

'I used to admire his cleverness. I thought it a fine thing.' She shakes her head slowly. 'Is this to be my whole life? I am become a ghost.'

'Hardly a ghost.'

'What, then?'

'You are still a woman.'

'I was a woman. Now I am a waste. A waste of a woman.'

'Don't speak thus, ma'am,' I say.

She turns to face me, and the grip of her hand on my forearm is sharp.

'Do you see me, Mister Read?'

Indeed I see her very clear: the freckles on her pale nose. The tiny hairs on her cheeks. I cannot stop seeing – these last weeks I am beset by noticing. And I cannot understand Captain Turnbull, who does not seem to see his wife at all.

'Yes, ma'am. I see you.' My breath has become a very uncertain thing, the exhalations juddering and suddenly too loud.

'I am not, then, invisible after all?'

I turn about so that she, her arm tucked in mine, must turn too. Before us, the binnacle is trimmed with brass, which Mr Flyte insists is kept polished to a shine. She and I are reflected there, our faces bent by the curve of the brass.

'Look,' I say. 'See? There you are.' I allow my finger to trace the line of her cheek on the rail's reflection. The helmsman stands mere yards from us; beyond him, a lieutenant is at the rail with a crowd of midshipmen. To any of them, it must seem as if nothing untoward is passing. Yet somehow the touch of my fingertip on her mirrored face is more intimate than anything our actual flesh could permit.

'See?' I say again. 'You would not be invisible, no matter what any man fails to see.'

We walk the rest of the hour in a new kind of silence.

I descend the ladder first and give her my arm to help her down. With her other arm she gathers her skirts. On the deck we are always in full view of all the men; below, in the cabin, her husband or her husband's steward will be present. Here, and here only, in this dark in-between space, we are alone.

At the foot of the ladder she turns to me.

Am I deceiving her, by not telling her the truth? But how can a body be a lie? It is real enough – she tests it herself, her hand on my cheek, her finger tracing my lower lip. She places her hand flat on my chest. Something trembles – my chest, or her hand, pressed so close that it makes no difference.

If I undeceive her, I could hang for my deception. And if I am caught thus, her hands on me, I may hang regardless. I think of Marston's warning. What price will I have to pay, for this moment?

'Ma'am,' I say. 'I cannot.'

She gives a slow, rueful smile. 'I had thought you different from all these other men. I thought you saw me. That you understood me.'

'I understand you well enough to know that this is unwise.'

She shakes her head impatiently. 'Must we always be wise?'

I lean closer – so close that her eyelashes tremble against my cheek. I kiss her only once, on her forehead, startlingly hot against my lips.

She lowers her head a little, and gives a sharp nod.

'Go on then,' she says. 'Put me back amongst his other specimens.'

'It gives me no pleasure to do so.'

'Pleasure?' she says, with a small, tight laugh. 'What has that to do with us?'

She is gone, the door closed behind her. I put my finger to my lips. Of course I wanted to kiss her more, and longer. But even more exhilarating than the kiss itself is the fact of my choice. I live my days by the ship's bell and the bosun's commands. Before that, I lived under Mr Twiner's rigid orders, and Ma's first of all. Yet today, it was I who chose to kiss Mrs Turnbull. I who chose to stop.

As I turn back to the ladder, something moves at the open hatch above. It's hard to see clearly, against the bright light beyond. But for an instant I can just make out Belling's face – and then he is gone.

A storm is rising from the west, and all hands are piped on deck and set to battening. Yet while I work I am running calculations in my mind: how much did Belling see, and how much dares he to speak of it? I am weighing his hatred for me against his fear of having his own petty thefts and misdeeds exposed.

Marston and I are set to work beneath the foremast, the storm already so loud that Marston must shout to be heard. 'Belling was asking after you at three bells,' he yells, pausing a moment to wipe his drenched face.

'If we all drown today,' I say, 'then at least Belling will be robbed of the chance to do me any mischief.'

This storm is shaping up nasty. Only a man who had never been at sea would think water is soft. Each wave that breaks across the bow teaches me again how hard water may be, and how sharp. Lewes slips and is swept towards the larboard rail and almost carried over, but I am able to grab him by one arm and hold him fast. He is a thin lad but in his soaked woollens he is no mean weight and it takes all my strength to hang on to him until the lieutenant comes to my aid and grabs him by his leg. The water drags itself down and does not take Lewes with it, and he is carried to the sick bay with a gash on his head, a flap of skin hanging like a slack sail.

The only blessing of such a storm is that there is no sign of Belling on deck, for he will be below with the other servant boys and the women. I think of Mrs Turnbull, and how she fares. Is she alone there, in her tiny cabin, or has she sought shelter in the great cabin itself? Has she anywhere to put her fear, amongst the sloshing barrels and the specimens that line the walls?

The captain has briefly disappeared below and I think perhaps he has gone to check on her. He runs back moments later, hunched over something clutched in his arms, and yelling for the surgeon. I move towards him without thinking, afraid of what I will hear next – but he turns and I see that what he holds is his polypus.

'The bowl,' he shouts to the bosun. 'I found it broken.' His hand is cut. The polypus, too, is wounded – at least one of its legs is gone. There is a grim slit in the jelly of its body, and the whole thing is aquiver. 'Where's the damn'd surgeon?' Turnbull yells.

Carson comes with his apron bloodied and his jaw tight.

'Can you not save her?' the captain asks, holding out the creature like a terrible gift. I do not know how long it can survive out of the water – but there's so much storm water in the air that it scarce makes a difference.

The surgeon shakes his head. 'I'm a surgeon of men, sir.'

'But can you do it?'

The creature has stopped its quivering, though in the rolling of the storm it is hard to be sure.

'I have men below with broken bones and worse,' says Carson, his voice calm but scalpel-hard. 'Why would I save this beast, even if I could?'

'Because I am your captain, and I order it.'

Carson doesn't move, so the captain tries again, in a different tone. 'And to men such as us, who prize knowledge, such a specimen is worth more than this ship.'

'I care for men more than knowledge.' Carson has dropped his voice, and I think it wise, for he will gain nothing by having everyone witness the captain's humiliation. But I am hard by them, and hear what he hisses to the captain. 'That's my job. And if you know what yours is about, you should do the same.'

The captain does not look up from his hands, which are kneading the strange dough of the polypus' body.

'I'm needed below,' Carson says, and turns without waiting to be dismissed.

The bosun calls for swabbers to the great cabin; Marston and I are sent below. The captain is there now, the polypus spread before him, quite dead, one arm draped over the edge of the table. Glass is shattered all about the cabin.

Mrs Turnbull's door is closed. There is no sound from within. Marston busies himself with swabbing the water while I sweep the shards, doing my best in the ship's wild yawing to avoid the captain, who slumps forward, both hands pressed to the wet tabletop, and makes no sound at all. He does not meet my eyes. I, who have seen many times how the polypus' lidded glass bowl is fastened securely in its casing, whenever the captain is not examining it.

By the closed door to Mrs Turnbull's cabin, I bend to gather fragments. Kneeling there, I lay my hand against her door. I stay like that for a moment, my palm pressed to the wood. I imagine her on the other side, her palm matching mine.

It pains me to see the polypus dead, for there was a kind of glory in its ugliness. But I cannot blame Mrs Turnbull for what she did. I do not know whether she was trying to liberate the polypus, or to kill it – or both. But I do know that tonight she made a choice of her own.

For three days I am not called on to escort Mrs Turnbull – and could not be spared even if I were. The weary old *Resolve* has taken a beating in the storm, and you may imagine to what hard shifts we are put, with the pumps and the rigging of a jury mast to replace our damaged topmast. The captain prowls the ship like an angry ghost, and I do not even see Belling. On the fourth day we put in at Southampton for repairs, and Mrs Turnbull is taken ashore, 'the seagoing life not agreeing with her,' as Marston hears the captain say to Ellis. I see her being lowered to the boat. I do not know if she sees me. There is a small smile on her face, and her chin is tilted up. She does not look back.

Belling tracks me down in the gunners' storeroom that afternoon, where Marston and I are set to taking stock of what was wetted during the storm. Belling is grinning as he comes down the ladder, and sidles into the narrow aisle where we work.

'Are you to take to wearing mourning, now that she has gone?'

I ignore him, so he tries again.

'And the captain is missing his sweet young wife. Positively dejected, he looks of late.'

I suspect it is his polypus the captain mourns, and not his wife, but I will say nothing of that to Belling, who seems to view Mrs Turnbull's departure as his personal triumph.

He leans closer. 'How do you think the captain will take the news, that his dainty wife is a slut who lets a ship's boy take liberties with her?'

I punch him in the face. His bony cheek is sharp against my fist – I warrant I have hurt myself more than him, though I refuse to look down at my knuckles nor to shake the pain from them. Belling staggers back against the bulkhead. He makes no move to hit me in return – only looks around quick to see if anyone has witnessed this, and presses one hand against his cheek.

'I'll go to the bosun. You'll be whipped for fighting.' He turns to Marston. 'You saw him strike me.'

Marston's face is grave. 'Indeed – I saw very clear. Saw you trip on the ladder and strike your head. A nasty blow – the kind of thing that might easily make you confused about what happened.'

Belling's eyes dart between me and Marston.

I lean towards Belling, and speak very slow. 'Whatever you fancy you saw between me and Mrs Turnbull, I invite you to take it to the captain. But think, first, how such gossip would reflect upon him. How a gentleman might react to such a slur on his wife, from a serving boy. Are you stupid enough to swing for such an insult?'

Belling peels his hand from his face and reassembles his smirk, though already his eye is blackening. 'Nonetheless, all your grand airs have come to nothing, and you're back to swabbing the deck, instead of promenading about like a gentleman on the poop deck.'

I must hope that this is enough to satisfy Belling for now. He shoots glances back at us as he climbs the ladder.

'Your punches need work,' Marston says to me, and bends back to his task.

That afternoon I take to the tops, for the first time in weeks. I turn my face to the clear wind and wonder if, ashore, Mrs Turnbull will yet find a way to see herself.

As for me, I am coming to see myself clearer than ever.

8

Late 1702 brings news of a victory at Vigo Bay, and we all trust
the war will not continue much longer – yet 1703 rolls over us
like a breaker. The Portuguese join our alliance; the Bavarians
have taken the part of the other side. We are called 'The Grand
Alliance', though below the decks of the *Resolve* this is held a
joke.

'Mighty grand, indeed,' says Marston, as he snaps his biscuit in
half to set the weevils dancing.

A sailor's time is little his own, but when I can, I escape to the
tops, so far above the deck that I can almost believe that Belling
does not even exist.

Off Malaga we meet with two French ships, one a mere sloop
but the other a sprightly frigate, very full of men and with forty
guns besides. We exchange fire with the frigate, and we lads are
tasked with racing the powder up from the magazine to the
gundeck. The captain has been very diligent in exercising the
guns of late and we get off broadside after broadside, neat as you
like, while the French are slower and squander their shot in the
water. Our guns grow so hot that when I brush one with my
arm as I set down the casket of powder, the hairs on my arm
shrivel and blacken.

We have the better of them already when one of our own
guns leaps backwards as it fires, striking me on my ankle. The
cannon only glances my foot, but it's enough to knock me down,
and I bite my tongue so hard that blood is hot and rusty in my
mouth. The strike has knocked all the words out of me so I can

do nothing but clutch my ankle and try to concentrate on the blood taste in my mouth, rather than the pain.

Marston stumbles over me. 'Jesus,' he says, seeing my ankle, already purpled. 'Are you alright? Best have the surgeon look that over.'

'I'm fine,' I say. 'It's just a knock.' I am afraid of the bone saw. But I am more afraid of Carson, the surgeon – I dare not have his keen eyes find me out.

A cry goes up from our men, for a boarding party has taken the French frigate. But I can take no part in the general rejoicing, for Flyte takes one look at me as I stagger on my ankle, which is already swollen fit to burst.

'No point trying to be a bloody hero, Mister Read – you're no good to me like that. Get to the surgeon.'

By the time I limp to the sick bay, it is overrun with the wounded. Carson has been given a few hands to help, and the whole space is thick with sound and stench. A trunk serves as the surgeon's bench, a bucket at its foot. I'm grateful for the dark down there, so I can't see what it contains. The injured men lie in hammocks, and the bone saw waits on the bench.

I show Carson my ankle. He takes it in his hands and tries to move it this way and that, though the swelling makes the joint stubborn and I cannot but grimace. He is quick and precise in his movements, and although he has small hands, his fingers are strong.

'You can you walk on it?' he asks.

'Aye, sir. But only slowly.'

'Show me.'

I hobble to the head of the nearest hammock and back. The surgeon is watching me very minutely.

'Sit,' he says, nodding to the trunk, and when I'm seated again he walks behind me. Unlike most sailors he wears shoes, and I hear them *tap tap tap* as he circles me.

'Fever?'

'No, sir.'

Still behind me, he puts a hand to my forehead. You could break a neck like that, I think – one twist, *snap*, and it would be done.

74

He lifts my shirt and puts an ear to my back. I can feel the shape of his ear against my ribs.

'Breathe,' he says, impatient, and I realise I have been holding my breath.

He listens for four slow breaths, then comes back around to face me, and bends once again to pick up my foot, holding it so that it lies between us like a slab of spoiled meat.

'Is it bad?' I ask.

'It could be,' he says. 'Could be very serious.'

This shocks me, for despite the pain I have not believed the bone broken.

'I can still work,' I say quickly. 'I can still get about.'

'This kind of injury,' the surgeon says. 'It's the kind that could be bad enough to get you discharged.' He's speaking pointedly, fixing his pale eyes on mine. I can't tell if he's threatening me or offering me something.

Carson speaks so quietly that I have to lean forward to hear him over the noise of the men in their hammocks, muttering and groaning. 'If a person had started something, say, and then found it wasn't to their liking. That it was too much, or not what they wanted. An injury like this could get you discharged without any scandal at all, if I tell them it's serious. If that's what you want.'

'No, sir. Thank you, sir, but that's not what I want.'

'It could be dangerous,' he says. 'Ignoring something like this.' He waves a hand towards my ankle, but his eyes are still on my face.

'I understand, sir. But I have no wish to leave the navy. And I'm a good sailor.'

'I don't doubt that. But I'm giving you a choice.'

I pause a long moment, before speaking. 'I don't know what I would be, if I weren't here, sir.'

Still he waits. I move my ankle from side to side, and fight against the wince that rises in me.

'I think I shall recover very well, sir.'

'Fine,' he says. 'In that case, I'd best do a venesection. And you'll find yourself on dull duties until it's healed – be prepared to pick a lot of oakum this next week or two.'

'Aye, sir.'

He unfolds a small blade and selects a spot with care. The swollen skin is stretched so tight that it slices easy. 'Be still,' he says peevishly, when I flinch. He holds a bowl below to catch the blood, and when the bowl is nearly full he bids me hold my thumb awhile on the wound, then he binds the whole lower leg. I thank him and limp back on deck.

All the rest of that day I wonder what Carson himself may know of secrets such as mine, and their keeping. I try to get the measure of it, weighing his small, neat hands against his flat chest; his high hairline, thinning, against his reedy voice. I never arrive at any answer.

The swelling goes down over the next days and weeks, and the purple bruise fades to green and then a dirty yellow. The wound where the surgeon bled me fills with pus, and takes on a foul smell; when I report to Carson he deals with me just the same as any other sailor aboard or, I fancy, even more brisk. He doesn't look at my face at all as he drains away the pus and swabs the wound with some strong spirit.

Henceforth, the surgeon never speaks to me if we pass on deck, nor accords me any particular attention. This, I decide, is for the best. I chose this. I chose it twice: once when I boarded the *Resolve*, and again in the blood-scented sick bay. The first time I chose in ignorance, knowing nothing of what it is to be a sailor. This second time, I know well enough the cost it demands. Saltblooded, wholehearted, I choose the sea.

Time moves slow in the 'tweendecks, and fast aloft. I learn the ship in all her seasons. In spring and summer we most fear the Spanish; in autumn and early winter we fear the storms. Beadle teaches me more of navigation and Lewes says, 'You fancy yourself a midshipman, with all your learning.' I ignore him, for in these long and shapeless years of war, it is some comfort to be able to look at the charts and to trace our path, from home ports to Dutch harbours, and up and down through the Bay of Biscay.

In early 1704 news reaches us of another splendid victory, at Malaga, with most of what remains of the French fleet trapped in Toulon.

'The war must surely finish now,' says Marston. I am not so sure, for a war is a stubborn thing. And can I wish for an end to this war, when I have lived in it these many years, and have no job nor home outside it?

Since the departure of his wife, and the death of the polypus, Captain Turnbull has fallen into a kind of apathy. He walks the decks in an abstracted way, barely speaking.

At first it seems better than if he had turned to anger. 'And at least we're no longer called upon to haul fresh water for his bloody creatures,' says Marston. Yet I fear that no good can come of a captain sunk thus into the barrel of his own despair. The specimens are left to die. From time to time, a sailor is ordered to Turnbull's cabin and returns lugging a barrel, and tips its murky contents overboard with a splash. The smell of dead fish from the great cabin is so strong that it seeps through the bulkheads, and I hold my breath whenever I am astern. Sometimes when the captain walks the deck his silent mouth is busy, muttering dumbly at some calculation that he cannot make come out right.

The whole ship sags under his listlessness. After a month of this we are told to head once more for Portsmouth. In November of 1704 we are told the old *Resolve* is to be broken up, her hull condemned, more caulk than wood. I think they may as well break up the captain too – he is done for as surely as the ship.

What the sea takes, it does not return. Not unchanged, anyway. On the beach you may find a piece of old glass that the sea has spat back – but it will be blunted and dulled and velveted all over by salt. And if a drowned body floats ashore it isn't the same body – the fish will take the eyes first, and the rest if they can.

So when I step on land at Portsmouth, now, I am not what I was. Nobody is, who goes to sea. It's not just the rolling walk, or the dislike of shoes, or the skin turned brown and wrinkled like parchment folded too many times. You could call it a kind of restlessness. Talk to a sailor, and you'll find they always have one eye trained over your shoulder, checking the horizon.

I went to sea a girl dressed as a boy, and I come back as something else entirely. I come back sea-seasoned: watchful of winds, and with an eye to the tides. I do not know if I have come back wiser, or better, or perhaps madder. But I am not the same. What the sea takes, it does not return.

9

'So what now?' Marston asks me in Portsmouth, our commission finished. 'Shall we take another commission?'

The way he says *we*, unthinking, I hold more precious than the pay we are given. Whatever Marston and I determine to do next, we shall do it together. Aboard the *Resolve*, I have learned to be a sailor; it is Marston who has taught me what it might mean to be a man.

It is not a difficult choice, both of us being fitted for the sea and for little else. Thus we are agreed that we shall take another commission – but until then we are giddy with having those two things rarest in the navy: our pay, and time ashore. Marston and Lewes are putting up at the Pelican, for it is hard by the docks and known for good ale. I leave them there to seek the mean back streets of Portsmouth, where I can afford to bespeak a small room of my own above an inn. I take off my stiff shoes and walk about, still adjusting to the stubborn stillness of the floor beneath me.

When I left them, Lewes was teasing that I was in a hurry to find a whorehouse. And what would happen if I did take a woman into my room? I figure there is little that would surprise a Portsmouth whore. I think of Mrs Turnbull too. I wonder if the captain will take again to keeping specimens now he is returning home. I wonder if his wife is awaiting him there, and if he looks at her as if through glass.

But for all my thoughts of Mrs Turnbull, in truth the luxury of flesh I crave today is my own: the luxury of having it to myself, and hiding nothing. For this, I have left Marston and come here alone. I pull fast the shutters, and make sure the door is locked, and in the darkness I take all my clothes off, lay them on the bed like a sleeping body. I wash, twice, in the water from the ewer, but my skin will not lose its sea tang – I am saltmeat now.

For near an hour I stroll about the small room naked, trying on this unfamiliar costume of womanhood, until the cold hardens my nipples to walnuts and sends me scuttling back to my clothes. The boards of the floor have great gaps through which creep smoke and voices from the taproom below – yet after the gundeck of the *Resolve*, packed with hammocks, my small room seems grander than any palace. I venture only to the baker for two buns, and eat them sitting cross-legged on my bed, relishing the extravagance of a meal eaten at my own pace, and without having to jostle with messmates for my share.

At night I go out again, still in my sailor gear. I walk fast in the alleys, to avoid the sailors I know and those I don't. Even when I reach a main street, the shops are all shuttered against the dark.

The man steps from a doorway as I pass and yanks me back with him, slams my face into the wall, and the mighty ringing in my skull is so loud I can hardly hear his panting. He is crushing me from behind, and with one hand he has my arm twisted up against my back, high and hard, fit to snap at any movement. He has his cock out now, pressing it against me, and me against the wall. I think of the butterflies in the captain's cabin, for the way this man is thrusting even while he struggles with my belt, he'd fuck the wall right through me and pin me to it too.

His hand is in my smalls and for a second or two he gropes about, seeking, then he shoves me even harder into the wall and my front tooth chips against brick. With my arm twisted behind me I cannot move, for my own shoulder blade is a knife in my back. I keep that little splinter of tooth on my tongue. I concentrate on that, and not on the man's hand still floundering about my privy parts.

The pressure on my twisted arm slackens as he fumbles.

'The hell,' he says.

He thought me a boy but I fight like a woman, for women know what it is to be cornered and I'll warrant there are few that have not found their face pressed against a wall at some point. I throw my head back and connect with his jaw, and hear the precise clash of his teeth as his mouth is slammed shut – but still he has my arm twisted against my back. I plant a foot against the wall in front of me and hurl myself backwards, and we land with me on my back atop him, and with my arm now freed. I roll off him, not neglecting to jab an elbow as I push myself up, and I get him in the balls or the guts, some yielding part, for he's curled around his pain now. All of this done in silence, for if anyone hears us and comes to my aid, it shall mean disaster for both of us, equally.

He staggers to his feet and he is still blocking my escape, and his pain might go either way: might make him mad or make him run, and so I ready myself to kick at him but it is to be running after all, and he's got his breeches up and he's hustling fast away and trying not to look back, trying to slow his pace so he doesn't look afraid. I do not wait to stare but run, only run. I hear myself call for Marston as I run though he is surely half a mile away – yet even his name in my mouth is a comfort.

By the time I reach the inn I have swallowed the piece of tooth, or perhaps it was spat out during the struggle. In my room I wash blood and brick-dust from my face. My newly chipped tooth is sharp against my tongue.

Ma raised me to fear what men may do to women, but I know that fear doesn't belong to women alone. Even in the navy there are stories of boys badly used on ships, and the men hanged for it, and sometimes the boys too, whether the men took them willingly or otherwise.

It was perhaps no more than luck that saved me tonight. Yet it is also true that he was confounded, and that bought me a few seconds. My doubleness made a space through which I was able to slip. It does not stop my tooth hurting, nor my hands from their tremors. But still I do not forget it.

Our next ship is the *Expedition*, another third-rater. I am glad to find myself again with most of the other *Resolve*s, though not Lewes, who has gone aboard a frigate. I cannot say I miss him, for he had a needling tongue – yet he has been alongside me since first I enlisted, and without him it feels as though the deck is aslant, or the masts at the wrong rake.

Belling, the servant boy, is aboard the *Expedition*, this time serving the new captain's wife. 'You would think Belling was the captain himself,' says Marston, 'the way he struts about.'

'I've the ear of the captain now, you know,' Belling tells me. 'The captain's wife is a dumb bitch but she likes me very well.' His tongue runs along his upper lip. 'I've great expectations.'

'Aye? And will you be thieving from her, and sniffing her skirts, as you did with your last mistress?'

He is quick as a cat, the way he turns and shoves his face in mine so I can smell the startling sweetness of his breath. 'You've a spiteful mouth, for all your quiet ways, Read. If you make trouble for me here, you'll pay for it.'

'You're well enough able to make your own trouble. I want no part in it.'

He is little liked by the other men – but in his hands my secret would be a nasty weapon indeed. When I pass him below deck, his stare takes up all the space around us; when he is near, my hands fumble over tasks I have performed a thousand times.

The *Expedition* herself is a fine ship and in good trim. Her song is different from that of the *Resolve*, for she is new and her planks still settling and learning their curves. Under full sail her hull makes a straining groan – the sound Mr Twiner used to make when hauling himself from his armchair when Madame rang for him.

Our captain, Norwood, starts good but fast turns bad. It is not his first command, but his first on a ship of the line, and while he starts civil and rather timid, he quickly grows angry. At sea none can countermand him, and he takes to snapping and ordering a man whipped for no reason other than a glance or a stumble. If I escape his cruelties it is only because I am beneath his notice, and have more reason than most to avoid a whipping, which would see me stripped before the lot of them.

I never thought to fear my own captain more than I fear the enemy. The chip on my tooth, where my face was smashed into the wall at Portsmouth, has lost its sharpness, for time and my tongue have smoothed it now, as the sea smooths glass. Still, when I see Captain Norwood order a man whipped at the grate for slipping on the icy deck, I run my tongue over that tooth again, and remember the violence that can surface in a man.

In March of 1705 we are sent to join Admiral Leake's fleet in the Bay of Algeciras for the defence of Gibraltar.

'Leake seems an unlucky name for a sailor,' I say to Marston.

Yet Leake does not prove unlucky, for the waiting French fleet is pounded by a westerly gale, and two of their great ships of the line are run aground, and their crews burn the ships rather than let us seize them. The gale whips the fire until the flames cast red light everywhere, through a shroud of thick smoke. All the world is a furnace now, and the hot wind carries the sound of screaming. I do not know if it is French sailors trapped or drowning – and though I do not believe in God, I see now that hell is real enough.

10

We are to sail for Portsmouth, our commission nearing its end. I pass Belling midships and for all that I am loaded with a roll of fresh cordage, he does not make room, jostling me. Shortly after, I drop my marlinspike back into my pocket and it clinks against something. I'd thought my pocket empty so I turn it out and inside is a trinket – a lady's brooch, not very fine wrought and I suspect the blue jewel in its centre is paste. But I recall Belling passing close enough to knock me, and I don't examine the brooch long, but look swiftly about me to ensure I am not watched, and hurl the thing over the larboard side, and whether paste or a real jewel it is decorating the seabed now.

Barely a few minutes later there is a great outcry as the captain's wife has reported a trinket stolen and we are mustered and called upon to turn out our pockets and then to empty our sea-chests and even to unpack our hammocks until Mrs Norwood, much embarrassed, starts to mutter she may have been mistaken and the captain is in a great fury which in fairness is nothing new. At dinner the men joke about it, and Beadle says, 'Perhaps Norwood will have his wife whipped on deck instead of the thief,' but it is no joke to me who might have hanged had Belling been less clumsy.

Despite his seagoing family, Marston has started saying that army men have a better time of it. Less disease; less of captains with too much power and not enough space. Ever since Blenheim all the talk is of Marlborough, and Marston longs to serve under him. There were twelve thousand dead at Blenheim, they say, but the story reaches us from the safety of distance and so we cannot smell the dead but hear only of the glorious victory.

Marston speaks of little now but the army – and even I begin to be persuaded, for though I have found my home in the sea, I have also found it in Marston. And I have come to fear Belling more than I fear the enemy, or the captain, for their belligerence is general, whereas Belling's hatred is shaped just for me, and is more deadly for it.

The army will surely take me and Marston, for it is desperate for men – back home, there are press gangs all over the country, snatching even men with families to support. So when the commission is at an end and the *Expedition* is paid off in Portsmouth, Marston and I take our leave of the navy.

'Here's to changes,' Marston says, when we toast one another in a tavern.

'To changes,' I echo. I do not wish to rob Marston of his cheerfulness, so I say nothing of my sadness at leaving the sea.

Enlisted, we are sent at once to Flanders, where the fighting over the Spanish Netherlands remains fierce. For some recruits the voyage to Ostend is a sore trial, and there is a great deal of vomiting and of groaning. Marston and I do not suffer, indeed to us it feels a rare luxury to be aboard and not at work with the business of sailing. But this high opinion we have of our own hardiness does not survive the first few weeks in the infantry. The men make sport of me and Marston for our rolling sailor's gait. 'You sway like a drunkard,' the lieutenant says, drilling us. We march to our first camp through mud such as I have never seen. All is confusion and disorder, our baggage and tents brought up behind us only after dark. The weight of a tent is no small thing; the weight of a tent all basted in mud is colossal, and pitching it we battle for hours with the slack, slick canvas until I feel myself still at sea and hoisting sails.

As in the navy, my greatest ally in preserving my secret is the furtiveness and havoc of this war – the mud and the mufflers over our uniforms and the crouching and huddling and chaos of it all. You could hide more than a pair of breasts in this whole mess. And we are all of us hiding something – we conceal our fear; smuggling it under our winter coats, clutching it close to our chests, hands clenched against the cold.

By three months in we have begun to lose our sailor's gait, and we walk landwise now. I do not regret that the men's teasing has stopped, but I am uneasy to think that my body is forgetting the ocean.

'Do you not miss being at sea?' I ask Marston.

He shrugs. 'We've not even been long on land. And there's not years enough in the world to make me miss Captain Norwood, nor shipboard rations neither.'

Not long on land, Marston said. Yet with each day away from the navy, I learn why *long* and *longing* are linked. After the sea's wide horizons, even the skies of the Low Countries seem miserly. I am not fool enough to miss Norwood, nor Belling – but I feel like a seal, ungainly and wrong on land.

I am not the only woman here – just the only one in men's dress. There are women enough who follow the drum. Each regiment has their own little trail of camp followers: the officers' wives, who come by choice; the wives of pressed men, or poor men, who come because they dare not stay at home and starve. Some of them work as cooks or nurses; others just follow, some even with their children trudging beside them. There are the whores, too, as essential to an army as its cooks. Every now and then the colonel makes a great show of having them chased off, and then there's general muttering and unrest amongst the men, and anyway the whores return soon enough, and all is as it was.

Then there are those people, men and women both, who come after battles to strip down the dead and steal what they can. These last are chased off too from time to time, but like the carrion birds they come back, for we will always have fresh dead for them to pick over.

At Ramillies, where battle lines are drawn, Marston places all his faith in Marlborough.

'Under the Duke we cannot lose,' Marston insists. 'We shall come about famously.'

I envy him his certainty.

Our regiment is in the second wave sent up to the ridge and we've been drilled long and hard in the loading and reloading of our flintlocks, timed very precise, so that six platoons fire at once while the others reload, and thus the enemy has no respite from our fire. I dare say the method answers very well in a drill, but in a battle I defy any man to keep to strict timings when your heart is its own beat loud in your head and all about you are shots and screams and the French answering with their own shot, though none so fast as us. We are very quickly upon them and then it is bayonet work which is ugly work indeed.

A Frenchman comes at me bayonet first, and I cannot fire for my own barrel is by now all clogged with mud. I block his blade with my musket turned sideways and he slips and staggers. Still he lurches at me again. In the mud I am like a barge, slow to turn. He jabs again and I dodge his blade, and he is swearing and though I speak no French, swearing sounds the same in any language.

He doesn't stop – neither of us can, for this is war and when it ends has nothing to do with such small folk as us. He charges me again and I charge back and is it my thrust or does he slip again, but either way he is on my blade now right up to his guts. Perhaps I have not kept my blade sharp enough, for it does not glide in smooth, nor come out smooth neither, for the blade snags and then jerks sideways so what's left is a slash rather than a stab – and there is no undoing what is done by a bayonet. His belly is a cracked egg and out it comes, all of it, more in him than I could imagine. His face purples and swells, then slackens, and I am grateful for the mud that covers him when he falls back.

I look around – for it is no small thing, to take a life; there ought to be a witness. In the navy I played my part in killing – but always at a distance, carrying the powder or manning the rigging. Today's fighting has a new weight, and a greater intimacy. What I've done to this man feels too large to witness alone. But close by me Marston is grappling with his own Frenchman and so it is for all the men and there is no time for pause but only more of the same: more mud and more French coming and if it is not to be their death it will be mine, so I must fight on.

I know this now: when you kill a man, you yourself must be his witness. Nor does such witnessing end with the dying. The men you kill you carry with you, nor can you ever set them down.

The crows come before dawn.

'Filthy creatures. Ungodly,' says Marston, and chucks a stone at a crow that is busying itself with a dead man's ear. Myself, I cannot find it in myself to hate the crows. Seems to me they do us good service, especially when haste or frozen ground do not allow for burials. If there can be no proper sea burial, nor even a landsman's churchyard burial, then there could be worse ends than being taken up by crows. It isn't pretty, but there is nothing pretty about these times, and the crows doing the tireless work of the dead is far from the worst of what I have seen in this war.

The talk in our camp is not about the battle itself, Marlborough's great triumph, but about one of the troopers.

'A trooper in the Royal Scots Greys was carried to the surgeon with half his skull blown off,' says Pascoe, a Cornishman in my regiment with a cheery disposition despite the pinched and sour set of his face. 'And they found it was a woman.'

From the men's reaction, the fact of her womanhood is more remarkable than her injury, or her survival.

'No,' says Marston. He is not even angry – just absolutely clear in his mind that such a thing cannot be. 'No fucking way.'

'It's the truth,' Pascoe insists. 'Kit Welsh, she's called. Followed her husband when he was pressed – served for years. Not just this war, either – the last one too. She fought at Schellenberg. Blenheim too, apparently.'

'No,' Marston shakes his head. 'People would know.'

'Well they didn't.' Pascoe pulls his muffler tighter about his neck. 'Anyway, seems even an English woman is too strong for the Frenchies.'

Had we not triumphed at Ramillies, I wonder if the men would be as cheerful about Kit Welsh's deception.

———————

After Ramillies, two weeks is all it takes for the Spanish Netherlands to fall to us – but nothing is free in war so there are further skirmishes fought, and yet more food for the crows. We are set to chase the remaining French, and the whole region is a rout, the enemy fleeing so fast that we come across their camps with tents still pitched and, once, a pot of water still hot over the abandoned fire. Marston makes great sport of washing his face in it and raising a toast to the fleeing Frenchies for warming his bathwater so thoughtfully.

The next dawn we come across a French column in retreat outside Louvain. Our company comes upon them quite by accident and had the French the sense to flee I doubt we would have pursued them for our colonel is as lazy a man as ever lived. But today it seems we've stumbled across the one set of Frenchies who are determined to be heroes, for they scurry for shelter on a low ridge and open fire, which obliges us to shoot. We look to have the better of them but they have grenadiers amongst them, which we discover only when two grenades land. The blast knocks time itself crooked, and sets my ears ringing, my skull a cathedral bell at full peal. And when the day has pieced itself together and I collect that I am not dead, I see Marston has fallen. He has taken the blast himself and mainly to the guts and we both of us know that he is done for.

Our men have overrun the small ridge now and the French are captured or perhaps dead, I do not care, for Marston is already grey and what he is holding at his stomach is not skin nor guts nor blood but an unholy mix of all three. He is swearing a great deal but I see now that it matters little for whatever you say when dying is a prayer.

His face is grave as I have never seen it – Marston who is never serious, and whose laugh drew men to him like a campfire.

'Marston,' I say, as though his name is some kind of incantation that will keep him with me. 'Marston.'

He does not know that I am a woman, but here crouched beside him in his own blood, I know for certain that I have never deceived him but given him the whole of me. I do not say to him: *You have been my only and my truest friend* – for he is dead now and it is too late for any such confession or any thing at all.

11

Word comes in autumn that men are needed for the cavalry, so I take my chance, for since Marston's death there is nothing to keep me in the infantry. Without Marston's easy laugh and his knack for finding joy even amidst the Flanders mud, I feel alone amongst the platoon, and cannot shake myself free of the weight of my grieving. And amid all the talk of Mrs Kit Welsh, the woman who concealed herself for years as a man, I fear the men's gaze will turn to me – and now I have no Marston to stand behind. In the cavalry, I figure that whatever slight disadvantage I have in height and weight shall matter less. If I am a little smaller than most of the others in my squadron, who would notice astride eight-hundredweight of horseflesh? I swear to the officers that I know my way around a horse, which is a lie, since the closest I ever came to a horse before now was sneaking into the stables at the big house to pat their noses when the groom wasn't there.

I know little of horses, but I love them nonetheless. It's the smell of them – chaff and hair – and even their shit doesn't smell foul but somehow like spring and grass, amongst the lean, wet autumn of the Low Countries. The patch atop their nostrils dares to be so soft, when all the world around us is so hard. I like to lay my palm there, and to remember that there can be such things in the world, when Marston is gone and all around me is mud.

I am no horseman, though, and daily I wrestle to keep my horse in line with the others. Worse, from the very first week,

Dan Jansenns, a tall blond in my troop, is watching me. We are all mustered for inspection but time and time again I must yank at the reins to keep my horse from grazing, for a horse's appetite is never sated. My horse jerks back and a wrestle ensues, so that I earn the glares of the men either side of me as I jostle them. And each time I look up from struggling with the horse, Jansenns is watching.

I avoid him as much as I can, but on the fourth night he comes suddenly upon me by the side of the tent. We are alone, and it strikes me that he has been at pains to make it so, for even now he speaks low, so that the others, gathered around the fire behind him, cannot hear.

'You lied when you enlisted, didn't you.' It is not a question.

I freeze.

'It's your hands that give it away.'

I look down at my hands. I had not thought them over-small. Nor are they delicate – they're strong, for they are sailor's hands.

'Look,' he says. 'No harm need come of it. I will tell nobody. And perhaps I can help you.'

'How?' I say. What kind of sordid deal can he be offering? I had not figured Jansenns for a predatory man; he is soft-spoken and handles his horse gently. My tongue goes again to my chipped tooth – the reminder I wear of what a man may do.

'I can teach you,' he says. 'For one thing, it's your legs ought to do the work, not your hands. Keep jerking at the mouth like that and there's not a horse in this camp who won't try to unseat you.'

A sound bursts from me – half laugh, half gasp.

'I didn't mean to alarm you,' Jansenns says quickly. 'I'll tell nobody, don't fear. And horseman or no, I don't blame you for wanting out of the infantry.'

I am giddy with relief. 'I should like to learn to ride properly,' I say. 'I'd like it of all things.'

After that, I fare better. Jansenns has none of Marston's easy charm, but he is a patient teacher. I tell him I was in the navy before the infantry.

'Aye,' he says, 'it figures, for you yank at the reins like you're raising a sail.'

My first horse is a grey called Sprightly, and under Jansenns' quiet tuition, the horse and I come to a good understanding, until I am on my way to being the horseman I claimed to be. But four months in, Sprightly breaks his foreleg in a rabbit hole on a long day's ride towards Aalst and I have to shoot him myself, and I cry for him and the warmth leaching out of him into the wet earth. I cry more for that horse than I have for Marston and I wonder at how this long war has frozen me like a puddle iced over.

After that I am given the charge of a mean bay called Rig who likes me no more than I like him, and though I now have the skill to manage him well enough, he never misses a chance to nip at me or to steer close to a wall and crush my leg between the stones and his unyielding flank.

We are a small troop of barely forty, with two other troops a little larger making up our squadron. The men are the same as any men: some kind; some mean; all more concerned with their own survival than with my body or its secrets. Jansenns is the closest I have to a friend, but he is unassuming and quiet, and still I feel closer to Rig, my spiteful horse, than I am to any of my fellow troopers. I do not wish it otherwise. In the coldest months, the impassable roads and the lack of forage for the horses mean that campaigning is paused and we are billeted in winter quarters. In the stone houses of the local villages, with their silent, nervous residents, we wait like tubers for spring. When the thaw comes, we flower again into war.

It has been seven years since I enlisted in the navy, and two since I left for the army. I am twenty-three years old. We advance southwards, for since the victory at Ramillies, Marlborough has driven the enemy back from Genappe and then Mons. But the news from France is bad, and I begin to believe that this war is a ship that will never make land.

1708, a stillborn summer, forever wet. At the river between Oudenaarde and Eename, our horses are bogged in the grasping mud. The French have made some gains in northern Flanders and it falls to us to push them back before they can besiege Oudenaarde.

We cross the river on the pontoon bridges, slick underfoot, the horses slipping and skittish. In the ceaseless rain, we wait. My horse's wet neck steams, and my boots fill with water. The infantry has had the worst of the fighting – we are set to guard the flank, and see little action until near dark, when we are led in an attack behind the French lines, their army near encircled now.

Charging, we outmatch them by so great a number that they make no stand against us, only scatter and try to run where there is no room to run, like the mice Ma used to catch in the bottom of a pail to drown. We loose our carbines at them on the first charge and from then on it is the bloody task of picking off those who live.

I welcome the dark when it comes, allowing the surviving French to creep off towards the canal. We are not ordered to cut off their retreat and I am glad of it.

'This is a bad day's work,' says Jansenns quietly, and none will disagree.

When we clean our swords, young Cooper turns his head aside and quietly vomits, and I pretend not to see. I clean my blade, and clean it again. I am thinking back to my navy days: the mercy of the sea, in covering our dead.

———————

Dan Jansenns has become my friend, as much as I allow anyone to be my friend since Marston's death showed me how such things may be wrenched from your life like a tooth. But when you work and fight alongside a man, and are quartered with him in a crowded tent besides, there is a kind of intimacy that cannot be resisted. Jansenns has long since finished helping me to master riding, but still he turns his curious, solemn gaze at me, and I begin to fear that he sees what others do not.

Jansenns is English but his mother's family is Flemish, and when we work alongside the Dutch he speaks with them in their language, and I find myself wishing I could understand those grave, thick-throated sounds. Even when he speaks English there is a gentle strangeness to the tone of his words, as if he is making each word anew. He is not a rattle the way Marston was, forever shaping the world into a joke. Instead, Jansenns has a quiet way about him. He is the tallest in our troop and must hunch over in the tents, and even outside he has the stoop in his carriage of a man who has always been taller than those about him. That diffidence becomes Jansenns well. There is a gap between his front teeth so that sometimes when he laughs there is a gentle whistling sound, and I find myself trying to make him laugh, to hear it again.

Perhaps Jansenns himself does not know, at first, why he cannot cease from staring. I am dressing in the dark, beneath my blankets, one dawn.

'What are you doing, thrashing about under there?'

'It's too bloody cold.' That's no lie – it's cold enough to freeze the teats off a cow.

Several times I borrow his shaving kit, in the forgiving dark of dawn.

'Barely keeping that beard at bay, you are,' he says quietly, as he watches me trying to raise a lather with the greasy soap, and scraping away at my chin.

'When I'm an old man like you I'll grow a fine beard,' I say. I have put it about that I am barely twenty, though I am three years older. He gives one of his laughs and there it is, that small whistle that I have come to like so well. But even as he laughs, he continues watching me in a measuring sort of way. I cannot tell if he is suspicious, or angry, or amused. I cannot tell if his eyes are measuring me for a dress or a coffin.

We are being drilled in shooting and reloading while mounted, an exercise that outrages my horse, Rig – yet as he lives anyway in a constant state of fury it signifies little, and I've learned to handle him well enough. Young Cooper has a new mount, an unsteady, wall-eyed grey, who startles sideways just as the order comes to fire, and Cooper takes a bullet to the guts from Bligh, a London fellow who has only lately joined our troop. Of the two of them, Bligh looks the worse, for his face is white and he sets to shaking and gibbering, while Cooper himself is mighty calm and even dismounts without help, before Jansenns and I can even reach him. He says something and for a mad instant I think he is speaking Flemish like Jansenns, for the word is a gurgle of blood in his throat. And we can see now the mess that the bullet has made of Cooper's stomach, and smell it too, the stink of shit which is death for certain, for a man may recover from a clean wound but not this, and besides there is too much blood. Now Cooper speaks clear: 'Goddamn you will none of you help me.' Bligh is still blubbering that it is not his fault and Cooper falls silent. An accident such as this seems a foolish way to die but in the end it means no more nor less than any of those other deaths in battle or elsewhere, for each death is absolute.

'Oh Jesus,' Jansenns says. He moves around so he's kneeling behind Cooper, raising him only a little, and holding him fast. But Cooper is too far gone for any comfort. He is in the deep dark by now, sweating and shaking at once, his face the slick grey of a fish belly.

The cold sound of steel, and now I understand that Jansenns isn't embracing Cooper. He is holding Cooper's head still so he can cut his throat. He does it very clean: tips Cooper's head back and slices across his neck, fast and hard. And we can see how close Cooper already is to death, already drained of blood, because there is no great spurt or spray from his neck, just his body falling limp.

In another place or time, there would be other forms of kindness. But this is the time we have, and the only kindness available to us, and so I see Jansenns' blade for what it is: an act of mercy. A war has its own tenderness, even if it is only the tenderness of blades.

'Do you blame me?' Jansenns asks me quietly in the tent that night, when the others are sleeping. 'For what I did to him?'

I shake my head. I wish I could say to him that sometimes in a war, *doing to* and *doing for* are one and the same. 'It was a hard thing to do,' I say. 'You did it well enough, Jansenns.'

'Dan,' he says. 'You should call me Dan.'

'Dan,' I repeat.

'And you? Am I to call you Read, still?'

'Or Mark,' I say. 'Read or Mark, as you like.'

———

Dan Jansenns has stopped watching me. He still stares from time to time, but not with the same appraising eye. You might think I would be relieved – yet I take it as proof that he knows. His looking has lost its urgency, for he has found what he sought.

How far may I trust Dan? And if he has seen what I am, then surely the others may see it too. For weeks I speak only when I have no choice, for to my own ears now my voice sounds too much a woman's, for all my habit of speaking low. I expect at any moment to feel the hand of the sergeant on the back of my neck, and to be hauled before the officers.

But the hand on the back of my neck does not come, and the men treat me still with the same cursing and swagger and casual, fond brutality, just as they treat one another. I begin to trust that I am safe as ever I was, for only Dan knows. Indeed I have come to understand his knowing as proof that he loved me before ever he knew, for attention itself is a kind of tenderness. I remember Turnbull, my first captain, who did not see his wife at all.

Dan cared enough to look properly – which is to say that he discovered in himself his affection for me, before he discovered my secret. I wonder, too, whether he found me out, or whether perhaps I showed him. Whether I let myself be seen, because I wanted him.

There is a time when a secret is not even spoken aloud, but is shared nonetheless. Its quietness is like no other – it is the quiet of a great church, where you dare not speak for spoiling the sanctity of the silence. So it goes, for many weeks, between me and Dan.

And when he does watch me, I do not shy away from his gaze. No longer afraid, I stare back.

You must not think I am largely concerned with Dan. I am busy with the business of staying alive, which is no simple thing as 1709 trudges on. We push south-west to Malplaquet, where the French are well entrenched and flanked on each side by woods. The day is a blur of blood: all morning the infantry charges follow one another, and it seems they gain or lose little ground, and such ground as there is begins to swell with the fallen. After noon it is time for the great press of cavalry, and our sergeant major gives a stirring speech about the glory we shall win for ourselves and for our country, but his great oration loses much by being cut short by the call to charge, so that even as we begin to move off he is still rushing through what he has rehearsed. Anyway, there is nothing of glory in what we do. Their cavalry meets us at each charge, and each time we are spared by the firing of infantrymen and we regain the field to charge again and then again, until it is like pumping water from a hull that will only refill.

We ride over the newly killed, but worse are those who are not yet dead for they cry out underfoot. The sucking clay mires our horses, and there is such a cannonade from our artillery and theirs that I can no longer hear at all. It's the heavy artillery that secures the day in the end, for now the French are being driven back by our fire and by the press of our greater numbers.

It is accounted a victory, as we hold the field. But it is no rout, and they retreat in good order. It is whispered that we have lost at least twenty thousand men.

'Another mighty victory like that and we shall be done for,' says Dan, and we have not the heart to laugh. Twenty thousand, a number so great that it will not fit in my head except to picture it as a great fleet: more than forty *Resolve*s, all sunk. That night the crows are made busy indeed.

Nonetheless, in our tent that night, Dan snoring lightly only yards from me, I find myself slipping towards an untroubled sleep. You would not think I could feel safe in such a time, while outside the crows strip the bones of the dead. Yet if there is safety to be found in this war, I am learning that it rests in the sound of Dan Jansenns' sleeping breath.

A week from the battle, Dan and Bligh and I are sent forward to clear a road, for in truth cavalry life has more of engineer duty and clearing obstacles than of battles. The route is blocked by heavy artillery left behind in the French retreat. The great cannons make for heavy work, and Rig does not like being set to hauling, being a horse with a very fine sense of his own dignity.

The French who stumble upon us are but three men, one of them mounted. By the ragged look of them they might be a tail of stragglers from the retreat, or even deserters – just three thin men with mufflers around their faces. They are startled to come across the road, and doubly startled to see us. The man at the front shouts an order and they retreat behind one of the guns. One of the Frenchmen fires first, and his companion's horse rears at the musket's report and pitches its rider off into the mud. Dan sees to the fallen man with his sword, though I think it a precaution only, for when he fell his head struck a rock loudly and he does not cry out nor even flinch when Dan's sword pierces his chest.

I get off a shot and Bligh does too, and I hit one of the Frenchmen, while the other fires upon us. His shot spent, he sprints for the trees and Dan makes to chase him but I call him back for Bligh has taken a musket shot to his chest. There is not much blood but he has turned a very bad shade of grey and breathes with a wet rattle, and though I hold his head and mutter some lies about how the surgeon will come soon, he is quickly dead.

Dan and I sit side by side on the road. It is the first time we have ever been alone – it ought to be a luxury, but it is a luxury vouchsafed by the dead all around us, and thus too dearly bought.

He leans his head back against the cannon.

'Mark,' he says. With his thumb he rubs at the mud that coats the back of my hand.

'No,' I say. 'I'm Mary.' And that is no more true than the comforting lies I told Bligh – for I am not just Mary. But it is what Dan wants to hear – and perhaps what I want to hear too, for it makes things simple. Here in the mud with Bligh's body by our feet, and two dead Frenchmen behind the wheel of the stuck gun, I have had enough of complications.

Dan gives a long, slow breath, which sets the whistle in his teeth singing. 'I knew,' he says.

'I knew you knew.' My own words sound very loud in the stillness, and I hear in them the echo of another word: *new*. In all the dreadful sameness of days and years that make a war, there might still be something new. A beginning, amongst so many endings.

'Would you still want me if I were Mark?' I ask.

'But you're not,' Dan says, impatient.

Still I want his answer, but he has stopped my questions with kisses, and I want that more, for Mark or Mary I am this desiring hot thing, Dan's mouth on mine and Bligh's blood still on my palms.

Around the fire that night Dan sets himself close to me, and he makes sport of it for all to see – 'Come here, Read, and sit on my lap for I swear you've less hair on your chin than any girl I ever kissed.'

The others join in, 'And less than your mother, Jansenns.'

Dan laughs back, 'I see you've met my mother then.' All the while with an arm around me and one hand slipping to the side of my breast. It's a kind of hiding in plain sight for we are known already to be steadfast friends, and he is made bold by the thrill of it.

For more than a year we continue thus, satisfying ourselves only with fumblings behind tents and his hand between my legs in the dark.

'We cannot keep going as we are,' he says. Yet what else can we do?

In spring of 1711 his uncle writes that he is giving Dan the running of his tavern, near Breda. It is the spur we have been waiting for, to break with the way things are. We agree that we must tell the officers, and be wed – for I will not have Dan otherwise. Do not mistake me: I would take him now, for I desire him and I care little for either God or sergeants – and I am certain I can love Dan no better as a wife than I do now. But if we keep our secret, and do not take up his uncle's offer, there is no call to leave the army, and nothing will change except the coming together of his body and mine. We shall still be stuck here, as though the thick mud of this place has swallowed us for good.

Dan readies himself to tell the officers. He shaves afresh, and asks me to help him brush the worst of the dirt from his uniform.

'It's my body, and not yours, that they'll be looking at,' I say. Nonetheless I help him brush his coat, for it is touching to see how anxious he is.

Dan goes first to one of the sergeants, a decent man called North. I watch the officers' mess tent from a distance, as first the sergeant major is summoned, then both our lieutenants and the captain too.

I am sent for last of all. I salute, but the assembled officers wince and wave away my salute and I see very clear that I must do away with all marks of soldiery, for this in-between place makes the officers uneasy.

'I understand you are to be congratulated,' says Sergeant North, 'and that Jansenns is to make you his wife.'

It is Dan, though, whose hand North shakes – and the other officers do the same. Dan, I realise, is the thing that changes the story. Without Dan, my story is a mortification to the army and navy both, for I am a woman who served and escaped detection. Dan changes it altogether, for I become a woman who was discovered, and my story becomes a love story, a novelty with a neat ending. And so the officers shake Dan's hand most heartily, and clap him on the back, and I wait by the tent door and none of us quite knows how to act, for I am still in my trooper's gear yet known now for a woman. It's a great relief to all of them when Sergeant North summons his wife and says he has asked her to give me some clothes 'more fitting to your station.'

Mrs North, an amiable woman with tiny hands, ushers me into her quarters. She calls the other women to her, and they gather around me in a crowd and touch me as if to prove I am real. There are sheets hanging to divide the great tent so that the officers and their wives may have the illusion of privacy. The women find me skirts and a stomacher, and a linen cap too, and Mrs North guides me behind one of the curtains as she helps me dress. I remember how Cecile used to dress Madame each day. The stomacher is too large but will serve well enough, once Mrs North has pinned it tighter. I think again of the butterflies pinned to the felt in Captain Turnbull's cabin.

The women bring me boots which they tell me belonged to Sergeant Newham's wife, dead of dysentery back in Aalst. The boots are narrower than what I'm used to, for all those years barefoot aboard the *Resolve* and the *Expedition* have made my feet unfit for any but the roughest boots, man-sized. I loosen the laces as far as I can, but still must take stilted little steps.

When I'm dressed, Mrs North faces me and presses a hand to each of my shoulders.

'There,' she says. 'And a fine woman you make, too.'

See? I think. *See how a woman can be made, with nothing more than cloth and some pins.*

She pulls the sheet aside, like the curtains of a stage, to reveal me to the gathered women. They move around me like some country dance to which I have not learned the steps. They run their fingers through my hair, which I have always worn fastened low at the nape of my neck. One of the wives tries to curl it, and though she pulls and twists it, it is kindly done and I do not mind. She herself wears only her shift, and when she raises the comb I see her underarm, a nest of dark hair in that scoop of flesh. I feel I ought to look away, for I know nothing of the intimacies of women and what they might show or hide from each other.

'Thank you for your kindness,' I say before I leave. Is my voice different? I fancy it still sounds low, beside the high trill of Mrs North and the other women. Is it years of training that have made my voice thus, or was it always so?

'There's no need to thank us,' says Mrs North. 'Indeed, Mary Read makes a most welcome addition to the camp.'

Thus I leave my dead brother's name in that tent, and walk back to Dan wearing a dead woman's boots and my proper name, stiff and unfamiliar.

The news has spread faster than any great news of the war, and the men of my platoon are already waiting, jostling one another to be the first to get a good look at me, though God knows they have had ample time to look at me over these last years.

'This is Mary,' Dan says, as if I'm meeting them for the first time.

We have all heard already of Mrs Kit Welsh, the woman who served in the Royal Scots Greys, but the men seem to find my story no less remarkable for not being the first.

'You're a sly one,' says Tanner, admiring and wary, both at once. He keeps looking at me and then away, shaking his head a little, as though he wishes he had the soldier Mark standing beside me, so he could compare us, one to the other.

They cannot allow me to be the same person, for I have seen too much: their bodies, their fears, their tendernesses and their moments of terror. Thus I must now play at being a stranger to them. I begin to think fondly of that period when my body was a secret shared only with Dan.

There is much teasing of Farrow, who is smaller and slighter than me, and the men laugh that he must prove himself a man now that I have cast such things into doubt. Then Tanner makes to rip open Farrow's shirt and they take to brawling, and I am very tired and glad to be able to retreat to the place allotted to me, a corner of the officers' tent, with a sheet pinned up for space of my own. I may not share with Dan until we are wed, though already I know well the slack shape of his sleeping mouth, and the different notes of his snoring.

＊

I cannot be discharged from the army – not officially – since my enlistment was a lie, and thus so was everything that followed. But they are happy enough to discharge Dan, for with Emperor Joseph dead, already there is talk of peace, if not with Spain then at least with France.

The chaplain presides over the wedding, and does it with good cheer, for his usual duties have been the consecration of the dead. The entire squadron has joined together to present us with a fat purse of guilders, and Collins and Tanner bring friends from other squadrons to meet us. 'Look!' Tanner says. 'You'd never know she passed as a man.'

But I know, I think, as I smile and nod and thank them for the coins and the notice. There is much laughter and Tanner drinks so much that he is sick against the wall of the tent and the laughter and the ribaldry are a little too loud, and over us all a fat full moon hangs like a blister, fit to burst.

'You will be in a hurry to be gone,' the men say, and it is meant as a jest, that we are impatient for our nuptial bed, but in truth it is they who want us gone for these men do not know how to reconcile the two people that I am: the man they knew and the woman they do not.

I am glad to have Dan's hand in mine as we walk away from the encampment, and the army. It does not do to make of a war your home, for you will find yourself as I do, stepping outside of the war and feeling afraid.

12

Half drunk, we take a room at an inn, and after all the goodwill and noise of the day, it is suddenly very quiet.

My body was to be the secret and the surprise, but his body is as much of a surprise to me. One cannot serve in both navy and army as I have and not see men's bodies. But they were bodies in motion: changing; washing; injured in battle, their wounds being dressed by the surgeons. Even when Lewes used to parade naked amongst the hammocks, I sought to look indifferent, and not to stare. So Dan's body is a new thing to me.

In our snatched fumbles behind tents and in dark corners, I have felt his cock before, urgent and hard through his breeches. Now Dan removes his clothes and approaches the bed, his feet bare on the splintered boards, and I have to stop myself from laughing – not that I don't desire him, but I want to say: *is that all it is?* His cock, a meek, fleshy thing hanging heavy. I know, then, the great fraud of being a man, and far from disgust I step to him and take him in my arms and feel myself caught in a slow-rising tide of warmth and pity. Even as his cock hardens and salutes, it is still such a tender thing, bobbing when he takes another step towards the bed, and I could almost laugh at the swindle of it, this almighty difference, his balls cupped in my hand like two egg yolks.

Our bodies manage very well together, and there is pleasure for both of us in what we do, for all its newness. Afterwards he slides down to lie with his head on my belly and his face turned towards my cunny.

'How could you keep this hid?' he asks.

'Did you expect me to run it up the flagpole?'

Dan treats my body like a great prize that he has brought back from the war. I am touched by all his little considerations: his coat set about my shoulders when my own is too thin; his arm to help me across a muddy street. Sometimes I almost laugh, for in these years past we have toiled side by side in muddy ditches for long hours, and I have not needed his help. But his small kindnesses give him joy and I do not wish to rob him of that, for there has not been much of joy in these long years, nor this long war.

We head north, through what the war has left behind, to Dan's uncle's tavern, near Breda. It is *De Drie Hoefijzers*, which means 'The Three Horseshoes.'

'That's three times good luck,' Dan says.

I haven't the heart to say that three horseshoes doesn't sound like good luck to me, not unless you're riding a horse with three legs. And when we finally arrive, the tavern doesn't feel like good luck, either – a squat building built in a hollow so that in winter the fog settles on us and never stirs. But Dan is so proud, the big key at his belt and the brass strip at the front door polished to a shine.

I thought being known for a woman would mean the end of watchfulness – but I discover that to be a woman is to be watchful all the time. A drunken young man in the taproom lifts my skirt when I have my back to him, while others laugh. Hands find my waist as I move through the crowded market square; men touch me for no reason, for having a woman's body is apparently reason enough.

When I go into Breda, the very way I move about the town is changed by my skirts. I hesitate at the mouth of the narrow streets behind the Grote Kerk, and hurry past the door of the tavern opposite the Spanjaardsgat, where once my fellow troopers and I might have drunk.

I write to Ma.

I am wed to Dan Jansenns of my troop and a good man. We have taken on the running of his uncle's tavern here, and the work is hard but we do it with good heart and are glad to be out of the army though I could hardly stay things being as they are. You may write to me here for I should like to hear how you fare.

A letter arrives in turn, months later and much dampened and creased. It is the only letter I have had of her:

I am glad to hear you are wed, although as you know being sadly deceived in my own husband who showed himself not a man of good character. But I must wish you joy of it though I cannot hold with foreigners. As to what passed before with you it is best not mentioned and whatever choices you made you have doubtless now repented.

It irks me at first that Ma speaks of my choice – she who made me into a boy before I could speak or walk. But it is true that I chose, after all, to enlist, and to stay in the navy and then the army ten long years. Ma made me a boy but it was my choice to leave, and mine to stay a boy thereafter. Mine too, to reveal myself to Dan and take to my skirts. Ma did show me, without ever meaning to, that each body may be a choice, and each day also.

———————

That summer, Dan teaches me to swim. He takes me south of Breda to where the Aa of Weerijs is barely twenty yards wide, and has grassed banks.

'Careful now,' he says, when I make ready to wade in at the edge, for I am a sailor and I cannot fear this tame water. But Dan takes a long bough and shows me how quick the ground drops away, and when he releases the bough the river takes it down and we do not see it again for the current is quick and heavy.

Few sailors learn to swim. If you fall from a ship of the line, swimming will make no difference, for the fall itself will kill you before you can drown. And in the winter months, the cold will kill you regardless. Some old salts cling to a superstition that learning to swim only prolongs the agonies of drowning – but I never held with that, for there is no man alive who, upon falling in the water, does not thrash and try to swim. I know of none who would surrender calmly to the depths, for the body has no notion of a quick death but will scramble for each breath.

Dan leads me slowly into the water. He's brought a cow's bladder for me to grasp but it has been blown too full of air, the whole thing so tight and slick I can't get any purchase on it, so he holds me instead, and I feel the water take on my weight.

'Take off your clothes,' he says.

'Is that the whole point of this?'

'I could look at you naked at home without freezing my balls off,' he says, and his teeth whistle with his laugh. 'Get on with it.'

And he is right, because the fabric would've dragged me under, and once I have tossed my clothes to the bank my whole body is lighter, and when I lean back the water answers me, lifting me up. Then I lean too far and slip below the surface and Dan hoists me up again, and we are so cold but laughing, and there are none to see us but if there were I would not be ashamed, not even naked, for the water and the cold have painted us bright with joy.

I look down at myself as we stand there, waist-deep. There are bubbles of air in the hair on my cunny, and when Dan brushes his hand there the bubbles take off in alarm like a swarm of tiny fish making for the surface. I lean forward and I am afloat, now, Dan's hand beneath my belly. I am a thing of water indeed.

———————

I learn to swim, but I do not learn to love the Low Countries, where the water gropes its long fingers inland. This region has been clawed back from the sea. That's not a fight that can ever be won – not in the end.

In the vale where the tavern sits, east of Breda, the mop is never dry for the water comes up between the flagstones. 'If I'd wanted to live in the mud,' I say to Dan, 'I'd have stayed in the army.' I fancy the whole tavern is sinking. When Dan laughs I hear the whistle of the air between his teeth and think the wind is blowing right through us.

I lie in our bed and dare not sleep.

'The dykes keep the water out,' Dan tells me, again and again. I know about the dykes the same way I know about God: I don't believe in them. I cannot trust the dykes, nor the dirt. Without the tavern, all is wet; within, we are barely more dry. I become accustomed to the smell of damp, the air heavy with water, and the mould that we can't scrub off the downstairs skirting boards. The hearth keeps one side of the taproom dry; on the opposite side of the room, the floorboards are softened with damp and the window frames rot. I scrape my fingernail along a sill and the black wood comes away like soap under my nail. The table legs are darker at the bottom where the wet soaks in. On hot days I watch the ground sweat water; at night I listen to the drip of a leak somewhere in the roof. *It's starting*, I think. I trust the sea to do what it has done before: to find me.

When I can be spared from the work of the tavern, I walk the edge of the sluggish canals. Sometimes I slip from my shoes and walk barefoot like a sailor, the ground spongy underfoot. In spring the canal water roils with carp and eels, the whole surface squirming and never still. They are breeding, or perhaps fighting. I watch them a long time – the fierce writhing mass of them.

Though I am become a woman in the world's eyes, I am not the one who has changed – it is Dan. How could things ever be the same, now that I am no longer his comrade but his wife? When we were soldiers together, he would never have given me an order, and if he'd tried we'd all of us have laughed at him and asked if he fancied himself an officer. And if ever I helped him with a twisted stirrup or washed his spoon along with my own, it was because I was there, and because he had done the same for me many days, without ever being asked.

An army has its ranks – we knew that well enough. But a marriage does too, and so in our home he is an officer now, and neither of us knows how to live thus. He is not a harsh man. But he is a man raised as a man, to believe women follow orders, and wives especially. That may be true, but it was not how we came to know one another, so we speak to each other in a new language, and it cannot be the same easy language of our tent.

I do not mind that he asks me not to wear breeches even when the tavern is closed, and nobody there to see us. In truth I like the airiness of wearing skirts, though they are awkward for the mopping. But the other parts of being a wife come harder to me. When Dan saw me for a woman he thought he had seen the truth of me. He doesn't realise that the man is also the truth of me, and that the stuff between my legs is not the end of what I am, nor the start of it.

Dan can no longer call me 'Mark,' and nor can he quite bring himself to call me 'Mary.' Instead he calls me 'Love,' and I believe him. He can never admit that he preferred it as it was, for some part of him fears that would damn him for a sodomite, or a poor husband. I suspect we never loved one another better than in the mud of the camps, but he does not wish to speak to me about the change that has occurred between us, for Dan's courage has never been in words.

'Can we not be as we were, to each other?' I ask him, once.

'We aren't who we were then,' he says, impatient. 'You're not, leastways. And if you were, we could never be wed. Is that what you want?'

It isn't, for I love him as well as I know how to love, though I fear that may not be enough, since such lessons as Ma gave of love were all taught with the back of the hand.

The tavern demands hard work, but it is nothing to the labour of the navy, nor even the army. We have taken on a girl to help in the kitchen. Together, young Ilse and I cook the meals, while Dan runs the taproom. Our neighbours are good folk, and if they show some reserve with me it is only because I have little Flemish. My strange history has not reached them, and Dan is at pains to keep it thus. 'Not everyone would understand,' he says, cupping the back of my head in his large hand. 'I've no wish to be fodder for the town's gossips.' Sometimes I think he is ashamed; at other times his eyes meet mine across the taproom and he smiles and I can believe that he likes our past to be our own private story, and ours alone.

I am neither miserable nor mistreated, and I am not fool enough to miss the war, nor the hiding. But I feel my life growing very small again, as it did at when I was in service at the big house. Most of all I miss the ocean and its restlessness. Even in the army we were often on the move. Here we are becalmed, stuck. At night, Dan's sleeping hand on my hip, I hear the wind dulled by the stubborn trees, and the old building settling deeper into the mud. I long for the clear singing of the ships, and I wish myself again up the mast, amidst all that sky.

In our first year at the tavern, our old squadron twice passes Breda. They visit *De Drie Hoefijzers* and are mighty noisy and joyful at first. Farrow and Tanner laugh very hearty about the time my horse ate the sergeant's stockings where they were hanged to dry, or the time a great alarm went up that a French prisoner had escaped, until Tanner and I found him fallen in the jakes and stuck there – but the laughter falls away for such things are not fit for a woman's ears. I want to say: *I was there. It was I who first found that Frenchman, waist-deep in shit, and we hauled him out together and I'll not soon forget the stink of him.* But we can none of us bridge the space between the soldier they knew then and the woman who stands here now, in skirts, with my tray to clear away their empty beakers. And when they speak of our cavalry days, Dan is forever hushing them and glancing about the room, for he does not wish the other customers to know my story. So although our old comrades leave with much noisy lamenting, and embraces for Dan, in truth they are relieved to go, and we to see them leave.

There are times when Dan and I are in bed and follow no orders but our own pleasure. This is why I like the dark – the same reason I like the water. I can give my body over to the dark or the water both. In such times I slip from man or woman the way we slip from our clothes. I am not Dan's wife nor his comrade, but only myself.

When Dan and I set sail on the raft of our bed, I can nearly forget the damp in the skirting boards, and the patient water pressing at the dykes.

———————————

We have been wed for two years in 1713, when the Treaty of Utrecht is supposed to be the end of the war. Philip is to remain the Spanish king after all, it seems, providing he renounces his claims to the French throne. There is fighting still, for the French and Spanish and Austrians have their own enmities, but the English troops who once trusted our beer are returned home, and the tavern is quieter now, and we can no longer afford Ilse to work in the kitchen.

I find that the quiet suits me well enough, for I am pregnant. A pregnancy starts as a secret between a woman and her body. This is the time I like best, and I do not even tell Dan. In these weeks the baby is mine alone. Later, when I tell Dan, he is overjoyed and kisses my belly and fusses over me though in truth I have never felt more well. But soon I wear the changes on the outside, and the baby becomes a thing for everyone else, and I must suffer the beery jibes of the drinkers at the tavern, praising Dan for having finally proved himself a good husband. Dan does not mind – some part of him, I believe, is glad of this, the final proof that I am truly a woman, which makes him truly a man. He has a renewed swagger to his walk as he passes amongst the tables and benches of the taproom. But I do not like going thus out into the world: my stomach bulging, low, and my breasts hardening and sore to the touch. I wrap my apron tighter about my stomach, and think of Ma yanking on the strings of my stays.

I have had little time for needlework amidst the daily tasks of the tavern but now I embroider a blanket for the baby. I stitch ships, and horses, the high waves off Cabrita Point and the tents in rows on the flatlands of Flanders. I sit up late to work at it and Dan does not begrudge me the candles but traces his finger over my stitches and points to the largest horse and says, 'That's Rig for sure – you've caught his mean eyes just so.' I teach him the names of the masts as I stitch each one: foremast; mainmast; mizzenmast.

The baby comes untimely. It has barely quickened when I am awakened one night by terrible pain in my guts, and then follows an immoderate flux, a great letting go, and the bed awash in watery blood. After an hour more of the pains, and before the woman from Breda can even be fetched, the baby slithers from me like a carp from a net. Afterwards follows the lumpen rope of the cord and the great fleshy placenta, which I must haul from myself like an anchor. Dan bundles the whole of it together in the soiled sheets and takes it away, but not before I have seen the child. It is fish-slick, half formed, its tiny head too soft to hold its shape, for it is calf-jelly not quite set. Its fingers and toes are webbed.

The softness of it, all wet and limp, sets me to thinking that the damp of Breda has got inside me somehow. I am rotting. I am a flooded field, where things will fester and not grow.

I give the baby no name.

I think of Mark, the brother whose name I was given, or took. Perhaps that is why there is no room inside me for a child, for I must carry Mark within me as well.

And what name have I? My mother named me Mary but did not let it be spoken aloud. I went to war to discover my true name. I was Mark all those years, or Read. Now I am Jansenns: Mevrouw Jansenns, or Mrs Jansenns, or Love. I slip between names. What keeps me tied to the world? I am untethered.

Dan takes the unnamed bundle and buries it. I would have preferred a proper sea burial, but Dan thinks it a mad request, a childbed fever, and tells me not to overtax my strength, and to lie still. Anyway we have no sea close by, despite being beset by water. I think of the damp ground, how you only have to scrape it to bring the water out, so perhaps beneath the dirt that little shroud is already become a ship.

There has been no baptism so there is no call for the churchyard, and I am glad there will be no churchman intoning over our small one, nor staring at it. Later I ask for the blanket I embroidered, for it would be some comfort to me to hold it again, but Dan tells me he buried the baby in it. I am glad the child went to its grave wrapped in stories that I stitched. I do not ask Dan where he dug the hole. I want no marker in the ground, no place to go and remember any of this.

The rich may do all the grieving they want – for the rest of us, there is work to be done. When the bleeding has stopped I am back to the stove, and the mop. In truth I am not sorry to be kept busy. But the hollow in which the tavern sits, and its dampening walls, close about me like the wet earth in which the baby is buried.

Late August 1714 brings news from England: the queen is dead. I never thought to feel pity for a queen, but she has died without an heir and everyone knows she has been pregnant time and again, and each baby born dead, or dead soon enough. A pair of Englishmen in the tavern raise a toast to King George, the new Hanoverian king, though Dan says that it will set the Jacobites rising again for they will not rest until they see the Stuart James on the throne – but I don't attend to Dan's words for I cannot stop thinking of the dead queen, her body a mangle churning out broken babies.

That winter something takes hold of Dan's lungs and won't let them go. If you'd wrung his lungs they'd have poured out water. His coughs rattle the shutters and bring up so much phlegm that we give up on handkerchiefs and by the end he is spitting into a bucket. Then he spits blood – not the startling red of new blood, but blood set thick and black, his lungs nothing but scabs. The doctor from Breda takes our money but offers us nothing in exchange save for prayers, and a jar of foul-smelling salve that I am to rub on Dan's chest.

I am used to a death that comes quickly, like at war. But Dan's death comes damp, slow and implacable.

From deep in his fever he calls to me: 'Mark Mary Mark.'

'I'm here,' I tell him, but I don't know which one of me he wants.

'I don't know how to do this,' he says, and I figure he means the dying. I cannot say to him that each person learns their own death in the doing. So I say nothing, and his breathing gets worse, until every rasping exhalation is a gamble, waiting on the next breath that may not come.

The going is so bad that in the end it is a relief when he is gone, and for all the gaps and silences of our marriage, I loved him too well to wish him to linger in such pain.

I clean his body, his skin already going hard as stale ship's biscuit. That night his ghost comes to me, dressed again in his cavalry blues, his face frosted over like a glass.

Am I to war again? he asks.

No, I say. *You need go to war no more.*

Then shall I stay with you?

I make no reply. If all my dead are to stay with me, it's going to get mighty crowded.

I won't take up much room, says Dan into the dark.

Nor me, said my brother, in a nightdress that covers his toddler feet. Marston and Flett, and the dead rising up from the battle-field, mud stiffening their hair. *Nor me. Nor me.* The baby, still soft-palated, watches me and makes no sound.

I cannot allow my life to become a rooming house for ghosts.

You have to go, I say. *Dan, I mean it. I can't be taking you everywhere.*

Dan nods, solemn as if receiving an officer's order.

What's it like? my brother's voice asks.

What's what like?

My life.

Dan was a good man – kind and true, and as decent a husband as any woman might ask for. But now he is dead I find I have already passed many miles through my grief, for ever since we were wed I have been mourning what we were to each other back in the army. I have already grieved for that, and for our child, and the truth is that when Dan dies there is little grieving left in me. I loved him – and having no longer any place to put that love, I feel instead a great wide emptiness, the world stripped back to its horizons. I take a very strong notion that it is a beginning, or an ending. Either way it is a mighty big feeling, and it sets me restless, waking at night from dreams of being again at sea.

I had taken Dan's name, Jansenns, but he took it back with him into the wet Flanders ground. Who I will be next I have not yet decided.

Dan is buried in the little churchyard. Through all the stiff ceremony of the burying, and the drone of the minister's words, I cannot see my way to the real stuff of Dan: the softness at the edge of his mouth; the sureness of his hands on the reins.

After, I lock the tavern door and scrub the house. I scour the black mould from the skirting boards and boil the sheets that Dan died in. I scrub until my fingernails are breaking and blisters sprout like mushrooms on the pads of my fingers.

I write to Dan's cousin in Oudenaarde, who was much aggrieved when Dan was granted the tavern. I tell him he is welcome to it, for Dan is dead. I pack my things into a bundle and bind it with rope, sailor style, and I head north-west on foot. I make for the sea the same way a river does: without thinking.

13

On the road halfway to Rotterdam, at the end of the first day's walking, I find a dead crow. Perhaps a fox got it, or a dog. Perhaps it died of whatever crows die of, and then a cart wheel ground over it. Either way, it's wholly smashed now, broken feathers and snapped bones. Everything about it is wrong, as if it's been badly sketched by a child. On an elm tree close by, three more crows stand vigil.

Most people see crows as vermin, and will stone them or break up their nests. But I've never hated crows. They're nasty buggers, but clever with it. And I admire the imperious angle of their heads. You'd be a fool to cross one. Ma chucked a tub of dishwater at a crow once, to chase it from the yard, and for years her clothes pegs were picked off the line, one by one, the clean linens slumping into the mud.

Even in the war, I didn't begrudge the crows our dead on the battlefields. It is an ugly sight, sure, but it seems to me that the ugliness cannot be blamed on the crows alone, for it is we who provide the bodies.

So it feels wrong to see the crow lying like that in the road, waiting for the next cart wheel, the next fox. I take up the body – the cold, stiff weight of it. It's easier to show mercy to crows than to men. Wiser, too, I reckon.

The feathers leave a grey dust on my coat as I hold the dead crow to my belly and walk a little way from the road. No time to bury it deep, but it is spring and the ground is soft and I gouge at the soil with a stick, and then my hands, to make a shallow trench.

The three crows are still watching me – they must've followed me from the road. They sit now on a branch of a dead oak and stare at me indifferently. For a moment I fear that in burying their comrade I have robbed them of a meal, and they will fly at me. I've seen at Ramillies how they can take the eyes from a dead man, and I don't much fancy having three crows coming at me, if they're inclined to be vengeful. But they stay motionless, staring only, so I get on with the burying. I do it properly, stamping the earth down flat. I could not bury my child myself, nor my husband. This at least I can do, and at the end of it my heart is the better for the work of my hands.

After that, the crows follow me everywhere. All that next day's walking, whenever I pause they alight in the nearest tree. When I reach Rotterdam and find an inn, the three of them settle in the tree outside, watching me with their black and unembarrassed stare. I take a turn about the dock, later, to see which ships have come in, and circling high above me are those three black shapes. Back at the inn, and my small upstairs room with its smell of boiled meat, the crows are lined on the sill, swaying side to side like a row of hanged men.

By dawn, when I'm wakened by swearing in the kitchen below, only the smallest crow remains. Where the other two crows have gone I know not, but this one has the look of staying.

I keep a cheese rind from breakfast. In the stableyard the crow awaits me on the fence. I toss her the bit of rind; she grabs it neatly, and makes no nod nor squawk, nor any show of gratitude. She takes it as if it is her due, no more and no less.

I go down to the docks again, mainly to see if the crow follows. She does – holding her distance, but keeping me always in sight. Twice she takes herself over the water and returns with a herring that she eats, unhurried, on the cobblestones.

I say she, though I've no idea – and I'm not planning on looking close enough, even if you can tell that way. But I think of her as a she, for the fierceness of the curve of her beak.

I toy with the notion that she means something. I even entertain, briefly, a godless thought that she might be some kind of spirit: a ghost of Dan, or the baby, or even Mark, come to haunt or to watch over me. But over the next two days I see enough to know this bird is no warning, nor blessing, nor guardian angel. The prodigious shits that she leaves on the windowsill are proof enough of that. No: a crow is always and only itself.

I can no longer delay seeking work, for I have little money. I go to the harbour still in my skirts, for with the babe only a few months dead, my body looks womanly, softer in the middle and larger in the chest than I was wont to be, and I fear that I can no longer pass as a man. Seeking sailor work as a woman will not be easy – but passing as a man has its own dangers. I have weathered one unmasking, when Dan saw through me, and I dare not trust I will emerge safe from another. But more than that, I haven't the appetite for concealment. I am done with hiding.

What if there were another thing: neither woman nor man, but sailor? Sometimes I think us sailors a different thing altogether from landlubbers. At the docks a frigate is newly arrived and I watch the topmen reef the sails. Barefoot amongst the rigging, they might be a different creature from the men who walk ashore.

If sailors are a singular thing, then man or woman doesn't figure in it. We are our own creature, as different from ordinary people as a whale or a seahorse. When my dead baby was born, its little body was much coated in white grease and between its legs nothing but a nub that might have shown it a boy or girl, or neither. Its toes and fingers were webbed, and I thought it was because the baby came too soon, its body unfinished or somehow wrong. Now I wonder if it was something else: a thing with splayed feet made for swimming, like the flat pads of a frog's feet, or an otter's. Every baby is a creature of water anyway – I felt it myself, the wet surge of liquid that poured from me before the baby came. They live in their own small sea all that time, in the narrow bay of the belly, and are born strangers to land.

So I stand at the docks in my skirts and am glad to meet the sea without lies – for man or woman figures less to me these days than it did. Perhaps my baby was born to be a sailor, and not a boy nor girl at all. And I too – a sailor first, hostage to wind and at home in saltwater.

———————

Most of the captains I approach have a little English; between that and my hesitant Flemish I am able to tell them of my years in the navy. Some of them doubt me, and I cannot blame them for it has the sound of a story, and I have nothing to prove it but my strong hands. Few are in need of more crew: the end of the war has left the world awash with sailors, for the navies have turned off their men, and privateering commissions too are done with, for the king cannot grant a licence to hunt enemy ships when there is no enemy. So I am far from the only sailor walking the harbour for work – but I am the only one in skirts, and that sets me at a grave disadvantage.

One captain will not hear me out beyond my first few words, but makes the sign of the cross and scurries along the harbour-side as though fearful of contagion. And the fourth captain is all too keen and would hurry me at once to his cocket-boat but it is I who rush away, for whatever he has in mind it is not work. But another man who has watched the whole of it points me towards the *Walcheren*, and says her *schipper* may have a use for me, for the talk is that they've had two men slip the ship and have cargo spoiling.

I go first to see the ship, for I will not take to sea on any old tub. The *Walcheren* is moored close enough for me to get a good look at her. She is an old East Indiaman, in the style the Dutch call *fluyt*: square-rigged and built for cargo and not for fighting. Widest by the waterline, with a narrow deck above, she has space for cargo, but a shallow draught. Even from the harbour I can see she is in good trim, so I seek the captain in the tavern where I was told he would be found. He is a shiny-faced man, balding though barely forty, his remaining hair combed across his pate in an unconvincing fashion. He is not carousing, but hunched over a table with another man whom I take for an agent or perhaps the purser, since they are deep in talk of barrels and lading and the price to be got for mace.

When I venture to interrupt them, the captain recognises my poor Flemish and answers me in English – he is English too, and introduces himself as Payton. In the warm tavern, sweat has made wet stripes of the hair that he pastes across his bald pate. When I tell him of my navy service he looks at me appraisingly, then pulls from his pocket a short length of cord, tosses it to me, and bids me make a hitch. I am relieved that my fingers have not forgot their work for I can still tie a hitch speedily and without looking. When I toss it back to him he nods and states a wage.

'I made near as much in the navy, sir – and that some years ago.'

'I don't doubt it,' he says. 'And since the war's end every port's crowded with navy men in need of work.'

'Not all of them speak English as I do, sir – nor trained in the Royal Navy way.'

He laughs. 'Your Royal Navy is bankrupted – the war dragged on too long, and her men and ships both are cast aside now. If I sailed to Portsmouth or Plymouth I could fill my ship with Royal Navy men.'

'Not with better sailors than me, though, I'll warrant. And you haven't time to wait until England, for you've cargo spoiling, I hear.'

He looks me up and down once more, very slow, then gives a nod.

When first I climb aboard the *Walcheren*, it is like releasing a breath I have been holding too long. Through her deck I feel the shifting of the water below, and I know myself at home.

'The hell's that doing here?' calls one of the crew, and I think he means me but he is looking beyond me to where my rolled kit-bag has been tossed up from the boat. The crow has settled on my bag, her head pulled down, or her shoulders hoisted up, if a crow can be said to have shoulders. She hunches as though angry at the wind.

'Is it yours?' the man asks.

I shake my head. Crows aren't the belonging kind. Even in my head, I've never made the mistake of calling her mine. She is no more mine than the sea.

'She's taken to following me,' I say. 'Won't cause any trouble.'

'We ain't feeding no bird. And we ain't having it shitting on the deck or getting in the way.'

'She'll stay out of the way. Catches her own food. Makes no trouble. And she's cleaner than that lot,' I say, gesturing at the rest of the crew already aboard, taking the measure of me and not trying to hide it.

'Bad luck, wouldn't you say?' Payton asks.

'Only if she don't like you.'

He looks intently at the bird. 'It's an ill-favoured creature.'

I pretend I haven't heard him.

Truth is that I feel safer going aboard the *Walcheren* with the crow as my witness. I do not fool myself that the crow will save me, if the men take it upon themselves to turn nasty. But she would witness, and a crow's witnessing is not a thing lightly to be dismissed. And if the men look a little askance at me as the bird settles on the rail close by me, all the better.

The man who objected to the crow turns out to be the bosun, a steady man named Cornelisz. His English is near perfect, and with Payton he sets the tone for the crew, which numbers only a little over thirty, nearly all Dutch. For the most they are not as young as those I served with in the navy, and being older and having homes and wives and lives beyond the ship, they are less concerned with the daily squabbles and pettiness of shipboard life. Below deck a private corner is fashioned for me with a piece of old sailcloth strung from bulwark to bulwark, and I am cloistered there. Even on duty, I keep myself a little apart. After losing Marston, and the baby, and Dan, I have little appetite for seeking out friendship with these men. I have the sea, and the crow, and find that is enough.

It is near a decade and a half since I first enlisted in the navy – I am thirty now, and if I do not climb the rigging as speedily as I did then, I do it nonetheless, my hands still sure and strong. My skirts I tie at at one side, to keep them out of the way. The years on land have not cost me the skill of navigation, nor of reading the wind. Such doubts as the men may have had about having a woman aboard are answered by my work, and soon enough the crew is functioning in an easy manner. I do not doubt that it's strange for them to have a woman aboard. But there is little that men will not become used to over time, and in all the strangeness of the ocean, a woman and a crow are not so strange after all, particularly when I prove myself useful.

'We sail first for America, for Virginia tobacco,' Payton tells me – and I take a breath so deep my ribs are fit to burst with the sheer possibility of it.

'You have not been to the New World before, then?' Payton asks. He is inclined to sweat, and to running his tongue over his fleshy lips.

'No, Captain.' I smile – for indeed, a new world is exactly what I am in need of.

I thought I had seen much of the world in the navy, but it turns out the world is far wider than I had any notion of. After my years in the damp tavern, sunk in its hollow, it is a balm for me to dare those great horizons, those audacious New World skies.

Under British laws, her colonies are supposed only to trade with British merchant crews – which may be another reason why Payton was happy to take me on, to bolster his pretence. Where there is money to be made, Payton does not scruple to break rules – the more I learn the canny ways of his captaincy, the more I understand why he was willing to hire a woman, especially when I discover that he is paying me less than any of the men.

We never see the *Walcheren*'s owner – he is from Utrecht, and leaves Payton to manage the ship, for he is rich already, and Payton makes him richer. I am glad of it, for de Brabander does not know that a woman is working on his ship. That isn't all he doesn't know – I quickly see that Payton cheats the owner, a job made easier by the fact that Payton is both captain and purser.

He is no common thief, to steal direct, but instead finds ways to deal on the side. It's a rare voyage we make when some small part of the hold is not taken up with Payton's own goods, for which he makes his own profits.

Life on a merchant ship is at once very familiar, and very strange. The ship itself holds no surprises, for the rules of wind and canvas are the same on any vessel. But the sounds and smells are different, and nothing like the well-ordered quiet of the *Resolve* or *Expedition*. On those ships we kept livestock for meat, but here on the *Walcheren* several of the sailors keep pets. Payton himself has a dog, a small, rat-faced thing, speckled black and grey, and Cornelisz has two cats that roam everywhere and are too lazy to hunt mice, but instead make a great play of taunting the dog. Once, the ginger cat tries to pounce on the crow, when she is on the rail. It ends with the crow unruffled, and the cat bleeding from a neat gash on the nose. Henceforth, both cats leave the crow alone.

When the men hear but a little of my past, they are full of questions: 'Is it true you served in the Royal Navy?'; 'How could a woman pass for a man?'; Madsen, a Dane, and the gruffest of the crew, asks, 'And have you ever killed a man?'

I don't flinch from his gaze. 'Several. And I could do again if pressed.'

The other men take this as a great boast, and Madsen claps me on the back, as if the question is a test that I have passed.

'I never met a woman like you before,' says Marshall, the youngest of the crew.

'I cannot say the same, for I have met plenty of men like yourself.'

He laughs, but it is an uneasy laugh.

'And you never wed?' asks Payton.

'I did. To a man in my own cavalry troop. We left the army together.'

'And where is he now?'

'Dead,' I say.

They fall silent. Perhaps they think I killed him too. I do not tell them the truth. Dan's slow death was a private thing, belonging to the two of us alone, and I have no wish to rehearse it out loud for the benefit of these strangers.

I do not know how long the crow will stay with the ship, or whether whatever makes her follow me is stronger than whatever keeps crows to the land. But she is resolute as only a crow can be, and if she misses land she gives no sign of it. Much of the day she passes perched on the bowsprit or the mainyard, staring windward, and descending when there is food to be had. When a storm blows in she comes below, bold as you like, and makes the head of my hammock her perch.

I call her 'Crow.' Any other name I give her would be a lie, for what would a crow call herself? Not any word I know. Her name is her own secret, clutched tight in her craw.

You might think a crow is black, but that too is a lie. Her dark feathers tell a host of other stories, and in the right light her black is all shot through with oily blues and purples.

'I never thought to see a crow take to the sea,' Cornelisz says, gesturing at the bowsprit where Crow sits.

I'll warrant he never thought to see a woman take to the sea neither, but if the strangeness of Crow draws gazes away from my own strangeness, then I am grateful.

For months after the baby died my breasts had been sore and the cries of the gulls were enough to set the milk starting. That is all left behind on the *Walcheren*, where I shake off the land, heavy with memory, and became once more my sailor-self. I fashion one of my skirts into trousers, the better to do my work.

As well as the tobacco route, we ply the Bahamas. Amongst the small islands of those parts, I am taught a new lexicon of colours, for in those waters we see blues so audacious that even Madsen the Dane will lower his marlinspike and say, 'Fuck me.'

The *Walcheren* does sweetly on such routes, for her shallow draught handles the many reefs and islands. Her song is harder to make out than the great orchestral groaning of the *Resolve* or the *Expedition*. When she sings it is the single, bright note of her square-rigged mainsail ringing with wind, or the busy hum of her headstay.

Payton used to be a privateer, but has been in trade many years. He is not petty except as it concerns me, and I see soon enough that his pettiness is all aimed at finding his way into my trousers. He finds excuses to touch me – not the casual touch of all sailors working and living close, where you are forever working with another man's armpit in your face as you fasten the fore-shrouds, or their hips and shoulders pressed against yours as you heave together to turn a hogshead of tobacco in the hold. Payton's touch is always deliberate: his hand finds the bare skin on the back of my neck and rests there a moment; if he climbs the ladder beside me he will put his hand right beside mine, his skin a little too hot.

I try to make a jest of it. My hammock is rigged above a barrel of salt pork, and the smell never leaves my clothes, so that Payton's dog takes to following me about the deck, and when Payton comes too close I ask if he likes salt pork so well that he must follow me too. He does not laugh. That afternoon I take to the mast, where even Payton will not follow. Only the crow comes, alighting close to me, and together we watch the *Walcheren*'s wake, and I contemplate the problem of Payton.

I will say of him that he is not hasty. Men of the sea rarely are – if you have the habit of waiting for tides and winds, you know that things move in their own time, and a wise sailor will not rush or scurry when to wait will serve just as well. There is in Payton a dreadful sort of patience, for he knows I have nowhere to go. From one port to the next is often weeks – longer if we're unlucky with winds – and upon a ship there is no place to hide nor run. Even in port, I cannot be sure that I would ever find another captain willing to take me on.

I soon learn that Payton likes nothing more than when I ask him questions about his craft – and I admit that he reads the tides and currents of trade the way a pilot reads the sea. If I enquire about his canny ways, he takes it as an interest in himself and will gladly spend hours holding forth about what he knows. If it costs me his hand on the small of my back as we lean together over a manifest, I count it a price worth paying. All that he can teach me, I will take.

———————————

Almost a year into my time aboard the *Walcheren*, a foul night drives Crow below with me. She perches on the side of my hammock and takes to worrying at the sailcloth curtain dividing my little space from the men's. I think nothing of it but she will not come away from it even when I offer her a piece of salt beef, and she is a bird very partial to salt beef. I go to where she is busy with her beak at the curtain and at first I think she has pecked a hole there, but when I look closer I see it is sliced, very neat – a tidy half-inch slice such as even Crow's ruthless beak could not have made. As for the culprit there is little question, for flush on the other side of the sail is the hammock of Marshall, the pilot out of Bristol, so close that I know the tuneless trill of his snoring.

Marshall is the youngest of the crew and I have liked him well enough, and along with Payton he is the only other Englishman aboard. He is a fine pilot but this matter of the curtain cannot stand so I go at once to find him on deck, and though I have my knife at my belt it is my marlinspike I take out, for its savage little spike is fit for what I need. I have it at his throat before he has even spoken.

'What in God's name?' he squeals.

'You know what, you little weasel. You'll patch the curtain yourself and if I catch you spying at me again, it'll be you who needs patching.'

He looks very young and slack-jawed and like to cry but I cannot be soft on him for a man who spies through a curtain one day is a man who will take more liberties the next, and as I have not the landsman's luxury of staying out of his way, I must needs teach him instead.

'I didn't see anything,' he says, and whether I believe him or not matters little for it's the trying that matters, not the seeing. I keep the spike of the marlinspike good and tight up under his jaw, so that he's on tiptoes, his eyes rolling back like a frightened horse. I count it my good fortune that the rest of the men are below or aft, not because I fear they might come to his aid, but because shame can make a man stupid, and could turn Marshall defiant where he should be remorseful, and that's how things turn ugly. But nobody has seen us and Marshall has not even gone for his own knife, which hangs at his belt. I figure it is the same knife he used to cut the sail and so I pull it from his belt myself and toss it overboard. A sailor's knife is a daily and precious thing and his was a nice one, too, with a bone handle carved very pretty – but it had to go for he must be taught a lesson, and if he bears me a grudge I shall sleep better if he has not a knife on him, at least for a while.

I thought the matter concluded but Payton comes through the hatch just as I step back and lower my marlinspike, and he demands to know what we are about. I say, 'Nothing. This is all dealt with,' and Marshall doesn't disagree for he has his pride I suppose if not his knife. But Payton says, 'I'll not stand for fighting on my ship,' and then Marshall blurts, 'She came at me, Captain, and has thrown my knife overboard what's more.'

So the whole story must come out, and Payton goes very calm and cold fit to freeze the sea, and three days later we dock in Southampton and he turns off Marshall and gives me a very signifying nod after Marshall has dragged his trunk to the cock-et-boat. We are delayed two days for we must find another pilot. The other men aboard the *Walcheren* take it mighty hard and grumble often of my having got rid of Marshall, though I had not sought his leaving nor started the trouble. But he is not here to blame and I am instead, and I am a woman and thus blaming me comes easy to them. Only Payton does not blame me but instead looks at me more carefully than ever, and when I see how scrupulous he is in having the cargo checked and turned, I know that his protecting me is the same, the same calculation of value and profit and loss.

Nonetheless, there are consolations to be found aboard the *Walcheren*. She is a trim ship, and once I've accustomed myself to the ways of a merchant vessel, its rhythms suit me well enough. The work may be dull but the sea does not begrudge us her wide sunsets, nor the calms that buff the water to a high shine. And I have come to love the nimbleness of the *Walcheren*. The *Resolve* and the *Expedition* were magnificent vessels but unwieldy: fit for a grand battle, and not for much else. The *Walcheren*, though a wide-bottomed cargo tub, turns sprightly in comparison. The *Resolve* and the *Expedition* were on the sea; the *Walcheren* is of it.

At ports, there is no begging shore leave from officers, and I see places I've not dreamed of. Ashore I go about woman-wise, and am not much troubled by men. In front of the merchants and planters we deal with, the crew call me Payton's wife, and if I have little appetite for that particular ruse, at least it allows my presence on the ship to pass without comment, and the men we treat with leave me alone.

When I came aboard the *Walcheren*, I put my age at thirty. Perhaps the men in port leave me alone because I am no longer young. Or perhaps it is my years of living as a man: the different way of taking up space, for the navy and the army have taught me well enough how to jostle for it, how to claim it. Even in the roughest ports, in my skirts, I take some of that man-swagger with me, each step proclaiming that I know my business, and it is my own.

One autumn dawn, blown off course towards Bermuda, Madsen gives a shout and we all gather at the larboard rail and there it is, a creature aglow, blazing like an underwater prophecy. It stretches the length of the *Walcheren*, trailing its own light through the dark water.

Payton says it is a sea-jelly, though he has never seen another that glows like this. Its body is a great fleshy bulb, with a tangled cord that drags behind. It reminds me of nothing so much as the placenta and the cord that I pulled from myself after the baby was born. Captain Turnbull would have been in rhapsodies over this creature, though no vessel in his cabin could begin to contain a thing so vast.

Mine is not a small life, that has such things in it. I have seen terrible things – I have seen Hanson slip his tooth from his scurvy-loosened gums; I have seen my husband drown in his own lungs. But I have seen this too. I have been privy to the sea's secrets.

14

Stories have it that ghosts cannot cross water, nor survive salt. But my ghosts have followed me aboard the *Walcheren*. Sometimes when we weigh anchor it is not the anchor that I see being hauled from the water but my dead baby, and I must clench my jaw into silence so that I do not startle the men. In the hold, Dan sometimes sits amongst the hogsheads of tobacco. He fidgets as he never did in life, and I do not know if it is being dead that discomfits him so, or if it is because he was a landsman who never took to sea. The features of his face are blurred; perhaps ghosts who pass through the sea are tumbled smooth as stones are. Once I look over the stern and see them in the water: my toddler brother Mark, and Marston. They float just below the surface, staring at the sky, their mouths open like the blowholes of porpoises.

I am particularly glad of Crow, for a crow is the opposite of a ghost. A crow is itself and harks back to nothing. Over time, I learn the many sounds of her. Crows don't sing, nor chirp, nor make the usual bird noises. Mostly she gives a slow croak, *crack crack crack crack*, like a hatch much in need of oiling, being opened very reluctant.

I fall into the habit of speaking to her. She makes no sign of listening, but when the two of us are alone I drop my words like stones into the sea. I tell her about the navy, and the army, and the big house, and Ma's hands on the corset strings. I tell her about Dan, and the baby, and the first sunset I saw at sea, stripped of all its land trappings, just the sun being lowered into a grave of water.

I had no notion of teaching her to talk, for I never thought such a thing possible, but one day when I come on deck and find her on the rail, I greet her: 'A fine westerly today, Crow,' and she turns her head and says, 'Crow,' very deliberate. After that I try to teach her other words, but it doesn't take. 'Fish. Hi. Hi! Mary,' I say, 'Mary. Mare-ee. Say Mary,' but she turns her head away and ignores me, like she knows that name has never fit me right. She says nothing but 'Crow,' and once startles Payton by saying it loud into his ear and he looks fit to shit himself, and Cornelisz is nearby and catches my eye, and both of us have a mighty struggle to hide our laughter.

In a tavern in Charles Town I see a man who has a parrot for a pet: a great colourful thing with straight red tail feathers as long as his forearm. It comes when he whistles, and snugs down into his neck. Beside such a creature, who would notice Crow, on a post outside the tavern with her back hunched against the wind. If I wanted a bird to coo for me, and do tricks, I'd have chosen a different bird. But I didn't choose Crow. She chose me.

She keeps me nearly always within sight. It is a feeling I'm not used to, after spending so much of my life trying not to be seen. A bird that can pounce from the top of the mainmast to skewer a sardine in the water, or snatch a crab from under a rock and find out its soft parts, is a bird that sees well, and clear. It counts, this witnessing. To live your life under the vigilance of a crow is a kind of covenant.

We are four days in Rotterdam and afterwards the men are teasing Madsen for he has been whoring and one of the women robbed him. He is shamefaced and broke, for he has a wife in Denmark, though from what I hear she will be more concerned with his stolen purse than with the women.

Payton comes to me quietly. 'You won't catch me at such places. Not this last year, since you came aboard.'

He presents his waiting to me like a gift.

I try to make light of it. 'Will you not think of the whores? They'll be missing you. And they've their living to make, same as us.'

'I don't think of them,' he says. 'Not at all, Mary. You know what I think of.'

His hand is on my arm, when Cornelisz strides close by. Payton drops his hand – but I am watching Cornelisz who, having passed us very intent and purposeful, is now toying aimlessly with the forestay. Cornelisz, with his quiet manner and his suspicion of Crow, has never gone out of his way to befriend me. Yet perhaps I have an ally in him nonetheless.

I have written to Ma to tell her I am aboard the *Walcheren*, though there is no easy way for her to reply, as Payton's prodigious looseness with the laws of customs and trade means we follow no regular route nor have a home port where a letter might be left. When we dock in Plymouth in the first year, I tell myself I am too busy to seek out Ma, for we are hard pressed, and when the cargo is loaded we sail on the first tide. When we return in 1716, this excuse will no longer serve, for there is some dispute over papers. Payton is sorting it as he always sorts such things, which is with shrewd dealings and money passed under a table in a tavern – so we shall be stuck here some days more at least. It suits me to be away from Payton, so I go in search of Ma. I cannot say that I want to see her – only that I do not know how she is supporting herself, for if she still lives she is a grand age now. I am not sure what I owe to her, but I would not see her starve.

I find a new family in our old rooms, and the neighbours tell me Ma is two years married to a man named Hepworth, and living outside London in Bethnal Green. I am both disappointed and relieved, but five months later we are docked in the Pool of London and I make the journey to find her.

Theirs is not a grand area, though the house, when I find it, is large and neatly tended. It's not just the fine polished brass knocker or the arched lintel that gives me pause. I don't know what stories Ma has told her husband, nor what version of me she might want to arrive at her front door. I am not sure she will want me there at all, for she did not write to me herself with her news or her new direction. It could be that a letter from her went astray – or it may be that she has left that part of her life behind, and me with it.

So I hesitate before taking up the stout knocker and letting it fall. But Ma is not the one to answer – instead it is a maid, who bids me wait in the parlour.

I need not have feared Ma's response, for when she comes, and her husband with her, she is little concerned with me, and asks nothing of my life. She is too busy making a great show of calling the maid for every sort of trifle, until I'm quite sure that none of my pretences over the years have been greater than Ma's pretence of being a great lady.

She introduces me to Mr Hepworth, a cheerful man with a face very red and a mighty jaw, the whole effect being of a shovel carved of ham. He had been six years a widower when he met Ma, he tells me, though he does not tell me how they met. He is 'in gin,' Ma says. I had not known there was a great deal of money in that trade, for the gin shops in London are cheap and dirty, and those in Portsmouth and Plymouth even more so. But Hepworth 'is in the distilling side, not the shops side,' Ma tells me several times, then once more she rings for the maid and straightens the white linen cloth beneath the teapot.

Hepburn seems only a little taken aback to see me, and to hear that I sail aboard a merchant ship. 'Your mother told me you were in the United Provinces, even since your husband's sad death,' he says. He does not ask me how I come to be at sea – for he is embarrassed. Or perhaps I do him a disservice – perhaps he does not wish to shame me, for most women at sea are there to follow their men, and he knows I have no husband living.

It is easy to speak little of myself, for Ma insists on show-ing me every thing about the house – the two dinner sets, and complaining of damp in the cellar in a way that makes me wonder if she remembers our rooms in Plymouth where, each winter, a determined stream ran from the window to the crack in the floor.

'We are thinking of setting up a carriage,' she says, 'for the roads hereabouts are very good now, even in winter.'

The third time she calls imperiously for the maid, Hepburn looks a touch abashed, and rushes to prod the fire himself instead. Whether he believes her to be the lady she claims, I do not know – perhaps, being rich, he has not the habit of suspicion. Regardless, he seems to dote on her, and who am I to say that what we love in others may not be their lies as much as the truth of them. As for Ma, there is nothing in her manner to suggest that she loves him, but it is very clear that she loves his clean house and the maid and the little crystal sugar bowl and the startlingly white starched cuffs of her mantua – and that is a kind of love too, I suppose.

I cannot say that Ma is happy – Ma not being inclined to happiness, any more than a stone is inclined to float. But she is calmer than I have seen her before, and her hands have not the rawness they had in her laundry-scrubbing days. She betrays no curiosity about the life that I lead, instead being at pains to show me again a new stomacher that the maid must fetch down, embroidered all over with glass beads. She bestows tight little smiles on her husband, like alms to the poor.

I had told Payton that I would stay the night with Ma – but she does not offer. I leave her standing arm in arm with Hepworth, and though I tell her that she may write to me at Plymouth or London, where they will hold a letter for me, none of us makes any mention of my calling again.

———————

It is late by the time I come aboard the *Walcheren*. I call out a low greeting, and there is a commotion below. As I descend the ladder, Payton is rushing a woman from his cabin, his shirt missing and his trousers unbelted.

I step back to make way for the woman, who shoulders past me, still adjusting her slip.

'Wait on deck,' he calls to her.

'I still need paying,' she says.

So he has been amongst the whores at last – it surprises me only that he has not done so earlier.

I try to ease past him, but he steps to block me. He glances up to the hatch through which the woman has gone.

'Look what you made me do,' he says. He pounds his hand hard against the bulkhead, once and then again, setting his small dog to whimpering from behind him. Payton's fist strikes the bulkhead close to my head, but I do not feel afraid – he means to hurt himself and not me.

'I did not think to see you return tonight,' he says. Now he drops his head. 'Jesus, Mary. You must forgive me.'

It is not like him to speak thus – this contrition is worse than his usual cocksureness.

We face one another in the cramped passageway. From the tip of his nose, a drip of something trembles – whether it is sweat, or snot, or tears, I do not wish to know.

'I'm sorry,' he says. He cradles his bruised fist in his other hand, staring at it and not meeting my eyes. 'It has been a long time, and there are so many temptations ashore.' Standing so close, he reeks of brandy and sex and shame.

'It's no business of mine,' I say. I try for a jovial tone. 'You are a man, after all.' I gesture at the ladder up which the woman climbed. 'And she looks tempting indeed.'

Still he will not let it rest, but steps yet closer.

'I missed you, you see. And you have been so very' – he pauses – 'so very unyielding.'

'Captain.' I say the word very slow and clear. 'What you do is your own affair.'

From above, the woman calls down. 'I won't wait all night.'

I slip past him and his cowering dog to my own cabin, and wish I had the sureness of a wooden bulkhead and door, instead of the sailcloth curtain.

15

These days aboard the *Walcheren* seem featureless, as if seen through a grimed glass. The days have smuggled in the years, until I have spent as long in Payton's crew as I did in the tavern with Dan. I am thirty-two; my closest companion is a crow. I think, sometimes, of that other life: the one in which I am a wife and a mother, and keep a Flanders tavern. That was supposed to be my life – but Dan and the baby are long buried, and in leaving the inn and taking again to sea, I have stepped out of that life entirely. Perhaps I have never been good at living the life intended for me.

My life on the *Walcheren* has become familiar and in many ways comfortable – yet I do not fool myself that there is not a reckoning coming. When I climb aloft, the crow beside me, I survey the sea's silence and wonder what shape my life may take beyond the *Walcheren*, and whether I dare to find out.

More than ever, now, we work the Bahamas. I am glad to have a good crew about me, for in these waters you must know your business. Don't be fooled by the clear water, its bright and innocent blue. There are hundreds of islands – thousands, if you count the low-lying keys – each of them with their own reefs and channels, and coral that looks soft as cake and would slice a hull, or scour your flesh down to bone.

It is neither reefs nor winds that we fear most in these waters, though, but pirates. Like the fishermen following the codfish to Newfoundland, pirates follow the trade routes. The Bahamas are rich pickings now because so many merchant ships pass by there: up in the Florida Straits, they may catch the Spanish ships, with their fabled riches coming back to Spain from their empire. A little further south-east, in the Windward Passage, are ships from Europe, or returning from Jamaica, heavy with sugar and sugar money. In summer many pirates will head further north; when those waters freeze, the pirates again come south and crowd the waters of the Caribbean.

But Payton is not one to miss a chance, and if there are pirates abroad he would rather trade with them than flee them, for their money is as good as any after all. In Charles Town, Payton has made the acquaintance of one Richard Thompson, who makes good money trading with the pirates in their nest at Nassau town, on the island of New Providence. Thompson runs goods between Nassau and Jamaica and Charles Town, for pirates cannot live on their prizes alone – and there are plenty who will trade with them, on easy terms.

Payton will only trade with Thompson, and not directly with the pirates, for even in his private trades he takes care to keep his hands clean – but it is close enough to make me afraid, for the pirates have a bloody reputation, and the pirate hunters the same.

'Will you tell de Brabander?' I ask him. The owner turns a blind eye to most of what Payton does, as long as the profits come in, but even he might hesitate at dealing with pirates.

'I give him no cause for complaint,' Payton says.

'Because he doesn't know.'

Payton lets his eyes linger on my body, all the way down and up. 'Plenty he doesn't know about. And I see no need for him to know all that goes on aboard this ship – wouldn't you agree?' He leans in closer, snatching my hand in his own. 'You cannot drag this out forever, Mary. You must make a choice.'

'I'm still mourning my husband,' I say.

He adopts a pious expression. 'And that does you credit. But how long can I be expected to wait?'

He leaves me, and I exhale. I am so tired. The work of keeping Payton at bay is harder by far than the heavy labour of hoisting sails or loading cargo. *You must make a choice*, he said. The choice I make daily, by evading him, he will neither acknowledge nor accept.

Can I not choose the sea, without having to choose Payton also? It would not be easy to find another ship to take on a woman – and many ships carry men worse than Payton. What price am I willing to pay, not to lose the *Walcheren*? Not to lose the easy companionship of the crew, and the job that I am good at? And how, among all this sea, has my world come to feel so very narrow?

———————

We do not sail alone to Nassau, for we are not mad. Thompson himself meets us off Charles Town in his sloop, the *Richard and John*, and we sail together to Harbour Island, where Thompson lives, off Eleuthera.

He has come aboard to talk with Payton and to show our pilot the shoals and reefs he must learn. Thompson is smaller than you might think, for one with such a large reputation, but he is big in voice and quick, and I suspect that few things would surprise him – certainly he is not taken aback to meet a woman aboard the *Walcheren*, only removes his hat and says to Payton, 'I see you have not told me the whole of your cargo.'

Payton says quickly, 'She is not cargo – and not for trading neither,' and Thompson reads Payton's face fast enough to say nothing further.

His sloop, the *Richard and John*, sails just ahead of us. As we draw closer to Harbour Island, he can see our crew becoming more watchful.

'Tell your men to unclench their arses,' he says to Payton. 'Not many ships would dare to sail here – but the pirates will no more attack the *Richard and John* than they would scuttle their own ships. No harm shall come to you if you stick with me.' He makes no effort to hide the menace in his words.

Thompson is as necessary to the pirates as a fair wind. He relieves them of their stolen goods and brings them what they need, and there is profit in it for both. Yet even under Thompson's protection, my breath tightens as we draw close to Nassau. It is the seat of the pirate empire, and I cannot say what laws of land nor sea may hold there.

I am up the mast as we come for the first time to Nassau, the town and its harbour laid out all at once before me. We have rounded the islands which shield the narrow harbour entrance – and here it is, Nassau, a scattering of shacks and shabby tents falling right down to the shore. This place figures so large in the imaginings and fears of all sailors these days that I thought it would be both bigger and grander. But the fort that overlooks the harbour mouth is a ruin; beyond it, the town is a makeshift and ragged thing. In the harbour is an ill-matched clutter of ships, in all the different styles of the many nations from which they have been snatched. Rotting on the shore are the prizes not fit for sailing nor selling, left instead to break up there. Above the town the Governor's House sits abandoned, staring back at me through empty windows, the glass smashed or stolen.

The reek of Nassau hits me before we have even pulled the cocket-boat up the sand. Woodsmoke and open latrine pits, and the seaweed on the shore rotting beneath a crust of flies. We walk into the town itself, Thompson keeping close at first so that all may know we are under his protection.

Outside an ale tent, a dead man swings from a tree.

Thompson sees me looking. 'He crossed Charles Vane in a trade,' he says.

The dead man turns in the breeze, as if to meet my gaze.

'And they'll just leave him strung up, right here?' I ask Thompson.

He shrugs. 'They'll cut him down when they tire of the smell.'

I scramble backwards to avoid two brawling men who spill from the ale tent. Others join the fight, and none move to break them up. The men nearby simply look on, one tall fellow shouting that his money is on Jennings' crew to win the brawl 'for they are vicious fuckers,' and there is a frenzy of betting and ribaldry to match the frenzy of the fight itself, and Payton takes my arm and hurries me past, though I look back over my shoulder.

We spend three days here, treating with Thompson and his fellows, and loading cargo. And what do I learn of Nassau? Nassau is a grand and glorious idea – and a shithole. It is a place that shows that it is possible to live otherwise, beyond the laws that don't serve us. Yet in this storied Republic of Pirates, all is shabbiness and ruin. Walking past the brothels and the fighting men and the cheerful trade in stolen goods, I can scarce credit that the world can contain both this and the big house of Madame, where Mr Twiner perhaps lives still, with his gloves and his trays.

I think again of those other lives I have left behind me – Ma; the big house; Dan and the tavern. By what strange sea-roads have I come to this version of my life?

On our second morning in Nassau, with Crow by my shoulder on the *Walcheren*'s rigging, I watch a pirate frigate sail into the harbour at dawn with a head on a sharpened stake, strapped above the figurehead. Whether the dead man was from a prize ship unwise enough to fight back, or the member of some rival pirate crew, I do not know.

'Don't look,' says Payton softly, and puts his hand on my forearm.

'You forget that I served in the war. There is little I haven't seen.' That is not true – I have seen nothing like Nassau. Still I refuse to look away. If we are to profit by these men, I will not deny the truth of what they are, and what they do.

Nassau is a world where anything is possible. I learn fast enough that a lot of what is possible is ugly. Yet there is beauty here too – the blaze by the shore on a clear night, when a rotted hull is put to flame, and some drunk fool casts powder on it so the flames eat the sky. The laughter rolling from the open-sided ale tents. I see things in Nassau that I never thought to see any place. I see Negroes working at the docks side by side with a crew, and not a man will pass comment on it. And Cornelisz points at a fellow with one leg, who is always to be seen leaning against the table in the ale tent. 'He sailed with Hornigold,' Cornelisz says. 'Lost his leg in the taking of a Spanish sloop. They say Hornigold's crew paid him out – and pay him still.'

I watch as the man slumps further over the table. 'They must pay him well,' I say, 'for I've not seen him sober.'

At the harbour there is usually to be found a preacher, a man with the red face of a drinker who stands with his back to the water and talks of God and damnation. It is said of pirates that they have no God but their money, and no saviour but their arms, but they seem to tolerate this preacher, though some make sport of him, and shout or spit.

Today the preacher reads from the Book of Jeremiah:

Fear ye not me? saith the Lord: will ye not tremble at my presence, which have placed the sand for the bound of the sea by a perpetual decree, that it cannot pass it: and though the waves thereof toss themselves, yet can they not prevail; though they roar, yet can they not pass over it?

He looks very smug to have found a bible passage ready-made, it seems, for sailors. But I do not know how he can recite it here, where the sandbar of Potters Key shifts with each tide, and the hurricanes are enough to swallow the shallowest of the islands. There is no sand that the sea cannot pass, eventually. A bible that claims God keeps the seas tidy and contained is a bible fit for landlubbers only. We sailors have need of something much stranger and looser.

———————

Payton accounts the first trip a success – he is aglow with profits, for the Republic of Pirates is growing fast. Henceforth we return regularly to Nassau. The pirates tolerate us for our connection to Thompson and the goods that we bring them; the merchants in Jamaica and Charles Town are careful not to enquire too closely as to the origins of the goods we trade.

Yet even under Thompson's protection there is no safety for me in Nassau after dark. There is not much safety for women any place, and in Nassau even less, for the men are either giddy with riches or furious with defeats, and most of them are drunk ashore for their captains will not stand for drunkenness aboard. Thus Payton has his uses, and I confess that in Nassau I cleave closer to him than in any other port.

But there is one woman in Nassau who seems to fear nothing. Young Anne Bonny is causing a tumult in the taverns, and she is bold indeed. She is lately brought from Charles Town by her husband, but he is now at sea, and she is not much concerned with him. In fairness, it seems most of Nassau accords with her view of her husband, which is that James Bonny is a man of no account, and a wastrel. So Anne takes lovers – plenty of them, if the rumours are to be believed.

With her husband away, she passes her time now in the taverns and ale tents, and usually in the company of some young fellow or other, their arms about her waist, their lips on her neck which is arched back very willing. But despite her fetching face and her bosom very much displayed to be admired, others amongst the men move warily about her. They keep a precise distance, as though she is a keg of powder, the fuse already lit – for she fairly swells with readiness for something. I am reminded of Marston's warning about Mrs Turnbull: *A bored woman is a dangerous thing.*

From the corner where I sit with Payton and the crew, I watch Anne Bonny carefully. She may be intemperate, but she is not a messy drinker – merely a determined one. She drinks as much as the men, until she has a heightened colour, an added quick-ness about her hands, and a great appetite, for she is a prodigious eater. I have seen her, when drunk, eat a whole loaf of bread, one piece at a time, each one smeared thick with good salt butter.

She is not yet twenty – younger than me by nearly fifteen years. Her hair is dark red and when she twists it about her hand it is thick as an anchor cable. The men have taken to calling her *Bonny Anne*, but she is not beautiful in the way of paintings. If she has beauty it is a fox's beauty, sharp and restless and very bright. She looks all about her, unsatisfied. She is ready to be mightily satisfied. Anne Bonny is full of *about-to* and *nearly* – it is a curiosity just to be near her, for she has made it very clear that she is waiting for something to happen. She is making something happen. She is the thing that is happening.

'A woman such as that is a disgrace,' says Payton. Yet I notice that he does not take his eyes from her. Nor do I.

When we leave the ale tent, three men outside have another woman circled and are pressing closer against her, their voices climbing over one another, 'Give us a kiss, you loose slattern, you slut, you nasty little jezebel.' I have seen that before: how even taciturn men become poets when it comes to hurling insults at a woman. At such times they become a very lexicon.

This is Nassau and we dare not intervene. But Payton grips my arm as we hustle past.

'I am not a man like them,' he says, his voice low and intimate in my ear. 'To prey thus on a woman.'

It is true that he is not like these hasty drunks who use fists and taunts. Instead he will use my wages, and the dreadful noose of gratitude.

We are three months gone from Nassau, Payton not wanting to miss the profits of the plantations' sugar harvest. On our return, the talk is all of Edward Teach. When last we were here he was but another man serving under Hornigold, but in these months since he has ceased to be a man and has instead made of himself a myth, called Blackbeard. Now he commands a company of seventy, and a six-gun sloop. Even Thompson speaks of him in a new way, for Blackbeard holds sway in Nassau almost as much as Hornigold or Jennings or Burgess.

Some in Nassau still call him Teach, or Thatch or Thach, though there is a rumour that none of these is his true name, any more than Blackbeard. At first I like the sound of such a man: one who chooses his own name, or moves between names, and shapes them to suit himself. I see him about Nassau, and it's true that from a distance he makes a fine spectacle, his great dark beard all in braids and ribands so that it hangs from his face like the limbs of Captain Turnbull's polypus. But when I am pressed near him in an ale tent, his beard is a mess of wax and smells very strong of tallow and sweat, and I suspect most myths are thus, shabby when seen up close.

'You want to know about Teach?' says the woman standing beside me, who has seen me staring at him. She is a whore, with little in the way of teeth. Before I can even answer, she pulls aside her kerchief and hoists one breast from her stays to shows me – in place of her nipple, a scar like a mouth puckered tight.

'Bit my nipple clean off, when I didn't please him.' She glances across the tent to where Teach stands. 'That's all you need to know about Edward Teach.'

Henceforth I never hear Teach mentioned without thinking of that woman. Yet Teach is far from the only pirate here with a fearsome reputation. I begin to learn the ways of Nassau's different crews. Hornigold and Jennings, foremost amongst pirates, and whom none dare to cross. Charles Vane, and his crew of Jacobites, very daring. Each pirate crew is its own small world, so that when they come ashore in Nassau, the air in the ale tents is thick not only with smoke and heat, but also with old grudges and old rivalries. On New Providence there are no kings, no governors, and no masters but captains – and between the crews a loose fraternity, which is not the brotherhood of sworn oaths or loyalty, but more the brotherhood of those who share a common enemy, and must rub along together or perish. A gallows fellowship.

Each time we make the crossing and return to Nassau, I find myself curious to see if Anne Bonny is still here. Thrice I see her in the ale tents, her cheeks flushed and her hands dancing their swift dance. And when she herself is not in the tents, her name is nonetheless bandied there, with much free talk about her and the lovers she has taken.

One morning I take the boat ashore before dawn, to escape from the snoring of Madsen the Dane, and the knowledge that Payton is lying in his cabin just yards from my own hammock. I walk the shoreline at Spencer's Point, watching for the sun to appear over Salt Key. And there she is, Anne Bonny, ankle-deep in the water and awaiting the same sunrise. I am surprised, for I had thought her dissolute ways would mean she keeps late abed.

I make to pass her by, but she turns, without leaving the water, and watches me.

'You're the woman who sails?' she calls.

I think of Blackbeard and his myth. It has not occurred to me before today that I myself could be the subject of stories or rumours.

'Aye,' I call back. 'On the *Walcheren*.' I turn to where the Dutch ship sits at harbour, her wide-bottomed silhouette unmistakable amongst the narrow sloops.

'The *Walcheren*,' she repeats. Still she does not leave the water. I bend to unlace my own boots. She watches me, unembarrassed, as I slip from them and place them beside her own. I take a few steps into the water, keeping still some yards between us.

'So you sail under Payton?' She lingers on *under*, an eyebrow raised.

'I am of his crew,' I say, very clear and definite. I am not sure why it matters to me that Anne Bonny should not think me Payton's woman. She herself has no great reputation for propriety.

'So you're a proper sailor then. I did not know such a thing was possible.'

'Nor did I – until I did it.'

She laughs and steps, splashing, towards me, holding out her hand.

'I'm Anne Bonny.' Her hand is small and cool in mine.

'I know who you are.'

'I'm sure,' she says, and though she is still smiling, I wish I had not said it. 'Perhaps you even know me by some other name? *The Great Whore of New Providence*, maybe?'

'It does not trouble you?' I ask. 'All that loose talk?'

She shrugs. 'Perhaps it would have done, when I first came to Nassau, a dutiful little wife.' She smiles again, and kicks with one foot, sending a ripple sweeping over my own shins. 'But things change. You ought not be surprised, for you said it yourself: all manner of things are possible that we do not know until we do them.'

We have made no arrangement, but the next day I go again at the same time, and am glad to see her there, once more trailing her feet in the shallows. Thence we meet each morning, and in Anne Bonny's company I do not feel unsafe, even in Nassau town, for she is not a woman given to fear.

Her husband is again at sea, and I ask if he is pirating.

She laughs. 'Oh, he claimed to be a great man among the pirates. You would figure him for a Hornigold or a Teach, to hear him speak when he was wooing me in Charles Town.' She grimaces. 'And now I find him fitted only to go turtling, or with some petty crew to harry fishermen from their catch, and to steal their canoes.'

On the third day that we meet, Anne and I sit on the ruins of an upturned cocket-boat, and Crow circles low above us and takes a perch on the keel. Anne laughs, delighted – it is rare indeed to see a crow so close, and so bold.

'She's yours?'

'She follows me,' I say. 'Has for years.'

Anne reaches out her hand and makes a *tch tch tch* with her tongue. Crow turns and, unhurried, sinks her beak into Anne's hand. Anne shrieks and jerks her hand about, but Crow has hold of the web of flesh between thumb and forefinger, and does not release it for several seconds, before taking calmly to the sky.

Anne's wound is tremendous neat: a V on each side of the flesh, deep enough that I have to press my skirt to it for ten minutes before the blood stops welling. I pinch the flesh, both sides, holding it tight between my own thumb and forefinger, and I do not need to say anything about why it is unwise to take liberties with a crow, because Crow has spoken for herself very clear in that matter, and it is my experience that what a crow has said no person may say better.

When I return to the *Walcheren*, Payton is waiting. 'That woman isn't a fit companion,' Payton says, when I return.

'Have you been watching me? Did you follow me?'

He doesn't bother to deny it. 'Do you want folk to speak of you as they do of her?'

'Perhaps they would do well to speak of neither of us, then.'

For the rest of the day Payton is tight about the mouth, and short with the crew. But there are few enough women in Nassau, excepting the whores, and though he disapproves of Anne, I suspect it suits Payton better to know I am with Anne than with men.

Next to Anne Bonny, so bold and notorious, I had thought myself meek and colourless, and my story of little note. Yet she never tires of asking me about my years in the navy, and the army. Even my years on the *Walcheren*, which to me seem largely drab, fascinate Anne.

'You sleep right there, amongst them? And they give you no trouble?'

'Payton wouldn't countenance it if they did. And anyway, I am very well able to fend for myself.'

I tell her the story of young Marshall, and how I caught him spying on me and held the marlinspike to his throat. She laughs long, her head thrown back and held there, as if the weight of her hair is so great that she cannot lift her head.

'All women should carry such a weapon,' she says.

'It's not a weapon,' I say. 'It's a tool.' I slip my marlinspike from my pocket to show her. She takes it and turns its spike to the light.

'Anything may be a weapon, in the right hands.' Anne smiles. And I am smiling too, and looking at my hands anew.

'Twas the crow that alerted me to his spying,' I tell her. 'She spotted the hole he'd made in the sail.'

Anne passes me back the marlinspike, and glances with distaste at the bird, perched in a buttonwood tree uphill. 'How do you stand it, having that creature always watching you so?'

'Forgive me, but you never struck me as a woman who does not like to be watched.' I am thinking of the ale tents: how she lets the young men kiss her neck, and throws her head back the better to allow it.

Anne smiles. 'And you have not struck me as a woman who likes to be watched. And yet here we are.'

What can Anne Bonny, so young, know of the different kinds of watching?

She is curious about my past, but speaks little of her own. 'You don't want to hear all that,' she says. 'Tell me again of how your ship grounded the French man-of-war at Gibraltar, and how it burned.'

I do not tell her that I see it still, sometimes – the burning ship upon the rocks. I suspect Anne Bonny is not troubled by ghosts.

We make several more crossings between St Jago de la Vega and Nassau, bringing cargoes of rice and tobacco. But in June, when hurricane season comes to the Bahamas, we are to sail again for Boston.

'And shall you return?' Anne asks, on our last morning.

'As long as there are profits to be had here, Payton will want to come back.'

'But what of you?' she asks. 'What is it that you want?'

I have no answer, for this is not a thing I have often been asked. When we sail that afternoon I look back to the narrow harbour mouth. I remind myself that Teach is the sort of man who thrives in Nassau: a man of savage appetites. And yet Anne Bonny is here too. What her appetites are, I cannot yet tell.

We work again the long route from Boston to Rotterdam, and then to London. A letter awaits me there from Ma's husband, Hepburn, writing to tell me Ma is gone. 'She is lately dead, of a fever, though it was a quick death and a merciful one – may we all be so fortunate though for the present I am sorely grieved.'

I ask Payton for a day's leave, telling him only that I am visiting Ma. I say nothing of her death, for I want to give him no more of me than I must. Crow follows me all the way to Hepburn's house, where she settles on the peak of the roof, and looks fitting indeed, for this is still a house in deep mourning. Some months have passed since his letter, but Hepburn greets me in black bombazine, without a button to be seen. In the hushed parlour, Ma's death gives us something to speak of, for we have nothing else in common.

'She spoke often of your brother Mark, at the last,' he says. 'She called for him.'

'That's what she said? Mark?'

'I'm sure she was thinking of you too,' he says hastily. 'She wasn't in her right mind, not by the end.'

But I am not angry, nor jealous. Indeed, for the first time since hearing of her death I find myself with tears starting, for I knew that when she called for Mark, she called for us both. She knew me by his name longer by far than he ever lived. She left me nothing else, so I will take that: my brother's name in her dying mouth.

16

At the hurricane season's end we sail again for Nassau. In each port on the way, we hear fresh news of pirate outrages. Teach, or Blackbeard, now commands a great sloop of war, the *Revenge*, and is seizing prizes all the way up the mid-Atlantic coast, and sinking what he cannot carry.

'The pirates' appetites have grown too great,' Payton says in Charles Town. 'They'll make their own undoing.' Payton thinks himself apart from the pirates, even as he grows richer by trading with them.

'Who would stand against them?' I ask. 'The governors won't – not while they're taking their cut of the pirates' profits.' It's well known that Teach pays off the governor of North Carolina, and other worthies thereabouts – and many pirates buy their safety the same way.

'Not all the governors are in their pockets,' says Payton. 'Anyway, it's bigger than just the colonies. If the pirates continue in this way, interfering with the trade routes, the king will crush them.'

'What would he care, from his castles in England? And surely the Jacobites and Spaniards must give him trouble enough at home, without concerning himself with what goes on here.'

Payton shakes his head. 'What do you think keeps him in his castles, and will fund his armies if he must needs keep the Jacobites or the Spaniards down? It's all the same – it's sugar money and tobacco money, flowing from the colonies. If the pirates cut off that trade, the king must act.'

Payton is no fool. But it is such a very great distance between the king and such men as Teach or Hornigold. The king sleeps under a different sky – he cannot feel the winds that buffet us in the Gulf Passage, and pirates cannot figure to him.

As for me, it is neither pirates nor kings that trouble me so much as Payton himself. In Charles Town he passes two nights ashore and comes back to the *Walcheren* mired in his particular combination of contrition and rage, so that I have no doubt he has availed himself once more of the local whores. You would think I would be relieved, knowing he has spent some of his lust, but he is furious at himself, and thus furious at me. He stamps about the boat so that Cornelisz says quietly, 'Jesus, he must have caught himself the pox ashore.' I know better.

That night Payton takes too much rum and corners me astern, weeping, and says to me again, 'Look what you made me do.' Men will blame anyone but themselves for their own desires. I pity the whores too, for I don't doubt they also bore the burden of his rage and shame, which is now grown so heavy that I fear the *Walcheren* will founder beneath it. He will assuredly take me down with him.

From the mast, I watch the crow brace her wings against the wind. It is time that I, too, begin to set my mind to new winds.

———

Late November 1717, and we land back in Nassau to meet with Thompson. The preacher by the harbour is more fervent than ever. 'Never doubt that a terrible judgment hangs over Nassau, this nest of piracy and sin,' he intones. Perhaps in a church his words might have been contained and echoed about and made grand – but here, amongst the tents and shacks of Nassau, his fine godly voice gets lost in all that big sky.

I hurry past him, for while it is profits that have brought Payton here, something different has brought me to Nassau. I weave through the streets, searching all the while for that distinctive head of dark red hair, and that defiant set of the jaw.

I find her coming up from Spencer's Point. Her hair is free of its cap, and she has caught up in her skirts a great trove of sweet-sop fruits. Anne cannot embrace me for her arms are full, but she runs towards me, calling my name. We sit together on a tree stump overlooking the water and she presses one of the green fruits into my hands. I watch her eat. When Anne eats a sweet-sop she eats a sweetsop more absolutely than anyone before her. She takes the seeds one by one from her mouth and lays them in a row on the ground before us, like jewels. No fruit has ever received such assiduous attention.

'I'm glad you're back,' she says, and places her hand, careless, in my own. 'I have not many friends in Nassau.'

'The rumours have it otherwise,' I say.

She shrugs, unabashed. 'That's different.'

I find myself disappointed.

'There's the cuckold,' says Payton. 'The husband of your friend who is whoring her way about the island.'

He points to the lean man walking by the harbour front. I look carefully. What is it about James Bonny that made Anne Bonny choose him? He has not much in the way of a chin, but he is handsome enough – and the pale woman by his side seems to find his company diverting, for she is giggling as he speaks.

'He does not have the look of a man pining for his wife,' I say.

'Can you blame him?' Payton says. 'Would you pine for such a slut?'

When we meet the next morning, Anne makes no mention of her husband's return. Instead she takes my arm and we walk our usual path along the beach. With her fingers she winkles a small crab from the sand, holding it up so that we can marvel at the silent applause of its claws. She places it in my hand, and the crab's cool and impotent scampering tickles my palm. I set it carefully back on the sand where it makes to scurry away, but Crow has spotted it and in an instant has speared its body on her beak.

'That bird of yours is vicious,' says Anne. Crow is picking the crab apart now on the sand.

'I've told you. I don't own her.' Yet I feel a jolt of pride at Crow's swiftness, and the precise click of her beak as she dissects the shell.

I find myself looking forward to these mornings with Anne. Yet I am not used to the company of women. Their bodies, the smells and sounds of them, are unfamiliar to me, having moved for so long in the world of men. We talk a great deal – and she is generous with her touch too, forever taking my arm, or holding a bitten sweetsop to my mouth to taste. I am unused to such intimacies – but Anne's ease with herself is so great that it allows for no unease in me.

We keep to our unspoken agreement to meet each dawn. But on my fourth night in Nassau I see her from the ship. She is tracing an unsteady path across the harbour front, scanning the ships at anchor. I climb into the cocket-boat as quietly as I can.

'Be careful.' Payton is standing above me on deck as I push off. His voice is low but there is threat in it, and I know it is not the dangers of Nassau that worry him.

I say nothing, only keep rowing towards Anne's stumbling figure. In the shallows I step from the boat and drag it onto the sand.

'Were you looking for me?' I ask her, trying to keep the hope from my voice.

She does not answer me, only grabs my arm and leans on me as we walk. I have not seen her so drunk before, and I wonder if it has to do with her husband's return.

'Will you look at that?' she says, with a sweep of an arm that takes in the stars, the heavy moon, and Nassau below it. There is a bonfire again, or perhaps one of the shacks is ablaze. In Nassau it amounts to the same thing, and men have gathered to drink around the fire. I can hear the preacher's familiar chant: *You are all damned in the eyes of God*. Tonight he has become part of the night's music. Somewhere a fiddle is playing, the notes flaring and fading into the dark like the sparks from the blaze.

'I wanted you to see it too,' she says, gesturing again all about us: the night sky and the water, and the great tumult of Nassau by dark.

Suddenly, she lifts her skirts to piss. She has been drinking hard and it is a prodigious big piss, so that although she has squatted wide, the dry sand soaks and spreads the puddle broader still and makes a great widening circle and she must stagger backwards to keep her feet clear, and she is full of laughter and still pissing, and grabs my arm to steady herself and in that instant there has never been anything more wondrous nor beautiful than the perfect full moon of wet sand that she has made.

———

Anne does not care to speak of her past – but often enough she has dropped maledictions about her childhood in Charles Town. To hear her tell it, the world of her father's house there had said to her one thing above all else: *no.* Nassau does not countenance that word. Nassau is *yes, yes,* all the time, and Anne wants it all. When she wades into the shallows, she hitches up her skirt above her knees, throws back her head, and closes her eyes the better to feel the warm water on her skin. In the ale tents she sits on the lap of whichever lad she is choosing to favour tonight, and calls loud for another jug, for Nassau refuses her nothing.

There is a tremendous urgency about Anne, for she is so concerned with now that it makes you look to your own now, to feel the seconds as they waste and shrivel under the New Providence sun, and to think how each second will not come again. When I walk the shore with her, I too begin to see Nassau afresh, in all its filth and glory.

I have told her almost everything of my own story, yet still I know little of her past. It is not shame that keeps her from dwelling on it – for Anne is not acquainted with shame. No – the past simply doesn't interest her. 'Why do you ask me?' she says, when I ask her of her youth. 'That's all done with now.' Anne is greatly enamoured of *now.* The past she will shrug off and leave behind like soiled linen. She is always going somewhere, and she is going there now, and if you don't wish to be left behind you'd best bestir yourself quick.

We sit together and she trails her fingers through the sand between us.

'My mother died,' I say. 'While I was at sea.' I have told nobody else this: even Payton still does not know.

'Will you miss her?' Anne asks.

I wrinkle my nose. 'I've had only one mother – so I'm shaped by her, for good or ill.'

'But will you miss her?'

I shake my head. 'No.'

'Well then.' She brushes the sand from hands and stands, as if the matter is dealt with, just like that.

Perhaps it is. Perhaps this is why I am drawn back to this beach each dawn, and drawn to Anne Bonny: so that I may learn from her not to carry my past with me. Dan's ghost settling at the end of my hammock. Marston's laugh smuggled in the creak of a rusted capstan. Hoisting a sack of rice in the cargo hold only to find it's my brother's toddler body that I hold instead, his weight real in my arms. Can Anne teach me to cut the rope of all the pasts I trail behind me?

If Anne is not interested in her own past, she is nevertheless too generous to deny my curiosity. In these long, hot Nassau hours, while Payton treats with Thompson and the pirates, I coax Anne's story from her. Thus I learn Anne backwards: first the new, and then, with much prompting from me, the old. From jibes against her husband, 'a miser, and a feckless coward,' and her time in Nassau, to stories of her life on her father's plantation back in Charles Town.

Finally, on the fifth morning she tells me of her childhood in Ireland, her father a respectable lawyer in Kinsale, Cork.

'Pa fell for his maid – his wife caught him at it, and she moved out.' She gives a small shrug. 'It was civil enough, at first – there was a separation agreement, and she even paid an allowance to my father, her family being wealthier. I think she was hoping they'd reunite, even after she found out he'd sired a baby girl with the maid.'

She drops a mocking curtsey, right there on the sand. 'Me,' she says, and twirls about, although the hems of her skirts are weighted with seawater and do not flare about her. 'Pa wished to keep me close by him, and as all the town knew his bastard was a girl child, he passed me off as a boy. Said I was the child of relatives, come to live with him to be trained up as a law clerk.'

Despite the bright dawn sun I feel giddy, drunk – for this part of her story is my own. Both of us bastards; both of us hidden as boys to hide our parents' shame, and to preserve an allowance. And I understand better now Anne's loud laugh, and her fondness for a stomacher so low that her breasts near tumble out of it. After being kept hidden so long, she delights in being seen.

Years passed, she says, the three of them living thus: her father, his lover, and her. 'Then word got out that Pa had set up house with the maid, and that the little clerk was their own bastard girl. So Pa's wife stopped the money – even put a statement in the papers.'

'I like the sound of this wife,' I say. I picture her hoisting her husband's shame into the wind for all the world to see.

'It was the end of Pa's law business, and we had to leave Kinsale. I was barely ten. He brought me and Ma to Charles Town to get away from it all. But soon enough Ma died, and it was just me and him.'

In Charles Town her father, Fulford, became a planter, and prospered.

'And you?' I ask. 'Were you allowed to be yourself again?'

'Far from it,' she says, with a grand sigh. 'For Pa fancied himself a fine gentleman now, and so I was to be a wealthy planter's daughter, to stay quiet and proper, and to make a good marriage.' She speaks as though this was a harder role to play than that of a boy.

When James Bonny told her he was a pirate, Anne liked the sound of it – the grandeur and the adventure. 'And I hated it at Pa's house – forced to play at being a fine planter's daughter.

The parade of rich puppies I was expected to choose from.' She grimaces.

So when Bonny asked her to elope with him, she saw a way out of her old life. James Bonny was a door and she walked straight through him.

She is still speaking, but I am completely overset by the story she has told me of her childhood.

I interrupt her. 'I can hardly credit it. The two of us both raised as boys.'

'I know,' she says, grinning. 'And for reasons so different and so similar.'

It is a kind of miracle. A miracle far grander than the curing of lepers or turning water into wine. The turning of girls into boys: what a bold stunt. Stranger still that we should be here now, the two of us, beside each other on the sand in Nassau.

'Yet we turned out nothing the same.' She says it carelessly, as though it signifies nothing. And she is right, of course – we are nothing alike. She so vivid and bold, her voice ringing out clear across the ale tents, while I watch from the edges. She so fiercely a woman, while I remain something else.

Yet for all our differences, still it is me she seeks out each day. Each morning she wades into the shallows with her skirts hitched about her knees with one hand, the other hand waving to me as I row towards her. And our shared past makes me believe in something – not God, and not chance, but something. It makes me believe so fervent that in the end I think maybe it's my own story I am believing. The story of my life has been altogether so unlikely and so strange that only now, suddenly, meeting another with the same story lets me think that such a life might count after all.

———————

Wading in the dawn waters with Anne, I step on a sea egg. Its spines pierce my foot and I yell 'Pope's balls,' a phrase I confess I've picked up from Madsen the Dane, who is fluent in profanity.

Anne snaps, 'Don't you blaspheme the Sovereign Pontiff in front of me, Mary.'

She is so rarely in earnest that I think she must be jesting. But she is entirely serious, hands thrust onto hips. I knew that she was Catholic, but it had not occurred to me that Anne, of all people, could be devout.

'My ma was a Catholic,' she tells me, squatting to examine my injured foot.

Her mother – the maid who bedded her father, and then died when he took her to the New World.

'Why hold on to it, with her dead all these years?' My whole life, the papists have been the enemy – it is the church of Spain and France. And Anne is not one for looking back.

'Because she's been dead all these years,' says Anne. From the sole of my foot she pulls one unbroken black spine, fearsome sharp, and holds it to the light.

Her mother's papistry is the only thing from the past I have ever seen her cling on to. I understand it well, having myself a mother not easily forgotten.

I watch Anne more closely. Her piety is like no other piety I have seen, but is no less fervent for it. She cannot go to mass but she prays wherever she chooses to kneel. She does not merely make her Hail Marys, but prays in her own way. I see her give thanks to her God for a handful of cockles, and outside the ale tent that night she gives the sign of the cross when one of her admirers pins a brooch on her bosom. She makes of the sky her cathedral, and I fancy no Spanish cathedral could be finer than this great stretch of stars.

17

News slinks into Nassau harbour like rats scurrying aboard a ship. A frigate comes from Boston with word of a new proclamation from the king, to curb piracy. A brig returns from Bermuda, its crew full of the news: an offer of a pardon to all pirates who surrender. At first we think it nothing but a rumour, or even a hoax to sow disharmony amongst the pirates. Then Governor Bennett of Bermuda sends his own son in a sloop to Nassau with the proclamation printed. Young Bennett is only a thin strip of a man, with spots still on his neck and a manner of bobbing his head like a bird. I take it as a sure sign that the governor dislikes his son, for it could go badly for the boy, walking into Nassau with his pile of papers, when no governors' men have troubled the island for years. Still I credit the lad with courage, for he comes ashore without flinching, and causes the proclamation to be pasted all over town, even on the doors of the taverns.

Those who can read are called upon to read it to the rest, and though I am a woman I am known to be good with words, and so when the paper is thrust into my hands, I find myself becoming a kind of prophet, announcing to those around me what is to befall them:

Complaint having been made to His Majesty, by great Numbers of Merchants, Masters of Ships, and others, as well as by the several Governors of His Majesty's Islands and Plantations in the West Indies, that the Pirates are grown so numerous that they infest not only the Seas near Jamaica, but even those of the Northern Continent of America; and that unless some effectual Means be used, the whole Trade from Great Britain to those Parts will not only be obstructed, but in imminent danger of being lost: His Majesty has, upon mature Deliberation in Council, been graciously pleased, in the first Place, to order a proper Force to be employed for suppressing the said Piracies …

There follows a list of ships to sail against the pirates, and it is no mean collection: *Adventure*, forty guns; *Diamond*, forty guns; *Ludlow Castle*, forty guns – and more besides.

Some of the men crowded around me are loud to scoff.

'Good luck to them, for they don't know the waters.'

'We'll raise a toast to them while we watch them founder on Potter's Key.'

But they fall silent as I read on, for the proclamation not only threatens them, but also offers them a way out:

We do hereby promise and declare, that in case any of the said Pirates shall, on or before the fifth day of September, in the Year of our Lord One thousand Seven hundred and eighteen, surrender him or themselves to one of our Principal Secretaries of State in Great Britain or Ireland, or to any Governor or Deputy Governor of any of our Plantations or Dominions beyond the seas, every such Pirate and Pirates so surrendering him or themselves, as aforesaid, shall have our gracious Pardon.

Word is spreading fast, and there is a great outcry and hubbub. I am jostled against Payton by a rowdy group in the road, led by Jennings. They climb to the very top of the ruined fort, where they affix a Union Jack to the old flagpole and hoist it high. In fact there is little wind and it hangs slack, a red and blue rag, but they raise toasts to the king and to young Bennett, whom they have carried down from the fort upon their shoulders, looking mightily discomfited.

Some of those who rejoice at the news of the pardon are the forced men, who had never wanted this pirate life and are thrilled to see a way clear of it. Even amongst those who came willingly to piracy, there are those who can see beyond the horizon of Nassau to something else: a respectable life, the money from their pirate prizes turned to some new profession.

'Hornigold is at sea, but he's sure to fall in with Jennings, when he returns,' hisses Payton from behind me. In the tight-packed crowd I have no space to draw back from him, and his breath is warm on my neck. 'He's always fancied himself a privateer, rather than a pirate. And if Hornigold takes the pardon, others will fall in besides.'

He's right that many will be quick to seize the pardon. Today has become their festival, and young Bennett will be lucky if he can stand by day's end, with so many insisting on buying him drinks, and he is much buffeted by fond thumps on the back.

A scuffle ahead draws Payton's attention and I slip away from him, stealing sideways through the massed men. I see Anne's husband, James Bonny, on the outskirts of the crowd that clusters around Bennett.

'Look at him.' Anne's voice sudden by my ear. 'See how he lickspittles the man?' she grimaces. 'He'll be the first to cry rope on other men for a taste of the king's gold.' She turns to me, grabs my arm. 'Warn Payton. He won't be safe, just because he does not pirate himself. It's enough that he traffics with pirates. People will snitch – my husband first among them.'

'You care mightily about Payton's safety, all of a sudden?'

'Not a bit,' she says.

A voice cuts across the general hubbub.

'I do not recognise the Hanoverian upstart as our king, and he has no more power to pardon us than he does to condemn us.'

It is Vane, his reedy voice loud. Like Teach, Vane is a man lately risen to command his own crew, where before he sailed under Jennings. And like Teach, Vane has of late earned a reputation for casual cruelty, which is no small thing in Nassau, a town built on theft and force. Vane and those other Jacobites gathered about him will take no pardon from King George, for they see him as a mere pretender, and would see James Stuart on the throne instead. I confess I have never understood their zeal, for I suspect a Stuart king would care as little for pirates as King George does.

Vane's man Rackham has joined the shouting, and he spits towards the flag above the fort. 'Have we not built this place for ourselves, and not for masters, or governors or usurping kings? Are we again to be supplicants, and not to rule ourselves?'

He has a handsome way of speaking and the men around him fall silent. John Rackham is a familiar figure in Nassau, and known as Calico Jack for the bright Indian calico prints that he wears. There are some who foster such names – Teach makes much of being called Blackbeard, and ties his beard up in evermore elaborate arrangements, for he is greatly attached to the myth of himself. Whether Rackham is such a man I cannot yet tell, though I am staring closely. Beside me, Anne's eyes too are fixed on him.

A boy runs up to Rackham and, wordless, hands him something, a bundle of black cloth, and Rackham does not just pass him a coin but flicks it behind his back to the lad, as a showman might. Then Rackham unfurls the length of black worsted and it is a pirate flag, the banner of King Death, white skull and blade and heart on black. Such a flag is only ever flown here in Nassau port, or during engagements – at all other times and places it is a death warrant.

There is some tussling on the fort stairs between Jennings' men and Vane's, and I am separated from Anne. But those celebrating the pardon are too jubilant for a real fight – they want only to get back to the ale tents. So the scuffle passes with nothing more than a few shoves and insults, and Vane himself lowers the Union Jack and raises in its place the black flag that Rackham passes to him, and though it hangs slack in the windless sky, nonetheless a great cheer goes up from Vane's crew, all the voices rising alongside the flag, 'No quarter! No quarter!' and it is no ship that they are raiding now, but all of it: a flag; a king; a governor; an empire. All the world which has found no place for them, and now wishes to take even this place they have forged for themselves. And part of me would not be surprised to hear my own voice amongst the others, joining that cry, *No quarter! No quarter!* But Payton has found me, one hand on my elbow while the other claims my waist. Even as he tugs at me and hisses, 'We must go. Now, Mary, now,' I am straining back to that great chorus clamouring beneath the black flag.

———————

Payton has always maintained that what he does is trading merely, and nought to do with pirating, but he knows well enough that neither navy nor governors will draw such distinctions, and he is readying us to leave as soon as we can. But he will not leave without a cargo, for no captain does so willingly, and Payton is sharper about profit than most. Nor can his dealings with Thompson so suddenly be concluded – thus we are stuck in Nassau for now, scurrying to complete our business and stow our cargo, and waiting for a load of tobacco promised by Thompson who furthermore owes Payton money. Nonetheless Payton sets a watch all night.

It is my turn at the watch, and long past midnight, when I see the small boat bobbing towards us – Anne has paid a lad to row her to the *Walcheren*.

'Why are you still here?' she says, before the boat is even made fast. 'James and his cronies are already planning who they will sell out, when the new governor arrives.'

'The governor is months away,' I say, reaching to help her aboard. 'And will have more pressing concerns than us.'

She grabs both of my hands in her own. 'Mary. Nassau will turn ugly.'

Only Anne could think Nassau is not already ugly.

'And you?' I ask. 'You must be glad, for once, that your husband turned out to be no fine pirate after all.'

She snorts. 'Would that he were – I'd cry rope on him myself, and be rid of him.'

I cannot tell whether she is in earnest.

'But you,' she continues. 'You must leave. You won't be safe here.'

I have served in the navy and army both. I have outlived my husband and my child. Yet nonetheless it strikes me that she is so fearful on my account – fearless Anne Bonny, who juts her chin at the taunts of the drunken men of Nassau.

I squeeze her hands. 'We sail as soon as Payton has finished his business with Thompson. A matter of days.'

When she is gone, for the rest of my long watch I ponder what it means that Anne, who is always urgent, has never been more urgent than in beseeching me to leave.

In these fevered days, all of Nassau is caught up in a great noise. There is the hubbub of the two sides arguing, and the clamour of work, as each side makes what preparations they see fit. Those who wish to reject the pardon begin to make the fort ready to repel the new governor when he comes; those who wish to flee are readying their ships.

A general council of pirates is called, and all the town gathers beneath the fort. We come too, keeping to the back of the crowd, for our fate also is caught up in this, and we must hear what the pirates decide.

Jennings speaks first, his crew hoisting him atop a barrel to survey the crowd. I can see why he wields power in Nassau, for he speaks well and his men are quick to cheer him on.

'A new governor's coming, whether you will or not, and those of you who refuse the pardon will find yourself set against the force of all the navy ships he can muster.'

'So we fortify the harbour,' yells Vane. 'Set guns in the fort. We'll send him on his way again.'

Jennings rolls his eyes. 'You want to make heroes of yourselves, but you'll only make corpses – and trouble for the rest of us, too.'

'We'll not so lightly forsake what we've built,' Vane says.

'What we've built? You mean this?' Jennings waves an arm at the ragged shacks, the rotting hulls abandoned at the harbour. 'Do you not want better?'

I concede it is a sorry sight. But Nassau has never been perfect – it is an idea, only, and the men who would fight for it would fight for that idea, and not for the reality, which is flooded streets and disorder and the reek of shit from the shallow ditch that runs down to the harbour.

'The Jacobites will come to our aid,' calls Rackham, standing beside Vane. 'The Stuart court in exile will send a fleet from France.'

'Keep your fairy stories for the children,' says Jennings. 'Nobody's coming to your aid. There's nobody but us – and they're offering a way out.'

'Even if we could trust the governors, we don't want their mercy,' says Vane.

'Then you're a fool,' Jennings says, and would say more but several of Vane's men rush at him, toppling the barrel on which he stands. Thus it ends in a brawl in which Madsen the Dane has his nose broke, and there is so much shouting and disorder that we leave knowing less than when we came.

I see Anne but briefly. Her husband has her by him, his hand tight on her arm. James Bonny is not a strong man but he has about him a feverish glow, his eyes darting fast. Men such as he will profit by such times, I doubt not.

Anne finds my eyes as he steers her from the crowd. 'Go,' she mouths, silent across the throng. 'Go.'

That night at last we weigh anchor. When we pass beyond the harbour mouth and Long Island, I take to the mast. If there are tears in my eyes, none can see them but Crow.

Boston, and thence London and Rotterdam. We do not return to the colonies until late 1718, and even now we stay well north, not daring to venture anywhere near the Bahamas. Yet my mind is beset by a northerly wind, driving my thoughts always south to Nassau.

In Boston, Cornelisz returns from a tavern with news of more pirate outrages: 'Teach's fleet blockaded Charles Town itself.

Threatened to send back the heads of his hostages if the ransom wasn't paid.'

All over the coast the name Blackbeard has become a word for fear. Each time I hear of him, I picture that Nassau whore and her missing nipple, and I think of Teach's teeth.

In New York, Payton comes aboard swollen with news, and in ill-humour. 'Vane, too, escaped from Nassau, and has blockaded Charles Town. Has ninety men or more sailing under him now, Rackham among them.'

'And Teach?' I ask.

He laughs at this. 'Took the pardon – but it didn't last. Plaguing the coast as far north as the Delaware River, they say. Has made himself a base in Ocracoke, and threatens to establish a new Nassau there.'

Could such a thing be possible? Nassau itself grew after an earthquake crushed the old pirate stronghold of Port Royal. Might the pirate base rise again elsewhere? And what kind of a place could a new Nassau be, under such a man as Teach?

In Bath Harbour we are loading the *Walcheren* with timber when a sloop comes in, and a cry goes up that it is Teach's *Adventure*. 'Look lively,' shouts Payton, and my hand goes straight to the pistol at my belt. All about the harbour men drop their goods to stare, and some run to spread the news, weapons already drawn. But the ship entering the harbour flies the king's colours, and from its bowsprit swings a head. The face is all drooped and much bloodied, but the beard that gave Blackbeard his name cannot be mistaken. Under any name – Edward Teach, or Thatch, or Blackbeard – he is dead. The uproar in the harbour is enormous, and even Crow takes to the top of the mast, shouting *Crow, Crow.*

Soon the story is all over Bath: a lieutenant called Maynard, out of Virginia, caught Teach run aground in Ocracoke. Teach, who used to have hundreds of men under him, and a governor in his pocket. Now the *Adventure* sits in Bath Harbour under an English flag, and under the bowsprit his head swings like a bell tolling the news.

I wish very earnestly that Payton will not go whoring while we are in Bath − not because I want him for myself, but because I account him more dangerous by far after each of his excursions to the whorehouses, when he comes back aboard vicious with remorse.

On our last night in Bath, Payton corners me by the stern. He grabs my arm, so tight I can feel my bone against his fingers.

'You know I make good money,' he says. 'I can offer you a good life.' With his free hand, he passes his sweaty palm again over his pate, flattening the strands of hair arrayed there.

'And is this not a good life?' I sweep my free arm at the *Walcheren* below us, the flint-grey sea all around. I force my voice to be calm. We are alone on deck, and there is no Cornelisz to distract or interrupt.

'You know what I mean,' Payton says. 'You have to make a choice.'

In these long years there have been days when I have thought it would be easiest just to give in to Payton. I have juggled in my mind the balance of cost and value − his desire, my peace. Indeed I have become nearly as cool in calculation as Payton himself. If I had not met Anne Bonny, perhaps I would have relented and let Payton into my bed. But Anne has woken in me a sense that I had forgot, since those early days with Dan: a notion of my body as a thing for myself, with its own desires. Where once I could think of Payton only with dreary resignation, there is now a vivid disgust.

'Think of what I'm offering you,' Payton says.

His grip on my arm tightens, his eyes intent on my own. A man may mistake something for an offer, when it is a threat.

I was splicing rope when he grabbed me, and I have my marlinspike in my hand still. I recall what Anne said to me about the same tool, back in Nassau: *anything may be a weapon, in the right hands.* If Payton pushes me further, it will come to that: blades and blood. He is a canny man and no weakling, for no sailor can be − but he is no fighter. I have been a sailor and a soldier, and can take him if I must. I wish it may not come to that − not because I pity him, nor because he does not deserve it. But what becomes of me then? At best, the end of my life on the *Walcheren*. At worst, the noose.

'Captain,' I say. 'Can we not continue as we are?'

'Enough,' he says. 'I've been mighty patient, Mary. Few men would be more so. Make your choice.'

Cornelisz comes through the hatch. Perhaps he came by chance; perhaps he heard Payton's angry words, for he is watching us, though he busies his hands with coiling a line.

Payton releases my arm as suddenly as he grabbed it, and walks away.

I meet Cornelisz's eyes, though neither of us speaks. The two of us have worked together for years and yet I know little of him. He has a wife in the Low Countries and gives me no trouble, except to grumble when Crow has been chasing his two spiteful cats. He has sailed under Payton since long before I joined the *Walcheren*, and the two of them work well together. Cornelisz must be twenty years my senior, and has never sought my company. Even now he bows his head to the line, his back to me, and it is clear he wants no thanks.

He has mentioned his wife in the past – it has never occurred to me before now to wonder if he has children too. I myself have never had a father. It strikes me that Cornelisz's children would be fortunate.

I am glad he was here today. But he cannot always be nearby – and I cannot be relying forever on any man to spare me from Payton.

When first I came aboard, the *Walcheren* was a raft, saving me from the wreckage of my marriage. Now she is an island on which I am marooned.

The next dawn, when Payton is calm, I say, 'We should make again for Nassau.' There is no safety for me in Nassau – not ever, and least of all in these strange times, with the king's edict against piracy hanging over the town. But I can no longer count myself safe aboard the *Walcheren* – and in Nassau there is Anne Bonny, and the chance, perhaps, of finding another crew. Not a pirate crew – not with the new governor arriving there any moment, to enforce the edict. But even under new rule, Nassau is Nassau still – amongst the ale tents and upturned hulls of the pirate nest, where many pirates must be looking to turn instead to trade, might there not be a merchant crew willing to take on a woman?

Payton is watching me carefully.

'Nassau is all in upheaval.'

I keep my tone light. 'It was ever so. But whatever the chaos there, men must still eat, and smoke – and we may profit by it, with a hull full of flour and Virginia tobacco.'

'I've taught you well,' he says, his top lip curling as he smiles. 'But we make for Charles Town first – for slaves must eat too, and their owners won't rob me as those Nassau bastards might.' Already he is walking away, but he calls over his shoulder. 'But we may yet return to Nassau, if the journey will pay.'

We sailors are used to waiting, and to chance. However small the chance, if it comes I will be ready.

———————

News from Europe: we are again at war with the Spaniards. Governors are granting commissions to captains to attack Spanish ships; apparently Nassau's new governor, Woodes Rogers, has granted Hornigold, formerly a ruler amongst Nassau's pirates, one such commission.

It is the new year of 1719 when we reach Charles Town. On White Point a mighty gibbet has been erected and twenty men at least hang there, all in shreds and tatters, ragged as an old sail. We fall silent as we glide by. Crow circles above the gibbet as if counting the dead.

I had thought to be done with wars after I left the navy, but whatever uneasy tolerance there once was of the pirates in these parts is done with now, and we have sailed into a kind of war.

Waiting for Payton at Charles Town is a letter from Thompson, concerning recent events in Nassau. I ask Payton if I may read it after him, but he ushers me near so that to read it I must be close beside him, the skin on his arm touching my own, the side of his sweaty thigh pressed against mine.

The new governor came in July 1718, writes Thompson.

... Woodes Rogers, who landed with more pomp than Nassau has ever seen, but I will allow he is an experienced captain at least, a former slaver and no fool. I myself have been appointed to his governing council but his arrival has not gone smooth for Nassau has never been a place to submit itself to any rule.

Rogers, Thompson writes, has been beset by the stubbornest of the pirates, and by a putrid fever that killed more than fourscore of his men. Each day more pirates fled Nassau to join Vane and his fleet. Hornigold and Cockram backed the governor, and were even sent by him to hunt Vane, but though they captured some of his fleet, still Vane eludes them.

But the new governor has shown himself in earnest for he has clung on, and only last month hanged eight pirates who had taken the pardon and then gone back to piracy.

Rogers had them brought to the gallows before a large crowd, made mainly of men who had themselves lately been pirates, and some who were still. And though the crowd turned restive and several times surged forward as though to free the men, who urged them on, they were hanged nonetheless and left to swing there, below the ramparts of the fort, and all who sail into Nassau now can see the governor is not to be crossed and that the old days of Nassau are done with.

Thompson reports that Rogers has not limited himself to the pirates:

He accounts himself a Godly man and has made of Nassau his own crusade, and is seeing off the brothel-keepers and their women, and this sets against him not just the whores but the men as well.

It would be a pretty thing, I think, if what loses Rogers the support of Nassau town, and scuppers all his schemes, are the whores and the men who will not be without them.

But the hanged men still swing beneath the ramparts, and Thompson reports that there has been no outright riot, though much muttering and unrest.

He writes:

I beg you accept my friendly counsel and do not risk these waters, for Vane and others are still abroad and our former association is no longer any guarantee of safe passage. Nor can I swear that Rogers would welcome you and it will serve neither you nor me to have our past dealings brought to light.

'So much for Nassau,' Payton says, and he tears up the paper, for any link to Nassau may be considered a danger now.

I turn away hastily, so that Payton cannot notice the expression on my face. I shall not see Nassau again. Not its ugly streets nor its beautiful sunrises. Not its ale tents, its scattered harbour, and the fires ablaze above night's black water. Not Anne Bonny.

18

Payton heeds Thompson's warning and we stay well clear of the Bahamas. Watching Payton at his work, I recollect what Captain Turnbull said about how a polypus can regrow a severed limb. Payton adapts himself to anything. With the Bahamas closed to us, he sets us to loading a cargo of tobacco and rice, and we make the crossing to Bristol, and to Rotterdam.

But I too must adapt. When I can, I cleave close to Cornelisz, who is no more friendly than ever, and yet does not bridle when I find excuses to work close to him, so that Payton may not corner me alone. Although we have had fine weather, Crow has taken to coming below with me when I go to my hammock. What she offers is not quite comfort – the silhouette of a crow is too hooked to be accounted a comforting thing – but it is her animal presence, and I am glad of it.

I cannot escape the *Walcheren* in England or the Low Countries – that would be going backwards, a return to lives that I have already escaped. It is time to move forward. Always my mind turns to Nassau. There, in the disorder and upheaval, where each day is crammed with unprecedented things, there may be a way to carve a space for myself.

We are returning to South Carolina in March, loaded with damask, pepper and mace, at least a hundred leagues from Charles Town. We must approach from the south-east to benefit by the trade winds, though they draw us too close to the Bahamas for Payton's comfort.

The sloop comes at us from the south, and at once we fear that they have some ill design for they are hard upon us. Payton has men at the guns, but we can make but an indifferent fight, with our four guns and not the men to operate them all at once. Fond as I am of the *Walcheren*, she is a tub not built for speed.

Cornelisz stands ready at the aft gun. 'Captain?' he calls.

'Hold off,' Payton says. 'Wait until she's alongside of us.'

The sloop is nearly within musket-shot when she hoists the black flag.

'Fuck,' says Payton, but already he is adapting, and his fingers are tapping on the wheel, and I fancy I can almost see him calculating already what the insurers will pay and what part of the cargo is his own secret stash, and not on the bill of lading and cannot be claimed for.

The pirates have six guns, and powder to spare it seems, for they send a shot just behind our stern to show they are in earnest.

We meet it with a volley of small arms – even I, from the rigging, fire my pistol, and Crow takes to the shelter of the sky. Our firing clears their decks but only for a moment and their men scatter but are not hurt, and Payton shouts to trim the topsails so that we may sweep them with our two larboard guns. The guns are loaded with chain shot to tear at the sloop's rigging, but the men time the shots badly against the *Walcheren*'s roll and so we strike their deck and not the rigging and I can see little damage done.

The pirates are close enough now that we can hear their shouts: 'We give no quarter. Stand down and you'll live.'

I drop back on deck, and Payton turns to me, speaking low. 'You going to be alright? If they board?'

'They're boarding either way,' I say. I will not deny I am afraid – but beneath my fear is a current of something else: an excitement I have not felt since my navy days. 'Better for me if they don't board angry. Better for all of us.'

'I'll protect you,' says Payton.

He would, I think – he'd fight for me, if it comes to it. I wonder whether that should mean something to me – whether I am supposed to be grateful.

'We'll give no quarter,' calls the largest of the pirates, a man with a red beard and the wide-armed stance of a bear. 'If you want trouble, you'll find it.'

'No trouble here,' Payton calls back, and all around me I see the rest of the crew exhale in relief. 'Not from us.'

The big pirate looks disappointed, but another man calls back. 'Then we grant you quarter, if you'll lay down arms, open your hatches, and drop and furl all sails.'

I would not know many pirates at such a distance, but Calico Jack Rackham is one, for his bright Indian cotton clothes are unmistakable, even across forty yards of water and on a crowded deck. When I saw him speak at Nassau against the pardon, he was of Vane's crew – but there is no sign of Vane now, and all those aboard the sloop are looking to Rackham, and hastening to his commands. They look a rough crew but they move in good order and speedily too: lashers and grapplings are made fast, and while half the men keep their muskets and pistols trained on us, the others swarm onto the *Walcheren*, Rackham himself swinging aboard lightly and standing watch as his men gather our tossed weapons. Rackham calls loud for our own captain to make himself known, and Payton steps forward and I will allow that he does a good job of hiding his fear.

'You know us,' Payton says. 'We traded with Thompson for years, and on his behalf. Where would you be without merchants like us to trade your prizes, and provision you? You're cutting off your own hand.'

'Now don't go putting ideas in my head,' says the red-bearded man, but Rackham silences him with a raised palm.

'Indeed, sir, you're known to me from Nassau,' he says to Payton. 'But did you not hear? Your friend Thompson has gone over to the new governor. Sits on the governor's newly appointed council, no less. Thompson's given up consorting with the likes of us. Denies ever doing it, furthermore.'

'Whatever Thompson's up to, we've done good service to your brethren, many years over,' says Payton. 'We're not in sympathy with the governor.'

'Sir,' Rackham says, 'let's stop wasting one another's time. If you're so familiar with me and my kind, you'll know it's your cargo I'm after, and not your fine speeches.'

Then Rackham speaks quick and low on matters of business: what provisions are aboard, and the inventory, and how many days' water. We wait in silence on deck while he directs some of his men, still armed, to check our stowed cargo, and to confirm that Payton has not lied. Then we are set to work to shift the cargo. I don't like to turn my back on the pirates, while they stand with muskets still loaded and aimed our way, but they look impatient rather than bloodthirsty, so we do as they order. Even with a few of their number helping it is hot work, but the pirates do us no harm, not withstanding the odd shove from the big red-bearded man when he deems that we've dallied too long. Crow has resumed her perch on the bowsprit and seems unconcerned by the whole affair.

The pirates themselves are concerned only with the cargo, and not with the unlikeliness of finding a woman aboard a merchant vessel – indeed, a number of their faces are familiar to me from Nassau, so perhaps my presence on the *Walcheren* is no surprise to them.

'How old's the ship itself?' Rackham is peering over the rail to see the state of our hull. There are captains who dress as rich men do, with white wigs and waistcoats trimmed in lace. But I've seen nobody else dress as Rackham does, which is all in a jumble of calico prints, bright even after the sea and sun have been at work on them. His trousers are striped and his shirt spotted, and on the back of his jacket is printed a great flowering tree in the old calico style, the branches spreading as his shoulders widen, so that to look at him from behind his whole body becomes a picture.

'You taking the ship too, then?' Payton asked. If Rackham takes the *Walcheren*, we will be left in our small boats, or perhaps marooned. Worse than that: there are stories aplenty of pirates who toss a crew overboard, or torture them or otherwise use them ill. But there is nothing in Rackham's manner that speaks of a taste for unnecessary violence.

I can see him weighing the options. He hasn't the crew numbers to sail both ships – not comfortably. He looks short-handed even for his own small sloop. The *Walcheren* is bigger, and better kept; Rackham's sloop is faster, but his hull is fouled, barnacles and weeds even above the waterline.

'We'll leave your ship,' he says, though he directs his crew to take two of our sails, which does not surprise me having seen the state of their own. Still I'm not unduly perturbed, for there is canvas enough on board for us to rig some kind of jury sail.

The cargo is stowed but Rackham's crew opens one of the barrels of salt pork and they eat like hungry men, with haste and not much in the way of manners. They found Payton's own cask of good brandy and rather than take it to their sloop, Rackham taps it right here on our deck, and draws a cup which he drinks, unhurried. Then he calls for more cups and passes the first to Payton, saying, 'Your crew, too, for they've not shied away from this day's work.' And so the cups are passed around and we drink, though Rackham's men wear their guns still and the red-bearded man, whom Rackham's crew call Tait, tosses his pistol impatiently from his left hand to his right.

I take the cup when it is passed to me, but sip it only. There's a tale from the battle of Sole Bay, back in the third Dutch War. A second-rater called *Royal Katherine* was taken, but the Dutch found so much brandy aboard that they got rolling drunk and let the ship be retaken before the day was out. But this isn't going to be another *Royal Katherine*. Rackham's men are drinking, but not drinking stupid, except for Tait, who is already sweating, eyes swivelling and eager for trouble. Nevertheless the brandy is loosening up both crews a little – for the cargo is stowed, and for all Tait's posturing we all know what's done is done and it will not come to blood today.

'Stay quiet and we shall pass through this soon enough,' says Payton in a low voice, his mouth so close that his wet lips brush my ear.

'You're English, yes?' Rackham asks him.

'What's it to you?'

'Listen.' Rackham waves away the cup that Tait holds out to him. 'We're short a few hands. Don't fear,' he says hastily, for he has seen the wary looks exchanged by our crew. 'I'll have no forced men on my crew – they've no stomach for the work. But if you're willing, you'll find us a fair crew, and you'd be granted your share of any prizes.'

There are merchant ships with conditions aboard so bad the crew rejoice at being taken, and would overset the cocket-boat in their rush to join the pirates. On navy ships, too, a crew attacked by pirates will sometimes join them to escape the navy with its paltry pay and many indignities.

Payton is surveying us, lips tight. The men stay silent, but eventually Cornelisz and Madsen shake their heads.

Cornelisz speaks first. 'We're too old for that game,' he says to Rackham, and the others murmur agreement. 'And I have my wife to think of.'

'We'll take no married men,' Rackham says to Cornelisz. 'They only prove deserters, or cowards. But honest sailors, unafraid of work, or of combat, will find us a fair crew.'

'We're wed,' says Payton at once, his hand on my arm. 'She and I.'

I do not throw off his hand as I would like, only move one very precise step away from his touch. Rackham raises an eyebrow, looking not at Payton but at me.

'Does he say that to save you, or to spare himself?' Rackham asks me.

'What's that supposed to mean?' Payton says. 'We're wed, I tell you.'

'You forget that I've been below,' says Rackham, with a jerk of his head at the hatch. Then he turns to me. 'That's a fine, fastidious husband you've got, who lets you keep your own hammock, and will not share his cabin.'

'He's no husband of mine,' I say, and Payton looks angrier than he did when the pirates first raised the black flag. I take a breath. 'And I am English too. And a sailor, who can hand, reef and steer as well as any man here. If you can offer me fair dealing, I will join your crew.'

One of his men guffaws, yet Rackham speaks politely.

'Lady, I had not thought to take on a woman.'

And I had not thought to ask. Yet if this is the chance the sea is offering me, I will seize it, for Payton is out of all patience with me.

Rackham looks at me appraisingly. I step forward, hoping he sees me for what I am: the knife and marlinspike at my belt; my strong hands, scarred by work. A sailor, sea-hardened and ready.

He nods. 'You'll find fair treatment with my crew. Your share of any prizes, too, no matter that you're no man.'

I think of how his men fell upon the salt pork and the brandy. Seems to me they haven't been taking too many prizes of late. I look Rackham's sloop over. She is nothing much to look at – if you saw her in a harbour, you'd guess she was there to be broken up, not readied for a cruise.

'Captain,' says Tait. 'Come on. We don't need some bitch on board.'

Rackham ignores him, and gestures to Payton. 'You've been sailing under him for some years?' he asks me. 'I've seen you in Nassau, I collect.'

I nod.

'See?' says Rackham, turning to Tait. 'Payton's known in Nassau for being a close-fisted fellow, with an eye to profits. He wouldn't keep her aboard if she weren't earning her keep. And if she's not earning her keep in his cabin, then I'll warrant she's useful on board.' He turns back to me. 'Join us, then, and you'll earn double what Payton pays you.'

In truth the money doesn't figure so much with me. Money for what – a fine old age? No matter how hard I stare at the future, I have never been able to make out an old age for me on its horizon. For that same reason, the hangman doesn't frighten me as much as perhaps it should. So neither the money nor the noose figure very large in my mind as I contemplate Rackham's offer. No pirate is safe – but under Payton's sweaty hands, nor am I safe on the *Walcheren*.

'What name d'you go by?' asks Rackham.

I like the looseness of that. I think of the names of Calico Jack himself, and Blackbeard – perhaps not many in the ale tents of Nassau stick to their real names.

If Payton weren't here, I might choose another name. But with him watching, I feel my name stuck to me like a barnacle to a hull.

'Mary Read.'

'Then join us, Mary Read,' says Rackham.

'Mary,' says Payton. 'You're not entertaining this madness, are you? Stay out of this, for God's sake.'

'It is no business of yours,' I tell him.

If this is a war, between pirates and others, there is no staying out of it. I have lived much of my life in the belly of war. War will have you, whether you will or no. The thing about war is that you must choose your side.

I gesture at the rest of Rackham's crew: Tait, squinting in the sun and still brandishing his pistol, and the others concentrating on the brandy. 'Would I find trouble from this lot?'

Rackham shakes his head. 'No trouble that you don't start.' He turns to the tall, thin pirate closest to him and says something I can't hear. The man crosses to the sloop and comes back sharpish with a long sheet of paper that crackles, stiff with salt air, as Rackham spreads it carefully against the side of the cocket-boat.

He doesn't ask me if I can read – just reads aloud to me.

Articles of Agreement between us aboard of the Camila, *John Rackham Commander, that we are to dispose of all the goods that are aboard amongst us, every man to have his full due and right share only the Commander is to have two shares and a half a share for the Ship, and whom the Captain please to take for the Master under him is to have a share and a half . . .*

'Fair dealing, see,' Rackham says. 'And note this,' and he jabs his finger further down the page and reads aloud again:

. . . and if we should take a Prize at Sea, that has any Women on board, no one dares, on pain of death, to force them against their Inclinations. Women taken in a prize are to be put ashore or given up to the hazards of the sea.

Payton looks at me and throws his arms wide. 'Come on. You trust a piece of paper?'

'Could I trust you?'

He doesn't respond.

I don't trust the paper any more than Payton does – each pirate crew has their articles, yet I have seen in Nassau what they are capable of. I don't trust a thing: not a man; not a piece of paper; not a solemn-sworn promise.

'Listen to me, Mary,' says Payton. 'If you do this thing, you can't undo it.'

'You used to be a privateer. Is it so very different?'

'Half the sailors between here and London have been privateers. It's not the same thing.'

'What's the difference?'

'A letter of marque. King's orders, that's the goddamned difference.'

'*A piece of paper*, you mean?'

'You know what I mean. You don't hang for privateering. It's different.'

'I've done both,' Rackham says, ignoring Payton's glares. 'Taking ships is taking ships. Never felt much difference myself, except I pay no commission to any monarch now.'

I'm not saying Crow chooses for me. Just that she flies to Rackham's sloop, up onto the jib line, and sits there like a decision that's already been made. She doesn't even look back at me.

'I'll come,' I say. Then again, for it seems too momentous a thing for two small words only. 'I'll join your crew, and willing.'

The rest of Payton's crew is staring. Do they fear for me, or envy me? Cornelisz is silent, but Madsen speaks.

'You don't have to do this.'

'It's my choice,' I say. Then again, louder: 'Mine.'

The thin pirate behind Rackham steps forward. 'Don't come aboard for the sake of any pretty notions. Being a privateer might be the same job, while you're at sea. But a privateer comes back to a grateful monarch and a nice house. If we get caught, we come back to a noose.'

I don't know whether he wishes to protect me, or only to assure himself that I'll be fit for the work.

'I've been a sailor too long to have any pretty notions,' I tell him. 'And I don't plan on being caught.'

He narrows his eyes, then turns to Rackham. 'You sure she's good for anything, Captain?'

I ignore the snort from the big man, Tait, and one or two of the others.

'Served five years in the navy,' I say. 'Army too – then four years here on the *Walcheren*. I'm quick, and good topside. You'll not find me idling. Ask Payton.'

Payton will not even meet my eyes now. 'You're really asking me for a good character, when you're going to jump ship?'

I just wait, and Tait once more passes his pistol from hand to hand, his eyes fixed on Payton, who spits over the rail, before muttering, 'She knows what she's about. Gets the job done.'

'I'm canny, too, in the ways of trade,' I say to Rackham.

'I taught you that,' Payton says. 'Have you forgotten?'

'Rest assured,' I say, 'I have forgotten nothing I learned from you.'

If Payton is grateful to have the *Walcheren* still, and not to be marooned, he gives no sign, scowling as we unhook the grapples.

'Don't be downcast. A woman aboard's supposed to be bad luck,' Rackham tells him, and gives him a clout on the back. 'Perhaps I'm doing you a favour.'

Payton snorts. 'I wish you well of her. But what of your own luck?'

'Don't worry yourself over me,' says Rackham. 'I don't trust to luck.'

I swing over to the pirates' sloop. When I look back, I fancy Cornelisz gives me a slight nod. I nod back at him, quick, so that Payton may not see.

Payton calls across to us. 'Governor Rogers is coming after the lot of you. He'll see you swing. You too, Mary.'

I keep my eyes very carefully on his. 'Look what you made me do.'

The sweet northerly wind takes us south and the *Walcheren* shrinks behind us. It gave me pleasure to throw Payton's own words back in his face – but he did not make me do this, and I am not fleeing him. I am sailing towards something. I don't know precisely what – no more than I knew when I left the big house and went to war, or when I marched away from *De Drie Hoefijzers* with my gear bundled on my back. I am making my way towards something that smells like saltwater and looks like the unexpected blue of Crow's wingtips, and feels just like the wind feels now, hard and soft at once on my upturned face.

I carry with me many things I did not choose: Marston's death, and Dan's; the baby that never lived. Ma, and all that she has done and been to me. Yet I chose to go aboard the *Walcheren*. I chose to step aboard Rackham's sloop, and to take to pirating. More intoxicating by far than the brandy in my belly, this knowledge: this is what I choose. This.

Rackham spots Crow that first day, as she circles slow above us. He takes to her right away.

'He's like an omen,' says Jack. He has taken Crow for male, and I don't bother to correct him. 'But an omen of what, eh?'

This is what I want to tell him: a crow is its own prophecy. When Crow sits on our bowsprit, what she announces is herself. *I am the event*, she says. *I am the thing itself. I.*

That night, at anchor, Rackham tells me how they came to be in these parts, on this unkempt sloop. His crew had lately seized the merchant ship *Kingston* in December, within sight of Port Royal, and scored a handsome cargo of gold watches and silk stockings. But privateers came upon them in late February down at Isla de Pinos.

'And I'll admit we were caught ashore, unawares and much the worse for drink,' Rackham says cheerfully, 'and we were obliged to hide in the jungle, while they seized the ship. Our only good fortune was that we'd brought ashore some of our prizes, thus we kept the stockings and some of the watches. These were the whole of our fortune, bar what Payton was kind enough to give us today.' And he laughs, unguarded. 'We may look a ragged bunch, but there is no crew with silk stockings so fine, I assure you.' He makes a small, mocking bow, and I laugh with him, for after Payton, it is a relief to have a captain who laughs readily at himself.

'How came you to break with Vane?' I ask him, for when I was last at Nassau he was still sailing under Vane. 'You did not find him a good captain?'

Rackham shrugs. 'I found myself no longer in need of a captain.'

'And how did it come about?'

'As to that,' Rackham says, with a wave to where the men are gathered, 'you have the crew to blame, for they chose me.'

I cannot disguise my surprise. 'In the navy, to rise up against a captain is mutiny and would see you hanged.'

'This is no navy,' says Rackham, grinning. 'Here, each of the company has a share in the company's business. And they choose their leader as they see fit.'

He takes his knife from his belt to trim the cord he holds. 'In November, we sighted a French navy frigate – twenty-four guns. Vane didn't want to take it on. I did.' He twirls the knife carelessly as he slips it back into his belt. 'Afterwards, the men elected me to lead them.'

I watch him as he lopes across the deck, and the easy way he laughs with his men. The more I see of Jack Rackham, the more I can see how a crew would choose such a man for their captain.

The *Camila*, as they call her, is a small Spanish sloop they took by great good luck, having only two small boats left to them after losing the *Kingston* and their brigantine. But even on my first day it is clear that the ship is in bad trim – her hull much fouled with weeds, so that she drags through the water like a woman wading in full skirts. The ship is iron-sick too, her nails and bolts eaten away by rust, leaving holes in her planks so that we are forever at the pump, which I account another reason Rackham was eager to take on more crew.

At anchor the first night he reads the entirety of the articles out loud, before the whole crew. I've read them carefully already, and the others have already signed them, but Rackham proclaims them again, as if it doesn't count unless the sea itself can hear. And there is a kind of poetry to it, his voice over the water.

He who first espies a Sail, if she proves a Prize, is entitled to the best Pair of Pistols on board, over and above his dividend. All plunder taken from a Prize must be handed over to the Quartermaster, on pain of a flogging and forfeiture of all possessions to the good of the Company.

The articles state the division of prizes. Rackham and the ship's master, the thin man Fetherston, are allotted the greatest part, yet still I will be granted my share, equal to the rest of the crew.

The articles enjoin the men not to gamble for money, nor to fall drunk aboard. Many would be surprised to know that a pirate ship may be well regulated, and its men submit to such restrictions.

'It's merely good sense,' Rackham says to me. 'I enjoy a drink or a game as well as the next man – but gambling and drunkenness at sea means nothing but quarrels.'

'From what I've seen in Nassau, no such rules apply ashore?'

Rackham grins. 'Assuredly not.'

When he reads out that each of us is obliged 'to keep their piece, pistols, and cutlass clean and fit for service,' Tait says low, 'Mary can polish my piece,' and the men ignore him. I can see already that he is one of those men whose dirty jokes are a habit and nothing more, if only because he is too lazy to stir real trouble. I prefer Tait's crass jests to the stiff courtesies of Payton.

Rackham offers me the quill. 'What say you, Mary Read? Will you sign, and commit yourself to our ship?'

'You barely have a ship,' I say. 'Not one fit for the name.'

'For now,' he says, with a grin that appears sudden as a sword slash on his face. I will admit it is hard not be swept along on the good wind of his confidence.

I sign my name: *Mary Read*, and it is a few letters only but as I write I feel a channel open beneath me, fifty fathoms deep, entirely new.

19

I quickly learn the chief figures amongst Rackham's crew. Fetherston, the calm, tall ship's master, with his thin face; Patrick the pilot; Corner, the quartermaster. Solemn-faced Davies, whom all call 'the Reverend.' Tait and Gibson, both of them old salts, forever laughing at each other's dirty jokes, and laughing even louder at their own. Howell the young cook.

And in charge of us all, Rackham. A pirate is well served by his legend, and so it does Rackham no harm to be known abroad as Calico Jack, for a ship that knows his fearsome reputation is more like to beg for quarter. Rackham is a man wise enough to know the uses of myth, but also wise enough to know its limits, and aboard the *Camila* he is just Captain, or Jack. It is true enough that he dresses fine – but he is not shy of work, and look close enough and you'd see his britches are shiny on the sides where the wheel brushes them, and where the lines rub. When Tait or the others make sport of him for his pretty ways, he ignores them, for such ways come natural to him, and still the crew jumps quick and uncomplaining to every one of his orders. And Rackham has no need to raise his voice when he gives an order, which I have found to be the mark of a captain who knows his business.

I have cause to see it only two days later, for we espy a sail to the west, and bearing closer upon them we find they are a brigantine under a Spanish flag. They have the advantage of speed, having much greater sail, but we have a shallower draught and are able to benefit by a channel passing closer to the reef. Rackham directs us very neatly to cut them off at the channel where they must round the reef, and they are taken without any weapons fired except for one pistol that Tait fires high as a warning. As it turns out they have little of value but some cloth and a quantity of rice, but I have nonetheless begun to learn a lesson of pirating, which is that for all Tait's bluster, and the pistols that the men keep ready, pirates have no wish to fight. There'll always be a few like Teach, proper mad bastards, in it for the blood and not the money. But most pirates know the rules: go in fierce, and fast, and the captains will beg for quarter, just as Payton did, and the Spaniards now do too.

Many merchants have insurance – if anyone's paying, it's a rich man in Europe, and nobody wants to die for the sake of a stranger and his profits. Sea folk are practical above all else. They won't tie a Turk's head knot where a bowline will do; they don't want to fight a battle over a cargo, when there's always the next cargo, and the one after that. So the Spanish crew mutter angrily but it does not come to blood, and the whole proceeding is done with before the wind has even finished clearing the gunshot smell from the air.

'Only stupid pirates take to killing,' says Jack, unabashed, as we carry the Spaniard's cargo of rice aboard the *Camila*.

We do not take the brig, which is too big for us to crew, but Jack takes all four of their twelve-pound guns.

'We've not the men to fire them,' I say. 'Nor the powder.'

He smiles. 'Aye. But the ships we chase down don't know that, do they?'

Indeed our little *Camila*, though still sorely in need of careening, and riding a little heavy under the weight of so many guns, begins to look very warlike.

I quickly prove myself useful up the mast, though on a sloop there is less call for top work. Off duty, I climb the mast for pleasure alone, to seek out the high, secret breezes, and the better to see the horizon's curve.

When I am up there, Rackham yells to me: 'Call your crow to you. The merchants won't know what to think when we come upon them with a woman and a crow on the mast. They'll soil themselves.'

I have never called Crow to me – nor would she come if I did.

'She goes where she likes,' I shout down to him.

I do not say: *and nor will I perform for you.* I have no wish to be a symbol, or an ornament to the ship. If I am up the mast it is not because it suits Jack Rackham's fancies, but because I choose to be.

———————

Off Hispaniola we chase down two periaguas and they are mere sail canoes but render up a quantity of turtle meat and a nice catch of fish and two nets. We feast that evening, and Crow walks her stately walk very close and hooks an eye from the largest of the fish.

'Keep that bloody thing away,' snaps Tait.

'Planning on eating the eyes, were you?'

He grunts. 'I've eaten worse, since Howell took over the galley.'

Jack has taken to the crow but Tait is affronted by her – yet I am quickly learning that he is forever aggrieved at something. Tait sees himself as much come down in the world from his privateering days. He speaks often of the glory days when Spanish ships used to come, unprotected, from the New World, and swears those galleons were so laden with silver and gold that they rode low, with water coming in at the gunwales. Of course he has pissed all his prize money away, and has ended up here with us, moaning about the good times long past, or making his dirty jokes, for he is a man who cannot hear mention of the Windward Passage without saying, 'I'll show you my Windward Passage.' He is no longer young, but Jack doesn't account it a shortcoming. 'The most useful thing about Tait is his two bad knees, for they can tell a storm coming better than any instrument or sky gazing,' Jack says. Tait carries on grievously when his joints take to aching, but it's a boon, for we know to batten down and seek harbour. He is missing two fingers on his left hand, and tells me a grand story about how they were sliced off when he led a boarding party in the taking of a Spanish galleon. I ask Jack, thinking for sure he will say Tait's fingers were crushed by a rolling water barrel, or in a bar brawl, but Jack nods. 'Still, the Spaniard knew his business,' he says. 'It was a lovely clean cut. A surgeon couldn't have done it neater.' That's the thing about Tait – at least half of what he says is lies, but you can never tell which half.

For the rest of the crew, they are an ill-assorted bunch, though they seem to find fellowship with one another. Amongst the older men are four or five who once served in the navy; there are also privateers, and young Howell the cook, who has been a sailor three years and still gets seasick in a fresh gale. He barely speaks but is an amiable lad and for that reason the crew tolerates his god-awful cooking. Another young fellow is known as Sheep because he was once a farmer, and I never learn how he came to be at sea, and indeed he is so quiet and has such a look of gentle surprise on his face that perhaps he himself does not know.

The quartermaster, Richard Corner, is an Irishman who has sailed with Rackham four years or more. He has taken gladly to a pirate's life, for before that he was a whaler, and says there is nothing to compare for suffering. 'The lowliest deckhand on a pirate ship lives like a lord compared to the whalers,' he insists. 'You cannot know, unless you've ever gutted a beast so large you can stand upright inside it and breathe nothing but the gut-stench for days.' He says months would sometimes pass between sightings of a whale, so I figure he learned it then: the way of stillness about him, and his knack for silence. The crew accounts him a good quartermaster, but Rackham prizes him above all as a lookout, and swears you will not find a keener pair of eyes than a whaler's, honed by years of straining to spot the beasts in any seas.

Corner and I sit by the rail and he tells me the only thing he misses from whaling is his soft hands. 'For all the hard work, and God knows we had plenty of that, we were elbow deep in whale fat and I had hands like a pair of lady's gloves, I swear it.' He turns his calloused and scarred hands over ruefully.

John Davies is called by all 'the Reverend,' which at first I think just a joke due to his sombre ways and his face which has the look of a trout, very downcast about the mouth. But I learn fast enough that Davies is a real reverend, or used to be, and came to pirating by what roads I do not know, though I suspect it had to do with drunkenness, for despite his solemn countenance he is a great one for drink. Nonetheless he still has a churchman's manner, and undertakes his shipboard duties in a particular and solemn way. I never before saw a man who could coil a line as if performing some holy rite.

He is handy with a musket in engagements, and does not scruple to take any prize that we steal, yet when we take a small fishing bark off a sandbar, the Reverend will have none of it, the day being Sunday, and he insists on sitting astern and reading his Bible for he will not break the Sabbath. He refuses his share of our prize even though the fishermen put up no struggle to speak of, and no blood has been shed. The others are glad enough to have his share between them, and Jack says, 'We may not have much of a hull, but we're the only pirate crew to boast its own chaplain.'

We have no ship's surgeon, but the Reverend is considered the nearest thing: for all his drinking he has steady hands and Corner swears that when of one of Vane's crew had an arm turn putrid, the Reverend took it off neat as any barber surgeon. Tait scoffs that he would trust the Reverend to take off his arm but not to trim his hair, 'For just take a look at the state of the man,' Tait says, and indeed I'll allow that there is an oddness in the Reverend's appearance, his hair kept very short and shorn completely at the crown as monks were once wont to do.

Noah Patrick, our pilot, is a former navy man. You'd think it a kind of magic, how the channels will part for Patrick, how he can slip the *Camila* through a passage where others will founder, and do it all while chewing his tobacco. His collection of charts is bundled together into one great book, his waggoner, and once when Tait handles it roughly, Patrick curses him up and down the ship and near kicks him off it, those charts being worth more than Patrick's share of any prize, for they are his profession. But when we sail he barely uses them, for his memory lets nothing go: not just where a sandbank is, but also the very moment the tide peaked last night and how full the moon, and thus whether it is a neap or spring tide, and what that means for the shifting of the sands. He does all of this without a glance at a chart – the same way you don't think when you pull on a shirt or tie a hitch, for the body knows its work.

Patrick argues for heading further east, along the south coast of Hispaniola. It is put to all of us to vote and we duly agree. Jack is our captain, but he has an easy way with the crew, and all decisions of any import are made by the whole company. It was enshrined in the articles that we signed: *Every man has a vote in affairs of moment.* Even I, no man, have my vote, and when I shout my *Aye* it feels a daring thing indeed, after a lifetime of navy and army discipline, and of Payton's officious rule.

The only time a pirate captain's word is absolute is during an engagement – this too is enshrined in the ship's articles. To do it any other way would be to see us hanged for sure, for in battle a crew must follow one voice or die.

In those first two engagements I play only a small part, for Fetherston and Rackham keep me working the rigging during the chase, and do not send me amongst the boarding party. I watch closely to learn the ways of pirating, which is at once different and similar to navy work.

'You need not keep me only to the rigging,' I say to Rackham, after the first engagements. 'I'm fit for rougher work, and you know it.'

'Boarding a prize is no game,' he says.

'Nor was I playing in my years in the navy and army. And whether I'm at the mast or in a boarding party, if we are caught, I shall hang all the same.'

He does not look angry, but his voice is firm. 'I station you where I need you most,' he says.

I know myself useful at the mast – yet does he keep me there because I am a woman, or because he doesn't yet trust me? I must show him that I have chosen wholeheartedly this life, and am fit for it. And I must silence the jibes of Tait and his friend

Gibson, and a few of the younger men. Tait has complained several times that if he wanted to be surrounded by lazy women, he'd have stayed in the whorehouses of Nassau. I must put an end to their complaining against me now before it takes on the weight of habit.

We chance upon a small brig off the French part of Hispaniola and chase it down but despite our flag and our superiority in the way of guns, the captain refuses to ask for quarter, though our guns have holed their mainsail and they are now at the waves' mercy and cannot get a shot at us. Even when we have our grapplers fast, their captain is still exhorting them to defend the ship and will not stand down, though Jack has warned him loud that they shall be spared if he asks for quarter, and slain if he does not.

Still the brig's captain will not relent. When Jack orders Tait and Fetherston and two others aboard, I dart forward too. I beat Tait to the captain, who meets my raised pistol with his, our muzzles close as two lovers about to kiss for the first time. It is to my advantage, I think, that he sees me at once for a woman, for it stays him a moment from shooting, confusion writ upon his face.

Pirates are thought fearless. I think pirates are not so stupid – for fearless doesn't get you anywhere, except dead. You want to feel frightened. You want that good, hard fear right in your guts, keeping your muscles clenched. You can't pretend old Death isn't there next to you, bloodied to the elbows, his hot breath on your neck.

So when I stand muzzle to muzzle with the brig's captain, I hold my gun steady, and let my fear do its work of sharpening my senses. The captain is young and seems not to know the rules, and is like to get himself killed for his stubbornness. Maybe he's heard too many stories of pirates and battles; maybe he's a hothead. He breathes loud and very fast.

'Keep your weapons and stand fast,' he yells to his men, not taking his eyes from my face.

His crew obey, for all that Tait and Gibson are yelling and roundly abusing the men with much slander, 'Useless dogs, shits, curs!' I dare a glance around the brig. Its crew's glares are fixed on their captain and not on us – indeed they look like they're minded to shoot him themselves, if he doesn't see sense.

'Call for quarter,' I hiss at the captain. 'Do it.'

He does not move, nor lower his pistol from mine.

'Listen, you little prick. Don't die for a hold full of rum. Isn't worth it.'

His head is swivelling wildly now, from me to Tait and Fetherston and the others of our crew who have surged aboard.

'They'll kill you,' I say. 'I'll kill you myself, if I have to.'

'I'm not a coward.'

'You don't have to be a coward. You just have to live.'

He steps back. 'Quarter,' he calls, and his voice wavers, so he calls again. 'Quarter.' I see his hold on his gun loosen and he is readying to drop it to the deck but I figure it will do me no harm with Rackham's men to be seen to take it myself, and so I give him a knock to the side of the head with my pistol butt, a tap merely but enough to make him cry out, and at the same time I grab his gun. He staggers a little and looks at me, dizzied and mighty aggrieved, but I am glad not to have had to shoot him, nor to have given Tait or Gibson an excuse to do so.

The brig turns out to be a pretty prize, having aboard her a fair quantity of pepper and powder. As Tait rolls a hogshead over the gangplank to me, he glances at the brig's young captain, who sits surly against the rail under Corner's guard, hand to his head where there is a little blood and already a fine lump forming.

'Nice to have a woman's gentle touch,' Tait says.

It takes us several hours to stow the cargo, and in that time neither he nor Gibson make one more remark on my usefulness.

I feel no guilt about this taking that we do. I give no quarter, for I have been given none. Nobody ever gave me anything. Not even a name – I had to live in my brother's name, just like I lived in his leftover clothes, once we were back in Plymouth and Ma had boiled the fever out of them.

I take because the world has taught me to take. Because the only steady witness I ever had was the crow, and the sea.

Was I more virtuous when I made my coin from wars, in the navy and army, and killing was my business? Or when I earned my living from trade, from tobacco and sugar harvested under a whip by slaves? Where there is money, blood will always follow – or perhaps it is the other way around.

I am a pirate now: a thief and a bandit and perhaps a killer. Perhaps I am become what I always was.

20

Near Trinidado in Cuba, Rackham has us set him ashore and leave him there three days. Clearly it is not the first time, for the men give many nods and winks, and Tait and Gibson wave him off with a great charade of thrusting. Three days hence when we collect Rackham, he comes aboard with a fresh swagger and an expansive mood. Whoever the woman is that he keeps there, she is a fine cook, for he has brought with him a great parcel of guava shells candied and sticky in syrup. When Tait calls him 'a veritable admiral of beard-splitting,' Rackham is in no ways perturbed but laughs along with the crew. I will say of Rackham that he does not keep his joy to himself but wishes to share it as he shares out the guava shells, and he slaps the men warmly on the back and laughs at the new haircut the Reverend has given himself, and listens earnestly to Corner's complaints about the state of the hull, and when he assures Corner that all shall be put right, it is easy to believe him.

Jack is not alone in taking his pleasure, for I stumble unawares upon Patrick tugging off Tait below deck. Patrick is mighty abashed but Tait is merely irritated, yanking the blanket across his lap and saying, 'Jesus, Mary – we've been long enough at sea. If you weren't such a pious bitch, maybe I would've asked you first.' In the navy, for all that there were rumours of such goings on, you can still be hanged for sodomy and thus it was a thing done very hasty and furtive, if at all. Amongst Rackham's crew, though, I begin to see that some take such things as a natural proceeding. Men such as Tait do it only at sea, because it's the only option, and because if the lantern's out and they have a need, then any hole will do. They do it without fuss, a casual trade – Tait muttering to Patrick: 'Go on then. You know I'll see you right afterwards.'

Rackham, overhearing, laughs heartily. 'Tait? He'd fuck a soft fruit, given the chance,' he says to me. Rackham is not one to begrudge any man his pleasure.

Two nights further east we are out of Spanish territory, and Rackham accounts it safe to go ashore, and even to make a fire. The sun has gone and taken with it the blue from the water. We tap a cask of rum and another of brandy and the men are noisy with our recent good fortune. Even the Reverend is jolly, and is prevailed up by the others to sing a song. Tait leans in, the better to hear the Reverend's fine deep voice, and singes his beard on the fire, and the men's laughter hangs over the flames like smoke. And when the fire grows low, Jack fetches a pamphlet and holds it aloft.

'*The Society for Promoting Christian Knowledge,*' Jack reads aloud, turning the slim booklet over, and back again. '*On Industry, Honesty and Godly Virtue.*'

He turns to me. 'Our esteemed new governor, Woodes Rogers, is of the puritan turn – he arrived in Nassau laden with this kind of falderal.' Now he raises his voice to address the company, announcing, 'And at last we have a use for it.'

He drops it on the fire, watches it flare, and the crew laughs again and Jack raises a toast, 'To the sainted Woodes Rogers,' and all drink.

I understand now that Rackham's crew seize joy as fiercely as they will seize a prize. I take my place in the circle about the fire, and take the cup that Corner passes me, and the fire's heat makes my face feel tight as a full sail. Such joy as these men take is not theirs alone, for I have a share in this. This is mine also.

Of course there is toil. The *Camila's* riddled hull keeps us at the pumps, and no ship nor crew welcomes idlers. It is the nature of the work that surprises me, though. I had thought, as most people do, that pirating was a business of battles and prizes. Indeed it is – for a few hours every few weeks, more or less, depending on what ships the wind offers up. Even then, the prizes aren't chests of gold or jewels, as the stories would have it. We take what we can get and much of it is lowly: fishing nets and the catch in them; a much-needed new cocket-boat.

Tait curses when we find three barrels seized from a Spanish sloop are filled with lime juice and not liquor – but I know a place in Boston where lime juice will sell for more per gallon than the best Jamaican rum. When we take a weather-beaten French sloop at anchor, and are in haste to leave so as not to miss the tide, Jack loads the bags of piemento but tells the crew to leave the lumber, for the *Camila's* hull has not the room for it.

'That's not lumber,' I say. 'It's logwood, prized for dyes. Stack it on deck – we shall have no trouble selling it to any Europe-bound ship.'

Some captains would be abashed to be thus corrected – not so Jack Rackham, who beams. 'See?' he crows to Tait and the others. 'Didn't I tell you she would prove her worth, and more?'

And I am glad now of all I learned from Payton, for when I put it to use here it increases the company's share, and thus my own. I took from him what I needed.

None of the tales about pirates say aught about lists, nor about rations and water butts, but I become used to sitting with Jack, pricing up bolts of damask, or trying to figure the best port to fence three hogsheads of mace. Having gathered quick that I know my business, Jack sets me to helping Fetherston, the ship's master, with the inventory. Tait helps too, when called upon to do so – I am surprised to find he has the prettiest hand of all aboard, though his spelling is erratic. I watch as, for Hispaniola, he writes *High Spainyolo*. I like to imagine that place, a great tall plateau of an island with houses all in the Spanish style, a place that Tait has summoned through his pen alone.

Tait will have it that he once saw a mermaid off Hispaniola. 'I swear it on my life,' he says. 'You should have seen the tail on her. The tits too.'

None of us will credit it. He drinks too much, and we've all been at sea long enough to know that mermaids are the imaginings of a drunkard in the grey part of dusk, who might glimpse a porpoise tail slicing the water and imagine a naked woman with the tail of a fish. Such a mermaid is made of no more than rum and lust. The porpoise becomes a mermaid, just as a seal basking with one flipper out of the water can easily be mistaken for a shark. We summon what we most want, what we most fear.

'Pining for a sweetheart?' jeers Tait, when he comes across me sitting at the stern, gazing over our wake. 'Did you leave some lusty lad ashore, and need your hammock filled?'

'Shut it,' says Jack quickly. 'You know Mary's husband is long dead.'

I ignore them both. If Tait knew the truth of it, he would scoff the more, for it is Anne Bonny I am thinking of. Her fingers drawing the crab from the sand and holding it out to me. Her chin jutted against the onshore wind as she stands calf-deep in the shallows.

To return to Nassau under Governor Rogers would be death. Yet when my hands are at work on the lines, unthinking, I return again and again to Nassau, and to those mornings on the shore, our boots left beside each other on the sand like the feet of ghosts.

Do I wish myself more like Anne – bold as she is, and careless of the jibes of Nassau's drunkards? Or is it that I want her? When I kissed Mrs Turnbull aboard the *Resolve*, so many years ago, I could tell myself that it was all due to Mrs Turnbull's confusion. She thought me a man, and I, playing that role, responded as one. Now I have no such excuse: Anne knows me for what I am, and I her. But what am I, if I desire a woman? Can I be something for which I have no name?

When the mood is upon him, Jack holds forth very prettily about 'the infamous Hanoverian who calls himself our King,' and how the French will send a great Jacobite fleet to join the pirates, 'rising up against the English governors and all craven dogs who do their bidding.' Hearing Jack speak thus, I could almost believe him that we are not common thieves but part of a mighty uprising against the Empire. Gibson and Tait egg him on with rousing cheers, and Howell the cook pounds a water barrel like a drum. Were Jack not a pirate he might have been a preacher, and I fancy his sermons would draw a fine crowd.

'Does he really believe in all that Jacobite falderal?' I ask the Reverend, who is standing close beside me.

He shrugs. 'He's not even a Catholic, as most Jacobites are.' He looks gravely at Jack, still holding forth to the rest of the crew, and speaks low to me. 'I suspect the Jacobite cause itself matters little to him. But it suits him, to set himself against the king, and all he stands for.'

Indeed – I begin to suspect that Jack is a man who finds *against* a very diverting place to be.

In a cove off Île-à-Vache, Corner's keen whaler's eyes have spotted a ship at anchor – but Jack recognises it at once and greets its captain with great cheer: it is a fellow pirate ship and its captain, Hayes, an old comrade of Jack's from both navy and pirating days. Their clipper is limping back from Brazil after a cruise that has earned them little but scurvy, and Hayes speaks low when Jack asks him where he sails next.

'We are to Virginia, to take the pardon.' And for all Jack's urging, Hayes will not be turned aside from that decision.

'If I were closer to your age, perhaps I'd think differently,' Hayes says. 'But I've been lucky to get away with it as long as I did. I've had my time, and the pardon is a mercy.'

But there is one man aboard, a Negro, who comes quiet to Jack and asks if he may join us instead.

'You don't fancy the pardon?' Jack asks.

'I do not,' the man says. Like most black sailors in the Bahamas, he used to be a slave – and thus I suspect he has more reason than most to be wary of white man's mercy.

Hayes does not begrudge the Negro his choice, though he says he is sorry to lose him as we will find no better sailor than Sam.

'Sam?' Jack asks. 'That doesn't sound like any Negro name I've heard.'

'That's what they call me,' Sam says with a shrug.

The next dawn, when Fetherston sets me and Sam to weigh anchor, and there is nobody else nearby, I ask him again.

'What is it, then? Your true name. Not the one your owner gave you.'

He just laughs. 'I'm not stupid enough to give my true name to just anyone.'

'I won't tell,' I say. 'Not a soul.' For I know how a name may be a secret or a sacrament.

He shakes his head. 'Your fool tongue couldn't say it anyway. Don't worry yourself with what's mine.'

He speaks English well, and though the words take a different shape in his voice, his accent is, in its own manner, no stronger than Corner's Irish lilt. Hayes spoke the truth when he said Sam was an able sailor, though Tait complains at the start and would see Sam given the worst and lowliest of the tasks, as newest aboard. But Jack will not have him wasted swabbing the deck when he is more use elsewhere. I do not think it a particular kindness in Jack, but only good sense, for we all benefit by Sam's quick hands and his easy way of handling the lines, and soon even Tait stops his muttering.

For myself I am glad to have Sam working beside me at the rigging. I am nearing thirty-five, and years of hard labour mean my shoulders ache when I haul a load, and another strong crewman is a welcome hand. Best of all, Sam sees no need to crowd each moment with words. With him at work nearby I can hear the *Camila*'s own song: her lumbering, porous hull suckling at the sea; the fine thrum of her mast against the wind. And Crow's song, too: her stark cry from the bowsprit, announcing herself to the sky.

I have been watching Rackham. His reputation is bold, but he seems to me to be a man of modest ambition, chasing after fishing ketches and small ships. South of Great Exuma we espy a Spanish galleon, and Jack guides us into the string of small keys where no such vessel can pursue, and we wait there amongst the sandbanks until dark.

'You've no appetite for such prey?' I ask him.

He only laughs. 'Too rich a prize for my taste.'

'I had thought your tastes more inclined to such things.'

'Do you long to tackle a first-rater, Mary? I didn't think you nostalgic for your navy days.'

'Nor am I,' I tell him, and it's the truth. 'Only I can't make it sit right with the story.'

'The story?'

'The story of you urging Vane to take on the French man-of-war, and him refusing. You charging him afterwards with being a coward, and the crew choosing you as captain in his stead.'

'Aye,' he says. 'It's a good story.'

Jack does not usually need much encouraging to hold forth, so I wait.

'Do you not see? I suspect you see more than most.' He is looking up to examine the sky, the stars prodigious bright tonight. 'Vane wasn't going to take on the man-of-war, no matter how I urged him. Nor would a crew mutiny in an engagement.

'Vane made the right choice – that man-of-war would've been the end of us.' He leans back slightly. 'But I didn't need to do something foolhardy. I just needed a reputation for courage. And mine was cheaply bought.'

'You never meant to take on the man-of-war?'

'I meant to take on Vane.'

All Jack needed was a little dissent – just enough to make itself known at the time, and to be stirred up later to a proper foment. I think of Blackbeard, and myths, and the stories we tell about ourselves, and to ourselves.

'So you don't fancy yourself against great gunships?' I ask.

Rackham smiles again. He gestures ahead of us: the night water; the unstinting sky. All of it ours.

'It's unfashionable in me, I'll own,' he says. 'But I've the gravest disinclination to die a hero.'

Tait and Gibson have taken to calling Sam 'Crow', and other such things that pass for wit with them. In fact Sam dislikes having the crow aboard, which is the only thing in which he and Tait are united. But where Tait thinks the bird unclean, Sam says it is unseemly to have a bird lower itself to live amongst men. When he passes the bird on deck he greets it with a solemn nod of the head. This formality delights me, though Crow gives no sign of noticing.

Jack likes to have a Negro in our crew. As with being a Jacobite, it fits well with Jack's notion of himself as a man pitched against the Empire and all its works. The plantations, and all the sugar and tobacco and money that flow from them, depend on the Negroes. 'But if we take the shipping routes,' Jack says, 'it all falls down: no slaves to pick the sugar; no riches for the planters nor the crown.' It's black money; sugar money; everyone getting rich on it except for men such as Sam, who does not speak of his past but has scars on his back that make even Tait grimace.

In attacking the trade routes and sailing with freed slaves, Jack would have it that we are not thieves but warriors for freedom. The Empire cannot countenance free black men – for what if, like dysentery, such a notion spreads? Freed Negroes such as Sam sail off the very shores where, almost within sight, their brethren labour to grow money for planters and merchants. 'And for men such as Rogers, too,' Jack says, growing more impassioned. 'Don't forget that Nassau's fine new governor made his money slaving.' Only a few years ago a slave revolt in New York State was crushed; stories are rife of smaller insurrections on the island plantations. Such rebellions are put down – and put down hard. 'But each free Negro aboard a ship is his own small rebellion,' Jack says.

He will hold forth at length on this topic, until the Reverend says, 'Are you setting up for a great man of politics, then?' But I notice that, for all his speechifying, Jack does not pause to ask Sam his views on the matter, nor does he try to seek out slave ships as prizes, to free the blacks of whom he speaks.

'There have always been Negroes amongst the pirates of Nassau,' Jack boasts. 'Teach had many blacks in his crew.'

'Teach didn't scruple to trade in blacks too, when it suited him,' the Reverend says to me quietly.

It's true that there are pirates who will free slaves if they seize a ship of them. But there are also copious stories of pirates who will keep slaves to sell at the next port, or who work them aboard without any share of prizes. Such a thing was common, despite all the loud talk in Nassau's ale tents of freedom and an equal share. Seems to me that for men such as these, the share figures more than the freedom. Seems to me there are men like that everywhere, and plenty amongst Nassau and its brother-hood of pirates.

For myself, Rogers' history as a slaver sits ill with his pamphlets about godliness and good conduct, for I've heard enough of the slave ships for me to know there's nothing godly about what goes on in them, or after. There are stories of the men sent overboard in shackles, when the slavers decided the insurance money is worth more than live cargo. There's a particular cruelty about the shackles, denying a man even the freedom of his own drowning. All sailors are reconciled to drowning, should it come to it – but those slaves were not sailors, and did not choose the ocean. And no man should drown with his hands or neck shack-led and iron-heavy, pulling him down so that he may not even raise his eyes to the light.

We watch for Governor Rogers like weather. At each place we stop to provision or trade, there is more news of him and his pardon. We hear of the men who have taken it, and those who have not, some of whom have been caught and hanged already. The date of the pardon has long expired, but there is word that an extension has been granted, and that since the new war with Spain, governors will give the pardon still, for they have need of privateers, and don't wish to be at war with both the Spaniards and the pirates at once.

As a kind of jest, Jack has nailed a copy of the king's proclamation to the mast. But whatever Jack's vanities, large and small, he is no fool, and he knows that you may drive a nail through the proclamation and yet not escape it. It is not the navy Jack fears, for he has a pirate's disdain for the navy and their cumbersome, deep-draughted ships, which serve them ill amongst the many channels and sandbars of the Bahamas. But the bounties offered in the proclamation are enough to turn any man against us:

For every Commander of any Pirate Ship or Vessel the Sum of One hundred Pounds; for every Lieutenant, Master, Boatswain, Carpenter, and Gunner, the Sum of Forty Pounds; for every inferior Officer the Sum of Thirty Pounds; and for every Private Man the Sum of Twenty Pounds.

The crew tries valiantly to make jest of such sums ('Hear that, Corner? Forty pounds you're worth, when all this time we thought you worthless'). Yet the belly has gone out of the laughing. With such bounties on offer, any sailor or landlubber who recognises our sloop can make his fortune by turning us in. Every stop to water or to trade is a mighty risk; every sail that passes may set the navy onto us, or come after us themselves.

The worst of the proclamation, though, is in the tail, for it is designed to encourage us to turn in our own:

And if any Person or Persons belonging to, and being Part of the Crew of any Such Pirate Ship or Vessel, shall, on or after the said Sixth Day of September One thousand Seven hundred and eighteen,

*seize and deliver, or cause to be seized or delivered, any Commander
or Commanders of such Pirate Ship or Vessel, so as they may be
brought to Justice, and convicted of the said Offence, such Person
or Persons, as a reward for the same, shall receive for every such
Commander the Sum of two hundred Pounds.*

Who aboard the *Camila* can afford to scoff at sums like this?
The men speak of what two hundred pounds would be to them.

'A plot of land in Georgia,' says Fetherston, 'and a Negro boy
to work it.'

If he is abashed to say such a thing with Sam sitting right
beside him, Fetherston gives no sign of it. Sam says nothing, only
keeps his head bent over the cord that he is splicing.

'I'd set up a tavern in Newfoundland,' says Corner, 'and die a
rich man, for nobody drinks as whalers drink.'

'A grand house in Hispaniola, where I need never be cold
again,' says Tait, rubbing his knees, which trouble him sorely in
northern climes.

'And you, Mary?' asks Jack. 'What would you do with two
hundred pounds?'

'Outfit a ship of my own,' I say at once. I have let myself
imagine it: an old sloop, or even one of the abandoned hulls in
Nassau harbour. 'Something small that I could fix up with my
own hands.'

The pardon's bounties are worse than rot in the hull, for a
ship depends on the trust of its crew, each man as much a part
of the vessel as the keel or the rudder. When that trust is gone,
what are we but an ill-assorted collection of scoundrels afloat?
We scan each other's faces the way we used to scan the horizon
for a prize.

21

Off Exuma we seize a Spanish merchant brig, and when we board there is some little trouble with the crew who will not all come on deck, even though their captain has thrown his own musket down and asked for quarter. Another young man at the bow is set on being a hero and will stand and fight, and so the air is loud with shots and yells, Jack and Fetherston cornering the young man on deck. Tait is first below to chase out the others and by the time I am down the ladder behind him there is already a Spaniard dead on the floor, his blood running into the gaps between the boards, and the cabin thick with smoke and the sharp smell of powder. Tait is bending over the dead man, and turns quick when I come in, his hand pressed to his guts.

'Shit,' I say. 'Shit. Show me where you're hit.'

He shakes his head. 'I'm fine.' But his hand is still clutched to his side, under his jacket.

'Show me,' I say, trying to make my voice soothing. 'It'll be nothing the Reverend can't fix.'

'I told you — it's nothing.' He pulls his hand out now and holds the palm to me, bloodless. But there is a lump under the jacket where his hand had been.

'What've you got there?'

'Nothing.' He speaks too fast, already turning away. I grab — he jerks his arm aside but I was not snatching at him but his jacket, which I yank open.

Tucked there, into the side of his breeches, is a pistol — but unlike any I've seen or used before. The handle is inlaid in elaborate patterns. Even the frizzle is curved all fancy, and the whole thing is polished until it shines like moonlight on water.

'Nice pistol,' I say.

He shrugs, and pulls his jacket back over it.

'Worth a fair bit too, I'll warrant.'

'If you say so.' He makes to leave.

I step between him and the door. The powder in the air is making my eyes sting and water. 'Fetherston's going to be happy to see that pistol, wouldn't you say?' Our articles are very clear: all prizes to be handed to the ship's master, to make a reckoning and allocation of our shares.

Tait says nothing.

'Mighty happy, I reckon,' I go on. 'And Sam, too, since he was first to spot the ship.' The articles state it: *He who first espies a Sail, if she proves a Prize, is entitled to the best Pair of Pistols on board.*

'Fetherston doesn't need to know about it. Sam neither.'

'I know about it,' I say. 'I signed the same articles as you, and all the rest of us.'

He shakes his head. 'You just can't keep your fucking nose out of other people's business, can you?'

'It isn't other people's business. It's my business. That's exactly what it is. That pistol's part of our prize. You pocket it, you're stealing from all of us.'

'This is why women have no place aboard. You bitches can't be trusted.'

'One of us is breaking the articles, and lying to the crew – and it isn't me.'

He pulls the pistol out, very slow. When he raises it, for a second I think he's handing it over. But he keeps raising it, until it's pointed straight between my eyes.

'I fought for this pistol,' he says.

'I know you did.' The gun is so close to my face I can feel the heat still coming off the barrel. 'That's how I know you're not going to shoot me with it now.'

'Don't think I won't.'

'I know you would if you could. But that gun's been fired not two minutes ago. And your own pistol too, by the look of that

214

poor bastard.' I gesture with my head at the man on the floor. 'You've not reloaded either of them yet.' With the back of my hand, I push the hot barrel to the side, and step to the ladder. 'Give it to Fetherston before the day's out.'

On deck too there has been blood: two of the Spaniards dead, and one of our men also, for the young farmer lad, Sheep, has taken a cutlass to the neck and died. He had no particular friends amongst the crew, being an odd and quiet fellow, but he was one of us nonetheless, and his death was an ugly one and serves as a reminder that skin is a very yielding thing when it meets steel.

Fetherston, too, has a nasty wound to his head, which the Reverend stitches exceedingly neat. Before Jack releases the crew of the brig, he questions them, none too gently, for news. Indeed they have it, for they tell us that Jack's old captain, Vane, is caught and sure to hang. He was wrecked in the Gulf of Honduras and was stranded some weeks on a small isle there, in great privation, only to be rescued and fall into worse trouble, for he was recognised by a captain who knew him of old, and carried him to St Jago de la Vega where he is to be tried.

It is an undignified end for a pirate such as Vane, a stalwart Jacobite who had once declared himself governor of the pirates, and swore to suffer no governor but himself. Jack is very sombre and quiet after hearing the news, as are the men, for they all served under Vane. Jack releases the brig and its crew to bury their dead, though he has hobbled the ship first and taken their mainsail. And though we came off best from that small battle, and took a second cocket-boat and a quantity of powder too, the news of Vane's capture is an unwelcome prize.

As for young Sheep, he is sewn into his hammock and given to the sea.

I have said nothing to Jack, nor to anyone else, of Tait's attempt to steal the pistol, which Sam now wears on his hip. But there is throughout the ship a fresh wariness, and even though we have had a fair cruise, there is for each prize a calculation to be done: the value of our share to be weighed not only against the value of our lives, but also against the bounty offered by the pardon. This dreadful mathematics makes for an uneasy ship, and a sense that we are sailing always upwind.

So when at last Jack begins to speak of the pardon as an inevitable thing, we are none of us surprised, for he speaks only as we have all been thinking.

'We have had a good long run, have we not, Mary?' he says.

For myself, each day of this cruise has been like something snatched from a fire. Yet if we must return to Nassau, I cling fast to the notion that at least Anne Bonny may still be there. What this signifies to me I cannot say – only that it makes the pardon a less dreadful thing. If Anne remains in Nassau, returning there may be not only an ending, but a beginning also.

'Will Rogers grant the pardon?' I ask Jack.

'We shall claim we were pressed by Vane – that he forced us to join him.' Such things are common enough. 'We'll tell him we broke with Vane only shortly before Vane's capture.'

'Rogers is not rumoured to be a fool,' I say.

'No. But he hates Vane above all else.'

That much is true – Vane's long and open defiance of the governor, and his audacious escape from Nassau, are well known. Jack's tale may well make Rogers more inclined to grant us the pardon.

'And this new war is a gift,' says Jack, 'for the governor is granting privateering commissions against the Spaniards. If we play this right, we can hunt just as we do now, with the governor's blessing.'

Yet later that day he finds me in the hold and takes me aside.

'It's safer for you not to seek the pardon,' he says in a low voice.

'Am I not of this crew, as much as any of them?' My voice echoes in the cramped hold. I had not meant to shout – but I had thought that after all this time Jack knew my value to the crew.

'You misunderstand me,' he says quickly. 'I'm thinking only of your safety. If the pardon is denied, we'll swing. The rest of us have no choice but to seek the pardon – we're known for pirates all over Nassau, and beyond. But you've been with us only these few short months. And of the crews we've taken since you joined us, only Payton could name you – and his own dealings with pirates have not been so very scrupulous that he will dare to cry rope on you. And even if he were to do so, who would believe it of a woman?'

It makes sense – who would countenance the notion of a woman pirate? Indeed, it is to my benefit – yet still some part of me resents the casual shrug Jack gives as he says it.

Nonetheless I am not fool enough to risk my neck over such a thing.

'Then we'll have to destroy the articles,' I say.

Jack fetches them for me himself. On deck, I tear the parchment very small and drop the pieces overboard. Jack and Crow watch me as I consign my name to the sea.

'If we can find work in trade,' Jack says, 'you shall have a berth on the *Camila* as long as you like.'

'Thank you,' I say, and I mean it, though I cannot trust to the future any more than to the *Camila*'s rotted hull.

The date for the pardon has been extended, but we know not for how long, and for three whole days we find ourselves becalmed. Stuck here, stagnant in the slack water, we joke that this shall be our luck, to miss out on the pardon through weather alone, and arrive in Nassau only in time to be hanged. At last the wind returns and Jack says, 'Good, we're away,' but all day he is stern and quiet and I warrant a part of him wouldn't have minded had the wind made the choice for him, and kept him from Rogers and his pardon.

As for Sam he is determined he will take no pardon, nor come to Nassau at all. When we cross the Grand Bahama Bank he asks us to set him ashore on Andros, where he will take his chances in joining a merchant ship, or perhaps another pirate crew. We leave him there, alone on the white stripe of sand, and heading inland. He does not look back.

22

We approach New Providence, heading not for Nassau but first to the south-west. There we spend near a full day ferrying the best of our cargo ashore, and burying it among the pines. We leave aboard only the cargo we can best afford to lose, when the governor's men come to claim it: some tobacco, which we know to be spoiling, and a quantity of spices. To bury the rest is heavy work, and as we dig there are many sideways glances amongst the crew. Jack makes us all swear, and swear again, that we shall all meet again at the appointed day, and that day only, to divide the spoils.

'And any man who comes sooner, to steal from his crewmates, will find his life forfeit,' he says, his voice uncommon stern.

I am watching Tait; the others, too, eye one another warily. Whatever easy fellowship we all had aboard the *Camila* has not followed us ashore. Was it the ship, then, that took this ill-matched band of thieves and sanctified us, and made us a crew? Perhaps it was the sea itself.

The next day we reach Nassau and find it much changed. It will never be a well-favoured town, nor a pretty one, but already the reforms under Governor Rogers are clear. We sail into the harbour under the eye of a battery established at the eastern entrance. The fort, too, is largely restored and manned with proper guns. Most of the junk and the rotting ships are gone from the harbour-side, and the roads cleared. The old Governor's House, too, is much repaired, and it is there that Jack leads the men straight away, saying gravely, 'If it's to be done, then it's as well to do it quick.'

For myself, I wait aboard the *Camila*, for until I know how the crew has been received by the governor, I dare not go abroad in Nassau, not even to seek Anne Bonny. I sit at the bow and am glad to have Crow perched near me on the rail, for few are better at waiting than crows.

What is now passing up at the Governor's House will see my crew live or die – yet it is to Anne that my thoughts go most often. Is she in Nassau still? Does she still make free at the ale tents as she once did, and does her husband still tolerate it? And as she walks the dawn shore, does her mind turn to me?

When Jack and the men come back, I can see from their very stride that the pardon has been granted. Tait swaggers, half cocky and half ashamed. Even Jack looks mightily relieved, and when I've rowed ashore I search his face for what has changed in him; yesterday a pirate fit to swing, and now an honest man again, made so by the governor's word. The pardon is a kind of baptism: you go in full of sin and come out washed clean.

Rogers himself comes down from the Governor's House to oversee the seizure of the goods aboard the *Camila*. He makes no comment to see me at the harbour with the crew, but it is clear he thinks me a fallen woman, to be in such company, for he turns away from me with a twisted lip. I recall those many puritan pamphlets that he brought with him to New Providence.

I watch him carefully, this man who has come to Nassau and reshaped it altogether. He is far from young, and no longer strong, but has the figure of a man who once was strong indeed. He walks uneven, from some old injury I'd wager, and his cheek has a splendid scar only partly covered by his dark beard, now largely grey.

Rogers' men empty our cargo hold and ferry it ashore, and he oversees them as they make a reckoning. It looks meagre indeed, laid out on the harbour-side, and Rogers himself prises open the hogsheads, rubs the damp tobacco between his fingers, and sniffs it close.

Jack clears his throat. 'As you see, Governor, we have but little.'

'And yet Vane was wrecked as early as February,' Rogers says. 'And somehow, these many months since escaping Vane, you have all survived, on' – he nudges one of the opened hogsheads with his foot – 'on nothing but spoiled tobacco and spices, without ever taking again to piracy.'

'We were singularly lucky, Governor, in turtling.'

Rogers raises an eyebrow. 'Lucky indeed.' Then he leans closer, his voice low. 'I have granted you your pardon. But I'm no fool, Rackham – and if we have a shared enemy in Vane, don't think I'll spare you if you prove untrue.'

He walks away, and I think the king has chosen his governor well. Our crew has their pardons, but Rogers is a man who will exact a price, and it will prove ill for us if we cannot meet it.

The pardon is also called the Act of Grace and indeed there is a solemnity in those who have taken it. Jack himself buys drinks for all, for he's wise enough to know the men need something to drown their shame. For all the changes in this town, it would take more than Woodes Rogers to shut down Nassau's ale tents, and tonight we drink hard.

Though I stay close by Jack's crew, my true role with them is not generally known, thus I am a source of much ribaldry from the other men in the tent. It troubles me little, even when I hear them joke about which of the men I am fucking, or perhaps all of them. I have slipped, neat as you like, through a gap in history. I wear trousers today, and most days, but my days of disguising myself as a man are long gone, for I am done with trying to pass as anything other then myself. Had I gone pirating in my man-guise, I must needs seek a pardon. But I am known here for a woman, and therefore can be no pirate. Instead, I am beneath the notice both of language and of laws. As for Jack's crew, they are happy enough to keep my secret, for if it becomes known that a woman has shared their work, it would make less of a man of them. Better for all that I should be seen as a lady of loose morals, kept by one or more of them aboard.

'Pardoned,' Tait says, and repeats it, 'pardoned,' rolling the word around in his mouth like it is a new liquor that he is savouring. Pardoned. Tait's deeds have not changed since yesterday: the same prizes stolen; the same men threatened, beaten, killed. Only that single word, pardoned, has changed all. It seems to me a mighty trick, that a piece of paper, a single word, may count for more than all those deeds.

All night I scan the tent for Anne, yet I do not see her. What if she has left Nassau altogether? What if she has reunited with her husband? Or, most frightening of all, what if she has not, and I must face at last the question of what I want from her?

I go back ashore at dawn, in search of her. Jack and Fetherston join me, having business to attend to in Nassau, and Crow cruises above the cocket-boat as Fetherston rows.

I am different now. I have emerged from my years on Payton's boat, like a tortoise from its long winter sleep. I shall never be like Anne, for she is bold and loud where I am quieter, more watchful. Yet this season of pirating has wrought a change in me, and something is awakened – a kind of daring that was not there before. Anne, of all people, must surely recognise it, for she is all daring, all fearlessness. What will she say, to see this new Mary Read, now I am become the pirate that her husband never was?

Word must have spread already that I am here – for we are still dragging the boat upon the sand yet here she comes, hurrying down to the harbour with her skirt hoisted in one arm just the way I remember. Her hair is pinned up hastily and she is running, her smile a lighthouse beam.

Except it is not me at whom she directs that almighty smile. I run to her but she is looking over my shoulder. I turn too and it is Jack she has seen, tall in his Calico jacket. She is gazing at him, her bright eyes kindled, and he is staring back.

Then she embraces me. 'I heard that there was a woman come in with the *Camila*. I thought it could only be you.' She leans back to look at my face, then in again to kiss my cheek. 'And I'm mightily glad that it is, for Nassau is dull since Rogers came – and all the duller without you.'

But already her hands are releasing my shoulders and she has stepped beyond me to Jack.

'So you're Rackham,' she says, though I can see she knows full well who he is. 'My husband was in your line of work.' She has a way of drawing back a little and lowering her voice, which makes Jack lean in closer as she speaks. 'Though he was not fortunate enough to do well,' she says.

'I've met your husband, ma'am,' says Jack, with a formal bow. 'And I think him fortunate indeed, though in only one respect.'

'If you've met him, then you'll know how little he deserves whatever good fortune he has found so far.'

Jack nods solemnly. 'Is he at sea at present? Does he still sail on the *Felicitous*?'

Anne shrugs as though she does not know. 'He is not here.' She repeats it, a pause between each word, and a little tap of her fingers on the palm of her other hand. 'He. Is. Not. Here. Now.' The 'Now' she says with great relish, and I never knew how a word can be laid out like a card placed face up on a table.

Anne and I walk together the length of the beach.

'How fares it with your husband, now the governor is come?' I ask.

'He's no better an informant than he was a pirate. Sometimes he runs cargo to Jamaica for Governor Rogers. But he's also known all over town as an informer.'

'And how do the two of you fare together?'

She snorts. 'He gives me no trouble, if that's what you mean. We each make our separate ways.' She stops walking and turns to face me. 'And you? You are rid of Payton?'

'Well rid of him.'

She cocks her head to one side as she examines me. 'You look different. This new life suits you well. You sail with Rackham?' There is a hint of reserve in her voice, that sits ill with her wide smile.

'These several months past. They seized Payton's ship in March, and I came aboard.'

'And are you Rackham's woman?' she asks. 'Rumour has it there have been plenty.'

'Of course not. I joined his crew. Nothing more.'

'His crew?' she says. 'You're a pirate now?'

Even Anne, it seems, struggles to imagine that a woman may do such a thing.

'I was,' I say. 'And a good one, too.'

'But you've not taken the pardon with them?'

I shake my head. 'Why, when none will believe I ever did such a thing?'

She leans forward, takes my hand. 'I believe it,' she says. 'Look at you: sailor, soldier, pirate.' She laughs. 'To see the two of us, anyone would think you the meek one – quiet as you are. But of the two of us, it's you who fears nothing.'

She smiles again. Yet having seen how she looked at Jack this morning, I know that she is wrong, for there is one thing I fear.

Rogers came to Nassau to make war upon us pirates, but since the new war with Spain, he has bigger concerns than pirates alone. The Spaniards are rumoured to be massing their troops against us, and the whole town is now on a martial footing in readiness for a Spanish invasion.

Many former pirates find themselves working for Rogers. Hornigold, once chief amongst pirates, is now chief amongst Rogers' pirate hunters; others, such as James Bonny, are known to be Rogers' informers. Half of Nassau is working for Rogers, and the other half whispering against him.

Rogers has enticed settlers back to New Providence with the promise of land, and there has been a great spree of building. But this has been done in the rough manner of Nassau and its men: hasty houses set up amongst old ruins, where poles have been laid as rafters and covered over with palm leaves, and the builders not much troubled about the ornament of doors and windows. Many of the new buildings are only tents of old sailcloth, so in a high wind, Nassau is a fleet in full sail.

Jack keeps a house in Nassau town – a shack, in truth, 'and constructed in the main of lizards and mildew,' Fetherston says ruefully, peering through a great gap between the boards of the wall. Nonetheless the shack is big enough for the crew and our hammocks, and Crow grows fat on lizards. The crew splits our time between the shack and the *Camila*. Some of the men drift away, taking on new work for Rogers, or joining other ships to try their hand at trade. But the core of Rackham's crew remains: Fetherston, the tall, thin ship's master; Corner, the former whaler; Patrick, our pilot; Tait and his friend Gibson, forever sniggering at each other's crass jokes; cheery, quiet young Howell, who cooks as badly on land as he did at sea. And the Reverend, who alone amongst the crew does not stay with us, for he has a small place of his own some ways inland, to which we are not invited, though he brings us cassava and proudly tells me it is from his plot there.

This new life we lead since the pardon is a drab one. Jack alone of the crew is not downcast – Anne is a mast he has spotted on the horizon of these dull Nassau days. Over these next few weeks, as he spends ever more time with Anne, his attention turns her glossy – I can almost see her growing with his stares, her cheeks flushing pinker and her hair taking on a new gleam.

And me? I watch, and find I can grieve even what I have never had. Was it only my fancy, that she used to look at me with that same fervent gaze that she now turns on Jack? Perhaps I imagined it, the same way a drunk or lonely sailor sees a mermaid where there are only waves. Yet I could swear I had felt something growing between us. I felt it, just as Tait can always feel a storm coming by his aching knees, or as Crow comes below long before the rain itself arrives. The body knows.

Anne is not unkind to me – indeed, she seeks me out as ever she did, and takes my arm just as willing when we walk together. Yet in the evenings, whether we gather at Jack's house or at an ale tent, the two of them draw closer and closer. I take early to my hammock, for I can no longer bear to watch.

The first time he takes her to bed, on the *Camila*, Anne comes to me the next day, plump with joy. 'My husband was never such a man,' she says, stretching her legs before her on the sand.

'Nor any of the men since?' The sharpness in my voice is ugly to me. Anne's other lovers have never troubled me before now.

She continues, oblivious, turning to me with a tremendous smile. 'He is a remarkable man, is he not? You must think so, to have followed him thus?'

'Yes,' I say. 'He is.'

She lies back in the sand. I feel that if I reached out to touch her hand, the heat of her would scorch me, for happiness comes off her like heat from a lantern.

———————————

Soon Anne is passing every night aboard the *Camila* with Jack, though she calls him always John. It is his true name but it sounds strange at first to hear him called so, when everyone else calls him Jack. 'John will get his privateering commission to hunt the Spaniards,' she says. 'You'll see. Rogers could not do better than to place his faith in John.' She makes of that more formal name a kind of intimacy, for it has become hers alone to say.

We all know that Jack is but the latest of Anne's lovers. Even the Reverend, not usually one for gossip, says to me, 'She has been not altogether so reserved in point of chastity,' which is a more gentle-manly way of putting it than the names they give her in the ale tents. But whatever her past she is mightily devoted to Rackham now, and he to her, and to see the two of them walk up the road from the harbour arm in arm, you would think they were prom-enading on some fine London street and not past the sagging tent of Mrs Hicks' brothel, and the *Felicitous* lying hull-up to be cleaned.

James Bonny is back in Nassau. We see him sometimes in town – more often in the company of women than men, for it seems he is not much liked by either the former pirates nor the governor's men. Having been a small-time pirate, he makes a small-time informant too. 'He is too shiftless even to make a great traitor,' says Anne, with a fetching scowl. 'He seeks advancement only when he can bother to rouse himself.' When he sees Jack and Anne, Bonny doesn't dare to challenge Jack, instead making a point of turning away, and studiously ignoring them. At other times he affects an expression that is supposed to appear heartsick, but merely looks sulky.

'For all the care he ever showed me, I am surprised he even noticed I was gone,' Anne says – though she is not a woman to go unnoticed.

———————————

We dare not retrieve our buried prizes for some weeks. When he judges it safe, Jack chooses a dark night, under only a blade of new moon. The walk is long, and longer when the night begrudges any light, and we dare not risk lanterns. I know the crow is above us but she is made for this dark and will not be seen. Assembled beneath the pines at the appointed hour, we dig in silence except for Tait's wheezing. When Fetherston's spade clashes against the first cask, a ripple of relief runs through the crew. Our prizes are still there. These are not great fortunes – scarce enough to live off for a few months, perhaps. But more precious by far than our share itself is the knowledge that our covenant has held. This is no small thing in Rogers' Nassau, ripe with informers and suspicion.

Each of us carries back to Nassau what is ours – for even under Rogers' new regime, there are still places in Nassau to trade in goods of dubious provenance. Rackham and the others sell a fair quantity of their gold watches and silk stockings to Thomas Stoner. Stoner is known for fencing stolen goods, but best known for having lost his balls – some say his whole tackle – when a powder barrel blew up aboard his ship some three years back. All the town knows the nature of Stoner's wounds and he himself makes a jest of it, proclaiming loudly that it is a great mercy to his wife, having already six children, and that if she gets with child again he will at least know the truth of it. 'Which is more than can be said for half the men in Nassau,' he says, 'raising other men's brats as their own.' Stoner drinks prodigiously and with good cheer, and answers to the name they have given him, 'Stoneless,' the wags of Nassau not being known for their originality. He buys from me a good quantity of gunpowder, and a pistol. I watch him as he counts out my coins, and wonder if we are alike, he and I, living somewhere between man and woman.

But nothing in me is missing, nor broken. Even now, when Jack and Anne's affection grinds at me like a stone in a boot, I know the truth of myself. Whatever I am, I am complete.

23

I hear the name Turnley before I meet him. Of all the men working for Rogers, few are more hated than Turnley. It's the particular disdain that people reserve for those whom they once counted as comrades – for Turnley was a pilot, and one of the brotherhood of pirates. I have never seen him in my previous visits to Nassau, for he must have been at sea. These days he is known in Nassau as 'Turncoat.' When first Rogers arrived he gave Turnley the task of making a great inventory of the ladings of every ship in the harbour, to identify which cargoes were come by lawfully. It was a task not guaranteed to endear Turnley to the men of Nassau, and he undertook it diligently, and is a great favourite of Rogers as a result.

We have careened the *Camila* and are caulking her poor sad hull, riddled with Teredo worms, when Turnley comes down, very smart in a blue coat in the style of Rogers himself.

'Turnley,' says Jack, with forced civility.

I had hoped never to see him again, but even after all these years, and his skin much lined by the Bahaman sun, I would know his narrow face any place: Belling, the servant boy from the *Resolve* and the *Expedition*, who used to steal from his mistresses, and tried to have me swing for it.

My throat tightens like a fist. I am accustomed to not being able to shake off the dead – I have become used to being followed by my ghosts. Yet finding Belling here is a new kind of haunting, more frightening by far. I left the navy these many years hence, in large part to be rid of him, and have since crossed whole oceans – and still I have not escaped him.

'I did not think to see you without your new master,' Tait says to Belling. 'Does Rogers let you out of his sight?'

Jack silences Tait with a glare. When I knew Belling he was a mere servant boy. It is clear that things have changed. Here in Nassau, where all things become possible under the harsh New Providence sun, Belling has not only found himself a new name – he has remade himself entirely. He may not be liked on the island, but it is clear that he is feared.

I have been staring, and now turn quickly back to my work, but it is too late, for Belling has marked me. I clutch the caulking mallet as I knock the oakum into the crack between boards. He comes to stand close, and speaks low so that the others may not hear.

'I heard there was a Mary Read come to Nassau. A rare thing, a woman sailor.'

Still I do not face him, but strike the oakum all the harder.

'So I had to see for myself whether it could be one and the same, for after you fled from the navy, we all heard of your marriage. Quite the sensation, that was. But I wasn't shocked. It was no surprise to me to hear that Mark Read was Mary Read, and a fine liar.'

I step back from the hull and turn to face him. 'I see I'm not the only one with a new name.'

He shrugs. 'Do you look to stir up trouble for me here, as you did back then?'

'Seems to me I could do nothing to worsen your reputation here.'

That silences him, but only for a moment.

'And you.' He rolls the word about his mouth like something sour. 'You – look at what you've made of yourself! A whole new woman – and a pirate too, by the company you keep.'

'These men have taken your governor's pardon,' I say. 'And I needed none.'

'Problem?' Jack asks.

I shake my head.

'We're old friends,' Belling tells him. 'From navy days.'

Jack comes to stand close by, for he knows me well enough to tell by my stance that Belling is no friend of mine.

'Nassau is a place of opportunities, now, for those wise enough to seek them,' Belling says to me. 'You'd do well to avoid men such as these.'

I pass the mallet from one hand to the other and back again, weighing its satisfying wooden heft.

'I knew better than to trust you when we were in the navy, Belling. I am not like to start now.'

I do what I can to avoid Belling — and I still think of him thus, for I cannot see him as Turnley. He does not seek me out, but when I do see him about the town he watches me very diligently. Sometimes he is in company with Rogers himself; sometimes with Anne's husband, James Bonny, talking close. Sometimes Belling is trailed by a blond child — apparently Belling has got himself a son, though the woman has not stayed.

'And who could blame her?' Rackham says.

As for Rogers, he is in the very air of Nassau. Even when he is not limping along the harbour front with Belling and his other men scuttling beside to take his orders, he is everywhere: in the rumours about him that men pass to one another; in the looming *Delicia*, his great thirty-gun man-of-war, at anchor in the harbour; in the soldiers from his company, who swagger about very proud — though not so bold that they dare to go alone, for this is Nassau still.

Each Sunday Rogers attends worship, and insists on his men attending too. They follow him in a kind of parade through the town to the service, which is held in the open, beneath the fort, the Spanish having twice burned down Nassau's only church years ago, and the pirates never having seen the need to replace it. I elect to go one Sunday — not to make a show of piety, but to watch this man who is so determined to shape Nassau after his own desires. He listens with great earnestness to the sermon, and prays without moving his lips, only squinting his brow very intent, head bowed to his hands.

In 1712, when Rogers made his name by his voyage around the world, he published an account of his journey. He has distributed copies throughout Nassau, much as he distributed his godly pamphlets, which I take as an indication of the regard in which he holds himself. Jack has got hold of a copy of the book, *A Cruising Voyage Around the World*, and brings it to the shack, where about the fire he reads aloud to us from Rogers' preface, in a voice very high and proper: 'I was not fond to appear in print; but my friends who had read my journal, prevailed with me at last to publish it.'

Jack reads a few more passages, but soon tires of the game – his fancies are often fleeting. I take the book and read every page. Thus it is through Rogers' printed words that I come to know him. Whether this is a trustworthy way of learning about a man, I am not sure.

I will say of Rogers that however dramatic the tales of his voyage, and however philosophical his musings may skew, there is always mention of heeling and tallowing his ships, and provisioning, and he most often ends each part with a note of the wind and weather, as a sailor's log does. 'Wind from the NNW to the NW by W moderate.' These observations are as a chorus in the song of his tale: 'Fair Weather. Very little Wind from WNW to N by E.' He is more like us pirates than we might think, which I do not account a comfort.

It is clear, too, that Rogers is neither weak nor cowardly. He writes of his own injuries as matter of fact as any other incident aboard his small fleet: 'We had only myself and another wounded; I being shot through the left cheek, the bullet striking away a great part of my upper jaw, and several teeth which dropt down on the deck where I fell.' The next day he continues very sanguine: 'In the night I felt something clog my throat, which I swallowed with much pain, and suppose it was a part of my jaw bone or the shot.' I have seen for myself the scar on his face, and now I learn, too, the origin of his crooked walk, for he writes of an attack on a Spanish galleon: 'I was unfortunately wounded by a splinter in the left foot, part of my heel bone being struck out and ankle cut above half through.'

He is not a man of wanton cruelty – at least, not according to his own account, where he praises himself handsomely for his civil treatment of prisoners. But he speaks casually of rewarding a *padre* with the prettiest of the slaves aboard, and putting them ashore together: 'The young Padre parted with us extremely pleas'd, and leering under his Hood upon his black Female Angel, we doubt not he will crack a Commandment with her, and wipe off the Sin with the Church's Indulgence.' Rogers' censure is all for the papists and their ways – his own involvement in this affair he counts as nothing. As for the slave girl, I fancy she would not consider his behaviour so civil.

Unused to being so long ashore, we have all of us fallen into a kind of idleness. I have claimed for my own a small lean-to at the back of Rackham's shack, and Rackham and Anne pass most nights together. Our work on the *Camila*'s hull is nearly completed, yet we remain stuck, for still Rogers has not granted Jack a privateering commission against the Spaniards.

Rogers approaches us at the harbour. Close behind him follows Belling, trailed by his son. Jack gives a cheery greeting, but Rogers speaks over him.

'Save yourself the trouble of speaking civil to me. You cannot imagine I will grant you a commission now.'

Jack takes a deep breath, and speaks with a strained joviality. 'Governor, you would not find a better privateering crew than mine,' he says.

Rogers looks over the *Camila*'s riddled hull. 'You may work at that husk of a hull all you like, if it keeps you occupied. But you shall have no commission from me.'

He does not stop to hear Jack's protestations – already he is walking away, his limp made worse in the soft and shifting sand.

Belling sidles closer to us. 'Haven't you heard? The *Accord* came in yesterday with news from England. It seems the Spaniards are backing the Jacobite uprising. Do you really think Rogers will trust a known Jacobite against the Spaniards?'

I exhale. 'Given that he seems to trust you, Belling, I could not swear to his judgment.'

Jack puts his hand on my arm. 'Mary speaks hastily,' he tells Belling. 'And the many Spanish ships I seized before the pardon will attest that I have no love for the Spaniards.'

'A word of advice,' Belling says. 'You won't win over a man such as Rogers with boasts from your years of piracy.' He stalks away.

'How can you let him lord it over you thus?' I say to Jack.

Jack smiles, and raps his knuckles against the *Camila*'s hull. 'I would suffer worse, for the chance of a commission, and some prizes that would buy us a new ship. Turnley has the governor's ear. Don't forget that.'

There is warning in his voice – we are ashore, but he is my captain still.

I watch Belling heading away from the harbour, trailed by his son, who can scarce keep up. The boy has the same sharp face as his father – a face born of hunger. And while I cannot find it in myself to pity Belling, I do pity his son.

It strikes me that of all those on Nassau, it is Belling who has known me longest. It is almost twenty years ago that we first met, aboard the *Resolve*. Our lives have unwittingly run parallel – from our poor beginnings, to the navy, and now to here. Along the way each of us has shed an old name. And each of us will cling fiercely to the new life we have built for ourselves. I fear that the two of us are more alike than I could wish.

Rogers will grant us no commission – but with the rumours of a Spanish attack growing ever louder, he will at least pay Rackham and his men for labour at Nassau's defences. It is dull work, cutting and hauling palisades, and for skilled seamen it is lowly work too. Patrick, the pilot, turns the pages of his waggoner at night with an affronted air, and most of Rackham's crew will work for Rogers only enough to divert any awkward questions about the real source of their money, for the sale of our buried prizes cannot be publicly known.

Rogers will not have women work at the defences, though if the Spaniards invade we shall not be spared. And so I must live on those of my old prizes that I can furtively sell to Stoner. I begin to fear that I may yet end up taking in washing – a more frightening prospect to me than being hanged for piracy. I used to brace the mainsail on the *Resolve*, that great expanse of canvas several tons in weight; am I now to be reduced to hanging linens instead?

To escape the dull and identical days I read Rogers' book again, for I have no other. Most often I return to his rescue of Selkirk, the man marooned on Juan Fernández. He was four years stranded alone on the island. When his clothes were nought but tatters he fashioned garments of goatskin, for he had learned to chase down the island's goats. He was much troubled by rats, until he befriended the island's cats by means of goat meat: 'by which many of them became so tame that they would lie about him in hundreds, and soon delivered him from the rats.' And thus, Rogers writes, Selkirk 'came at last to conquer all the inconveniences of his solitude and to be very easy.'

I trace his name in the dry dirt floor of my tiny lean-to: *Selkirk*. It is just a few letters shy of selkie, the creature neither seal nor human, which young Flett spoke of on the *Resolve* before he was killed.

Who was Selkirk, in those long years, goat-clad and passing his nights in a nest of cats? When he was rescued by Rogers and came aboard, he could barely speak: 'he had so much forgot his language for want of use, that we could scarce understand him, for he seemed to speak his words by halves.'

Was Selkirk a man, in those four years, or did such notions fall away along with his words, his old clothes and habits, even his name? Who would any of us be, marooned and entirely alone? And would such a thing be a losing of oneself, or a finding?

Tait and the Reverend fall into a quarrel. It is some ordinary scuffle over Tait's laziness in our work on the *Camila*'s hull, but I've noticed that such fights are more common and more vicious since we came to Nassau. The Reverend calls Tait a useless layabout and wastrel, and Tait curses the Reverend for a sodomite, very loud, the better for all to hear.

'That's rich, from you of all people,' I say, thinking of Tait and Patrick's shipboard arrangement. As for the Reverend, he has said nothing in his own defence.

'Buggery's not merely a shipboard ration for your friend the Reverend, though, is it,' says Tait. 'Ask him about it. Go on. Ask him about his man in the hills, and what they get up to together.'

I knew the Reverend had his own place inland – it had not occurred to me that there would be someone else in it. Nor had I thought to ask who was tending his cassavas and his plot for all his months at sea. I have been a poor friend to the Reverend, to take his loneliness for granted.

Still the Reverend says nothing, and Tait laughs and strides away. I do not understand how Tait and Patrick may swap frigs behind the water butts when at sea and yet scorn the Reverend for a sodomite because he takes his buggery ashore. Such are the stories men tell of themselves and they follow no logic that I can trace. And I begin to understand that there may be more reasons than drink why the Reverend is a reverend no longer.

Since he has Anne on his arm and in his bed, nothing dampens Jack's mood – not Rogers' stubborn refusal to grant him a privateering commission; not even news that the long-awaited Jacobite uprising has ended in blood and ignominy after a battle in June at Glen Shiel.

'If we must endure the Hanoverian king a little longer,' says Jack, 'at least I have a fitting queen by my side.' And Anne sits on his lap and the two of them laugh as he tips her back to kiss her.

Like many Catholics, Anne is a Jacobite – Jack seizes on this as yet more proof that he and Anne are in sympathy. He stands behind her with his arms wrapped tight about her and his head leant forward upon her shoulder, and calls her names, 'My darling, my puss, my Jacobite queen.'

We have many loose hours for such things, stuck as we are, awaiting a commission. On deck, Jack restlessly turns over one of Rogers' puritan pamphlets. 'Just listen to the name of his company,' he says, reading from the back: '*The Co-partners for Carrying on a Trade & Settling the Bahama Islands*. Can't you just smell the stench of balderdash coming off that?'

'It's a tautology,' Anne pipes up from by the rail, where she's chewing on a strip of salt beef. '*Co* and *partner*. They mean the same thing.' She'll jump at any chance to show off the learning she gleaned when she was supposed to be a law clerk.

She pulls a string of fat from between her teeth, slow and luxuriant as any fine lady untying a sash from her dress. Crow watching me as I watch her, and Jack does too.

At last the *Camila* is permitted to sail – though in a meagre way, ferrying supplies between Nassau and St Jago de la Vega, Jamaica, to supply Rogers' men and the new settlers he has enticed to Nassau. Thus I find myself a merchant once more, and for Rogers himself – but I care not why we sail, as long as I am once again at sea, and the crow on the wind above me.

Anne comes with us – it was never in doubt, for she and Jack will not be parted. She has done but little sailing: she made the crossing from Ireland to America as a child, and lately sailed with James Bonny from Charles Town to Nassau. Yet already she talks of the *Camila* like an old friend, caressing the rail and praising her nimbleness, though even with a freshly cleaned hull the *Camila* is no prize.

'Be more women than men aboard if you carry on this way,' Tait says to Jack.

'There'll be one man fewer if you keep idling,' Jack says. 'Mary does twice the work you do.'

Tait grunts. 'Causes trouble, is all I'm saying. Men arguing over women.'

'Mary can take care of herself. And Anne's mine.'

Jack says it very sure, as though that's the end of any debate. *Anne's mine.* I would never say that about Crow, let alone about Anne. I look at her, wearing a pair of Jack's old trousers hitched about her thighs the better to feel the sun as she lays abaft. I wonder if James Bonny, her husband, used to think of her as his.

Three days out of Nassau she straddles the bowsprit and edges forward. There's a decent swell and the *Camila* is pitching mightily but Anne sits there and laughs, her hands before her on the bowsprit not even clasped tight.

'Can you swim?' I call.

'I don't plan on falling.'

'Nobody plans on falling. Doesn't stop them doing it.'

Anne turns back to grin at me over her shoulder. 'The sea ain't got me yet.'

And Jack is watching her from the wheel and I think he might caution her to come back but he is grinning too, and I see for sure now that those two are far beyond caution.

24

When Patrick takes out his waggoner, Tait likes to brag over the charts, pointing out all the places he has been. If Patrick lets him, Tait will bore us all night with accounts of his travels, his finger on Patrick's charts tracing his lifetime's voyages. He claims to have rounded Cape L'Agulhas, and to have sailed the Red Sea too.

'He is all talk,' Anne says to me, quiet.

I smile. 'With his talk and his charts, he'd make the sea small enough to fold away and put in his sea-chest.'

I have known other men like this: men who measure themselves against the sea, which is a fool's game, for they will always find themselves wanting.

What I know: you could draw a chart as big as the sea itself, perfectly matched in scale, enough to paper the whole world over, and it would be useless by the time the tide goes out at Algeciras, shifting the sand channels and nudging the wrecks. The sea is new each day.

Anne, who has already forgot her husband and her father both, is the same. She remakes herself anew, and does not look back.

————

At anchor in St Jago de la Vega, Fetherston is at work stripping the running rigging and through mischance or carelessness he slips and falls right over the side, and before even a general cry has gone up, Anne has leapt into the water. She can no more swim than fly but she is in there nonetheless and doing her darndest to swim to him though she herself is floundering fast. Within a few moments Fetherston has surfaced and is swimming very strong for the *Camila* and Anne is in real trouble now, but by good fortune the cocket-boat is down already so the Reverend and Jack drop into it and in two smart strokes they are upon her, and the Reverend pulls her from the water.

Who amongst us can fail to smile as she wrings the water from her skirts, laughing fit to burst? Jack says, 'Anne, swear to me you'll not do such a thing again,' and she brushes him away and says to me, 'Well then, I had best learn to swim.'

Jack wraps her in a blanket and warms her feet in his hands, and Fetherston thanks her gravely though he can swim like an otter, and in truth it is a great deal of fuss about nothing, but Anne is not troubled by that, being partial to a great deal of fuss. And afterward no man in the crew will hear a word against her and indeed there are several brawls in Nassau when strangers talk too free and call her *slut* or *whore*.

The only one aboard the *Camila* who does not take to Anne is the crow, who watches her very intently, keeping always at a distance.

'What does that damned bird want from me?' she asks, seeing Crow staring from the rigging.

A crow can want nothing from people. It's the other way around, I'm learning. Jack thinks Crow a noble symbol of our company, and back when we were pirating and she chose to land on the bowsprit, he used to say, 'There, see – that will set them quaking.' Tait wants to see in Crow a rogue and a plaything, so he throws food for her, and when she deigns to snatch at it he says, 'See, I've set to dancing now.' The Reverend wants her to confide in, and I have seen him lean against the rail for an hour at a time, speaking low and serious of theology and other grave matters. He has learned that a crow will swallow secrets as surely as the sea does.

———————————

Anne makes herself useful aboard, and though Fetherston is still the ship's master, she now serves in the office of scribe or log-keeper. Her years of pretending to be her father's law clerk have left her with a neat hand and a prodigious memory.

She is so much younger than me, but in these weeks aboard the *Camila*, the sea's tannery has been at work on her face, so already she has the browned skin of a sailor and there are deep creases that form at the corner of her eyes when she smiles, which she does a great deal.

The Reverend being an Anglican and Anne being Catholic, I think at first they might be at odds, now we are all living in close quarters aboard the *Camila*. But Anne and the Reverend deal very well together for each has made their own terms with God, both of them being lax as regards certain of the commandments, and in earnest regarding others. So the Reverend drinks and steals, but is diligent in keeping the Sabbath. Anne, who is not a great one for her marriage vows, will tolerate nothing of blasphemy and will reel off a prayer at the sighting of an albatross, or a good catch of barracoutha in the nets. 'Look,' she says, lifting one of the dead fish in both hands, and raising its huge, ghastly face close to her own. 'Mary, look at his face. Have you ever seen anything uglier? Anything more magnificent?'

In Charles Town we collect a cargo of rice. Tait, not usually one for diligence, fusses over the cargo, for he's heard the old story of the ship sunk by a load of rice that went damp and would not stop swelling, tearing the hull apart. Being Tait, he swears blind that a friend of his, indeed a cousin, drowned in that very ship.

'By nightfall it'll be his own father who was drowned,' the Reverend says to me.

'Aye,' I say. 'And by tomorrow, Tait'll swear he was on that ship himself.'

When Tait once again cautions us about how to arrange the sacks of rice in the hold, I roll my eyes to Anne. 'The rice thing is just a story to frighten people who've spent no time at sea.'

'And less time still in the kitchen.' She heaves another sack atop a barrel. 'It's rice, not gunpowder.'

But while Anne and I laugh together, I don't begrudge Tait the story. Corner told me once of a whale that was beached at Nantucket and rotted, the bloat building up within its great belly until one day it exploded, raining whale parts and stench along half a mile of beach. It's a fine story, true or otherwise. And so I won't tell Tait his rice story is most likely a nonsense, any more than I would tell Anne what I think of her popery. It is a serious thing, to take a person's stories from them – for what remains, then?

———————

Month after month has dulled the crew's initial relief at the pardon, and the men grow restless. This merchant work for Rogers pays little, and we've long since exhausted our buried prizes. Rogers will pay no wage to a woman for sailing work, but Jack has paid me a portion of his own wages, on condition I tell nothing to the others, 'For it will only set Tait to bellyaching, and God knows we need no more of that.'

I see how it galls Jack to hear of lesser captains, with lesser crews, profiting handsomely from privateering, while we haul cargoes from Charles Town to Nassau under Rogers' orders. Tait has brought aboard two hens in a coop and whatever glamour there is in sea work is not to be found in these days aboard the *Camila*, with her leaky hull and the smell of chicken shit very strong below deck. Without the promise of engagements or prizes, each day is the same.

Finally Jack gathers us all on deck.

'What if we keep working for Rogers, but pick up the odd prize as we go? Just in a small way.'

'The courts make no such distinction,' I say. 'They will hang us all the same.'

'So we won't be caught,' he says. 'We'll target none but enemy ships, and take only prizes small enough to be concealed, and quick to sell.'

At the mention of selling, the men's attention sharpens. The lack of ready money has worn us all down. I warrant that poverty has made more pirates than bravery.

'Rogers will be watching us,' says Corner.

'Belling too,' I say. 'Or Turnley, as he calls himself now.'

'Even Rogers can't watch us from Nassau when we are at sea,' says Jack, quick. 'Let alone Turnley.'

Still the men are silent.

'I ask you to take no risk I don't take myself,' says Jack.

'It'll be no comfort to me to hang beside you,' says the Reverend.

'Are you a coward, then?' says Tait. He has shown no eagerness for Jack's proposal, but will never miss a chance to taunt the Reverend.

'Nobody need hang,' says Jack. 'Rogers thinks us under his thumb, but he's given us the perfect cover. We sail under his orders. Who's to know if we pick up a prize as we sail? And now we're at war, enemy ships can hardly go crying to Rogers or the other governors.' He is bright-eyed now, and louder.

'I sail with you,' Anne says, stepping forward to place a hand on his shoulder. 'Pirating or not.'

The crew shifts and mutters. Perhaps they're persuaded by Jack's assurances; perhaps they're ashamed to be seen more cowardly than a woman. Perhaps it is nothing but common greed, after all.

'Aye,' says Corner. 'I'll come.'

One by one the others speak too. 'Aye. Aye. Aye.' The voices are low but they join together to make a fair rumble. And I speak too: 'Aye.' For as soon as Anne was decided, there was no question.

Of all of us, it is Anne who takes to our return to pirating with the most naked enthusiasm. James Bonny wooed her by telling her he was a pirate, then proved himself a poor pirate and a poor husband. Now she sees a chance to make good that disappointment, and she is all enterprise and excitement. We seize a fishing ketch on the Grand Bahama Bank, and she is second aboard, and though there is little resistance from the fishermen, I watch Anne arrange herself near the prow to her best advantage, one foot up on the low rail and pistol propped on her knee and aimed at their captain. If she had not been a pirate she would have done well on the stage. I credit it to the ceremony and drama of the papists, for they do love a procession and the waving of a smoking censer and the ringing of bells.

From that very first meagre prize, Anne understands the trick of piracy: to raise the black flag sudden and give a show of arms to force a surrender with fear, and not with fighting unless it cannot be helped. First Anne takes the flag itself and embroiders on the skull a mouth with huge teeth, fearsome sharp. Then she comes to Jack with a new notion.

She stuffs one of the Reverend's threadbare shirts with bundled net and rags and lashes it to the foremast, and below it a pair of my old trousers too, likewise stuffed. For a head, she winds a ball of tarred rope and jams a hat on it. The head is too heavy to stay upright up but perhaps she meant it thus, for the way it hangs gives the whole figure the uncanny feel of a snapped neck.

Then she kills one of Tait's chickens, and Tait complains most bitterly for he is a great one for eating eggs. But Anne assures him the prizes we seize will buy him all the chickens he could want, and promises him the carcass besides and asks Howell to cook it for him just as he pleases.

Anne bleeds the chicken over a pail. How tender and how merciless those slender fingers, which do not flinch from slicing the neck clean through, and holding the bird steady while its wings and legs are flailing still and the blood steaming in the air.

She daubs the blood very thick all about the neck and chest of the figure she has made, and the Reverend mutters crossly for he had thought to have the shirt back, but Anne, having once begun a thing, never stops at half measures. The shirt being white the effect is very shocking, and blood pools on the deck below. And though we know it is all artifice, the smell alone is enough to transform that bundle of tarred rope and old clothes into something alarming – indeed all that morning I do not like to turn my back to it. In the awful weight of the lolling head, and its slumped posture against the mast, the figure reminds me of nothing so much as those statues of Christ on the cross that the Catholics hold so dear, all rib bones and wounds.

Tait alone seems unconcerned by the figure. We bear south-east in search of prey and he spends the whole day chewing chicken bones as he works, his fingers slick with chicken grease, and his beard too, for he never shaves save when ashore and you can always tell how long he's been from at sea by the length of his coarse red beard.

Up the mast Corner spies a small Spanish cutter, and we give chase. The Spaniards have the weather gage of us but with Patrick at the helm we are able to close with her. We are within firing range but Jack says they will not be fool enough for we have twice the guns and twice the sail. When we come aside them under our black flag, they are standing by their guns but their eyes are fixed on the figure tied at our mast, and on Anne, astern, who has been sure not to wash her hands of the blood. Her hands, red to the wrist, and the silent figure, do more persuad-ing than our guns, which are not needed, for their captain calls something and the men surrender meek as you like, and we board them nice and easy and score for our efforts a good cargo of damask and three butts of Madeira.

By the next day the chicken blood has hardened to a black crust. We are close enough to shore that the flies come for it, until the figure wears a shimmering beard of flies. Jack says Anne's ruse was a pretty trick and has served us well, but even he will not suffer the stink any longer and tosses the whole thing overboard, where it floats face down like a drowned man.

Anne has scrubbed her hands clean but along with the stuffed figure they have done their work. They have made a declaration, to ourselves as well as to our prey: that we are sworn to blood; that we sail under a blood flag.

25

You may think it a kind of torture for me to see Anne and Jack always together, and to hear them at it at night. It may be hard to credit that this time is a joyful one, for me as well as them. Remember that my life has not been such that I expect to receive what I desire – and I have become good at finding happiness where I may. We are again at sea, again pirating. If I have Anne's friendship, and nothing more, that is no small thing, for her friendship is as generous as every other part of her. Neither do I scorn Jack's friendship. Since Marston's death, and Dan's, I had not thought to find such companionship again – yet there is a vividness in Jack, and a thrill in the way he speaks of the sea, that has begun to feel very much like a home.

The crew, too, is buoyant with being back to hunting. Howell, the cook, takes our jibes about his cooking in good heart, and even the Reverend and Tait have largely stopped carping at one another. From his lookout post at the mast, Corner sings his whaling songs, and Crow hovers above us, riding the same winds that fill our sails.

And Anne? She is never jealous of my place amongst the crew. Instead she delights in it, and asks me to tell her again about my time in the navy, and about all our previous engagements aboard the *Camila*. 'You're a new Gráinne Mhaol,' she says. She tells me stories of the Irish pirate queen who routed the English two hundred years ago, and Jack sings us a ballad of her life. In his song she is named Grace O'Malley – but Anne, raised in Ireland, always calls her by her Irish name, and it sounds better thus.

Gráinne Mhaol, Anne tells me, commanded twenty galleys or more. None amongst her pirates were braver than the pirate queen herself, who birthed a child aboard one of her ships, and when the very next day they came under attack from Corsairs, rose from her birthing bed and fought fierce as ever and led her men to victory.

'Jesus,' Jack says, 'And you thought the two of you were tough.'

Anne slaps his arm, for she will not countenance blasphemy even from him. Myself, I am not so shocked to think a woman could fight, still bleeding, fresh from pushing out a babe. There are those who mistake being a mother for being soft. It's not a mistake I could ever make, raised as I was by Ma.

'Mary would take on the Corsairs, and others too, for she's our own pirate queen,' says Anne, and places on my head a little loop of cord, for the Reverend has been teaching Anne her knots and she has fashioned it into a circlet, a rough crown.

I am no queen, nor have ever wished to be. But with Anne beside me, telling me her tales of Gráinne Mhaol, I feel for the first time a lineage, spreading out behind us like a wake.

Jack fences our prizes to his man at St Jago, and when we return to Nassau harbour and Belling is ferreting over the ship to make his inventory for Rogers, we have nothing aboard but what is on the manifest – not even the black flag, which Anne has tucked beneath her skirt for safekeeping, our coins tied inside it.

James Bonny is still in Nassau, and I suspect him of being the source of most of the rumours about Anne that continue to swirl about the town. They say that back in Charles Town, when she was still Anne Fulford, she tormented her wealthy father with her wild ways. They say she stabbed a maid, and thrashed a suitor who tried to take liberties with her.

If Anne hears the whispers – *slut, whore* – she simply pushes her shoulders back and holds her head all the higher, or else grabs Jack by the neck and kisses him then and there, which is for Anne a kind of hoisting of the flag.

Her intelligence is not the kind for discoursing about philosophy, or for trading witticisms. Jack fancies himself a philosopher – he and the Reverend can pass hours talking of politics, theology, and sin. But Anne is not interested in ideas, only in things she can touch. Jack tries to recite some pretty verse to her, for he is full of words, only some of them his own. He bestows words like he is bestowing prizes.

'Don't give me poems,' she says, taking his face in her hands. 'Give me gold.'

She is smart – smart enough to get this far, through all the many strangenesses of her childhood and her early life. She has a prodigious memory, and can recite whole passages from the legal papers she used to handle for her father. But mainly her intelligence takes this form: she puts her shoulder to the world and pushes. That is her cleverness, or her courage: nothing but a kind of doggedness, and an almighty anger too, when she fancies herself wronged. She has not hesitated to walk away from a father, a husband. Nothing is easier to cut than a rope pulled taut, and Anne is pulled very taut indeed. It is a skill I have not yet learned from her, this cutting loose and walking away. If I had, perhaps I would not be here, unable to stop watching her and Jack.

When James Bonny sees us about Nassau he makes his hang-dog face, but I do not account him a threat. It is not he who troubles me, but Belling. What course his life has taken to lead him from the navy to the pirate republic, I do not know. But I know that he watches me. Governor Rogers is no friend to us and observes us closely, but not as close as Belling. When the two of them pass us by, Belling at Rogers' heels, it is Belling who turns to stare after me, watching me until I am out of sight.

In an ale tent we fall to talking with Phipps, a pardoned pirate whom Jack has known of old.

'Heard a story, when last I was in St Jago.' Phipps smiles. 'A sloop very much like yours has been doing a spot of pirating.

Along the same sea-roads that you yourself have lately been frequenting.'

'Did you indeed?' says Jack. 'It's funny how these stories spread. I lately heard a story too.' He leans back, tipping his chair. ''Twas a story of a man who cried rope on two fellow sailors. Only the brotherhood of Nassau would not stand for such squealing, and the snitch was hanged long before the pirates ever were. Strung up from a tree above Toxes Point, the coins of his reward heavy in his pocket, to make him hang all the faster.' He takes a slow sip of his beer. 'Perhaps you've heard that story?'

Phipps swallows, shaking his head.

'Would you care to?' asks Jack. 'For it's a story I'm happy to tell you again, if needs be.'

'No need,' says Phipps, spilling what remains of his beer in his haste to stand. 'Only wanted to give you a word of warning, friendly-wise.'

'Then consider me grateful,' Jack says, beaming. 'Most grateful. For we're all of us in need of friends, in these dangerous times, wouldn't you say?'

'Is it true?' Anne asks him, when Phipps has fled the tent. 'About the man hanged for snitching?'

I answer. 'True or not, what does it matter? What matters is that Phipps believes it.'

Jack smiles at me. Of all that I have learned from Jack Rackham, the most useful is what he has taught me about the value of stories.

———————

On the next crossing to Charles Town, Anne and I are on the long watch when I espy a light in the dark.

'How close?' she asks.

'Here,' I say. 'Lower your head a second.'

I place the fingers of one hand on the back of her head and push lightly. 'Do you see it?' I lower my own head at the same time.

'No. It's gone.'

'Exactly. That means it's a long way from us, for now.' If you lower your head and the light disappears, it's all the way at the horizon. I learned it in the navy – a neat trick to make the dark give up its secrets.

I raise my head and the light reappears. She raises her head in time with mine, but I leave my fingers where they are.

———————

In Charles Town in September, all the talk is of the recent trial in Boston of the pirate Furlow, captured and hanged along with all his company. Jack brings aboard a gazette with an account of the trial, listing crimes committed 'piratically and against the Peace of his said Majesty his Crown and Dignity.'

Jack is usually hungry for news, but today he presses his lips together tight, and folds the gazette in half, and in half again, very precise and deliberate. The noose means something different to him now, for Anne is growing fat in the belly and reckons herself four months gone. She has refused to countenance the idea of remaining in Nassau without us, 'with my husband mooning about, and Rogers looking down his puritan nose at me.' Jack determines to put her ashore with friends of his in Cuba. I am surprised that she agrees to it, but since she is with child, she is both fiercer and more languorous. She can spend three hours on deck doing nothing but laying back with hands on her belly – but when there is a sail spotted she is the first to the guns, the loudest voice amongst our cries as we draw within halloo of them.

Together, we let out her skirts, to make room for her stomach. As we stitch, she asks me to tell her again about my own time in the birthing bed, though I have told her that it was not a birth but a death, my baby too small and my body caught unawares. 'Tell me anyway,' she says, and takes my hand and presses it to her belly as if to a wound. I have by this time stood beside her at six or more engagements, yet this is the first time I have seen her afraid. So when Jack brings to her his notion of refuge in Cuba, and paints her a pretty picture of Trinidado, which to hear him tell it to Anne you would think is built principally of Catholic churches and mangoes, she brightens and says, 'Yes, yes that is just the place for me. It will serve very nicely.' Henceforth whenever Jack grows maudlin at the thought of being without her, she is brisk and cheerful, and will not be distracted from the vigil of her hands on her belly. The child is his, but has little to do with him now, and she is beguiled by her own transforming. She paces the deck, staring down at her growing belly, a woman who has swallowed the moon.

In January, when she is huge with child, we make for Cuba. We sail warily, for this is Spanish territory, but Jack insists Anne will be safe with his friends. The bay to which he directs us is the same one where we left him those many months ago – but if Anne knows that she will be staying with Jack's lover, she is unconcerned, for nobody could doubt Jack's devotion to her. Ever since Anne became preoccupied with her belly, his attentions have only become more doting.

'If there were room on deck, he'd leave her presence walking backwards, like a courtier,' the Reverend says to me, watching Jack's solicitous arranging of cushions beneath Anne's feet, which in these last few weeks have swollen, the top of each foot fattened like dough left to rise.

Jack takes her ashore, and is four days gone. It is an uneasy wait and when he returns, resolute and tired, we are all of us glad to be gone from Spanish waters. The ship without Anne is a duller place, and Jack too a different captain: smaller, and in some way diminished.

Time becomes burdensome during the months of Anne's absence – and Rogers has the whole of Nassau scurrying with preparations for the long promised Spanish invasion, which comes to nothing. And all of a sudden this war is done with – in Europe men have sat about a table and traded islands like so many pieces of eight, and signed a treaty, and the real-life battles fought and not fought count for nothing against such manoeuvrings.

For once, Jack cares nothing for such details – without the threat of the Spanish we are again at liberty to sail, thus we are straight to Cuba, with Jack standing at the prow as though his leaning thus will make us faster. Tait mutters to me, 'Patrick may as well stay in his hammock, for we've no need of a pilot. I swear we could navigate by Jack's straining cock.'

We wait three days offshore and they return: Anne and Jack but not the baby, who has been left with a wet nurse. 'And anyway,' Anne says, when she has done with embracing me, and all the crew besides, 'we cannot raise a baby aboard a ship, nor is the pirate life one for children.' I do not know that our life can fairly be described as a pirate life, for we are still merchants in Rogers' employ, and since the war's end our pirating, such as it is, must be done with more care than ever. But for Anne, pirate is no longer a thing she does, but a thing she is.

Jack is bright with pride. 'A fine, fat son,' he says. 'A jolly lad, with his mother's eyes.' Jack kisses Anne as if to make up for all that they have missed these last weeks; she kisses him back just as urgent.

When we've weighed anchor, I ask Anne: 'The woman you stayed with – she's Jack's woman?'

'No,' she says at once. 'Not anymore. I mean, she has been his woman, but it's not like that now.'

'And she was happy, taking in his new lover?'

Anne waves her hands impatiently. 'I told you – it's not like that.'

'So tell me what it's like.'

She tries. As we sail for Nassau, she tells me about going ashore, that first day, and the long ride out of town on a hired mule. How they came to the Creole woman's house, so deep in jungle that the sun didn't hit it until near noon. How children stood watching in the doorway, the tallest chewing a long strand of hair pulled halfway across her face. How the woman came out and laughed to see Jack there.

'And you'll never guess her name: Camila,' Anne whispers to me. 'Marie Camila.' She says it the way the Creoles say it: long in the 'a', and with a twist to the 'l'. I search her face for anger or jealousy, now she knows that we sail aboard a ship named after Jack's earlier lover. But she leans her head back and says it again, 'Camila,' and gives a hearty laugh.

Jack left Anne there, with the promise that Camila would care for her until the babe came.

Whenever Camila moved about the house, Anne watched her. She watched her for days, until she realised that although she was still watching Camila, she wasn't afraid of the woman anymore. She was watching her because she liked to.

Some nights a man came to the house, and slept in Camila's room. Most times he was gone before dawn, and Camila never said anything about him, though on those mornings she moved slow and heavy as a snake. Of Camila's children, a girl and two young boy twins, Anne gave up the game of guessing which, if any, might be Jack's. She asked Camila once, and Camila said, 'Everything in this house has to belong to Jack?' She laughed, leaning forward so her breasts almost fell out of her shift, and cupped them in her hands. 'These? Do these belong to Jack?' She stopped laughing 'And you?' She looked at Anne. 'Do you?'

Anne had no answer. In Nassau people used to speak of the republic of pirates. Those weeks with Camila, Anne says, waiting for the babe to come, she got to thinking about a republic of women.

Back on the ship now, Anne is still leaking milk for the baby she left behind. A few times each day great wet circles grow on the front of her shirt, and she keeps working and never says a thing except to laugh, and she has about her the unapologetic smell of milk, sweet-sour. But it is the only mark of the baby on her – for she gives no sign of missing him.

'A child is a very pressing thing,' she confides. 'It wants everything, you see – it has no notion of enough.' And I think such a child is very like Anne, which may be why she is not better suited to mothering. I cannot but suspect that she liked her baby best when it was part of her.

I ask her about the birth itself.

Camila put water to her lips in between the pains, and had the good sense to stay quiet. A woman from Trinidado town was sent for, and she and Camila stayed with Anne all the time, though even from my own sorry labour I know that birth is something a woman always does alone, no matter how crowded the room. It's a matter between a woman and her body.

When the time came for Anne to push, Camila gave her an old piece of rope to bite down on and said, 'Now. Push now.'

The baby boy came out covered in white grease, Anne says, like the fat on the underside of an uncured hide. He took the nipple right away, and Camila made Anne drink rum while the woman from Trinidado stitched her up where she was torn.

'It is the strangest thing,' Anne says. 'For when the baby comes, it's not like meeting anyone new. It's not a surprise. You look at that little crumpled face and you recognise it like an old friend. You say: *There you are.*'

From the start, the baby looked bonny and like to live. 'He did not need me,' Anne assures me. 'Indeed he will do much better with the wet nurse, for she has patience I do not, and four fat children of her own to vouch for her milk.'

She tells me Cuba is an island of rivers – 'five hundred of them, they say.'

I think about the impatience of rivers. Anne loved Cuba, but the rivers taught her how to leave it, and how to leave her baby too. A river is a river because it's always leaving. The sea doesn't do that – the sea goes in and out like breath. But rivers just go.

April, and we are again in Nassau. Since Anne's return, Jack has been very lavish with her favourite sweetmeats and fineries. Our modest prizes do not make us rich, but he does not begrudge her what he has. And she takes such unabashed glee in any little fancies that when he gives her the merest riband to tie about her hair, the way she beams and holds her head just so, you would think it is a jewelled crown.

She has Jack for finery. Instead, I give her the only gift that I can: I teach her to swim.

I take her in the late afternoon beyond Toxes Point and amongst the shelter of the stunted trees that grow in the dunes. We take off our shifts because in the water they will only become shrouds. I fold mine into a neat square; Anne tosses hers to the ground, a long white sea-jelly stranded on the sand.

The water beneath our feet is warm but there is an unseasonable cold northerly that makes my nipples clench. Anne's belly is soft where the baby grew.

We wade in together until the water reaches my navel. Anne gives a small sigh as the sea relieves her of her body's weight. She takes a step further and leans back so that the loose tendrils of her hair fan out around her head. Beside her, I lean back too, our necks arched and staring at the immoderate blue of the sky.

I take her hands and wade slowly backwards, towing her, and showing her how to trail her legs and to kick them. How to trust her body to do what it must, for the body will rise if you let it. I teach her how to keep afloat, arms sweeping forwards and backwards. She copies me, her hands almost meeting before her, like hands in prayer, and then pushing the water in a sweep to her sides. That great expansive movement, as if ushering something in.

The process of dressing is more intimate than our undressing earlier. Fabric clings to our damp flesh. I help her pull her shift down over her head and she looks at me all the while.

I am first to kiss her. You might think me the more diffident of the two, but the pirate in me is done with diffidence. I have learned to take.

The men are at Jack's house tonight, so Anne and I go to the ship – not because we are ashamed of what we will do, but because some things are too important to be done on land.

In the cabin we are too busy to trim the lantern wick so the light flares for a while and then shrinks and goes out. I am glad of the total dark because it means that what I learn of her body I learn by hand, slowly, which is a different kind of attention.

I wonder what name Anne will call me now, a new name for this new thing. In the dark, with all our pasts and stories set aside, she might speak my true name – it might rise from her mouth like something surfacing in water. I listen for my name to emerge. I wait, my ear close to her mouth, and all that long night my name is *Yes*.

26

The crew comes aboard in the morning – we are to sail tomorrow and there is work to be done.

Jack does not need to ask us where nor how we passed the night, for below deck has the good salt smell of sex. And Anne wears her body very heavy today, like a woman caught midway through yawning.

'And I see you two have found ways to divert yourselves,' Jack says.

There is no question of hiding it from him. Jack is not an easy man to deceive – and Anne is not one for hiding. Even while Jack stands there, she lets a single finger trail, very deliberate, along the back of my neck. And, anyway, on a small ship such as the *Camila*, where Tait's chicken coop is crammed atop the water barrels, and a man may not get up for a piss in the night without waking all of us, there is no room for secrets.

'If I care for Mary, it does not follow that I care less for you,' says Anne, and indeed she kisses him then very fierce.

'I had fancied the two of you were growing fonder of one another.'

'*Fond*,' says Anne, and I am glad to hear her speak so scornfully. 'Fond' is such is a soft word for a thing that is not soft. A small word, for a thing that is not small.

'Call it what you will,' he says, and laughs. 'Are you only to take your pleasure with Mary, now?'

'No,' says Anne. 'At least, not only. I take my pleasure where I may.'

'I am not a man opposed to pleasure,' says Jack.

It is perhaps his own great confidence that renders him unconcerned by us. Less than unconcerned, for he is proud: he moves about the deck with a new swagger.

Tait may joke about 'Jack's growing harem' but there is never any question of such a thing. I desire Jack no more than he me, and what each of us has with Anne is our own. Tait sidles up to me and says, 'I never figured you for a beard-splitter,' and pats me on the back hard enough to spill my drink. He seems relieved, as though what has passed between me and Anne is the answer to a question I had not known was troubling him: the question of what I am. If the question has not been answered quite to his satisfaction, it has at least been answered. 'Mind you,' Tait says, 'Jack is more generous with his woman than I would be.'

Jack says, 'If you ever find a woman to tolerate you, then the question might arise, but for now it does not,' and even Tait joins the general laughter.

Henceforth, some nights she comes to me; some nights to Rackham. When she comes to my makeshift cabin she walks towards me like a bride, barefoot and serious.

She walks to Jack the same way.

'I'm generous enough to share,' he says to me a few days later, when the two of us are turning hogsheads in the hold to check for damp. 'It's good for her to have time with another girl. You're like a sister to her. Like a mother.'

I do not let my anger surface – I am learning that women's love lends itself to laughter and to those soft words: sister, mother, girl. These words have nothing to do with that angry need in us, me working her over until my fingers are slick with her and my hand cramps. The weight of her as she makes her way up my body, her chin shiny and a long string of fluid stretching from my mouth to hers and it might be spit or something else, and it might be hers or mine.

Jack continues. 'It hasn't been easy for her, you know, to give up the child. Such things change a woman.'

I stay silent, thinking only that Anne has barely mentioned the baby. Let Jack believe she comes to me in grief and not in desire.

Let him think that what I do with her does not count – for I admit I think the same of him. When she comes to me smelling of him, the cummy sourness deep inside her, I kiss her all the harder that she may go back to him with me beneath her finger-nails. Once she gets a hair of mine stuck between her teeth – one of the dark curls of my bush – and though she laughs and grimaces and tries to yank it free, I would have it stay there, send her back to him thus, my hair in his mouth when he kisses her.

This is the flag I would sail under: the *Camila* its own republic, sailed off the shores of either this or that, into some wide undiscovered sea.

Still Anne comes. Still she goes.

We sail again for Charles Town, under Rogers' orders, but with Corner up the mast always alert to any small craft we may target.

There are people who have never loved aboard a ship – I pity them, for they know nothing of how a hammock with two in it will force you down atop one another, jostling for the lowest point. They can never understand the way a lantern throws light about the tiny space of a cabin, or how in high winds you move together with the swell even when you do not move at all. If you have neither loved nor fucked aboard a ship, you cannot know what it is between Anne and me, how on cool nights we enter my cabin like entering a warm mouth.

Anne is greedy for everything. She is hungry for saltfish and for preserved plums; for my body, and the pleasures of her own. Hungry for Jack too, grabbing him as he passes and kissing him in a way that I recognise, for it's how she kisses me.

Who can begrudge her, for she shares as well. She wants everything, but she will hold out to me a guinep, already bitten, and say through juice-stickied lips, 'Mary, you'd better taste this.' I take whatever she offers me.

We have half a day ashore in St Jago de la Vega and while the men seek a tavern Anne and I walk the line between water and land. From a boy on the beach she buys a nest with eight tiny eggs, speckled the palest green of clear sea over rocks. I would have paid the same for the nest alone, which is a small miracle, woven as neat as any corn dolly. They are wailing bird eggs, the boy tells Anne. We have nothing to cook them with but Anne has a flint, so she sets the eggs aside in the sand, and lights the nest itself, which sparks with the burnt hair smell of feathers.

'I didn't want to burn it,' I say into the smoke.

'Why not?'

I shrug. 'It was beautiful.'

She waves a hand at the nest of fire, sparking and pulsing. 'Is it not beautiful now?'

Seafoam lies like lace at the edge of the water. We place the eggs atop the ash, and their shells char to black but do not crack. They're still hot when we pick them up to peel them. We eat them hasty and hungry, and when a trail of yolk runs down my wrist, she licks it clean.

These long salt days at sail. What we have built is neither the republic of pirates, nor the republic of women that Anne imagined when she was in Cuba with Camila. This is something different, something newer and more strange than anything history shall record of Nassau and its pirates. This is our own republic, the republic of salt. Salt on the wind, and on my cutlass blade. The white tide-mark of salt on Jack's bright clothes when they have dried in the sun; the white crust of salt on Anne's eyelashes after we swim. Sea salt, saltmeat, the salt on Anne's flesh when I take her in my mouth. Saltblood. It is the sixth year of the reign of King George. These are the first days of the first republic of salt. We are away.

'Your crow's still watching me,' Anne says. We are in my tiny lean-to room at the back of Jack's Nassau shack, and Crow has settled on the sill.

'No,' I say. 'She's watching me.'

'Same thing, when we're like this,' Anne says. She pulls the blanket higher, to cover her breast.

I pull it down again, for to cover any part of Anne is a shameful waste. Crow's gaze does not move.

'Why do you need to go through life with that thing watching you?'

Who else is going to watch me? I want to say. *Who? Is my life not also worth the witnessing?*

———————

Some weeks after I first took Anne to bed, Jack says to me, 'She will not be made to choose, you know.' He gives a small laugh. Was his indulgence of me and Anne just the indulgence of what he thought was a passing fancy? 'I cannot say that I understand this new thing between the two of you.' He looks at me, very long and searchingly. 'Do you understand her, Mary?'

'Do you?' I ask him.

This is what Jack has never learned: understanding has nothing to do with it. Not with truth – nor love neither. A ship does not know how it floats but it trusts the water nonetheless. There's a reason those kneeling in church close their eyes as they take the Eucharist bread – the same reason you close your eyes to kiss. All communion is blind.

When Jack and Anne first came together I was jealous. Yet now that I myself am also with her, that jealousy has gone, wind passing over water. I cannot resent Jack, for I know Anne would not come to me without having him too. Her notion of herself as a woman, as a papist, demands it: she must take a man for a lover, even though she wants me also. Being with Jack gives her permission to be with me. It is all knotted together – the three of us a matted nest of cordage that cannot be unpicked. Wanting Anne to myself would be like wanting to sail a square-rigged ship upwind. Would mean wanting someone who wasn't Anne at all. And the one thing I know beyond any doubting is that I want her.

The more you give, the more she takes. And my God, the skin on her. The way she is lit up, like the sea-jelly I saw from the *Walcheren*, aglow like a lantern to show the bulge of its inner workings.

Let Jack think what he will. I care not, for I am learning to trust my own pleasure – for pleasure is its own truth, and does not lie.

———————————

I likewise find pleasures elsewhere. In Charles Town Jack takes aboard a young man of good family. He is not long past twenty, and his name is Gladstone, and his father puts it to Jack that his son wishes to be a sailor. The son himself gives no sign of this, being the sort to drift with the currents. He has the easy manner of a man who has thus far found life a good game, bolstered by his father's money and his own good looks. But his father is out of patience with his aimless youngest son – and Gladstone comes aboard cheerful enough.

The rest of the crew is wary of him at first. We dare not refuse him, for his father is an old friend of Rogers and has sought a Nassau vessel for that reason. And we must curtail for a while our taking of prizes – though I suspect young Gladstone, vague and cheerful, would make a poor informant. I will allow that he is not work-shy – and Jack takes to him quickly, for Jack fancies himself a gentleman and enjoys Gladstone's fine ways, which dredge up in Jack his own finest manners, to match.

When Gladstone confides to me that he wishes above all to be an artist, I think it unpromising, for a ship needs muscles and not art. But Gladstone persuades me to his way of thinking, for he does magic with lines. With just a damp finger on a dry deck, or a charcoal stub on the back of one of Jack's old *Boston Gazettes*, he can conjure anything. He turns his stare onto Crow. One sweep catches the precise hunch of her back. Another, the beak, its cutlass curve. Two short lines, the hooked claws. He takes Crow down to but a handful of marks, yet in his sketches she is more herself than in her flesh.

I find myself edging nearer to him, to watch him draw. He draws Anne too – she basks in his gaze, and when he is done she traces with a finger the arc of her own throat as Gladstone has sketched it, and she seizes the sketch and rushes to show Jack, calling, 'John, look – is it not the very image of me?'

When she and Jack are together at the prow, Gladstone nudges me. Jerking his head towards Jack, he licks his finger and draws a line on the salt-dry deck. There is the haughty angle of the jaw, made just that little bit haughtier. There is the back of the neck arched just so. I never knew four lines could be a joke, but there it is: Jack in all his magnificence and arrogance.

I take Gladstone to my hammock on his fourth night aboard – not because Anne has gone to Jack this night and not to me, but because of the artist's attentive and nimble fingers. He is a man – you may think that my tastes no longer run in that direction. But being with Anne is the opening of a door, not the closing of anything. So I bring Gladstone willingly to my hammock and he gives me no cause to regret it.

The next dawn there is much guffawing amongst the men, and far from being angry Anne winks at me, very slow, and says, 'The sea is ever full of surprises, is it not, my Mary?'

Gladstone and I pass many nights together on that voyage, and the next. None of the crew like him – least of all Tait, whose mood has lately been fouler than ever, for he is up half the night coughing. He calls Gladstone a pretty boy and a wastrel, which is unjust, for during his shifts Gladstone works diligently enough, and more than Tait. But I will allow that even when he works, there is in Gladstone's every movement a kind of indolence, the easy manner of a man who has never been poor.

Ashore just south of the St Lucie rivermouth, Gladstone and I squat by the water, where I am gutting fish for Howell to ruin later. Tait storms over and throws to our feet one of Jack's *Boston Gazettes*. There, sketched in the margins in charcoal, is Tait: a few lines merely, but merciless and unmistakable.

'You pert little prick,' he says, and grabs Gladstone by the shirt-front, hauling him to his feet.

'I don't see your name there,' says Gladstone. 'Not even your face.'

It is a bad move, and only makes Tait flush more red – for he has been forced to acknowledge himself in what Gladstone has drawn: the belly, and the slack jowls, and the air of bluster and foolishness.

'You're a fucking weasel,' Tait says. 'A lazy, rich wastrel – and getting balls deep in Mary is the first bit of hard labour you've ever done.'

'A slur to my honour I could stand,' Gladstone says. 'But not to Mary's.'

'Jesus,' I say. 'Don't make this about me.' I care little for Tait's insults – they have for a long time been part of life, and figure no more in my mind than the smell of bilgewater or the sting of salt.

But Gladstone ignores me and continues, stepping close to Tait. 'I must demand satisfaction.'

Tait laughs in his face. 'You calling me out? You may think yourself a princeling, but that's not how we do things around here.'

I could almost laugh too, were it not so deadly serious. Sailors and pirates settle their fights there and then, with fists and whatever is at hand, and not with the great ceremony of a gentleman's duel.

'If you're too much a coward to meet me in a duel,' Gladstone says, 'then I will fight you here.'

'Enough,' says Jack. 'This stops now.'

'Like hell it does,' Tait says. 'I'll meet this young braggart any way he likes.' He turns to Jack. 'Jack – will you be my second?'

'We're not doing this,' Jack says. 'Your foolishness will cost us all. Kill the kid and Rogers will see you swing. All of us, perhaps.'

But Tait is red-faced and will stop for no man. 'He wanted the duel – he shall have it.'

Fetherston speaks close to Tait now, his hand on Tait's arm. 'You heard Jack. Don't be bringing down a world of trouble on us all.'

Tait will not be soothed. Thus the Reverend grudgingly agrees to be Gladstone's second and Patrick will do the same for Tait, and all of us are silent and very solemn, for somehow Gladstone's stupidity has turned an ordinary quarrel into this ponderous and formal thing. Tait and Gladstone are measuring out their paces on the beach, Gladstone fussily kicking driftwood from his path to clear the way.

'The insult was to me,' I call. 'If anyone is to have satisfaction, it'll be me.'

'Shut up,' Tait says, not even looking up.

'I mean it. If we're doing this duelling nonsense, then by rights it's I who must be satisfied first.'

I care nothing for Tait's insults, and have never been troubled by questions of my own honour – but I care about this crew, and Gladstone's rashness will end in disaster. If Tait kills Gladstone, his father will insist on revenge – and if Gladstone kills Tait, the crew are like to kill Gladstone anyway, for though Tait is a hard man to like, he is one of our own.

'This is no business of yours, Mary,' Gladstone says.

'You're wrong.'

Tait throws his hands wide. 'Leave me to deal with the kid. I'm not going to fight you, you dumb bitch.'

I pull out my pistol.

'You are,' I say. My hand, as it clutches the pistol, still has fish-scales glinting on the skin; it seems incredible that a thing of such moment can happen when I still have the reek of fish guts on my fingers. 'You'll fight me now, as you've wanted to do since I came aboard the *Camila*.'

'Mary,' says Anne. 'Don't get drawn into this.'

'I'm already in it,' I tell her, not taking my eyes from Tait. 'Draw your pistol and fight me, Tait – for if you fight the lad you'll kill him, and it'll hang us all.'

'I can handle this,' Gladstone says, and I have no time even to laugh, for already Tait has drawn his pistol and there is no talk now of seconds nor of rules nor paces, for Tait will wait for no count. He shoots – it clips my left shoulder only, I feel no pain but only a great knock, like a kick from a horse. The sun is behind Tait, his great bulk a black doorway cut out of the sky, and I shoot. He drops at once and the Reverend rushes to him but neither God nor physicking will save Tait for I have shot off a piece of his skull and even from here I can see that he is done for.

Gladstone reaches me first, shoving Anne from his path. My shoulder bleeds excessively, and so he grudgingly makes room for Anne to bind it, though he stays close to get in her way. The wound has not yet begun to hurt – there will be time enough for that later.

The Reverend has laid his jacket over the mess of Tait's head, and it might be for Tait's sake or for ours, for it was a nasty sight, brains and skull together mashed to a sort of gruel.

When the binding is done and the others gathered about Tait's body, Jack comes to me. 'An ugly business,' he says, shaking his head and squatting by me on the sand.

'You could have put a stop to it.' It strikes me that it's unlike Jack not to be in control of what passes among his crew. After I challenged Tait, he made no attempt to stop us.

'Why didn't you step in?' I ask. 'Tait was your friend.'

'Aye. And he was a thief and a scoundrel.'

Those things may both be true, I own.

'And he had the pox,' Jack continues. 'Spanish gout or the like – some kind of whorehouse pox, anyway. You've heard him coughing. Have you not seen his arse?'

'I make it my business to try not to.'

'Pustules all over. And he's had the gleets, shitting green. The Reverend could do nothing for him – Tait wouldn't have lived many weeks more. But if he'd killed the kid, we'd all have swung, for Rogers is looking for an excuse to be done with me.'

'That's why you didn't stop me? You were happy enough for me to kill Tait – is that what you're saying?'

'I'm saying nothing.' He stands. 'But Tait was a problem, and now he's not.' He smiles. 'So let's bury him and be done with it.'

'Will there be trouble from the rest of the crew?'

'I'll see that there isn't. He shot you first, remember.'

'You knew he would.'

'Aye. But I knew he was like to miss, too. He's not had a steady hand for months. And you' – he places his hand on my good arm – 'I knew that you would not miss.'

For all Tait's faults we will not deny him a proper sea burial. We row the body back to the *Camila*, and sail from shore until we can anchor again in five fathom water. The Reverend recites a psalm, and the men join in, in the way of habit, having little to do with Tait, and even less to do with God.

Because of the pustules, nobody wanted to wash nor shroud him, so Jack made Gladstone do it, which pleased the crew who saw it as a kind of penance for Gladstone's role in this sorry mess. Being no seaman he has made a bad job of it, not sewing Tait properly into his hammock, nor thinking to weigh it down with shot – though in fairness we are short of shot as well as most everything else. When Fetherston and Corner slide the body into the water, the shroud unfurls around Tait, and he floats there naked, his arse up, boils and all. Already a few fish are nudging at his side with their blunt yellow noses. Gladstone has turned grey and is sick over the rail.

Fetherston takes a grappling hook and cranes down to force the body below the surface but Tait's pox must have been further gone than even Jack knew, for the hook strikes him under his arm where the flesh is all wasted with pustules, and the skin splits, bloodless and white.

'Jesus,' says Rackham. 'Stop making it worse. Come away, the lot of you, before the sharks sniff him out. Nobody wants to see that.'

My shoulder heals fast, but I think often of Tait. You might think I would be casual about death, having seen so much of it. But the opposite is true – I know death too well to treat it carelessly. I deal in it. I've hauled the dead from the decks, and heaved pails of water to wash away their blood. I know the right measure to weigh a body to send it down for good. I know the exact weight of a man's life.

Gladstone never forgives me for saving his life. Some men would rather be dead than ashamed – men who have, like Gladstone, lived a tidy life, out of the way of death's hot breath. Thus he keeps his distance from me, and the men keep their distance from him. Indeed, you would never believe so much distance could be found on a small sloop.

He quits us as soon as we land again at Nassau; he will find a berth on the next ship back to Charles Town, he declares, for the sailing life is not to his liking, which surprises none of us.

He has not touched me since the duel, but he kisses me at Nassau harbour as though it is a mighty farewell. I have known he would leave since I killed Tait – and I have no time for swooning in his arms when there is a ship to unload, and good sugar spoiling in the *Camila*'s damp hull. I go to say something and he puts his finger to my lips and says, 'Don't speak,' and is baffled when I laugh, because I had only wanted to hurry him along, and not to make any grand speeches or laments.

My shoulder heals. I do miss Gladstone's body – I miss the things that it could do. But Anne is newly fervent since she saw me with him, and she kisses the tight new scar on my shoulder, and when she comes to my hammock there is no part of me that misses him.

But I will allow he taught me something about lines, and how few of them it takes to conjure something. Sometimes when I look at Crow I fancy I see her more clearly, broken down into sweeps and curves. When I look at Anne I see the line of her jaw, or the jut of her shoulder, and I am glad to see her for a moment as an artist might – and if that is all he gave me I am still glad of it.

27

Even after Gladstone's leaving, we remain very quiet in the pirating way, seizing only a small French barque that we overtake off Eleuthera, which furnishes us with a purse of coin and a surprising quantity of smoked fish, of which we are soon heartily sick. The *Camila*'s hull is daily springing new leaks, and trawls sluggish through the days. It is clearer than ever that we need a new ship.

We return to Nassau, where Rogers has hanged another man for a pirate. It is Tennant, a small-time pirate who took the pardon and yet was caught about his old ways, and now he hangs from the fort, his tongue a thick blue lizard lolling from his mouth.

'They mean to make an example of him,' Jack says, shaking his head. 'But you hoist a man up like Christ, you risk making a martyr out of him.'

'That's blasphemy and you know it,' Anne tells him. 'And Tennant was no Christ.'

He surely was not – only last month I saw him drink so much that he pissed himself and it took two men to drag him from the ale tent. But Jack has a point. A man gets larger, hoisted thus, for all that he's dead. A man with a small life, made of small crimes, gets set on high like that and it makes people crane their necks to stare. There will be some who will be frightened and swear off piracy. But there are others who will see such a man, hanging thus with the sun behind him, and mistake him for a much grander and more dangerous thing: not a man but an idea.

In Nassau we sometimes encounter stories of ourselves. It is like turning quick and catching my shadow doing something quite apart from myself. Many times I hear the story of Jack and how he won the command from Vane. In an ale tent I overhear a fine tale about how I came to kill Tait. There is no mention of pox, nor of arse pustules. Instead it is a grand story of duels, in which I challenge Tait to spare my lover from certain death. It is a good story.

Several times I have heard it put about that Anne joined Jack's crew before me. That story suits me well enough, for the less known about my time pirating, the safer I shall be.

And I will own that it makes a neater story, for Anne joined our crew for love, whereas I joined for something different, which refuses to fit into any neat tale.

I must hope that none of the rumours concerning me and Anne reach the ears of Rogers, nor of Belling. I see Belling often now in company with James Bonny, and it seems to me that it is a friendship that can mean no good for us.

In port I sometimes don a skirt, but at other times I wear my trousers. I make no effort to act the man, but this is how some see me, in my sailor's gear and with my hair tied at the nape of my neck, navy style. A costermonger in St Jago de la Vega calls me 'sir' when I buy a melon, and I take no pains to correct him.

For years I feared being exposed for what I truly am. It is still a new thing to dare to believe that what I truly am is this: both and neither. That this is neither a disguise nor a costume, any more than my body itself can be these things.

I used to envy Anne, for she has always known precisely who she is, and the masquerade forced on her as a child didn't budge her knowing. I played the role longer, and after so many years I did not know what was left of me except for the playing. Only lately have I come to see it different – that the playing itself can be the truth of me. When I swing myself up the mast, or grind my hipbone between Anne's legs, or confound the men of Nassau, who fall silent as I shoulder past them in the crowded harbour front, I know myself for what I am. It has taken me a long time to learn the way of it: to trust that a self that changes is a self nonetheless.

Lately I am become my crow-self, which is to say, myself. I see more clearly; my hands are quick and sure on the lines; my body apologises for nothing, not its joys nor its aches. Crow casts her wings wide against the sky. Anne beside me and the sea below me, and the fierce sun above. All is light, all is light.

———————

Anne wants her marriage to Bonny annulled. The name Anne Bonny grows heavy on her. I fancy it is the papist in her, too, that craves the annulment, for she is very attached to ceremony. And she is a great one for walking away and starting fresh. Jack will marry her, and gladly, if she can shake off this old marriage. But some things stick, and a marriage sticks like tar.

'And what about you?' Corner asks me.

I shrug. 'It doesn't concern me.'

He rolls his eyes. 'Come now. We've known each other too long for such dissembling.'

'I mean it. It has no more to do with me than what Anne and I do in my hammock has to do with Jack.' I smile at him as I make fast the line, and he laughs.

Anne and Jack go to ask James Bonny if he will agree to have the marriage annulled. Apparently Bonny makes no objection, for it is generally known that Anne has birthed a child to Jack, and there is no question but that she has long been lost to Bonny. He has never been the kind of man to fight for something, or he might've made more of a success of pirating. But he is smart enough to demand a payout – I'd wager that even shiftless James Bonny can see that Anne wants it bad enough to pay.

The paying isn't the problem. The problem is the witness that Bonny has suggested for the signing of the papers.

'He says we shall meet with Turnley tomorrow, and do it then,' Jack says.

As soon as I begin to speak, Anne places her hand on my wrist. 'I like Turnley no better than you do. But it'll smooth things over, him being so much in favour with the Governor.'

I try to tell them that they are wrong. Belling has changed his name but not his character. He is not a man who can be used to curry favour, for he serves his own interests only. You can see it in the way he goes about Nassau with an air of grievance on his narrow face, casting quick, rat-like glances side to side.

'We cannot pick a fight with Bonny – not now. And Nassau is not so full of educated men that we may afford to pick and choose,' says Jack, and I own that he is right, for there are not so many in the ale tents of Nassau who can read or write – and fewer still who have the ear of the Governor.

But the next day Jack and Anne do not return from their appointed meeting, and the rest of us wait on the *Camila* for hours, Fetherston pacing until the Reverend snaps at him to be still, and even patient Corner is uneasy.

Jack returns to the harbour alone, long after dark, and we row by lantern to meet him.

'Where is she?' I call, jumping from the boat in waist-deep water, the quicker to wade to where he waits on the sand.

'She's fine,' he says at once. 'She's at the shack. She is not hurt.' Fetherston raises the lantern to Jack's face now and I see why he has reassured us that Anne is not hurt, for Jack himself has a fine bruise coming up on his left eye, and a long gash upon his brow.

'Jesus Christ,' I say, and Anne is not here to chastise me for my blasphemy.

'You were right about Turnley,' Jack says. It gives me no satisfaction. 'There were six of Rogers' men there to meet us, with Turnley himself ordering them about, playing at being a general. They dragged us to the Governor's House.'

The Reverend tries to check Jack's wounds, but Jack waves him away and continues. Governor Rogers was incensed by the notion of an annulment, and threatened to throw Anne in prison. 'And to make me whip her myself, if she will not return to her husband.' Jack spits – the gobbet that lands on the sand has blood on it, for Rogers' men have knocked out one of his teeth.

'He doesn't just want to be governor,' Jack says. 'He wants to be pastor, too, and all of us his flock.' His fury is doing him good, the colour returning to his face.

'You should've heard Anne,' he says. 'She swore very prettily that she'd return to Bonny, and keep loose company no more.'

She and Jack cannot now be seen together, and so I go to her. She insists she is not hurt. Instead she is newly determined. In the heat of the dark house she kisses me.

'Back to James Bonny?' she says, and we laugh, for if ever there was a man who did not know what to do with Anne, it is that feckless fellow.

'So we have no choice, you see,' she says, her breath on my cheek.

She is right. Rogers and Belling have given them no choice. No other chance, now, for Jack and Anne, but the sea's chance, and they will take it.

28

Anne has promised to return to Bonny, but to her relief Bonny himself wants no more to do with her. He is only a pawn for Rogers and Belling, and is aggrieved that the governor's interference has robbed him of the payment that Jack and Anne had promised him. As for Belling, he has left Providence for some time, gone aturtling, and I count it wise in him for if he and Jack were to meet again it would not end well for Belling.

Rogers is realist enough not to insist on Anne's reunion with Bonny, with both of them unwilling. Nonetheless he has made it deathly clear that Anne and Jack must stay apart – and they take care to do so, meeting only furtively, when Jack and the crew are not at sea. They still ply the trade routes for Rogers, but I do not sail with them – not with Rogers' renewed scrutiny over us all. Anne must be seen to have broken with her wanton ways, so Rogers orders that instead of keeping with pardoned pirates, she is to live instead with some virtuous woman. Virtuous women being in short supply on New Providence, Anne is sent to live with me, to keep her from sin.

We savour the joke of this as we savour one another. We take a small shack of our own, so that all may see that Anne has indeed renounced loose company. It is a threadbare thing on the west of the town, with a worn sail for a roof, and for more than a month we live quietly there. I miss being at sea, but it amuses me greatly to be cast in the role of duenna or chaperone. You might mistake us for two respectable women, if you did not look too close. We cook together and eat together and take in some piecework and mending for money, for Anne can stitch fine and I can stitch fast. Her finger grows a new callous from the needlework and I feel it when she touches me.

There are no words for what we do and so it can neither be named nor outlawed, and we live openly together as part of this new charade of Anne's reform. I think of what she told me of her time in Cuba, with Camila: how she imagined a republic of women. With the crow on the roof, our shack with its dirt floor is our own small republic, and I am as happy as I could ever be on land.

Nothing lasts – least of all in Nassau. When the *Camila* is in harbour Jack comes to us in the dark, or Anne creeps to his shack. And Rogers is ever watchful, when we pass him about town. If it is true that he's been cut loose by his supporters back in England, it has not broken him but given him a renewed and furious vigour. He drills his remaining men in the July sun, and another captured pirate swings from the fort. Jack, when he comes to Anne, is restless. And for all the joys of Anne and our bed, when the two of us walk down to the harbour for the cool of the evening breeze, I find myself looking beyond the horizon of her face, to seek the sea.

Anne does not need to tell me she is pregnant again: I know her body well enough, and better perhaps than my own. There is as yet little to see, but with my mouth and my fingers I discover the truth. Her breasts are of a sudden hard and tender, her belly low and full, and there is now about her movements the same drowsy weight that I remember from last time. She is perhaps a few months gone. Soon Anne's body will betray her, and announce to Rogers the truth that they have kept hid. It will be the end of our private republic.

'What will we do?' I ask.

She places both hands on her belly. 'John has a plan.'

The *Camila*, with her doomed hull, is fit for little, and an ill ship to trust with a new beginning. But lately in the harbour is the *William*, belonging to the privateer, John Ham. She's a neat little sloop, by reason of which Ham is known as 'Catch-him-if-you-Can,' for he has done a pretty business these many years harrying the Spaniards.

Jack summons us to come to his shack after dark the next night. The rest of the crew is gathered there, even the Reverend, come from inland.

'We'll take the *William*,' Jack says.

'That's open war.' The Reverend stands. 'That's not a little bit of pirating, on the quiet, as we've done from time to time since the pardon. Take the *William* from under his nose and Rogers will hunt us down.'

'It's already war,' I say. 'There's a dead man swinging under the fort. And look at Jack's face.' His bruises have healed in the month since the governor's men beat him, but the fresh scar on his brow is still dark pink.

'There's no future for us here,' Jack says. 'Not with Rogers set against us. And Anne cannot go back to Bonny.'

He says nothing of the baby, so I, fluent in secrets, do not mention it either.

'That's you – not us,' says Gibson, who has been in a foul mood since Tait's death. 'You're asking us to piss away our pardon, just so you can shack up with your latest bit of skirt.'

I expect Jack to turn on him, for ordinarily he will countenance no harsh words about Anne. But Jack keeps his voice low and calm, and speaks as though he is discoursing with the Reverend on theology.

'You say I'm asking you to waste your pardon. But a pardon is nothing. It's the absence of something, merely. The pardon dictates no pirating. Fine – but what's left to you, after that? Taking the pardon is the easy part. But making a living, afterwards? Making a life? What does your life look like now?'

'It won't end in the gallows,' Fetherston says. 'That's good enough for me.'

'Is it?'

Jack has a way of handing you a question like he's handed you a box of powder with a lit fuse. And what answer have the crew? They have little money left, and even fewer ideas. Just stale days of work hauling cargo for Rogers.

'The *William*'ll be guarded,' says the Reverend. 'Ham's no fool.'

'He sleeps ashore,' says Anne, very quick. 'And he sets but a light guard, thinking himself safe here, so close to Rogers. Two men only, and these aren't keen fellows either – they pass most nights asleep, if not dead drunk.'

It seems that Rogers is not the only one who has been watching what goes on in Nassau town. While I have been gazing at the sea during our night-time harbour strolls, Anne has been more alert.

The *William* would be a prize indeed. She has only six guns but is trim and fast, and made for waters such as these: a shallow draught for the reefs, and nimble as you like. And the word in Nassau is that she is to sail by the end of week – so she'll be well-provisioned, too, sitting there loaded with powder, water, food.

'A small crew could manage her very well,' Jack says.

Gibson is still shaking his head. 'Rogers will send after us.'

'Good luck to him,' says Jack. 'There's few ships here could catch the *William*, and fewer still who've pilots to match Patrick.'

The *Delicia*, Rogers' great man-of-war, which sits at the harbour like a floating fort, could never keep pace with a sloop in these waters, and we could escape her amongst the islands and the sandbars. But there are privateers enough in smaller vessels that would snatch at the chance of a reward and Rogers' favour. No place will be safe for us, hereafter.

'Think of it,' says Jack. 'A fresh start. No pardons, no masters.'

'No more bloody worms in the hull,' says Fetherston.

Jack claps him across the back. 'A swift ship beneath us – think of the prizes we shall take.'

'On the *William*, we will be a new Nassau, afloat,' Anne says.

She is bright-eyed, her hands moving fast and her words even faster, as the crew begins to make its plans. Anne likes nothing so much as to start again.

———————————

I come upon Jack by the shore, and take a place beside him on the sand. He sits leaning forward, his elbows on his bent knees as he stares to sea.

'Why did you not tell the crew?' I ask. 'They would have followed you all the more willingly, if you'd told them about the baby. Told them that you have no choice but to leave.'

'For that very reason,' he says. 'It's their lives. They must choose for themselves, and not from blind loyalty to a captain.'

When he speaks thus, I understand better than ever why they would follow him so blindly. Why I have done so.

———————————

We allow ourselves four days to prepare. When the dark comes on the elected night, it comes with rain, and we are glad of both. It is a good fat August rain, and a good thick dark, so that as we make our way down to the harbour I can scarce see the others around me.

Fetherston, Gibson, Howell and Patrick are waiting already aboard the *Camila*. The rest of us – Jack, the Reverend, Corner, Anne and I – avail ourselves of one of Rogers' launches, and row out in silence, met by the flash of a lantern from the *Camila*. There is a gusty northerly and even in the shelter of the harbour the ships are noisy at anchor, a great straining and clashing of cables and of water on wood. It takes both me and Jack rowing to get us through the heavy waves.

We draw near the *William* at the same time as Fetherston and the others, in the *Camila*'s boat. We had thought to approach the *William* from both sides but in this wind that will not serve, and we must both come to the lee of her or be thrown against her by the waves. When the sloop looms above us, Anne and I fend off her hull with our hands, while Jack and the Reverend secure the ladder, which is far from easy in the wet and resolute dark, the launch jerking beneath us.

Jack is first aboard, the rest of us following close behind. Jack and Anne together slip through the hatch, and I am just behind them. Anne was right: there are only two guards, both below to avoid the rain. Anne has her pistol on the men already and is threatening to 'blow their damned heads off,' which is bluster only for below deck the mess alone would not bear thinking of. Anyway it does its job and one man, who seems drunk, surrenders very meek at once. The other tries to yell for help but any sound would be lost in the storm and anyway Jack puts an end to it very neatly with the butt of his pistol.

'Quicker to finish them off,' says Fetherston, when Jack tells him to bind and gag the drunk man and his unconscious companion.

'Stick to the plan,' Jack says calmly, and watches closely as Fetherston secures their bonds. For speed we cut the anchor loose – I cut the cable myself, and we are away. At the harbour mouth we are hailed by the watch aboard the *Delicia*, but Jack is ready for this, and waves at the severed cable and shouts through the angry rain that we have snapped our anchor cable, and must take her outside the harbour, or in this wind she will be broken up against the other ships. The rain is doubly our blessing, for not only is it harder for the watch to make out who we are, but no sentry wishes to prolong anything on a dirty night such as this, and they are happy enough to wave us on. We limp through the harbour mouth, but as soon as we are beyond it we hoist all the sail we have.

The bound guards have surfaced to consciousness now, and Jack gives them both a choice, for we could use two more men: 'Join us, if you will – and if you go along with us, you shall have your share and sign our articles as men among equals.' But the men want none of it and that does not surprise me, for in taking the ship we did not treat them too gently and Anne in particular was mighty fierce.

'Join your crew of hellcats, and swing for it?' the drunk man slurs. 'Not on my life.'

'As you wish,' says Jack cheerfully, for he has never liked having pressed men aboard, and thus we let them clamber into the launch to make their rough way to shore.

As they battle their way against the wind, Jack calls after them: 'And give our service to John Ham, and tell him we shall be happy to return his ship to him when we are done with her.'

Rogers will send men after us. A pirate is never safe, but what we've done means Rogers will take it personal. Our crew has had their chance at a pardon, and they took it. There are no second chances. And Jack and Anne have doubly betrayed Rogers, having sworn to him that they would live virtuously and apart. He is their enemy twice over now, and will want his vengeance, for such a double slight will do nothing for his standing in Nassau.

So we sail hard through the night, which in such wind and amongst the reefs and sandbanks would be a deadly undertaking under any pilot but Patrick. But we know Rogers too well to stop, for he will have his vengeance.

And what is vengeance but a kind of loyalty? For there's none will attend you so faithfully, nor follow you so close, as an enemy. In Rogers, we have made our own enemy – chosen him the way you might choose a lover. Perhaps we chose ill, for he is not a man to let go easy.

Jack calls an order, and the Reverend and I, together, trim the head sail. The *William* slices neatly through the heavy swell. A thrill crests in me like a wave – we have made our choice, and cast our fortunes in with the sea. Nonetheless, every rope I see that night is a noose.

We had no thought of beginning our raids so close to Nassau, and in truth I would have preferred to head east without delay, but near dawn we espy a schooner run aground on a sandbank, its mainmast half down and in no state to flee us. Thus we take it almost without effort, and its crew, already much battered by the storm, are quick to ask for quarter. There is little aboard but some piemento and a small quantity of sugar, and we want none of the ship itself, damaged as it is, though we take her anchor, having need of one. Our crew nonetheless are giddy with the ease of the prize, and with their own daring, to strike at once and so close to Rogers.

'An auspicious start,' announces Jack, for men are always keen to read a thing as an omen if it bodes well.

We are away. After the *Camila*, the *William* is tight as a good rum barrel. Her hull has been cleaned recently and she is tarred below the waterline. Nothing swings loose in her except hammocks. Upwind there is none swifter, and she tacks dainty and quick. Such a sweet little sloop she is, the whole of her an instrument for moving. She is a joy to sail, and so tidy when we seize her that even Gibson, usually slovenly in all things, takes some pains to keep her so.

Of the crew, only the Reverend is subdued. While the rest of the crew is drunk on our own boldness, the Reverend is quiet, and sets about his work with his jaw gritted tight. I think of the man he has left in Nassau, where he surely may never return, and I have some sense of what it has cost him to follow Jack on this voyage.

By the next night the storm has passed south and left us behind. We anchor briefly south of Exuma, and Jack has us each sign the new ship's articles. Even Gibson and Howell, who can neither read nor write, make their rough mark beside where Jack has written their names. Then Jack holds the paper over the rail and sets a lantern flame to it, 'for a man may as well sign his own death warrant as to let this fall into the navy's hands.' It is a pretty piece of pageantry, for the articles are made all the more solemn for being committed to the fire. Again I am struck by Jack's flair for showmanship – he has somehow taken those written words, with all their dull details — *two shares and a half a share for the ship and whom the captain please to take for the master under him is to have a share and a half* — and with nothing but flames has made of that page a sacrament.

<hr />

I counsel Jack to take us west, but he will not yet venture so far from New Providence for he has first a task to finish. Jack and Anne will have their vengeance upon Belling, and so despite my warnings that we should not tarry, we sail south-east, for an islet where Belling is said lately to have been turtling.

We spot his sloop at anchor and it is easy to take it, for there are but four men aboard and they are not on a martial footing. Jack and Anne compel them hard, with some blows from Fetherston, to tell us where Belling is hid. But Belling is ashore with his young son, the men swear, gesturing at the dunes.

Jack, Fetherston, Anne and I go ashore but the storm has left a heavy swell and we cannot even land the launch but must needs leave Fetherston to keep it beyond the waves while we wade the last distance to the beach, our weapons held above us. If Belling had not already had the good sense to flee inland, he will certainly do so now. We make the bleak beach, where the wind has taken even Belling's footprints. Jack fires his pistol in the air and shouts some curses, scanning the long, bleached grass of the dunes above us. Belling and his son must be cowering there, but we are running out of time to pursue them. Jack and Anne stride up the sand, looking for tracks and shouting imprecations.

It's not a movement that I spot — rather, a stillness amongst the grass which itself is never still in this wind. An eye, and a slice of face, topped with white-blond hair. From this distance I cannot make out whether it is Belling or his child who is lying there among the grass — though it matters not, for where one is, the other will be.

'See anything?' Jack yells. Perhaps he has noticed that I have frozen.

I stare a moment longer at that unblinking eye.

'We've waited too long already,' I call to Jack, turning back to him. 'Rogers' ships could come upon us any moment.'

Jack is in a black mood as we wade back to the boat, and Anne swears mightily.

It gives me no joy to conceal anything from Jack and Anne. Nor do I begrudge them their vengeance on Belling – indeed I have some vengeance of my own that I would serve him. But I don't wish for his scrawny young son to witness it. And though Anne is still swearing as we row back to the sloop, it is she herself who has taught me that I need not carry my past always with me. Belling has done harm enough already – I don't want our new life to begin with a slaying. I don't want Belling amongst my ghosts.

Back on Belling's ship, Corner has already set the men to taking down the mast, and shifting anything of value to the *William*. Then things take a different turn, for Gibson says we should press Belling's men. Since Gibson took the pardon he has a notion of himself as a fine gentleman and is lazier than ever he was. Jack nods, brisk, and says he will take all four men.

'You sure?' I say to him, quiet so as none of the others can hear. Jack has always said he finds pressed men work-shy, and not fit to trust. 'You've never liked having pressed men aboard.'

'I like Turnley even less. And if I can do him a mischief by this or any other means, I shall not miss my chance.' Jack keeps his pistol on the four men as they ready to climb aboard the *William*.

At the last instant Jack and Anne elect to leave one man – not as a mercy but only so that he may bear Belling a message. The lone man is left adrift on the crippled sloop with his message from Jack and Anne, given with many oaths and imprecations: that if ever they lay hands on Belling, they will see him whipped to death.

The three pressed men show us no resistance, Belling not being the kind of man to inspire any great loyalty. Two of the men, Carty and Earl, are no strangers to pirating, for Jack knows them of old as Nassau men before Rogers' coming. The other is but a boy, a shy scrap of a thing called Noah Harwood, who seems if anything relieved to be taken. He is in positive awe of Jack, whom he takes for a gentleman. Harwood is timid around women, and when Anne or I pass him below deck he shrinks back in mortification, as though he'd sink into the bulkhead rather than be brushed by my arm. But he is able and quick, and his reverence of Jack makes him a willing hand.

Thus we have our crew: Jack, with Fetherston as master, and Patrick as fine a pilot as any in the Bahamas. Howell, a decent sailor and a terrible cook, and the Reverend, our own surgeon. Corner, the former whaler, is quartermaster, while Gibson, Anne and I make up the crew, along with Carty and Earl, and Harwood for a cabin boy and general factotum. Jack recites for them the ship's articles, already burned, and they chorus their agreement, Harwood's voice high and quiet.

The reciting of the articles is not to be our only ceremony, for Anne has another in mind. Once we are well clear of Exuma she gathers us on the deck.

'I am to wed Jack after all,' she announces, 'for I consider myself divorced from Bonny under Brehon law.'

'What the hell's that?' says Gibson.

'It's the old law, back in Ireland. Long gone, but my father taught me about it when I was his clerk.'

'What difference does it make?' asks the Reverend.

'Gives women the right to divorce their husbands. Gráinne Mhaol left her second husband under Brehon law. Husband or wife could end a marriage after a year, if they wanted.'

'Gráinne Mhaol did a lot of things,' Fetherston says. 'Doesn't mean you can.'

'Listen,' says Anne. 'Under Brehon law, a woman could leave a marriage for a host of reasons – God knows Bonny fits enough of them.' She counts, finger by finger: 'Impotence. Hitting and leaving a mark. Spreading lies about his wife. By law I can divorce him – entitled to much that's his, as well.'

'Much of nothing's still nothing,' Jack says.

'Doesn't matter. I can be free of him, that's what counts.'

'Free so as a pastor or a governor would recognise?' I ask.

'Who cares for them?' she says.

Jack says to me, low-voiced, 'That old Irish law can't sit right with her popery. She can't have it both ways.'

'Don't let her hear you talk that way,' I whisper. For she will – she will have it every way. It does not surprise me to see her here, holding forth in her sudden fervour for this ancient law. Jack may mistrust this Brehon law business, but he will wed her anyway, for laws of God or man trouble him little. And he sees in Anne the same thing I see: something in her ardent to be absolved.

The Reverend will have none of this wedding, which raises a fury in Anne. I have never made the mistake of thinking the Reverend left the church as a non-believer. He left because he had some private disagreement with God, which is a very different thing – and he is steadfast today in refusing to countenance the marriage. Fetherston says he will take the Reverend's role and says some words, a gabble of words supposed to sound pastor-like: 'In the sight of God on this solemn occasion I come to wed these two.' The Reverend cannot bear the mangling of his liturgy and strides astern and makes a show of continuing his work, and causes an almighty clattering and creaking as he checks the pump.

Anne, impatient, interrupts Fetherston and takes over the ceremony herself, speaking loud over the Reverend's racket: 'I take you as my wedded husband, to live together after God's ordinance in the holy estate of matrimony.' And she knows all the words, for her memory is sharp for such things, and her first wedding is not so very long ago, though none would dare mention that now.

When she promises to obey Jack, Gibson snorts the loudest, for Anne may obey Jack as a captain, but never as a wife – but Anne is in a place now where Gibson's jibes cannot reach her, nor the chortles of the rest of the crew, nor the Reverend's clanking at the pump. I understand why she waited for this marriage to be done aboard and not ashore, for this is a serious business, too big for land, and fit for the solemnity of water. Her marriage

288

to Jack is not countenanced by a pastor nor a steeple, but by the crow on the bowsprit and the patient sea.

She has her face set against the wind as she continues: 'and serve you, love, honour, and keep you, in sickness and in health; and, forsaking all others, keep only unto you, so long as we both shall live.'

I am right here, close enough to touch her, as she says, 'forsaking all others, keep only unto you.' There is no doubting her sincerity. It is a particular talent in her, how she may believe one thing and do another. How she may swear herself to Jack with a fresh bruise on her thigh from my thumb. Just as she and the Reverend have each made their own accommodation with God, Anne has made her own accommodation with marriage, and it is no less sincere for including me in it.

What a performer she is: she has been a boy, a woman, a harlot, and now again a virgin bride. She is Catholic, she is divorced, she is twice married, she is Anne Bonny or Anne Fulford or Anne Rackham, she is a law clerk, she is a pirate. She loves Jack she loves me.

That night I hear Jack and Anne – the noises, big and small. We have rounded the eastern tip of Exuma and headed west again to a sheltered bay that Patrick knows of, and in the light swell the *William* strains patiently against her anchor. I press my hands to the bulkhead between Jack's cabin and mine, and listen to the slap of water, the low thrum of voices on deck above, and Jack and Anne, their words and the noises between their words. It is their wedding night, after all, no matter that she has borne his child and left another husband in Nassau. She can shake such things off like water from oilcloth. She will remake herself again and again. She is doing it right now.

Do not think me jealous. This is something different. I am athrill with it: some part of it is mine too, their wedding and now this night, all of us together within the *William*'s bounds. In this, too, I have a share.

29

Now we cross the Exuma Sound and come along the northern coast of Harbour Island, where the prey is small but easily had. Over several days we take a number of fishing canoes, and a small schooner. The pressed men, Carty and Earl, prove themselves solid enough. They are not with us by choice, but choice gets mighty blurry once you're beyond sight of shore. Once at sea, it makes little difference how you got there. You do the work, same as anyone else, or you'll find yourself overboard. And when a storm comes in hard from the north and the waves are over the bowsprit, the only choice any of us has is to live or die. So Carty and Earl do their work well enough, and better than some. As for the boy Harwood, though he remains shy he is eager to please and quick as a rabbit, and fast finds favour with the crew and with Jack in particular.

'He's a good lad,' Jack says, gesturing at Harwood, who is swabbing the deck very diligent. 'And has the makings of a good sailor.'

'You like Harwood,' I say, 'for you like nothing so well as to be worshipped.'

He laughs. In these bright autumn days aboard the *William*, Jack and I find much to laugh about. He is not my lover, and I have no wish for him to be. But he is Anne's husband as sanctified by the sea and Anne's own choice. He is her lover and so am I, and he is our captain both, and so we are bound together, Jack and I. If this is a kind of love, I account it a very pure one, for we want nothing from one another. I am free to enjoy him from a distance. Anne ought to have come between us but instead when I catch him watching her, as she bends to the capstan, I feel closer to him than ever, because I am watching her too.

Sometimes, when the *William* has all her sheets filled and is running neat downwind, Jack turns to me and squints, half laughing, into the sun, and waves an arm at the spray and the wide horizon.

'How do you like this, Mary?' he asks, and though he is my captain and my friend, I think: *You did not make the sea, Jack, nor grant it to me.* I have been a sailor these many years, and came to the sea long before I came to Jack's crew.

And does he think he has given me Anne? Does he think that she, too, is part of his munificence, his captain's divvying up of prizes?

We make north-west to the Berry Islands, and there come upon a sloop, larger than us but not so swift. They do not ask for quarter even when we have raised the black flag and hailed them, so we are obliged to shoot upon them, and they meet our firing with their own and do some damage to our windlass, before our chain shot shreds their mainsail and we are able to board. Anne and I are back to back on their deck, and having fired our pistols in boarding, it is cutlass work now, each of us against one man. I have disarmed mine and knocked him to the deck with the hilt of his own cutlass when another runs from the poop deck and has his pistol straight at me and when I hear the gun's report I think that is very likely the end of my story altogether – but it is he who drops to the deck. Beyond him I see Jack, pistol smoking, and we have just time to exchange a quick nod, for against my back Anne is still hard pressed by a tall, pale fellow and it takes both of us to get him down. Even so it is not until Anne has her cutlass at his neck that he asks for quarter, for he seems to take it very personal that he has been bested by women. By this time his captain, too, has realised they are beaten, and gives a general call for quarter.

Once they are disarmed Jack treats them civilly enough for they acquitted themselves well in the engagement and showed no lack of courage. Their captain even agrees to take a sip of rum with us, and the rum will do him good as he sports a nasty cut on his hand. He tells us his name is Isaacs and he is Nassau-bound, from South Carolina. But he knows already who Jack is, for he says Rogers has sent after us a sloop captained by a Doctor Rowan, and that Isaacs saw him not two days ago, and hailed and spoke with him.

'He has twelve guns, and more than fifty men aboard,' Isaacs says, 'and instructions from Rogers not to return save with your head hanging from his bowsprit.' Isaacs speaks mighty bold for a prisoner. 'And Rowan says he's not the only ship sent out with the same orders.'

'Rogers can send as many ships as he likes,' Jack says, 'but he'll not catch the *William*.'

Nonetheless you may well imagine we move tremendous quick to steer a course back south, for though I share Jack's faith in the *William*'s speed, and in our crew, a twelve-gun sloop on our tail is not a comfortable thought.

Except for the news he gave us, we profited little from Isaacs' ship, not having the numbers to take his sloop itself, nor room on the *William* for her cargo of lumber. Thus we could take only her powder and fishing tackle, and the crew is restless.

'I wouldn't mind swinging for gold or rum,' Gibson grunts. 'But not for fishing tackle.'

With Rogers' vessels in pursuit, we have all risked too much to be satisfied with the kind of small prizes we have lately been taking. Thus we agree to head south, to Hispaniola, the better to target the shipping routes there.

South of Acklins Key there is a dead whale afloat. We know it first by the almighty stink, and next by the birds that crowd on it, though the nearest land is a good five leagues away. A whale makes its own island, and the birds cluster there, hundreds of them, picking at the bloated white flesh, and circling above.

When the crow lands upon the beast's head, a score of affronted gulls takes off, all of them together, a sudden white sail hoisted.

Crow settles above one of the whale's eyes. Leisurely she winkles the eye from the socket, like a cockle from its shell.

Even hours later, I cannot rid myself of the smell of rotted flesh. I've never been one for signs or omens. But that whale is too big to mean nothing at all.

South, we sail against the wind, and ever mindful of the ships Rogers has sent after us. But three leagues north of Hispaniola we come across a merchant sloop, and the taking of her is well worth our while, and the little powder we spend before her crew begs for quarter, for she has a great quantity of both rum and salt, and two sheep which we are glad to have after weeks of salt-meat and biscuit. Jack considers keeping her but though larger than the *William*, having a burthen of some thirty tonnes, she is by no means so fast, as we proved in the seizing of her. Instead he has them sink the struck mainsail, loaded with shot, so that they cannot so swiftly raise the alarm.

As we leave the sloop and its crew, Jack calls back to them: 'Tell Governor Rogers of Nassau that it was Jack Rackham who dealt with you thusly. And send my fondest regards to him – from me and my good lady wife.'

We pass a night in a sheltered bay on the north coast of French Hispaniola, and after we have filled the water butts, Jack lets the crew make free with the rum. It is as bad as any I have tasted but it is plentiful, and the crew still in exalted mood after today's rich prize. We have a fire and Corner butchers the sheep and while we set aside one for salting, the other we eat tonight, and even Howell's cooking cannot ruin the pleasure of fresh meat.

The Reverend is in a merrier mood than usual, for he has been busy at the rum, and when we are picking at the sheep bones, he takes a sweep of sailcloth and drapes it around himself like a cloak. Sitting on a driftwood log with his knees splayed, he holds his cup high like a sceptre or a gavel, the firelight shining on his wet teeth.

In a low, grave voice, he intones: 'You, Jack Rackham, and your crew, have most wickedly and wantonly committed divers crimes—'

The others join in:

'Taken the sloop *William* from Nassau harbour by cover of night.'

'Seized prizes, and given no quarter to the men defending them.'

'Left the women of Nassau's brothels wanting more.' (This from Anne.)

'Evaded the saintly Woodes Rogers and all those he sent to chase you down—'

Jack raises his hand for silence, and the Reverend speaks again. 'What say you to this charge, then? How do you plead?'

Jack shouts, 'Guilty,' and the others join him, and I hear myself joining too, 'Guilty Guilty Guilty,' sounding around the fire again and again like spilled powder catching alight.

The crow turns her back as if bored with us and all our human clatter.

The Reverend stands. 'Then I sentence you, Rackham, and all your crew, to a fate more terrible than any other: Howell's cooking, and no rum.' Howell swears, but the Reverend speaks over him. 'And to be hanged by the neck until you are dead.'

'And to be whipped roundly,' says Gibson.

'We're already dead, shit-for-brains,' calls Fetherston. But then the others join the jest:

'And then starved to death.'

'And then ridden to death by the bony hips of Elsie Pox of the Three Keys.'

'And then run through with a cutlass.'

'And then hanged again, and hoisted in a gibbet to make young sailors piss their trews and cry for their mammies.'

'Enough,' says Jack. 'Enough.'

Is he thinking, as I am, of the bodies hanged from the fort at Nassau? The men we have seen in gibbets, a cage of air and bones?

But for now there is meat in our bellies and more rum to be had, and the *William* at anchor in the bay, laden with prizes. Anne's head against my shoulder, the small hairs on her shins lit to a shimmer by the flames. Jack nearby and my crew about me, and with each breath we hoist the black flag in the face of death and we will give no quarter.

Truth is, for us, death isn't a thing we have glimpsed a few times in a gibbet, in some far-off port. Death is right next to us, sniffing our salt beef and trailing a finger over the side of the cocket-boat to test the water. We are pirates; death is beside us in the rigging and in our hammocks and right here, around this fire, with a pitcher of bad rum and the patience to wait for all of us, each one.

Our sweet luck continues, for the very next day, further east, we catch sight of another sloop, and we are quick to overhaul her. This crew, though, is not so ready to ask for quarter and must be persuaded with our guns, which she answers with her own and we take some damage to the *William*'s prow. When we board the sloop it comes to close fighting and Gibson takes a blow to the back of the head and is killed. I myself am called upon to kill a man which I never enjoy though I do not scruple to do it, for he has me close against the rail and would have killed me first had I not been quick to get my knife up under his ribs. Two other merchants are dead with him by the time the crew is subdued, and the Reverend is kept busy with a number of wounds amongst our men.

We send Gibson to the depths with few words. He was a rough fellow and along with Tait was a great one for lewd jokes. The Reverend says Gibson came from Bristol; Fetherston says he thinks there was a wife at some point, and perhaps a son, though where he does not know. Nobody offers anything further. A man's life seems very small once he has quit it.

Aboard the prize sloop is a good cargo of cloth and limes. One of her men asks to join us, and Jack is glad to have him for we have lost Gibson, and this new fellow showed himself brave enough in the fight. We could use more hands, too, for we will keep the small sloop – and each ship having its own peculiarities it is useful to have amongst us one who knows the particular ways of this one, which the man tells us is called the *Evangeline*. He himself is called Dobbin, lately of Philadelphia, and is young enough that he accounts pirating a great adventure, and comes aboard merry as you like, despite the mutterings and cursing of his former crew, who wish him to damnation as we set them in the launch to make their way to land.

These seagoing days, Anne comes to my hammock with a new urgency. Her belly is growing, but her appetites grow too. When we kiss, I taste on her the salt and sweat of the battle. Gibson is dead; Rogers pursues us. This republic of salt is a fragile thing. Each day I see her stomach filling out, and think of sand counting down in an hourglass, time falling away.

30

We are by now feeling very sorely the lack of a base. Without a haven such as Nassau, there is nowhere to sell our prizes, nor store them. Even with the *Evangeline* to share the load, the *William*'s decks are crowded with barrels, and she rides low in the water. And provisioning our tiny fleet is not easy, for this isn't the navy – no commissary, no storehouses, and not much room for stores aboard neither. Water and fresh food mean going ashore – and each stop is a delay we can ill afford, with Rogers coming after us.

But Jack has some acquaintances near where the town of Monte Cristi once stood, just within the Spanish part of Hispaniola. More than a century ago, the Spaniards destroyed the town itself for trading with pirates – but it seems there are families in the area with long memories, who carry on the same trade, and thus we send Jack ashore. The next night, at the appointed hour, he comes down to the bay with three men, and we shift off most of our cargo, and the crew is well pleased with the coin we get in its place.

But coin is not all the men give us, for when the unloading is done, Jack is hasty in weighing anchor and will not have so much as a lantern lit aboard. Only when we are a league from shore, the *Evangeline* leeward, close by, does he allow the lamps lit, and passes me a creased piece of paper.

It is a proclamation that Rogers has caused to be printed. Jack's man in Monte Cristi, Juan, had it himself from a south-bound ship only four days ago.

Whereas Jack Rackham, George Fetherston, John Davies, Andrew Gibson, John Howell, Noah Patrick & two Women, by Name: Anne Fulford, alias Bonny, & Mary Read, did on the 22d of August last, combine together to enter on board; take, steal and run-away without of this Road of Providence, a Certain Sloop call'd the William, *Burthen about 12 Tons, mounted with 4 great Guns and 2 Swivel ones, also Ammunition, Sails, Rigging, Anchor, Cables, and a Canoe, owned and belonging to Capt. John Ham, and with the said Sloop did proceed to commit Robbery and Piracy upon the Boat and Effects of James Gohier Esq., on the South Side of this Island; also upon Capt. Isaacs, Master of a Sloop riding at Berry-Islands in his Way from South-Carolina to this Port:*

Wherefore these are to Publish and make Known to all Persons, Whatsoever, that the said John Rackham and his said Company are hereby proclaimed Pirates and Enemies to the Crown of Great-Britain, and are to be so treated and Deem'd by all his Majesty's Subjects.

Given at Nassau, this 5th of September, 1720.

Sign'd WOODES ROGERS.

Jack takes back the paper. 'I don't doubt that Juan would turn us in himself, if he didn't know he'd hang alongside us – for he can ill afford the attention of the authorities.'

The proclamation is passed about the ship, and Anne speaks it aloud for those who cannot read. Some of the men have a new swagger about them, for though the proclamation is merely telling our own story back to us, it is somehow grander in print. The Reverend is sombre. As for Anne, she is outraged that it names her *Fulford*, her father's name, or *Bonny*, and not Anne Rackham – and there is no point arguing with her for once her anger finds a mark no storm can shift it.

We sail swiftly west again, going ashore only once, for water. There, Corner espies several head of fat cattle grazing, and seeing no herdsman in sight we steal two, hastily butchered on the sand. If Dobbin, the latest to join the crew, finds such tasks below the dignity of what he had imagined of a pirate's life, he has the good sense not to show it, and proves himself a hard worker.

We are done with the butchering when two men step unawares from the woods to the east of the bay. We seize them at once – two Frenchmen, in search of the same stream where we filled our water butts. They are only poor men who have been hunting wild hogs, and they are fit neither to rob nor ransom, but they have seen us with the stolen cattle, and thus we have no choice but to bring them aboard. But Jack treats them very civil, for he speaks their tongue, and we share with them our meal. They confide to Jack that they have not eaten so well for some time, which means they must be poor men indeed for Howell's cooking has not improved. They show a willingness to work, and we are glad to have extra hands aboard, for we are short-handed to sail both the *Evangeline* and the *William*.

With the Frenchmen aboard, we waste no time in leaving Hispaniola and making for Jamaica's north coast. There we come across a sailing canoe and when we hail it from the *William* and raise our flag, we are met at once with a pistol shot and a barrage of cursing. The sole figure aboard is a woman, standing to face us and getting busy with reloading her pistol. This gives Jack pause, for while our men may not scruple to have women on the crew, they are not so sure about shooting one. But the Reverend and I get the grapples onto her canoe, and I clamber down before her reloading is done, and match her swearing with my own as I wrestle the pistol from her. She is a wiry thing some years older than me and with only a single tooth, and she fights me so fierce that were it not for the Reverend's help she would overset the whole boat.

She will not stop her thrashing and so we bring her aboard the *William*, for although she is a devil for pinching and biting, I do not want her drowned. While I bind her, the crew shifts her cargo aboard, but it is nought but some provisions and fishing tackle.

'We should never have hailed her at all,' Anne says, and I cannot disagree, for the vicious old fussock is still shouting and swearing that she will see us hang. Now that she has her bearings enough to make out that Anne and I are women, she yells that we ought to conduct ourselves better and that we are a pair of hussies and harlots and many other base slanders, and my brandishing my machete close to her face has no effect and nor does Anne giving her a slap, for Anne is not one to take insults mildly. Still the woman curses us and wishes us to the devil.

'Good lady,' Jack tells her, very mild, 'we have been the devil's these many years past, and are not like to change our ways now.'

His charms are wasted on her. The two Frenchmen talk soothingly to her, but as she speaks no French, their words seem to alarm her more than anything and she shrieks that we consort with infidels and foreigners. In the end I gag her, for her mouthing off will only cause her harm and indeed Anne's pistol hand is looking mighty twitchy.

Jack and I hold a hushed council astern; I think we should keep her aboard and not risk her broadcasting our whereabouts, but the crew wants her gone for she is like a lit candle set down on a barrel of powder. In the end we keep her pistol and set her back in her canoe, though we have taken her small sail, so she will at least be slowed in reaching shore. That she will raise the alarm I have no doubt, for even as we leave her she is shouting imprecations and calling damnation down upon us.

———————

Anne is not yet five months gone, but already her belly stands proud, and all the crew now know she is with child. I help her once more to let out her skirts and trousers, my stitches following the neat row of holes from where we let them out last time, for the baby boy that she left in Cuba. If he still lives, he is not yet a year old. Jack mentions him, sometimes – 'when my son is big enough to sail with me,' he says. Anne only smiles.

Crow has taken to staring at my belly. When I stretch out on the deck, she hops close to my stomach, her head cocked, then hops back, satisfied. She knows what I have not yet admitted to myself: that my own body is changing.

It is six months since I was with Gladstone – this thing growing within me is too late to be any babe of his. My monthly courses have for many years come very irregular, if at all, so they are no help to me. I toy with the idea that Jack's seed could somehow have lingered on Anne – on her finger, on her tongue – and found its way to me. I even toy with the idea that my body is somehow echoing Anne's. My life has been fat with miracles. I have been girl and boy, man and a woman. I have done things that the world ought never have permitted. What's one more miracle aboard the *William*, on this stolen cruise where each day is a marvel already?

The crow continues to stare at my belly. Perhaps she can smell something turned sour, something gone awry in me. I know for sure that crows do not believe in miracles.

As yet, there is little to see – the merest bulge. But I feel it growing in me, so heavy that it throws my balance askew. It takes space like a man does, without asking. I feel it catching, something snagging and pulling within me when I reach for the boom.

Anne has noticed nothing. Her own babe is news enough for her and for Jack, and for me too. Jack lets her have the cheeks of every fish, scooping them out very particular, for she likes nothing so well. I rub her feet when they pain her, for already they have begun to swell. Who would notice my body's changes, beside Anne's growing belly? She draws the eye as a fire does.

———————

Further west along Jamaica's northern coast, five leagues from Port Maria Bay, Corner spies a schooner. They have more guns than us but no appetite for a fight, and call for quarter as soon as we send some musket shot over her bow. Jack gives his orders and they strike their sails and surrender their weapons and come aboard very meek. Their captain is one Thomas Spenlow, and he has given us our richest prize yet, for he has aboard fifty rolls of tobacco, and nine bags of piemento – and his schooner, too, is a handsome vessel. Spenlow himself is a melancholy man who reels off a long litany of mischances and sufferings that have plagued him on this voyage, including pox and groundings, and pirates taking his schooner not six months hence and carrying it off, along with ten slaves. On that occasion, he says the pirates were swiftly captured by the navy and his ship, the *Neptune*, returned to him.

'I undertake to treat you no worse than those last who seized you,' Jack says, 'though I can't promise to be so obliging as to be immediately captured.'

Spenlow does not laugh. But being a former navy man, he gravely gives Jack his word of honour that, having surrendered, he will make no effort to escape. Jack says, very civil, 'I trust you'll forgive me if I keep your weapons and lock you in your cabin nonetheless, sir – for we pirates find that honour figures very little in our lives.'

Spenlow nods forlornly, as if he had expected just such a misfortune, and is led below with his crew.

It falls to me to take them their evening meal. We let the men come above to eat, and as young Harwood shares out the food, Spenlow and I fall into conversation, for he is much fascinated by my presence on the ship, and Anne's.

'Are you not afraid of being hanged?' he asks.

He speaks terribly polite, as though we are in a parlour taking tea, and not perched on the windlass, discussing the gallows.

I shake my head. 'As to hanging, I think it no great hardship. If not for the threat of the noose, every cowardly fellow would turn pirate, and infest the seas.'

He shakes his head. 'I confess I would not wish to see you hanged.'

I smile. 'Then we are in agreement, for I don't plan to be.'

We pass a busy night for we have now three ships to sail and not enough men, even with the two French hunters we snatched from Hispaniola. They have proved willing enough hands, for though they are not sailors, like most poor men they are accustomed to hard work. We work our way westward, keeping our fleet always at least a league from land, and the next day we are off Dry Harbour Bay in the late afternoon when Corner hails us from the *Evangeline* to say that he has espied another sloop. We raise the *William*'s black flag, and Corner fires upon her with two of the *Evangeline*'s guns. Seeing our numbers they know they cannot fight, but instead climb into their launch and make for the shore. But we bring the *William* alongside them and Fetherston hails them, and Jack calls out.

'We're English pirates, and if not quite gentlemen we are not savages. If you ask for quarter you have nothing to fear from us. Come aboard, and although we'll relieve you of your cargo, you'll pass a more comfortable night amongst us than skulking ashore.'

Such an offer is mightily persuasive with both the *William*'s swivel guns trained on them. And so the men agree to come aboard and hand over their weapons, though with a degree of reserve for which I cannot blame them.

Their ship is called the *Mary and Sarah*, at which Jack laughs loud and says, 'We must find another name for her, then, or our Anne will be jealous of this Sarah.' The joke is lost on her captain, one Dillon, who watches grimly as we take stock of his lading, which is tobacco largely and some sugar. He seems particularly alarmed by the presence of two women aboard, and stares as Anne and I work together to check his cargo.

'It's not just that it's unnatural,' he says to Jack, low-voiced. 'You're courting ill luck.'

Jack claps him on the shoulder. 'Seems to me that the ill luck might be yours and not mine, no?' Dillon turns away and says no more.

We do not keep them long, for we have now more prisoners than our own crew, which is an uncomfortable position. We have not men enough to sail a fleet of four ships, without grudging labour from our prisoners – and thus we elect to cut loose Spenlow's *Neptune*, and the *Evangeline* too. It is heavy work to shift all the cargo aboard the *William* and the *Mary and Sarah*, and being a Sunday the Reverend will have no part of it, which sets the rest of the crew into a foul mood. Jack leaves Spenlow his ten Negro slaves, never liking to trade in them.

'Do you not wish to free them instead?' I ask.

'We have not the room to take them,' he says, his voice unusually stern. 'Nor can I have our crew all but outnumbered by strangers – let alone men who cannot sail.'

All of this is true enough, and perhaps prudent – though there had been no hint of prudence in the fine speeches Jack has previously delivered about the ills of the slave trade.

That night I catch the Reverend alone by the bow.

'I must speak to you,' I say. Keeping my back to the others, I open my shirt a little and show him the small swelling of my belly, down low.

He puts a hand to my stomach, where the rounded flesh is hard as a coconut.

'You have not fucked Jack, despite what Tait used to say?'

I shake my head, impatient. 'Never.'

'And it's months since that fool Gladstone was aboard.'

I nod.

'Does it pain you?'

I nod. 'Sometimes.' I place my fingers atop the swelling, hard by my ribs. 'Right here.'

'Have you come to me as the ship's reverend, or as her surgeon?'

'Which do I need?' I ask, but he does not answer.

306

31

We run into a piece of ill luck, for Corner is piloting our second ship, the *Mary and Sarah*, and not having Patrick's skill, nor following him close enough, runs upon a sandbank and is grounded. We dare not wait for the tide to free her, so must ferry her cargo to the *William*, her decks crammed with barrels now. It is hot work but I am not disheartened. We started with the *William* alone, and here she is still, loaded with rich prizes, and she runs so sweet beneath us that I cannot find it in me to miss our small fleet. The song of the *William* is high and tremendous neat: the wind plucking the tight lines of her rigging; the *shh* of her bow cutting the water. I have Anne beside me, and the crow rides the wind above us. I want for nothing.

We follow the retreating coast south, for we have reached the westernmost tip of Jamaica. We espy a large periagua, already rowing madly to shore, for the fishermen within it spotted us first. Jack fires a single shot in the air, to hail them, and when we come alongside he tells them they need not fear us for we have no more room for prizes, and they look a meagre prize at that. He invites the nine men to come aboard and drink a bowl of punch with us, and they do it willingly enough.

We anchor there, within sight of land, and the fishermen find us in a merry mood, and eager to share the punch, which Howell has mixed with a generous hand, not stinting on the rum nor the sugar, even though it is only morning.

Anne has reached that point in her pregnancy when she is no longer Jack's, nor mine, but entirely her own. Her hands are at all times on her growing belly, and when she leaves my hammock she swings her legs down with a small sigh. When Jack surveys our prizes he speaks not of his riches but of his son's, for he is sure the child shall be another boy. Anne agrees. 'He's like to be a hearty lad,' she says, 'if I can judge by the kicking he is giving me.' She rises four times each night to piss, and her appetite, which was always good, is an untamed thing now, and Jack jokes that we must lock away the salt beef or she will eat everyone's share, and the sugar too, for she likes to scrape her knife along the edge of a sugar loaf and lick it straight from blade, her eyes closed the better to savour it.

She makes no mention of her first child. It is always now with her: the baby in her belly is all, while the boy left in Cuba has faded over the horizon. I do not doubt that when she held him in her arms, she loved him as giddily as she loves the idea of this new babe – for Jack and I have learned well enough that this is Anne's way, and she will never be otherwise.

She sits beside me. We are all full with punch and sun and our bountiful harvest of prizes. Jack does not usually permit us to drink so much at sea but since we dare not go ashore he makes an exception, for perhaps he knows that after these many recent engagements the men stand in need of a proper rest. The fishermen's fear has turned to relief, and there is something of relief in us, too, not to be obliged always to meet every man as an enemy. The Reverend is in a singing mood and Anne rests her head on my shoulder while he sings. Howell, ordinarily so quiet, joins the song, his voice high and surprisingly clear, and I marvel that the sea may still discover new things in us, even if it is just a fine singing voice in our cook.

A sail comes into sight from the north. This is an evil of our position in this bay, we realise only now: a ship may round the point and be upon us quick, for to the east we have not the benefit of a wide horizon. Still Jack is not unduly concerned for the ship drawing closer is neither big nor fast, and we weigh anchor with all speed and as soon as we come about, Jack has us loose one of the guns. The sloop draws off at once and Jack says we will not chase it for at any rate we are overburdened and the men half drunk.

'What if it is no pirate or merchant sloop, but a privateer set after us?' I ask.

'Some privateer, to sidle away at a single shot,' he says. Nonetheless he sets a course southward, and the nine fishermen have no choice but to come with us, for Jack will not wait to set them down, and they are happy enough to stay for there is punch remaining yet, and we continue to drink as we head south, not anchoring until near nightfall, north of Negril Point.

Out of the gloom to the north comes a ship. It is not the same vessel we fired at earlier, but a narrow Jamaican sloop. This time we do not even weigh anchor, but slip it at once, a thing no sailor does lightly – but there is no mistaking that this sloop has some ill design for she comes hard at us. We stand off and make good speed, but having the advantage of the wind, she is gaining on us, and Corner calls from the mast that he can see the English flag.

A man hails us across the water. 'Strike for the king's colours.'

Jack roars back: 'We will strike no strikes,' and signals to Fetherston who is at the bow swivel gun, and fires immediately – but if any of the enemy crew are hit, they give no cry.

It ought to be something momentous, to bring about this battle – some grand betrayal, or strategy gone wrong. Not this everyday thing: a foolish choice of anchorage and too much rum. Such small things, yet we are like to be undone by them. Can this be how the world turns, on such petty things, barely worth the noting?

Anne runs to fetch more powder to the guns. Half our crew are still below, rum befuddled and slow.

The sloop comes about and is lining up for a broadside. I knock Anne down with me as I dive for the deck. Above us there is a great splintering of wood and the boom is down, the mainsail hanging, a broken wing.

'Call for quarter,' shouts Dobbin at Jack.

'No quarter,' I yell over him. 'If they take us, we're dead for sure.'

One of the fishermen from the periagua is beside me, his eyes flaring and a string of spit hanging from one corner of his mouth.

'This's got nothing to do with me,' he says. 'I'm not going down with you bastards.'

'You'll swing anyway. Think they'll believe you just came aboard? You want to live, get to the swivel gun.'

He shakes his head, but follows me, swearing, as we scramble to the stern-mounted swivel gun. Jack is trying to bring the *William* about, but with the maimed sail we cannot manoeuvre and Jack yells to the crew to man the oars but all is chaos, the shouts of men and gun-smoke white under moonlight, and the trembling fisherman in my way as we try to load the gun's breach. He fumbles, sending grapeshot skittering about the deck.

The enemy sloop is close enough for small arms fire now, but they fire high. I do not mistake it for mercy – only as proof that they mean not to kill us but to capture us. We shall die either way, and I would choose a quick death on our own deck over the noose.

There's such smoke astern I think we are alight, but then I see Patrick on his knees putting the lantern flame to his waggoner. The huge book, each page a painstaking chart, burns in an instant.

He sees me watching. 'I'll let no other man have the joy of them,' he says, and I know then that we are done for.

Their grappling hooks are on our larboard side. I have a pistol in each hand but through the moonlit smoke it is hard to find my mark. I get off two shots and the second is met by a cry in the murk.

Most of our crew have retreated now below, but Anne is beside me again, a cask of powder in her hands.

'I'll not hang,' she says, wrenching open the cask so that powder scatters all about her. 'You understand?'

I do. I think of the nest on the beach, and how she set it ablaze.

I grab the lantern from Patrick, my eyes on hers. It would be quick, to ride the blasted bones of the *William* to the bottom of the sea. I am thinking how a thing may be beautiful even as it burns. I am thinking that if the only gift you can give is the gift of a quick death, that is a gift nonetheless.

Someone snatches the lantern from behind. I swing to fight – but it is Jack.

'You can't,' he says, panting. 'That's my wife – my son.'

I lunge for the lantern but he holds me off with one long arm and with his other he throws the lantern over the rail where the black water swallows it with a hiss. They are boarding us now, twenty men at least, with much clamour and some shots, but it is Jack that my pistol is trained on.

'Quarter,' he yells over me to the men. 'We beg quarter.'

I turn from him to face the raiders. Though I know my pistol is not reloaded, still I work the trigger, my body wanting very dearly to believe. There is a hollow click and nothing more, and then a sound very loud and sudden – the butt of a musket striking my head, for I am on my back now and one of the boarders stands over me, sees me still awake, and brings the butt down again.

32

I wake shackled. Waking is a bad business, for I am sick upon myself, and my head pains me so that I am grateful for the darkness, and the silence of the bodies crowded all around. By the stink of it, someone has pissed themselves; perhaps it is me, though there is no way of knowing for we are all of us soaked. By the rhythm of her breath I know that it is Anne beside me, and it is some hours more before my head is clear enough to grasp that all the rest of our crew is there too. I account for each one: Jack. The Reverend. Fetherston. Howell. Corner. Young Harwood. Dobbin. Carty. Earl. The fishermen, too, huddled together and shackled. Only Patrick is missing. I ask after him, and Jack says, 'Dead,' and there is nothing further to be said. Whether he was killed in the battle, or whether he followed his own book of charts into the flames, I do not know.

For two days and nights we sail thus, under close guard in the hold of the Bermudan sloop. The captain himself descends to see us on the second day. He says he is Barnet, of Jamaica, and has a commission to hunt pirates.

'I was at pains to take you alive,' he says, 'for Governor Rogers will not rest until he sees you hanged.' He speaks civil and without malice, as though he is simply pointing out to us a rising northerly, or a good harbour.

By the light behind him in the hatch, we are sailing east, and I figure that we are headed for St Jago de la Vega.

Harwood has taken to beating off, all hours of the day and night. Wretched, shy young Harwood, pressed from Belling's men, who used to blush if he so much as passed too close to me or Anne below deck, is now at himself, setting his shackles rattling each time.

'I'll swing for sure,' he mutters, when the Reverend tells him to stop. 'And I've had few enough pleasures in my life. Damned if I won't take my pleasure where I can.' And I can't bring myself to begrudge him that, so I turn away and try to ignore the shaking, and the small wet moan he gives at the end. I wonder if any life is granted an allotted amount of pleasure and of suffering – and whether I have met my account in each. But the rubbing seems to bring Harwood little pleasure, just a mounting anger – and he barely stops after each turn before he starts again, keeping at his poor cock until Jack says, not unkindly but tired: 'God's sakes, boy, you'll worry it right off.'

For the rest of the time, we are largely silent, for what comfort could words offer each other, or ourselves? I hear some whispering between Jack and Anne, and turn away.

Jack speaks to me only once, low-voiced.

'You've lost your crow now. I'm sorry for that.'

Whatever he should be sorry for, it is not that – for Crow will find me, sure as the sea. Right now she may be above, perched on a crosstree, or following Barnet's ship from a distance. She will follow me all the way, for we are bound together, and while I don't know why, I do know that it was her choosing – for when has a crow ever done anything otherwise?

At Port Royal we are brought ashore, blinking against the light. Under escort of the militia, we are taken in a wagon. When we pass beneath the arch of the gaol at St Jago de la Vega, Crow is waiting on the archway.

As we are led, shuffling, past one of the prison dormitories, a man sets up an almighty swearing and shouting. It is Charles Vane, for some reason still here, though it is more than a year since he was caught. Despite his prison house pallor it is unmistakably him, and he screams at Jack, 'Traitor turncoat coward,' and does not cease.

If Jack shouted back it would hearten me, but he keeps his gaze fixed ahead, and with each step his shackles scrape the floor like a dreadful cough.

───────────

Anne and I are quartered alone – they are little used to women prisoners and instead of the large dormitories that house the men, our room is a small one above the kitchen. We can neither see nor hear the rest of the crew, though the gaolers are free with their talk, and tell us the crew is quartered below. We are close enough, though, to hear Vane, and he kicks up a great shouting several times a day, hollering Jack's name and many curses.

The rumours swirl about the prison, as to why Vane has not yet been tried. One gaoler swears that Vane has promised the governor a great hoard of treasure, buried on some distant island, if they will free him. Another says that they dare not hang Vane for fear the Jacobites will avenge him. More likely there is a witness to one of his crimes who is not here to speak against him, and so they hold off his trial – and there are guilty men aplenty to be hanged in the meantime.

Whatever the cause, Vane is still here, and still wishing damnation on Jack. It seems he sees Jack as the start of all his misfortunes – though if my own life has taught me anything it is that every man is the start of his own misfortunes.

As for Anne, she never once speaks of Jack.

───────────

Our window has no bars, this room not being intended for prisoners, and the window being anyway too small to pass through. But it is no obstacle for a crow, who finds me on the second day and hops briskly inside to busy herself with spearing lice on her beak, before taking once more to the sill.

From the gaolers we have no trouble – once the novelty of our story has worn off and they have wearied of gawking at us, they are civil enough, and give us no trouble. I had feared indignities from them, but already there are rumours of Anne's father – that he is a planter and a man of means, and that if they treat Anne well, some of his money will come their way. Anne is at pains to encourage such rumours, and when she talks to them she speaks prettier than I have ever heard. It is a beautiful performance: they know her for a pirate, in ragged trousers, and yet when she speaks to them in that soft voice, she is somehow a wealthy planter's daughter and very fine. When she asks to write to her father, they bring her the means and she thanks them ever so gracious. The letter itself she troubles over for many hours, until her fingers are blackened where she has smudged the ink, and she will not show me what she has writ.

We are less than two weeks gaoled when Jack and the men are taken to trial – we hear it from the gaolers, and from the shouts of Vane who is filled with glee and yells, 'You will swing before me after all, Jack Rackham.' Anne is quiet. We are to be tried separately from the men, we have been told.

By evening the gaolers have the news: the trial is done, and they are all to hang. Even Vane falls quiet, for whatever his anger at Jack, he must surely know that Jack's fate will be his too, when his own trial comes.

How to grieve for Jack? Jack Rackham of the unstinting laugh, Calico Jack who strode the decks of the *William* and threw his arms wide the better to admire the sea. My captain, who seized pleasure with both hands, and loved words, most particularly his own. Who taught me the power of stories. Who ushered me into a pirate's life, but lost it for me too.

Did he in truth believe in his grand notions of a republic of pirates, or was he just enthralled by his own voice? And can I grieve for him without forgiving him?

As for Anne, she does not weep but only asks the gaolers, very prettily, if her letter to her father has been posted yet. She rubs her belly as though it is her sole job now. She rubs it as though her skin is a deck that she must polish to a high shine.

They bring Jack to see Anne, by special favour, before he is to be hanged.

There is a red mark on his lip that might be a bruise or might be a sore. The bright patterns of his calico clothes, already faded by the sun, are lost altogether now in prison dirt.

I turn to face the wall and pretend to sleep – in part to give them time alone, and in part because I have nothing to say to Jack Rackham. I rest my right hand on the lump in my belly, and stare at the crow on the sill, her head the black executioner's hood.

Jack and Anne speak in hushed voices and for a long time. Whatever passes between them, it is theirs alone.

When they at last fall silent, Jack walks to where I lie.

'Will you not farewell me, Mary?'

I say nothing.

'I am your captain.'

I sit up to face him. 'You were, until you proved yourself a coward.'

He speaks in an urgent whisper. 'I wanted only to protect Anne and my son. That's why I asked for quarter. I swear it on my life.'

'That's not much of a stake.'

'I did it for Anne,' he says. 'For love of her.'

He whips out his love like a quick-drawn pistol in the face. Like it's an argument that can never be answered.

'Did you ever truly believe in any of it?' I ask.

'Any of what?'

I want to say: *The republic of pirates. The* William *and her crew. Us: me, Anne, and you.* Instead I just wave my hand – south, to the sea.

He meets my eyes. 'What d'you want from me, Mary?' He gestures at himself: the soiled clothes; the mark on his lip; the sores the shackles have left on his wrists.

I have felt many things about Jack Rackham but I have never before pitied him. I can see, now, what he is. I see it clear as anything: he is a man as any other. Any grand ideas I had of a republic of pirates, or a new world, suddenly seem flimsy as a paper boat setting out in water.

I lay my hand on his arm. I am thinking of the *William*, and how sweetly she sailed upwind. How swift and willing.

He looks down at my hand, and speaks low. 'I wish it were not a land-man doing the knot.' He swallows. 'I'd trust a sailor better than a hangman to know his business, and to get the knot right.'

I'm sure it will be quick, I want to tell him. But I cannot know if it's true, and for all Jack's faults, I don't want my final words to him to be a lie.

Anne is sleeping next morning when Daly, the youngest of the gaolers, brings us our food. He glances at Anne.

'Did you hear what she said to Rackham?' he asks me. 'Looked him straight in the eye, and said: *If you had fought like a man, then you need not die like a dog.*'

There is no point in telling the gaoler that this is a lie, and that nobody heard what Jack and Anne said to each other yesterday – not even I. Let the man believe what he will. 'If you had fought like a man.' They are fine words, but I doubt they are Anne's. They have the sound of something a pamphleteer might come up with.

All that day I find myself caught up in crying. Anne does not cry, nor move to comfort me. In a strange way I think I am sadder than she to farewell Jack. When Jack failed her, and was condemned, she left him in her wake. I have not her talent for forgetting. I think that Jack will number among my ghosts.

It is done, and they are hanged. Young Daly, the gaoler, tells us they have hanged Rackham, Fetherston, Corner, Davies and Howell at Gallows Point in Port Royal, and that Rackham, Fetherston and Corner are to be carried to Plumb Point, Bush

Key, and Gun Key, and hanged in gibbets. 'For a public example, and to terrify others from such-like evil practices,' Daly says sagely. As for the pressed men, Harwood, Dobbin, Carty and Earl, they are to be executed tomorrow. I do not know whether they will account the extra day a blessing.

I think of Jack being fixed in the gibbet and raised like a sail.

So this is the final disbanding of our crew. Fetherston, our steady ship's master. Corner, with his whaler's patience and his sharp eyes, who will now keep a blind lookout from the gibbet. Howell, the worst cook in the seven seas, as Jack used to boast – and keeping hid within him all the time that high, sweet singing voice. The Reverend, my old and solemn friend. Somewhere in New Providence, his man is tending their cassavas and waiting.

Anne refuses to cry. She sleeps in my arms as Jack hangs at Gun Key, and I picture him there, his gibbet the shape of a cathedral door – and the light will shine through them both the same.

33

The gaolers argue loudly about what we should wear to the trial. Some say we should wear the trousers we were seized in, as proof of our wickedness for all to see. Others insist it would be an offence against propriety, and not to be permitted. In the end they bring us petticoats and stomachers to wear. Anne thanks them sweetly, but I am not much comforted, for it seems to me they would only dress us so if they were certain already that they had enough evidence to hang us on, and do not need us in our trousers to further sway the court.

The night before our trial Anne is calm and oddly still.

We have not fucked these many weeks, though we still sleep close, back to back, or my hand on hers and hers on her belly. If she has noticed my own belly's growth, she has said nothing, though the bulge is clear to see, if you look close. But today she puts her hand directly on my stomach.

'Listen,' she says. 'Whose child is it?'

I shake my head.

'I'm not angry, nor jealous,' she says. 'Is it Gladstone's?'

'Don't be stupid. If it were his, it would nearly be born by now.'

'Who else have you bedded?'

'Only you.'

'Apart from that,' she says, impatient, as though what she and I do together counts for nothing.

'Only you,' I say again.

'Why are you lying to me?'

'I've never lied to you.'

'Did somebody take you against your will?'

'Nobody raped me, Anne. Nothing happened.'

'Something did.' For there it is: my own body testifying against me, my belly round and unyielding under her fingers.

I've seen her kneel in prayer, and mutter her Hail Marys. Anne believes the same way she does everything else: fiercely. And being a papist, she makes more of Mary, and the virgin birth, than the drab and polite church I knew. Maybe that's why Anne lets herself believe that I could have a babe inside me, where no man has been since Gladstone, so long ago.

'It's not a baby,' I say, but her finger is on my lips, and none too gently.

'Listen to me,' she says. 'Tell no one. Not ever.'

———————————

I lace her stomacher, and she laces mine. If you did not know us well, you might notice nothing of our bellies. You might not see how, when we stand face to face, my stomach arches to meet her, and hers to me.

Even in the early morning the courtroom is hot, and the press of so many people makes it hotter still. Before the day's business can begin there is a great deal of intoning of jurisdictions and it goes on so long that I am shocked when at last I hear my name, and Anne's. Even then, the reading of the charges alone feels interminable.

> . . . *and then and there, piratically and feloniously, did make an assault, in and upon certain fishermen . . . and then and there, piratically and feloniously, did put the aforesaid fishermen, in the said fishing boats then being, in corporal fear of their lives . . .*

Those words, 'piratically and feloniously,' come around again and again, like the refrain of a song.

> . . . *and then and there, piratically and feloniously, did steal, take, and carry away, the fish, and fishing tackle . . . and then and there,*

piratically and feloniously, did make an assault, in and upon, one
James Dobbin, and certain other mariners . . .

I could almost laugh to hear Dobbin invoked here as a
victim, when they have already hanged him for joining us
thereafter. In this courtroom he is pirate and victim at once:
they have not scrupled to hang him, and then to use him to
hang us too.

> *. . . piratically and feloniously, did steal, take, and carry away, the said*
> *two merchant sloops . . . did piratically, feloniously, and in a hostile*
> *manner, shoot at, set upon, and take, a certain schooner . . .*

I lean close to Anne, and whisper, 'What manner is there but
hostile, when you're shooting at something?' But she only looks
ahead, sitting very upright.

Still the man's voice going on, droning like a blunt saw working on a mast.

> *. . . did piratically, feloniously, and in a hostile manner, set upon,*
> *board, and enter, a certain merchant sloop, called the* Mary *. . .*

The charges mount in the stifling air. All these words, tightening
around me until I can feel Ma yanking again on the strings of
my corset.

Finally the court president turns to us. 'What say you? Are
you guilty of the piracies, robberies and felonies, or any of them,
in the said articles mentioned, and read to you today?'

And together, at once, we reply: 'Not guilty.' What does it
matter that it is not true? What have these men to do with us,
and with our lives, and what do they know of our choices?

They summon witnesses. First is the ranting woman from the
canoe, much tidied now in her best mantua, but no less angry.
Dorothy Thomas, her name is, and pointing at me and Anne she
says that when we seized her boat, 'I knew them to be women
by the largeness of their breasts.'

323

The crowd in the courtroom do not even pretend to hide their measuring eyes. I imagine tearing open my stomacher and showing them my tiny breasts, man-flat. Even clothed, anyone may see that I've no breasts to speak of. Nor are Anne's large, even now she is with child.

But it will make no difference. I can see already that this actual thing, my body, will not stand against the story being written in this room. What does the truth count, against such a good tale?

The two Frenchmen are called next, speaking through an interpreter, and telling the court how we were part of the crew, 'very active on board and willing to do anything.' That they themselves worked with us willingly enough, the Frenchmen do not mention. I cannot blame them for that, nor would I tell the court of it.

Thomas Spenlow, the morose captain who complained of his bad luck, tells of the taking of his schooner. Then comes Thomas Dillon, of the *Mary and Sarah*, who tells the court he saw us dressed as men when we were attacking a prize, and as women at other times.

For the most part, though, the witnesses speak of us as though we disguised ourselves as men – indeed, to hear them dwell on it, you would think it the greatest part of our crimes. Anne is mightily affronted at this claim she lived as a man, and sits stiff and ladylike, her chin slightly raised, and looking strictly forwards, and ignoring the stares of the crowd.

The stories of our man-disguise are a nonsense, for we both wore skirts at times, when ashore, or anchored. But a person who wears skirts aboard a ship would be a person who longed to trip and pitch overboard, or have her back broken when her skirts catch in a trailing line. We were known as women in Nassau, and wore what we wished, and not to hide as men.

I have long since understood myself as something altogether more spacious than the narrow port of either woman or man. As for Anne, if sometimes she acted the part of a man when seizing a prize, it was only to help frighten our prey into asking for quarter, for men have not learned to fear women as they should.

324

The court turns to us, an afterthought. Have we any witnesses, or any questions to put to those witnesses already deposed here? And we say no, for there is nothing to be gained by such arguments, and nor would they listen. If I were to tell my story it would have to start all the way back: with Ma, and the navy, and Captain Turnbull and his sea creatures, and Dan and the dead baby, and Payton. That is too long a story, and most of its witnesses are dead.

When the gentlemen of the court are ready to make their deliberations, we are taken into a small room at the back, which by the smell of it is above the stables.

'Listen to me,' Anne says, her voice very low. I had feared for her, during the trial, and wished to shield her from the scrutiny of all those staring men. But I see now that she is Anne Bonny still, for she is unabashed, and terribly calm.

'Listen,' she says again, taking both my hands in hers. 'I can fix this. But you must accord with what I say.' She puts one hand on her belly, and one on mine. 'You're with child. Do you understand?'

I shake my head. 'You know it's not—'

She cuts me off. 'I can do this. But you must be with child.'

I stare at her. I have not always understood Anne Bonny, though that has never stopped me from loving her. But I understand her less than ever now.

'Let me do this one thing,' she says. 'I can save you.'

The verdict is read: we are guilty.

'You, Mary Read and Anne Bonny, are to go from hence to the place from whence you came, and from thence to the place of execution; where you shall be severally hang'd by the neck, till you are severally dead. And God of his infinite mercy be merciful to both your souls.'

It seems to me that no god's mercy may be considered infinite if it cannot find sufficient mercy for the babe within Anne's belly. I am not innocent, and nor is Anne – but her baby is. When the hatch drops and Anne swings from the noose, will the child feel the swaying? Will the child die at once, or will it swing there some minutes, feeling her womb grow cold around it?

I confess that it is not only for Anne's child that I am afraid. I, who have never feared to drown, don't want to drown in air. Standing beside Anne in the dock, my hand is at my throat, which has become its own noose, tightening so that I can barely breathe.

Then Anne steps forward and speaks.

'We submit ourselves to the mercy of the court, and of the sentence passed upon us. But I beg to inform the court that both Mary Read and I are quick with child. We plead the belly, for which there are many precedents in law, and we ask the king's mercy. And we submit ourselves gladly to examination by a jury of matrons, as the law dictates.'

She does not falter. All those years of work as her father's law clerk were not wasted, because she speaks as clear and fine as any of the gentlemen in the room. Clear and fine as she recited the Brehon law when she announced she could divorce Bonny, or the wedding vows when she wed herself to Jack.

'For according to the laws both of this country and of nature, it is not justice for the sentence to be visited not only on us, but on our unborn babes.' Her hands are on her stomach now, cupping its roundness, and I think of the stuffed and bloodied figure she rigged against the mast before we attacked that sloop. This is her greatest performance.

'And if it please the court, it would not be any kind of justice to let these unborn children, innocent and free of sin, to suffer for the sins of their mothers, or their fathers neither.'

There is a mighty outcry in the courtroom, and a great deal of pushing and manoeuvring as the crowd tries to get a better look at us, and at our bellies specifically. Anne attends to none of it. She stands there, her belly proud before her, a shield. With her right hand she reaches for my stomach, and if you did not know you might think it a reassuring pat, but she is pressing the fabric of my skirt close to my skin, the better to display the small bulge there.

Her eyes stay on the court's president, the stern-faced man who read the verdict, and is now turning to consult with the others.

It is several minutes before he faces us once more, and speaks, his voice weary, as though Anne's appeal has delayed him from some important occasion.

'We are agreed that execution of the aforesaid sentence should be respited, until an inspection by a jury of matrons can be made.'

Anne turns to me, her hand on my arm and her voice low and sure.

'I told you, back when they attacked us on the *William*,' she says. 'I told you that I will not hang.'

Back in our cell, she is giddy and breathless.

'They'll send people to check,' she says. 'To know for sure that the children have quickened.'

I don't say, *Not children — child*, for there is no stopping her. And if this lie is to spare me, then I must enter into it fully.

'It's called a jury of matrons, which sounds grand, but it will just be a handful of women the judge has pressed into duty. It might take them a few days to rustle up the women. Some of them may be midwives, so they may know what they're about.' It's a warning to me, though she will not say it any clearer.

There are clues that what I harbour is no baby — will any of these women be looking for them? The lump in my right armpit, as big as an eyeball, and about the same texture. My bones sharpening beneath my skin as I grow thin — but who would wonder at that, on prison fare?

The women come three days later. They walk into our cell in a file, solemn as a funeral procession. There are six women, two of whom claim to be midwives, and I'll allow that there's a practised turn to the way they handle us.

They undress us to examine our bared bellies. One of the women presses her hand flat on Anne's stomach to feel the child move; an older woman pushes her aside and takes her place. 'Better to use your cheek,' she says, and kneels to do it herself, her cheek against the stretched skin of Anne's belly. I remember Carson, the surgeon on the *Resolve*, his ear against my back to hear my breath. I think of how that surgeon kept my secret for me. Nothing about these women, and the brisk way they go about their job, suggests that they would be willing to do the same.

'It kicks,' the woman says with a nod, not to Anne but to the other women.

And now she kneels before me, her cheek pressed to my navel. It is such an intimate thing – her skin so soft against mine, for all that her decision may send me to the gallows. What does she hear there, her ear to my belly? Does my body keep its secrets, or will she?

The quickening that I remember from my own pregnancy, so long ago, was nothing so violent as a kick. It was a flutter, the merest thing, like when you set a pan of water to boil and the first reluctant bubbles drift to the surface. I resist the temptation to make my belly give a great jolt, but try to tense my muscles to give the lightest quiver – a heartbeat, that's all, but in my guts. The woman stills; her brows draw together. I do it again, lighter this time.

She says nothing, but stands to continue her inspection. When she prods my breasts I wince, remembering the great tenderness of my breasts when I was pregnant with Dan's child – though the woman is not so gentle that I have much need to exaggerate my pain.

'Your milk's not in,' she says. Her voice is passive, but it's still an accusation.

'It's too soon. And I've never had much to show for myself up there,' I say.

Silence.

'When did you last bleed?'

Truth is I have barely bled for years – not regular. Maybe I am too old – I am nearing thirty-six after all. Maybe it's the shipboard work, or the shipboard fare.

'Months ago,' I say.

'How old are you?'

'I am gone thirty,' I say.

The words catch on my dry mouth. Anne and I were tried as a pair, and she has made this plea for both of us, together. If my lie is discovered then she may swing for it too, and her unborn babe also.

Still the woman is staring very hard at my face, which I know to be lined and sun-marked. Can she believe me barely thirty?

She passes me back my clothes, which I hold before my nakedness.

'What will you tell them?' I call after her.

She pauses at the door. Her eyes give away nothing. It was a mistake to ask her – if I were pregnant I would surely never doubt her answer. She knows it too.

But she looks at my stomach, and at Anne's, and then back to mine.

'We'll tell them the truth,' she says. 'That's our solemn sworn duty.'

We are reprieved.

'When the babies have come,' Anne says, 'they may hang us yet.' Still she says 'babies.' If the ship of our lie is to float, we must not acknowledge it. 'But my father will come first,' she says, and she will hear nothing of doubts.

But she is right about her father. He replies to her, and writes also to the gaol, for we are furnished now with better food, and blankets, and clean straw for our bed. A local woman is hired to wait on us: Ginty, she is called, and she brings for Anne skirts and shifts and stomachers, everything of the finest quality. Ginty bustles about each day to sweep our room and to lay out our food, all done in a grand manner as though we were in a hand-some house and not a prison cell. Anne does not stint to share her food with me. But as she grows bigger she is always hungry, while my body has forgotten its appetite.

Anne's babe is grown so big that when it presses against her skin I can make out the shape of feet, or even fingers. I press my lips to her belly. I remember when Captain Turnbull of the *Resolve* hauled aboard a mermaid's purse, the egg case of a shark, so fine the light passed through, and within I could make out the tiny shark in its own complete and watery world.

It is not until January that they try the nine fishermen whom we summoned aboard the *William* for a bowl of punch. The gaolers tell us of their sentence, and again when they are hanged at Gallows Point several weeks later. It is a hard thing, and those men must account their bowl of punch very dearly bought.

Sometimes at night when the dead gather about me, those nine come too, set back from the others and all in a row. In their hands they hold empty punchbowls, and their mouths are open and thirsty and will never be filled.

34

'You're lucky,' Anne says. 'We both are. So lucky.'

Strange luck, this.

I think of Ma, her dead son and her living daughter, and the swap that made me a boy. Maybe this is the Read luck: this sneaking of children. This looseness that allows our children to be other than what the world thinks. A messy kind of magic, this, and not enough to save me, but to buy me a few more weeks or months, me and Anne, and the crow. Sometimes I feel giddy with the audacity of the trick.

Crow sits in our small window, so that all of the world I can see is but an outline to a crow. When she flies away, it's never for long. She's getting fatter. She's glossy with this place, for the lice are a feast for her.

There are rumours amongst the gaolers that, once the babies come, there could be a reprieve, or a commutation to a lesser sentence. Anne talked about it a lot, at first. Lately she avoids it, because she knows she will not be here. Her father is coming, and he is in correspondence already with the court. He will work the rich man's magic and make some kind of deal, and she will be released. I am glad of it.

As for me, there will be no baby. Anne and I are still skirting that truth like a reef. At first, we didn't mention it because the secret could see us hanged. Now, we dare not even whisper it, for it makes too stark the difference between us: that she is with child, and I am dying.

Anne grows and grows. Her belly is a globe, her breasts swell and harden until I can see the net of blue veins cast under her skin. Even her hair gets thicker, and takes on a new shine.

I grow too. My skirts, fine new ones from Anne's father, hide the worst of the difference – you have to look close to see it. The bigger my belly gets, the clearer it is that the growth is all on one side, and the skin puckers and sticks to whatever is growing within me. The rest of my body is wasting quick, for I throw up most of what I eat. Still the gaolers do not know the truth. They watch me, but not as a crow does. And my body has always been a nest of secrets. It is good at this.

When her baby moves, Anne grabs my hand too and presses it to the skin.

'Feel now,' she'd say. 'Now. Did you feel that?'

I do, and it shocks me how strong it is: that real, determined push against my palm. This little one will be like its mother. It will wait for no one.

'I think it's a boy,' she says. 'He's so strong already. Ginty says if you carry high, like I am, it's a boy.'

I agree with her that the baby is strong. I don't agree that it's a boy.

I dream that I am indeed pregnant. When my baby comes it is a crow. It comes out slick-feathered and beak-first, meeting the world crow-wise and sharp. It shakes its feathers three times and looks at me without turning its neck. 'Hello,' I say. 'It's you.'

We share a cell and a bed, Anne and I, but we live in different tenses now. She speaks of 'after': 'after the baby comes,' she says, or, 'after my father arrives.' Her baby is coming and her father is on his way, and brings with him the promise of a new beginning. For Anne, there will be more sky than this cell's small window permits.

For myself, I live only *now*. I am wise enough to know that, and not to grasp at hope.

There is no space between us – indeed, we sleep each night closer than ever, her within my arms. But there is time between us instead. 'You'll see,' she whispers to me in our bed at night. 'All will be well. You'll see.' But she loses me at the 'will,' for that is yet to come, and therefore cannot be mine.

The crow leaves the sill to hunt, or perhaps just to check if the world is still there. *What do you see?* I would ask her if I could. *What ships lie in the harbour? Is the wind offshore and propping up the waves? How high the tide, and are the anchor cables straining tight? Have you flown as far as the key, and visited Rackham's body swinging in its gibbet? Crow, have you cracked the shell of his tar and tasted him, and does he taste of tar or salt or forgetting? Does he taste of Anne?*

Under which name will they bury me? Am I to go into the ground with no shroud of a name around me?

I was born into my brother's name; I wore my husband's name a while; I have severally been Mark and Mary Read, and Mary Jansenns. What is the name Crow gives me in the black nut of her skull? Will Anne ever speak of me, and by which name?

And by which name will I know myself?

The gaolers bring the news: Anne's father has come through with the money and arranged for her a quiet release, if not a pardon.

'I'm sorry,' she says, over and over. 'I'd take you if I could. If he'd pay, and if they'd let me.'

Of her old distaste for her father, and for his money, there is now no sign. Now she seizes it with both hands, and I am not surprised, because for all Anne's skill with words and laws, this is her true talent: survival.

I walk with her to the door where Ginty waits, Anne's belongings bundled in her arms. The growth in my belly has crept round to my left side, right down to my hip, so I cannot walk without limping.

'Go,' I say. I put my hand to her belly. 'Go, and keep her safe.'

'I'll keep trying,' she says. 'I'll keep asking my father. I will not let them hang you.'

I place a palm on either side of her face. 'They're not going to hang me. I promise.'

We both know that I speak the truth.

———————

Will Anne ever go back to Cuba and find her first child there? Will the child she now carries learn about Jack Rackham, or about me?

She does not visit me – nor do I expect her to. I have always known that Anne would leave me here. You might mistake Anne for a sea woman, but she was a child in Kinsale, and grew into a woman at Charles Town – river ports, both of them. It's why she loved Cuba so fiercely, that island of rivers. The sea has nothing on the impatience of rivers.

Leaving is what her father did, when he took Anne and his mistress and fled to the New World. It's what Anne did herself, when she ran from Charles Town and her father. It's the same thing she did when she left her first husband, and later when she left her babe in Cuba. By the time Jack was hanged, she had long left him behind and was busy arranging for her own salvation.

I envy Anne her riverblood – her knack for leaving. She steps lightly through life, unburdened by ghosts. They cannot catch her – she's already gone.

I told you already: she is a woman made of rivers. Raised at rivermouths, all her life has been one leaving after another. What else did she know how to do but to leave?

35

April 1721

It must now be clear to all that what I carry is no baby. I can no longer stand without a great deal of effort, and what little I eat comes up again. The crow never leaves the window now, but keeps her vigil.

If the gaolers can see that I have lied, they have no need to hang me for it, for the noose would be a waste of good rope. I carry within me my own death. Whether it is more or less lenient than the court's sentence of gallows, I have not yet decided.

When I was in Flanders and felt the damp closing in all about me, a child grew in my belly and I thought that it would save me. I was right, but not in the way that I thought. It is true that I can be saved and damned, both at once. That the things that save us kill us.

Ginty visits me in the prison to tell me that Anne's baby has come. 'Fat as anything, with hair such as you've never seen.'

'A boy?' I ask.

'No,' she says. 'A girl.' And I can no longer stand, but I turn my head to the side so that only the crow may see me smile.

Anne, her father and the baby are to leave Jamaica soon, Ginty says. They will go to Charles Town first, and where thereafter

Ginty does not know. They will not be taking her, for Anne will need a new life now, and a new name.

————◆————

Vane is condemned — Vane is hanged. So few remain, now, of Nassau's republic of pirates. I smile to think that Anne Bonny is one of them.

My dead come to me, though there is scarce room for them all in here. There is Mark, though he wears my face. Jack Rackham comes, waving his pamphlets and trying to speechify, but his mouth makes only the shapes of silence. There is the Reverend, head bowed in prayer or drunkenness, or perhaps for him they were the same. Marston, with the laugh that made him welcome everywhere. There is Corner, riding astride the bloated body of a whale. Tait, with his great pustuled arse quite bare. The nine fishermen in a row, each holding out an empty punchbowl.

Dan comes too, wearing his tavern apron and not his cavalry blues. Our baby toddles across the cell floor, wet with Flanders mud and towing its afterbirth behind it like a toy on a string.

I never did learn from Anne to leave my ghosts behind. Yet I am not she — this I have learned, and made my peace with it too.

————◆————

The eager reverend comes a second time, entreating me again to make my final testament. He says he wishes to absolve me, though I know he wants only to sell my story. Needing neither coins nor absolution, I send him on his way.

My dying is nearly done with me. I am thirty-six, which is no mean age — least of all for a pirate. I would have liked to pass more days at sea, and to see again a whale shrug the ocean from its back and surface into sky. Yet I never thought to live long, for my life was already granted on sufferance, stolen from my brother and kept secret.

For years I felt myself a stowaway in my own life. But the sea has taught me this: such days as I was granted, they were mine.

I wish they would bury me at sea, for I do not trust the earth, its stubborn refusal to budge. O bury me instead in the deep dark down. Bury me where the sea eats sound, where water speaks its own name and can teach me the crabwise patience of shelled things, coral growing into bone.

And if there is to be a reckoning, it must come to this: that I have never lied to the sea, and I have kept my faith with crows. That I have followed my own story, and written it too. There is a crow on the sill; there is salt on the wind. I have known my body for what it is, and I have let it love where it found love. I have learned the songs of many ships. And while I shall be granted no sea burial, I am the sea's forever.

<hr>

The air grows very grudging. I am glad to be alone for this, and not on the gallows. Each death should be a private matter – just me and my old shipmate Death, and Crow watching from the windowsill.

I know my crow name now. I knew it all along. I know it, and it fits around me like water.

Anne said to me, after she left her son in Cuba: 'When the baby comes, it's not like meeting anyone new. It's not a surprise. You look at that little crumpled face and you recognise it like an old friend. You say: *There you are.*'

I see my old witness Death, bending low over me. Blackness all around, the black of crow feathers, so dark it turns to blue.

I say: *There you are.*

Historical note

This novel broadly follows the historical record, though this is often sketchy and contradictory. I depart from the historical accounts with Mary's crow (an invention on my part), and with my explanation for Mary's final 'pregnancy.'

The more sensationalist versions of Mary and Anne's stories claim that they were in disguise as men during their time as pirates. This is not supported by the evidence (for example, Governor Rogers' 1720 proclamation, concerning the theft of the *William*, names them both as women). However, the true story of their lives is no less extraordinary than the myth. Accounts of their childhoods suggest that both were (for different reasons) partly raised as boys, and that Mary served in both the navy and army before becoming a pirate. Mary and Anne were the only documented women pirates of piracy's 'Golden Age.' That they served together on Rackham's crew, and were both reprieved after pleading the belly, is more remarkable than any imagined tale.

Mary was buried in St Catherine Parish, Jamaica, on 28th April 1721. Anne's fate is not known, though historians tend to agree that her father likely managed to purchase her freedom.

I am indebted to the writers and historians whose work has informed this novel, and has provided me with countless hours of fascinating reading. All errors are, of course, my own.

I drew most heavily on the transcripts of the trials of Rackham and his crew, and the (pseudonymous) Captain Charles Johnson's *A General History of the Pyrates* (Vol. I, 1724, https://www.gutenberg.org/ebooks/40580; Vol. II, 1726, https://www.gutenberg.org/ebooks/57005) – although these various texts do not always accord with one another. As well as fascinating information (some of it possibly apocryphal), Johnson also provides several irresistible phrases, which I have borrowed, including his description of Anne as 'not altogether so reserved in point of Chastity'. I have also quoted from Governor Rogers' 1720 proclamation (https://www.postandcourier.com/gov-woodes-rogers-pirate-proclamation-in-the-boston-gazette/pdf_d53297f8-dd54-11e8-a5bb-f382533ea96d.html), George I's 1717 edict against piracy (https://www.thegazette.co.uk/London/issue/5573/page/1/data.pdf), and Woodes Rogers' *A Cruising Voyage Around the World* (1712; https://www.gutenberg.org/ebooks/55538). I have modified Rogers' original words slightly, to avoid confusion. Rogers wrote of the enslaved woman and the minister: 'we doubt he will crack a Commandment with her.' When quoting this passage in *Saltblood*, I have amended this to 'doubt not', to clarify the meaning for modern readers. In Rogers' time, 'doubt' was often used to mean 'suspect' (for example, Rogers writes of his unwell sailors: 'if we don't get ashore, and a small Refreshment, we doubt we shall both lose several Men').

Other illuminating primary sources included George Roberts' 1726 *The Four Years Voyages of Capt. George Roberts* (https://play.google.com/books/reader?id=OWsBAAAAQAAJ&pg=GBS.PP6&hl=en_GB), and a collection of depositions, pirate articles, and more, compiled as *Pirates In Their Own Words*, edited by E.T. Fox (Fox Historical, Devon, 2014).

Aside from these contemporary texts, the most useful source was Colin Woodard's *The Republic of Pirates: Being the true and surprising story of the Caribbean pirates and the man who brought them down* (Pan Books, London, 2014). I also found helpful Eric J. Dolan's *Black Flags, Blue Waters: The Epic History of America's Most Notorious Pirates* (Liveright Publishing Corporation, New York,

2018), and several books by David Cordingly, including *Heroines and Harlots* (Pan Books, London, 2002), and *Life Among the Pirates* (Abacus, London, 2014). Phillip Thomas Tucker's *Anne Bonny: The Infamous Female Pirate* (Feral House, Port Townsend, 2017), while not generally reliable, did raise the fascinating prospect of Anne's awareness of the Brehon law.

No source specifies the actual ship(s) on which Mary served in the Royal Navy; the *Resolve* and *Expedition* are my own creations.

A selection of further references is below:

Creighton, Margaret S., and Norling, Lisa (eds), *Iron Men, Wooden Women: Gender and Seafaring in the Atlantic World, 1700–1920* (Johns Hopkins University Press, Baltimore, 1996).

Dear, I.C.B. (ed), *The Oxford Companion to Ships and the Sea* (Oxford University Press, Oxford, 1988).

De Pauw, Linda Grant, *Seafaring Women* (Peacock Press, Pasadena, 1998).

Falkner, James (ed.), *Marlborough's Wars: Eyewitness Accounts 1702–1713* (Pen & Sword Military, Yorkshire, 2020).

King, Dean (ed.), *A Sea of Words* (3rd Edition) (Holt Paperbacks, New York, 2000).

Pennell, C. R. (ed.), *Bandits at Sea: A Pirates Reader* (New York University Press, New York and London, 2001).

Rediker, Marcus, *Outlaws of the Atlantic: Sailors, Pirates, and Motley Crews in the Age of Sail* (Verso, London, 2014).

Stanley, Jo (ed.), *Bold in her Breeches: Women Pirates Across the Ages* (Pandora, London, 1996).

Stark, Suzanne J., *Female Tars: Women Aboard Ship in the Age of Sail* (Naval Institute Press, Annapolis, 1996).

Wheelwright, Julie, *Amazons and Military Maids* (Pandora Press, London, 1990).

Acknowledgements

I am grateful beyond measure to my agent, the incomparable Juliet Mushens, who loved this book fiercely from the start, and has been the most superb advocate for it.

I was ably supported by the entire team at Mushens Entertainment, particularly Rachel Neely, Kiya Evans and Liza DeBlock. I'm grateful for their commitment, kindness and encouragement.

My editor at Bloomsbury, Emma Herdman, has been a delight to work with from the very first start. Her passion for this novel has been a gift and a joy, and her wisdom has improved the book enormously. Particular thanks also to Charlotte Greig for her devotion to the novel, and her skill.

The team at Bloomsbury has shared Emma's enthusiasm for *Saltblood,* and I am vastly indebted to them for all their energy, hard work and creativity. Thank you to Katy Loftus, whose copyediting was at once rigorous and sympathetic, and to Lin Vasey, for her diligent and careful proofreading. Any remaining errors are, of course, my own. Thank you to Lauren Whybrow for masterfully shepherding the book through production, and to Carmen Balit, for the beautiful cover design.

Thank you to Eris Young, whose insightful sensitivity reading made this novel stronger and more capacious.

Thank you to Alan Haig, whose indefatigable pedantry was both incredibly useful, and a great source of amusement on the family WhatsApp chat.

While writing this novel I had the great privilege of working as a mentor for The Writing Squad, whose brilliant writers taught me considerably more than I taught them. Without the many conversations that we shared, this would have been a lesser book.

Thank you to A and M, beloveds, and to the Haig and North families for their belief in me, and their excitement on my behalf. I'm also hugely thankful to the many friends who have tolerated hearing about this project over many years, and have provided joyful distractions from it.

A Note on the Author

FRANCESCA DE TORES is a novelist, poet and academic. She is the author of four previous novels, published in more than twenty languages, with film rights optioned by DreamWorks. In addition to a collection of poems, her poetry is widely published in journals and anthologies. *Saltblood* is her first historical novel. She grew up in Lutruwita/Tasmania and, after fifteen years in England, is now living in Naarm/Melbourne.

A Note on the Type

The text of this book is set in Bembo, which was first used in 1495 by the Venetian printer Aldus Manutius for Cardinal Bembo's *De Aetna*. The original types were cut for Manutius by Francesco Griffo. Bembo was one of the types used by Claude Garamond (1480–1561) as a model for his Romain de l'Université, and so it was a forerunner of what became the standard European type for the following two centuries. Its modern form follows the original types and was designed for Monotype in 1929.